Danny Bronson was about to toss the folded newspaper onto the bright yellow welcome mat, then stopped, frowning. The door to the apartment was ajar, which was unusual. Even in a nice neighborhood like this, people were cautious about leaving their doors unlocked, much less open.

Feeling slightly uneasy, he looked around, then back at the door. Maybe he should call the police. If this was a robbery, the guy might still be inside. He might even have a gun. On the other hand, if the woman who lived here was sick or hurt...

After a short hesitation, he approached the apartment and peered through the opening. He couldn't see a thing. It was pitch-black inside. And silent as a tomb, which convinced him that if a robbery had taken place, the robber was long gone.

He gave two short knocks. "Ms. Lamont? You okay?" When there was no reply, he pushed the door wider. "Ms. Lamont?" he repeated, embarrassed that his voice was shaking. "You in there?"

He swallowed hard and walked in, cursing softly as he bumped into a table. At last he located a switch and turned on the lights.

Calling out her name again, this time much louder, Danny walked around a chair and hurried down the hall. He stopped in front of an open door, searched for the light switch and flipped it.

"God Almighty."

In the middle of the room an enormous brass bed held center stage. And on that bed, lying on her back with her arms spread wide, was Ms. Lamont—dead.

Watch for Christiane Heggan's next release

DECEPTION
coming in October 1998
from MIRA Books

CHRISTIANE HEGGAN

Suspicion

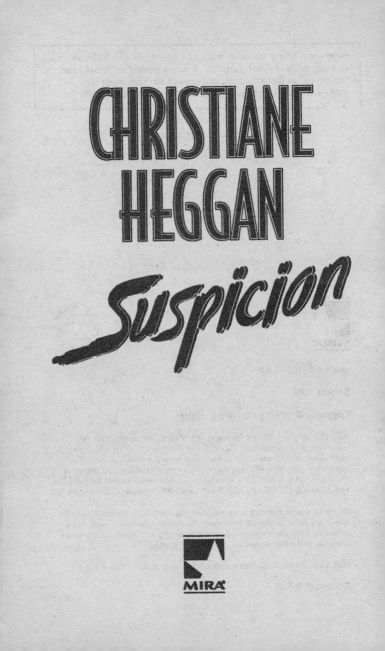

MIRA

ISBN 1-55166-305-8

SUSPICION

Copyright © 1998 by Christiane Heggan.

To Larry and Millie Criswell

Thanks for the grand tour of Washington, D.C.,
and for your friendship.

One

As the twelve jurors filed back into the courtroom, their eyes downcast, defense attorney Kate Logan felt her heart skip a beat. Not a single one of them had looked at Tony.

"Kate…" Tony shot her a quick, worried glance. He was a small but wiry young man, with Latin good looks and a tough exterior that didn't match the gentle man she knew him to be.

"Stay calm," she said, wishing she could take her own advice. "Let's listen."

From her bench, the Honorable Margaret J. Hawthorne, a severe-looking woman thought by many to favor prosecutors, turned toward the jury box. "I've been advised that you have reached a verdict," she said in her resounding voice. "Mr. Foreman, is that so?"

The foreman, a middle-aged businessman who had been scrupulously attentive throughout the trial, rose. "Yes, Your Honor. We have."

"Please hand your verdict sheet to my court clerk."

The clerk took the sheet of paper to the judge, who unfolded it and read the verdict before handing it back to him. Without a change in expression, Judge Hawthorne looked at Tony. "Will the defendant please rise?"

Tony and Kate rose together. The court clerk turned to face them and read out loud, "We, the jury, find the defendant, Antonio Fuente, guilty."

Before the people in the gallery could react, a cry of utter despair rose in the courtroom, creating instant chaos among the more than one hundred Puerto Ricans who had come to hear the verdict.

Kate didn't have to turn around to know that the heart-wrenching protest had come from Maria, Tony's mother.

"No!" the woman's voice echoed with the kind of anguish only another mother could understand. "You can't do that," she cried at the twelve solemn-faced jurors. "He didn't do it. My Tonio is innocent."

The judge, who hadn't given Kate a single break during the two-week trial, banged her gavel several times in an attempt to regain control of the courtroom.

"Silence! Silence! Sit down, Mrs. Fuente. One more outburst like that and I'll have you removed from my court." She looked at Maria over the rims of her glasses. "Is that understood?"

Reaching behind her, Kate took her housekeeper's hand, which was clasped on the wooden railing, and pulled her down gently, but firmly. She waited until Maria was once again seated before turning back to face the bench. "We apologize, Your Honor. Mrs. Fuente is under great stress—"

"Maybe so, Counselor, but I won't tolerate that kind of behavior in my courtroom."

Kate was tempted to snap right back at her. Would it have killed that cold bitch to show a little compassion? Instead, she forced her tone to be respectful. There was still a sentencing hearing to go through, and making an enemy of Judge Hawthorne now could have disastrous consequences.

"It won't happen again, Your Honor."

"Good."

Kate waited until the courtroom was perfectly quiet before adding, "May it please the court, I move that the jury be polled."

"Very well." Arms resting on the bench, Judge Hawthorne turned her head toward the jury box again. "Polling the jury simply means that I'm going to ask each one of you to state your personal verdict out loud. You need not, and will not, say anything further."

After a quick glance at each juror to make sure her instructions had been understood, the judge let her gaze rest on the man in the first seat. "Juror number one, what is your verdict?"

The man answered without hesitation. "Guilty."

"Juror number two, what is your verdict?"

"Guilty."

"Juror number three, what is your verdict?"

"Guilty."

The answer was the same with all twelve jurors, including number eight, an African-American woman with tears in her eyes and a tremor in her voice as she said the word "guilty." No doubt, Maria's grief had touched a few hearts, Kate thought bitterly. But it hadn't changed the verdict.

As the judge dismissed the jurors, Kate glanced at Tony, who, as the last shred of hope vanished, had fallen back against his chair, his eyes closed. A knot formed in her throat. She had known him since he was a small boy. She had watched him turn from a mischievous child to a rebellious teenager before finally settling down. She knew he could never hurt another human being, much less murder the woman he loved.

Kate heard the sound of rustling paper and looked up at the bench.

"The sentencing hearing will be held in this court on Tuesday, January 2 at 10:15 a.m." Judge Hawthorne snapped her desk calendar shut. "Until then, the prisoner will be escorted back to his cell." Then, with a final rap of her gavel, she added, "This court is adjourned."

Oblivious of the deputy who was approaching, handcuffs in hand, Maria stumbled out of her seat and threw herself into her son's arms. *"Oh, hijo,"* she sobbed, hugging him fiercely. *"Hijo mío."*

"Mom, please don't cry. It's going to be all right." Tony threw Kate a helpless look.

Too upset to talk, Kate wrapped a comforting arm around Maria's shoulders and held her back as handcuffs were snapped around Tony's wrists.

"Take care of my mom, Kate." All signs of toughness were gone as Tony's eyes filled with tears, not for himself, Kate knew, but for his mother, whom he adored.

"I will." She gripped Tony's arm and squeezed it. "Please don't lose faith, Tony. I know that it looks as if the system has turned its back on you right now, but this fight isn't over. First thing tomorrow morning, I'll file for appeal."

"Sure, Kate."

She watched him being led away, a proud young man who was trying desperately not to succumb to the terrible blow that had been dealt to him.

The crowded courtroom began to empty. At the prosecutor's table, Ted Rencheck, a small, pretentious man with big political aspirations, was accepting congratulations from two colleagues. Knowing he wouldn't miss a chance to come over and gloat, Kate pulled out a set of keys from her purse and handed them to Maria.

"Go wait for me in the car, Maria. I won't be long."

She was gathering her papers and stuffing them into her briefcase when Rencheck approached her. "You should have taken my deal, Kate."

"Some deal." She closed her briefcase, remembering the long, drawn-out argument they'd had in his office three weeks earlier. "You wanted my client to plead guilty when you knew damn well he was innocent."

"He could have gotten twenty years and been out in seven. Now he could get twice that—" Rencheck paused for effect "—or he could get life."

Kate turned to face him, forcing a thin smile. "And then again, he might get off on appeal."

Rencheck laughed. "Appeal? On what grounds?"

"You'll have to wait and see, won't you?"

The assistant U.S. attorney let out another chuckle and walked away, his female assistant running to catch up with him.

"Jerk," Kate murmured under her breath. As she turned around to leave, her eye caught a movement to her left. Glancing over, she saw that Mitch Calhoon, the detective who had investigated the case, was watching her.

Kate had met the homicide detective six months ago when Tony had first been apprehended. Although there was something appealing about the man—a latent strength combined with a rather boyish sincerity—she had quickly come to realize how wrong first impressions could be.

Mitch Calhoon had been concerned with only one thing—to see Tony convicted. Even under her cross-examination, which had been brutal at times, he hadn't wavered from his steadfast insistence that Tony had murdered Lilly Moore.

She wasn't surprised to see him in court today. Most detectives insisted on hearing the verdict firsthand. Calhoon was no exception. It was common knowledge that his arrest/conviction ratio was higher than anyone else's in the Washington Metro Police Department. No doubt he wanted to keep it that way.

Aware that he was still looking at her, she strode down the aisle, pushed the double doors open and hurried toward the exit.

A blast of frigid December air hit her as she stepped outside, but it wasn't the cold that instantly commanded her attention.

Held back by a half-dozen uniformed policemen, more than two hundred people, most of them Hispanic, had assembled in front of the courthouse to protest Tony's verdict. Some were carrying placards proclaiming Tony's innocence. Others were more verbal.

Maria stood facing the demonstrators, her rapid-fire Spanish eloquent and passionate as she tried to pacify them, but they weren't listening. They were accusing the justice system of having used Tony as a scapegoat, and Kate knew why. Two weeks ago, just as Tony's trial had begun, three young Puerto Ricans had blasted through a Washington delicatessen with machine guns, killed the two Italian owners and run off with eight hundred dollars in cash. Although the police knew the perpetrators and had searched their neighborhood with a fine-tooth comb, they hadn't found them. Either the three youths had fled across the state line or someone in their neighborhood was hiding them.

Afraid that this latest act of violence would jeopardize Tony's trial, Kate had made every effort to postpone it. Rencheck, true to form, had refused to delay the proceedings.

Pushing through the crowd, a female reporter for Channel 4 shoved a microphone in Kate's face. "Mrs. Logan, do you feel that Antonio Fuente's verdict was in retaliation for the killing of those two men two weeks ago?"

"No, I don't," Kate said, anxious not to have this demonstration escalate into a riot. "As you well know, the jury included two Hispanic-Americans—"

"As well as three men and women of Italian origin," the reporter interjected.

The demonstrators, either tired of listening to Maria, or inflamed by Kate's presence, suddenly turned hostile.

"You sold out, lady," a man in the front row shouted at Kate. "It's all your fault Antonio got the shaft."

"That's true." A dark-haired woman elbowed her way forward. "Whose side are you on anyway?" They moved closer, angry-faced men and women who looked as though they could explode at any moment.

Before Kate could respond, a strong hand had gripped her arm, pulling her back. Startled, Kate turned and saw Mitch Calhoon. He held her tightly, with an understated possessiveness she wasn't accustomed to.

"What do you think you're doing?" she asked, trying to free her arm.

He didn't answer. And he didn't relax his hold. Instead, he turned to the officer closest to him. "What the hell is this?" He had to shout to be heard. "What are those people doing here?"

"They have a permit, Detective. It's in order. I checked it myself."

"A permit for what?"

"Peaceful demonstration."

"Peaceful, my ass. I want them out of here." He motioned to another policeman. "Now."

The officers responded immediately, drawing their batons and gesturing for the crowd to step back. At first, the demonstrators resisted, but after a few minutes, the placards and the fists came down and they walked away.

"May I have my arm back now, please?"

As if he hadn't realized he was still holding her, the

detective glanced at Kate, then at her arm. "Sorry," he said, releasing her. The dark blue eyes moved quickly over her face, lingering longer than necessary on her mouth. "Are you all right?"

"Of course I'm all right." She'd be damned if she was going to admit to him that, for a brief moment, she had been afraid. "They weren't going to lynch me if that's what you thought."

"Maybe not, but I've seen too many such demonstrations turn sour to take a chance." He glanced at the dissipating crowd. "Where is your car?"

"Across the street, and I can get there by myself," she said, anticipating his offer to walk with her. Not wanting to sound ungrateful—he had, after all, helped her through a potentially dangerous situation—she gave him a brief nod of her head. "Thanks for your help, Detective Calhoon. I suppose you're right about crowds. One never knows which way they'll turn."

Then, signaling to Maria, who had been standing discreetly aside, she waited until her housekeeper had joined her before taking her arm and heading toward the parking lot.

Two

"*We, the jury, find the defendant, Antonio Fuente, guilty.*"

Sitting at her desk in the plush office she had occupied since joining the law firm of Fairchild, Baxter and Rendell three years ago, Kate closed her eyes as the words she had hoped would never be spoken echoed in her head.

The case had been doomed from the start. Everyone had told her so. Even Douglas Fairchild, who had known Tony even longer than she had, had warned her it would be a tough fight, perhaps a hopeless one.

Her eyes, red from lack of sleep, focused on the open folder in front of her. It contained the closing arguments she had presented to the jury only yesterday. Believing in her client's innocence, she had delivered her speech with all the passion and conviction she could muster. The jury, eight women and four men, had listened to every word, and for a while, Kate had dared to hope that the case wasn't so hopeless after all.

She couldn't have been more wrong. After deliberating for less than twenty-four hours, the twelve jurors had returned a guilty verdict.

Who could blame them? As Ted Rencheck had been only too glad to point out, the case was a slam dunk. Tony's girlfriend, a law clerk at Fairchild Baxter, had been found smothered to death in her apartment. The only fingerprints the police had found there, besides Lilly's, were those of her boyfriend, Tony Fuente.

But it was the testimony of Lilly's upstairs neighbor that had been the most damaging.

Chuck Winslow was sixty-three years old and a retired school janitor. He and his wife of forty-one years lived one floor above the apartment Lilly Moore had occupied.

On the night of the murder, Winslow had been on his way to the basement to empty his trash. As he'd reached the second floor, he'd heard shouts coming from Lilly's apartment. One of the voices had belonged to Lilly, the other to a man. They were arguing, Winslow had claimed, and the man sounded very angry. Winslow had also heard Lilly call her visitor by name—Tony.

By the time the ex-janitor had returned from the basement, all was quiet in apartment 2A and he hadn't given the incident a second thought. It wasn't until the following morning, when the police had come knocking at his door, that he learned of the tragedy that had occurred on the floor below.

Although Tony had admitted to being in Lilly's apartment that night, he had emphatically denied having quarreled with her. In fact, he said they had been talking about taking a vacation together after Lilly graduated from law school later on that month. When he left Lilly's apartment—fifteen minutes *before* Chuck Winslow claimed to have heard him and Lilly argue—Tony was the happiest man on earth.

At the time he was arrested, and through the entire trial, Tony had also maintained having seen a station wagon parked across the street. He wouldn't have paid much attention to the car if it hadn't been for the man behind the wheel—an unusually large man wearing a dark knit cap, who seemed to be dozing.

Hoping to identify the mystery person, Kate had distributed a rough sketch throughout the neighborhood, but no one fitting that description, or that of the car, had been seen in the vicinity.

In the end, the jury hadn't believed Tony. It didn't matter to them that he adored Lilly, that he had turned his life around and was putting himself through college by working long hours as a bartender. Only two things had mattered: Antonio Fuente had once belonged to a gang and he had a hot Latin temper—a point the prosecution had reiterated continually.

Feeling restless, Kate stood up. As she did, she caught her reflection in the small antique mirror directly across from her desk. God, she looked awful, she thought, running her fingers through her shaggy red hair and wishing she had never cut it. After she'd left her husband, Eric Logan, a year ago, she had felt an overwhelming need for change, for self-renewal. At the time, chopping off the rich, fiery mane Eric had loved so much had seemed like an important step toward that goal. Thank God it was beginning to grow back, but until it was restored to its original shape and length, she would have to make the best of what was there.

Peering into the mirror, she studied her features a little more closely. She looked tired. Tears shed in the car as she had driven Maria home had washed away most of her makeup, and her green eyes, usually so bright, now looked dull and weary. Even her mouth had a sad, downward slant to it. Tony's trial had taken its toll on her. Just as it had on Maria.

With a sigh, she moved to the window overlooking the Capitol. Just beyond it was the Mall, the vast, grassy, gravel-pathed pedestrian strip that stretched for several blocks, all the way to the Washington Monument.

Kate never tired of the view, of the huge crowds that mobbed the area every day, of the grandeur of the monuments. Even now, with the trees barren and the skies a pewter shade of gray, there was a symbolic beauty to this city that was breathtaking.

She had fallen in love with the nation's capital the moment she had set foot in it eighteen years ago. She had been a freshman at Georgetown University then, a wide-eyed country girl full of dreams and ideals.

The daughter of two Iowa schoolteachers, she had never wanted to be anything but a lawyer. But rather than seek employment in one of the capital's many law firms after her graduation from law school, she had accepted a position with the U.S. attorney's office.

"I want to make a difference," she had told her father, by then a widower. "I want to truly serve the people. And to do that, I need to prosecute criminals, not defend them."

Her father had understood. But not Eric Logan, whom she had married during her first year of law school. A marketing assistant at Hollbrook Industries, Eric couldn't understand why, after all the time and money she had invested in her education, she had settled for such a menial job.

After a while, Kate gave up trying to explain it to him. Too late she realized that he had married her not because he loved her, but because he thought that as an attorney, she would be able to provide him with the kind of luxuries he regarded as essential.

"Living in style," as Eric called it, was the reason he had insisted they live in his stepfather's luxurious home in Potomac, Maryland, where he had spent the past several years, rather than in Kate's modest Bethesda apartment.

At first, Kate didn't see any harm in it. Rose and Douglas Fairchild had welcomed her with open arms, and the house was certainly big enough to give the newlyweds all the privacy they needed. But when Alison was born a year later, Kate began to wonder if being raised in such luxury would give the child a false sense of values.

When Kate suggested to Eric that they start looking for a place of their own, he was so adamantly opposed to the idea that she quickly dropped it—for the sake of family harmony—and never brought up the subject again.

Three years ago, following a complex murder case Kate had brilliantly prosecuted, Douglas, who had tried to lure her to his firm before, made her another offer—a six-figure salary and a junior partnership in Fairchild Baxter.

Her initial reaction was to say no, as she had previously. She still felt the justice system was unfair, that it leaned too heavily in favor of the defendant, especially if the latter happened to be wealthy.

Knowing that, and knowing that an office with a view and a handsome salary wasn't enough to sway her, Douglas had laid his trump card on the table. Along with the high-profile clients Kate would be expected to represent, she would also be able to take on cases that were important to her, cases the firm might otherwise reject.

After a great deal of consideration, she agreed to give Douglas's offer a try, partly because she was fond of him and hated to disappoint him again and partly because she hoped, foolishly, that the huge increase in salary would save her marriage.

But while her decision to leave the U.S. attorney's office proved highly successful careerwise, it did little to improve the situation between her and Eric. Disillusioned with his lack of advancement at Hollbrook Industries, Eric had begun to go out at night, sometimes until late. Although he emphatically denied it, Kate was certain he was seeing other women.

It wasn't until last December, when she caught him having lunch in an out-of-the-way restaurant with a stunning nineteen-year-old, that she decided she'd had enough. Indifferent to Eric's claim that the girl meant nothing to him, that he loved Kate and didn't want to lose her, she packed her and Alison's belongings, moved out of the Fairchilds' house and filed for divorce.

Life as a single mom hadn't been easy, especially with a daughter who held her solely responsible for the breakup of their family. But somehow they had survived the first year. And at times, that's exactly what it felt like—survival.

"How did it go, Kate?"

At the sound of her ex-father-in-law's voice, Kate turned around and met Douglas Fairchild's concerned gaze. In his early sixties, he was a short, round man with thinning gray hair and pale blue eyes that seldom showed any kind of emotion—a characteristic that had served him well in the courtroom. He came from a long, illustrious line of Washington attorneys and had inherited the sixty-year-old firm from his father, a former Supreme Court judge.

Kate sighed, walked back to her desk and sat down. "They found him guilty."

"I see." Unbuttoning his impeccably tailored brown jacket, Douglas lowered his chubby frame into a chair facing Kate's desk. Although his face was grim, she knew he wasn't surprised at the verdict. "How did Maria take it?"

"Badly. One of the jurors was close to tears and couldn't bear to look at her."

"Did you poll them?"

Kate nodded. "They all stuck to their verdict."

Douglas gave a troubled shake of his head. "I feel terrible about this. Maria and Tony are like family to me."

It was true. Prior to working for Kate, Maria had been in the Fairchilds' employ for nineteen years. When Kate had divorced Eric and moved out of the Fairchilds' mansion, it was Douglas who had suggested that Maria go with Kate so Alison, then twelve years old, would have someone she knew and loved to look after her when Kate was at work.

"He didn't do it, Douglas," Kate said with the same earnestness she had demonstrated in the courtroom. "I've never been so sure of a man's innocence as I am of Tony's. They convicted the wrong man."

Douglas's eyes locked with hers. "Are you absolutely sure of that?"

Kate stiffened. "Are you saying you aren't? That you think Tony lied to us?"

Douglas sighed and pinched the bridge of his nose. "Frankly, Kate, I don't know what to think anymore. Since hearing Chuck Winslow's testimony last week—"

"The man lied! Someone got to him and offered him a lot of money in exchange for that phony testimony. I'd stake my life on it."

"If that was the case, we would have already seen signs of his windfall—an occasional dinner out perhaps, or some new clothes for his wife. But you told me yourself that his lifestyle hasn't changed one bit since the murder. He and his wife never go out, they don't entertain and they still ride around in that battered old pickup truck."

"He's being cautious, that's all," Kate said stubbornly. "I'm sure whoever bought his testimony warned him about not flaunting the money."

Douglas looked skeptical. "I don't know, Kate. I was

there the day Winslow testified, remember? He didn't sound like a man who was lying. In fact, I thought he made a very credible witness. Even under your cross-examination—and you were tough on him, Kate—he never faltered."

Kate leaned back in her chair and steepled her fingers. She had always had a great deal of respect for Douglas, but there were times when she couldn't quite figure him out. Maybe he had been defending the rich and mighty too long. He had become jaded, almost cynical.

Well, no matter what he or anyone else said, she would never believe Tony killed Lilly—not even in a moment of passion. Right now, however, she was too damned tired to argue about it.

Remembering that Douglas and Rose were leaving for Bermuda in a few hours, she asked, "What are you doing here anyway? Shouldn't you be home packing?"

Douglas's lips pulled into a smile. "Are you kidding? Rose wouldn't let me within ten feet of a suitcase. Besides, I didn't want to leave without finding out about Tony."

With a flip of her hand, Kate closed her file. "I wish I could have given you better news."

Douglas watched her for a moment, his expression unreadable. Then, in that fatherly tone he used only when they were alone, he said, "I hope you're not blaming yourself, Kate. You did a great job in that courtroom—the best, considering what you had to work with."

"Thank you for saying that, Douglas."

"I mean it." He leaned back in his chair and crossed his hands over his slightly protruding stomach. "You know what you need to lift your spirits? A vacation. Why don't you come to Bermuda with us? Rose would love it."

It was a tempting offer. She could think of nothing more appealing at the moment than lying on a warm, tranquil beach, pretending not to have a care in the world. But there was Tony's appeal to prepare and a daughter to supervise.

"Alison would never forgive me if I went without her, and as much as she would love to play hooky for a few days, taking her out of school so close to Christmas wouldn't do her grades any good." She smiled. "May I have a rain check?"

"You bet." Douglas's expression sobered as he asked, "How are things between you two?"

Kate shrugged. "Status quo, I'm afraid. She still blames me for divorcing Eric and I still let it get to me."

"I know my wife would wring my neck for telling you this, but don't you think it's high time you told Alison why you divorced her father?"

"No." Kate shook her head. "She's been through enough. Besides, she wouldn't believe me. You know how she idolizes Eric."

Douglas made a face as if he had suddenly smelled something foul. "Don't remind me."

Kate held back a smile. It was no secret that Douglas didn't like his stepson. The only reason he tolerated Eric's living in his house was Rose, who adored Eric.

As Douglas stood up, Kate did the same. "Enjoy your vacation, Douglas," she said, circling her desk. "I'll see you when you get back."

"All right. But if you change your mind, we take off at one." At the door, he turned around. "Give my love to my granddaughter, will you? And tell her if she behaves herself, I'll bring her those earrings she saw in Hamilton the last time she was there."

Three

Juggling his briefcase, a bag of groceries and his keys, Mitch Calhoon opened the front door to his Kalorama Road town house, bent to pick up his mail, and kicked the door shut behind him.

The place was just as he had left it that morning—a mess. A basket of laundered clothes he had meant to fold and put away sat in the center of the living room, yesterday's newspaper was scattered all over the floor, and an empty coffee cup was on the cocktail table.

Vowing to give the entire house a thorough cleaning before going to bed, he walked across the living room and into the small but efficient kitchen.

When he had returned to Washington a year ago, he could have purchased any of the grand old Federal homes that lined some of the capital's most famous streets. His years as a private investigator had been financially rewarding, and as a single man he had nothing else to do with his money. But when the Realtor had taken him through Adams Morgan with its smorgasbord of ethnic restaurants, outdoor vendors and street musicians, Mitch had made his choice right there and then. The Realtor, sensing a hefty commission was passing her by, had tried to discourage him, reminding Mitch of the 1991 riots that had spilled into Adams Morgan from neighboring Mount Pleasant. Mitch had been unfazed. He liked the area. It was everything Washington wasn't—hip, undisciplined and unpredictable.

Today's mail still in his hand, Mitch set the Safeway bag on the counter and started to sort through the pile of sale circulars and Christmas catalogs. Spotting the electric bill, he set it aside and threw the rest into the trash.

The muscles in his neck and shoulders felt stiff and he rolled his head, trying to loosen them. At any other time, he would have attributed the condition to the long hours spent at his desk, typing those tedious police reports. Today, the tension he felt was caused by something else entirely—the Fuente verdict.

Assigned to the murder case six months ago, Mitch had handled the investigation as he had dozens of others— efficiently and expeditiously. Nothing about the case or the witnesses he had questioned had led him to believe that something was amiss. Until a week ago when, on his way to pick up his car, which was being serviced, he had seen Chuck Winslow examining a brand-new Explorer. After questioning the salesman, Mitch found out that this had been Winslow's second visit to the dealership.

The same question had nagged Mitch all morning. How could a man on a janitor's pension with no savings afford to even look at a twenty-five-thousand-dollar car?

Curious to see if Winslow's financial situation had changed since Mitch's initial investigation, he had made a few discreet inquiries. And found absolutely nothing. Except for a small pension and two hundred dollars in a passbook account, Winslow had no money.

A less obstinate cop would have called it a dead end. But Mitch's gut feeling told him something wasn't quite right with the good janitor. And if there was one thing he trusted, after eighteen years in the business, it was his gut feeling.

Unfortunately, Rencheck hadn't shared his concern. After seven years as an assistant prosecutor, he had just announced his candidacy for U.S. attorney, and he wasn't about to jeopardize his long-standing winning streak.

"So the man was looking at an expensive car," Rencheck had told Mitch the following day. "Since when is that a crime? The man can dream, can't he?"

At the suggestion that Winslow may have been motivated by more than his civic duty, the prosecutor had laughed. "Come on, Calhoon, you know as well as I do that if someone had paid Winslow off, he would have spent some of the money by now. He's just too damned stupid to do otherwise." Then, with a smile that hadn't quite reached his eyes, he had added, "You did a good job on this case, Mitch. Don't screw things up now."

Realizing he still hadn't put the groceries away, Mitch began to empty the bag, which contained the usual staples—coffee, milk, a loaf of bread and a pound of American cheese. On his schedule, regular meals were practically nonexistent. When the urge to eat something more substantial struck him, he usually ordered Chinese from a nearby takeout or stopped to pick up a pizza on his way home.

To offset the damages made by years of junk food, Mitch put himself through an exercise routine that would have made younger men cringe. Apparently, his efforts had paid off. At thirty-seven, he was blessed with the same hard body he'd had during high school when he'd led his football team to a state championship three years in a row.

His sports exploits, combined with an excellent academic record, had earned him a scholarship to George Mason University in Fairfax, Virginia. But Mitch never graduated. When his father, a Fairfax police sergeant was killed in the line of duty, Mitch had left school and joined the force, determined to continue the work his father had loved so much.

He'd just been promoted to detective when he met Ava.

Before his thoughts took him too deeply into a past he had worked hard to forget, Mitch opened the fridge and extracted an ice-cold Budweiser.

He was debating between leftover chow mein and a Swanson frozen entrée for dinner when his doorbell rang. Beer in hand, he went to answer it. It was his best friend and fellow policeman, Tom Spivak. The two men had worked together on the Fuente case before Tom had been pulled out to investigate a high-profile murder.

The veteran detective was a big man with a linebacker physique, a ruddy complexion and a fiery shock of red hair he kept in a military crew cut. Although he had recently been passed over for sergeant, he was an excellent cop.

"Am I interrupting one of your culinary adventures?" Tom, who liked to tease Mitch about his poor eating habits, gave an exaggerated sniff.

"Why?" Mitch deadpanned. "Were you thinking of joining me?"

Tom chuckled. "Not on your life." He patted his flat stomach. "After all I went through to get back in shape, I've sworn off junk food forever. I'll take one of those, though." He pointed at the Bud in Mitch's hand. "I'm off duty."

Back in the kitchen, Mitch took another beer from the refrigerator and tossed it to his friend. Leaning against the kitchen counter, he crossed his ankles. "What's up?"

"I dropped the girls off at ballet class and thought I'd stop by to see if you'd heard about the Fuente verdict."

Mitch's hand went to the back of his neck. He squeezed hard. "I was there."

"You don't sound very happy."

"I'm not." He gave Tom a long, thoughtful look. "I think Chuck Winslow may have lied on the stand."

Tom's eyes registered surprise. "You're kidding."

"I wish I were." He told Tom about seeing Winslow at the dealership.

"You told Rencheck?"

Mitch let out a short, bitter laugh. "He said I was making a big deal out of nothing."

"Sound advice considering he's just won a conviction."

Mitch tipped the can of Bud to his mouth and took a long swallow. "Yeah, except I'm not buying it. There's something about Winslow that doesn't ring true."

"Did you check into his finances again?"

"That's the first thing I did. Unfortunately, nothing has changed."

"So why is this still an issue?" Tom asked after taking a sip of his own beer.

"Because the guy wasn't just window-shopping, Tom. Maybe he wasn't planning to buy the Explorer any time soon, but he was looking at it as if he intended to buy it. That much I could tell. And so could the salesman."

"Is that all you're basing your suspicions on?"

"No. I keep thinking about his court testimony, too. For someone so unsophisticated, he handled Kate Logan's cross-examination remarkably well. Much like a man who had a lot at stake."

Tom's mouth curved into a mischievous smile. "Are you sure you weren't influenced by Kate Logan's moving summation? I understand the woman was nothing short of brilliant."

"That had nothing to do with it." Although that was true enough, he couldn't deny Kate Logan had impressed him very much. More disturbing was the fact that since meeting her six months ago, he hadn't been able to get her out of his mind.

"What are you going to do?" Tom asked.

Mitch smiled. Tom knew him well. Too well perhaps. "What makes you think I'm going to do anything?"

"You've got that restless look about you, and I'm not sure I like it. The last time you followed one of your hunches, you nearly got yourself killed."

"Stop worrying so much. You sound like an old lady."

"Then tell me I have no reason to worry, that you're not thinking of doing something stupid. Like getting Rencheck pissed off at you. And believe me, he'll be pissed big time if he finds out you're reinvestigating a case he's just won."

"It's happened before."

"But not to Rencheck. This is a man who wants to be U.S. attorney real bad, Mitch. You foul up his chances and there's going to be hell to pay, so watch your back, will you?"

Mitch took one last swallow of his beer. "I intend to do just that." Then, because he knew his friend hadn't come all this way to discuss Tony Fuente's verdict, he added, "Now, why don't you tell me why you're really here?"

Tom chuckled. "As a matter of fact, smart-ass, I came to invite you to a dinner party on Saturday night. Nothing fancy. Just us and our new neighbor. Her name is Shannon. She's new in town—"

Mitch raised his hands in mock fear. "Oh, no, you don't. After the last barracuda Mary Beth introduced me to a couple of months ago, I'm through with blind dates."

"This one is different, I swear. She's attractive, bright and—this is the best part—she's totally devoted to her career and won't make any demands on you. In fact, she told Mary Beth marriage is the furthest thing from her mind at the moment."

"No."

"It's just a dinner, Mitch, not a lifetime commitment."

"I don't care. The answer is still no."

Tom sighed. "Mary Beth is going to be disappointed. This is the third invite you've turned down this month."

That was true. Ever since Mitch had rejoined the Washington Metropolitan Police Department a year ago, Mary Beth and a number of other well-meaning policemen's wives had made it their mission to pair him with some of the capital's most eligible young women.

None of them had turned out to be anything more than a passing interest. No matter how much Tom praised the advantages of married life, Mitch's own experience with matrimony had left him with a bitter taste in his mouth. The women he did date occasionally were women who, like him, had no need for serious attachments. Those relationships, although not terribly fulfilling, accomplished one goal. They helped fill the void.

"Tell Mary Beth I appreciate what she's trying to do. But she doesn't need to worry about me. I'm really a very happy fellow." To prove his point, he gave Tom a broad, silly grin.

Tom crushed his empty can with a single squeeze of his big hand and tossed it in the trash. "Why don't you come for Sunday dinner and tell her yourself? She's making her famous lasagna."

"No surprise guest?"

"Nope. Just the Spivak clan. On its best Sunday behavior."

Mitch wrapped an arm around his friend's shoulders and walked him to the door. "You're on, then. I'll bring the Ruffino."

Kate's house was located in Cleveland Park, a quiet, upscale neighborhood in the District's upper northwest. It was a classic two-story Colonial with green shutters, a screened porch and a large backyard.

Kate had chosen Cleveland Park not only because of its small-town charm, but also because of its proximity to Potomac, where Alison's grandparents lived, and to Georgetown, where Eric would be moving after his marriage to industrial heiress, Megan Hollbrook. As much as Kate had wanted to distance herself from her ex-husband after the divorce, it was important for Alison to be near him, to feel she could see him as often as she needed to.

As usual, the first thing that greeted Kate when she came home was the deafening sound of rock music blasting from Alison's CD player. Angry at the teenager's blatant disregard for their neighbors, Kate dropped her briefcase on a chair, shrugged off her camel-hair coat and hurried up the stairs to her daughter's bedroom. Ignoring the No Trespassing sign hanging from the knob, she flung open the door.

Alison was stretched out on the bed, her right ankle resting on her left knee and her foot beating in time with the music. In spite of the noise, she seemed totally absorbed in the schoolbook she held.

At times like these, when her face was free of hostility, Alison's beauty, caught somewhere between womanhood and childhood, was almost breathtaking. Long, silky blond hair framed a delicate face with high cheekbones, beautiful gray eyes she had inherited from her father, and a small, petulant mouth.

Unnoticed, Kate marched to the wall-to-wall bookcase and stopped the offending sound with a push of her finger.

Alison jumped off the bed, a look of shock on her face. "What are you doing?"

"Turning this earsplitting machine off," Kate said, bracing herself for another fight. "Something I wouldn't have to do if you didn't constantly challenge everything I say."

"You said not to play my music loud. That wasn't loud."

"Mrs. Lieberman disagrees. She's complained twice already."

In a gesture that was meant to be arrogant, Alison flipped her long hair behind her shoulder and thrust her chin forward. "If we didn't live in this stupid house, we wouldn't have to worry about nagging old neighbors like Mrs. Lieberman."

"This stupid house," Kate replied a little testily, "is your home now, whether you like it or not. So I suggest you adapt." She nodded toward the bookcase. "And that means no loud music. You break that rule one more time and I'll take your CD player away." Then, half-expecting Alison to retreat to her bed and sulk as she often did, Kate headed for the door. "Dinner is in forty minutes."

"Well, I *don't* like it," Alison said, following Kate down the stairs. "In fact, I hate it here. This house is too small. And it's miles away from my friends."

"Maybe it's time you made new friends."

"I tried. They all hate me because I'm rich."

Kate held back a sigh. "Alison, how many times have I told you that you're not rich. Your grandparents are rich. Maybe if you stopped acting like such a spoiled brat, you wouldn't have so much trouble making friends."

The moment the words were out of her mouth, Kate

regretted them. Harsh criticism was hardly the way to improve the relationship between her and Alison. What Kate needed was patience and understanding, both of which Alison kept pushing to the limit.

"I'm sorry, baby," Kate said, stopping at the bottom of the stairs and turning to face her daughter. "I didn't mean that."

"Oh, you meant it all right," Alison spit. "I heard you talk to Grandma on the phone the other day. I heard you tell her how much I had changed."

"You have."

"You've changed, too. First you divorced Daddy for no reason at all. Then you forced me to leave Grandpa's house where I've lived all my life. You never once asked me what *I* wanted to do, who *I* wanted to live with. That's not how it used to be. We always had family conferences where everyone had a chance to express their opinion."

"This was different. The decision that you should live with me was one your father and I made together." Her voice softened. "I'm sorry if you felt left out, baby. We didn't think it was fair to ask you to choose between your father and your mother."

"So you chose for me."

"It was in your best interest. I know you don't agree with me right now, but someday you will."

"No, I won't."

Rather than pursue an argument she couldn't possibly win, Kate took a deep, calming breath and walked into the kitchen. With its blue tile countertops, oak cabinets and pleasant smells, the room never failed to cheer her up. But tonight the magic wasn't working.

Aware that Alison had followed her, Kate opened the refrigerator, pulled out the meat loaf she had prepared before going to court that morning and slid it into the oven. "Look, sweetie," she said, hoping that the sight of her daughter's favorite dish would turn the girl around. "What do you say we call a truce for a couple of hours and try to have a nice, peaceful dinner. I've had a bad day."

Alison's transformation was immediate. For a moment, she was once again the sweet, compassionate young girl Kate knew and loved. "Oh, my God, I totally forgot. The verdict came in, didn't it?" She searched her mother's face, saw the grim expression and let her shoulders sag. Tears filled her eyes. "They found Tony guilty."

Kate nodded.

"Oh, no." Leaning against the island, Alison lowered her head in her hands and wept hopelessly.

In two short strides, Kate was by her side, enveloping her in her arms. Six years older than Alison, Tony had spent a lot of time at the Fairchilds' house when he was growing up, and the two had formed a strong friendship.

Kate continued to hold her daughter tightly, stroking her hair. "I'm not going to abandon him, Alison. I'll be working very hard on his appeal."

Suddenly, Alison pulled away from her mother's embrace. "This is all Detective Calhoon's fault," she said in a voice full of hatred. "If he hadn't brought up Tony's association with that street gang years ago, the jury would have had a different opinion of him."

"Detective Calhoon was just doing his job, darling."

"Well, his job stinks."

Kate smiled. "If it's any consolation, I agree with you."

Alison wiped her tear-streaked face with the back of her hand. "When is the sentencing?"

"January second."

"Why so late? Tony will go crazy."

"The judge's docket was full. That's the first date she had available."

"Can I see him?" Alison asked after a while.

"Sure." Kate took a strand of hair that clung to Alison's wet face and tucked it behind the girl's ear. "I'll see if I can arrange a visit for you sometime next week."

"Thanks."

Her face expressionless again, Alison began to set the table. As Kate busied herself with the rest of the meal, she threw an occasional glance toward the teenager. God, how she missed the way they used to be, more like sisters than mother and daughter. That moment they had just shared, however short, had made her realize how badly she wanted her sweet, young daughter back.

"You need to be a little more patient with her," Rose Fairchild had told Kate a few days ago when the two women had met for one of their weekly lunch dates. "She's had to deal with an awful lot lately—the divorce, a new home, a new school. And puberty." The gray eyes, so much like Eric's, had twinkled with amusement. "It's been a while since I was a teenager, but surely *you* remember what it was like, don't you, dear?"

Maybe Rose was right. It wasn't easy to be thirteen. Maybe Kate was the one who was being too demanding, not Alison.

Holding back an uncharacteristic sigh of self-pity, Kate took a Sara Lee pound cake from the freezer and set it on the counter to defrost. Alison was the most important person in her life and she would not give up until she had won her back. No matter what it took.

Four

In spite of Kate's efforts to salvage what was left of the evening, Alison had remained cold and distant throughout dinner, answering Kate's questions about school in monosyllabic sentences that only added to the tension. At eight o'clock, claiming to have homework, she had retreated to her room, looking more sullen than ever.

Now, alone at the kitchen table, Kate stared pensively into a mug half-filled with cold coffee. What did she have to do to set things right between her and Alison? The only person the child seemed to care for these days, besides her grandparents, was Eric. Not that he wasn't deserving of his daughter's love. If one was to discount his lack of parental guidance and his inability to say no, Eric was a good father. He was fun, understanding and generous to a fault.

A knock at the door made her jump. She glanced at the kitchen clock on the wall. Ten-fifteen. Who could it be at this time of night?

She stood up and went to the door, cautiously peering out the narrow side window. But before she could make out the shape on the front step, her visitor knocked again, this time more insistently.

"Kate, it's me. Eric. Open the door."

"Eric." Not bothering to conceal her irritation, Kate punched in the code on the security system and opened the door. Her former husband stood on the threshold, dressed in jeans, a navy duffle coat and black Reeboks. With his blond good looks and youthful physique, he looked more like a college student than a thirty-eight-year-old divorced man. "What do you want?" she snapped.

If he noticed the edge in her voice, he didn't show it. Instead, he walked past her. "I need to talk to you."

Kate let the door swing shut behind him. "You could have picked a better time."

"This couldn't wait." At the kitchen doorway, he glanced toward the second floor. "Alison asleep?"

"It's ten-fifteen on a school night. Of course she's asleep."

It wasn't until Eric had stepped into the kitchen and was in full light that she saw the changes in him. The year-round tan he worked hard to maintain seemed to have faded, and there was a haunted, almost desperate look in the handsome gray eyes.

Her first thought was for her former mother-in-law. "What is it? Has something happened to Rose?"

"My mother is fine." Raking both hands through his hair, he began to pace. "It's me. I'm in big trouble, Kate." He turned pleading eyes toward her. "I didn't know where else to go."

Her eyes narrowed. "What kind of trouble?"

"I'm being blackmailed."

"Blackmailed." Kate took a couple of seconds to digest the news. "By whom?"

"A woman." He averted his eyes. "A woman...I slept with a couple of nights ago."

"Oh, Eric." Kate slowly shook her head as a sense of déjà vu swept over her. Eric had always had a weakness where women were concerned, but when Rose had told her that he'd changed now that he was engaged to Megan Hollbrook, Kate had wanted to believe it—for Alison's sake. "You slept with a woman two months before your wedding? Have you lost your mind?"

He stopped his pacing and leaned against the kitchen counter. "Believe me, Kate, you aren't telling me anything I haven't told myself a dozen times already. All I can say in my defense is that I was drunk."

"Apparently not too drunk to have sex."

"No. Although I doubt that a lack of libido would have made any difference."

"What do you mean?"

His eyes flashed with sudden anger. "I mean that even if I hadn't been able to screw her, that bitch would have made it look as if I had. Just so she could squeeze money out of me."

Kate took two fresh mugs from the cupboard and filled them with coffee. "Why don't you start at the beginning?"

Eric took the mug she handed him with both hands and stared into it for a moment. "I met her at Lyle Wanamaker's birthday bash on Saturday night."

Kate knew Lyle well. A rich playboy who liked to live on the edge, he had a deplorable influence on Eric. "You went there alone?"

He nodded. "Megan's bridesmaids were giving her a shower. I didn't want to go without her, but she insisted I should, that Lyle would be offended if I didn't at least make an appearance."

"And within minutes, you had a leggy blonde attached to your arm," Kate said sarcastically. "Some things never change, do they, Eric?"

"It wasn't like that." He still wouldn't look at her. "She was the one who came on to me. Her name was

Gina Lamont. She said she was a model and that a friend had brought her to the party. But I had her pegged for what she was—a high-priced call girl—the moment I laid eyes on her.''

He set the mug down, and without asking her if he could smoke, he reached into his coat pocket, pulled out a pack of Salems and shook a cigarette out. Kate started to object and then stopped. He was upset enough as it was without adding to his misery. Having no ashtrays, she reached inside a cabinet, pulled out one of her mismatched saucers and set it on the counter.

Using a solid gold lighter, Eric lit the cigarette and drew on it deeply before releasing the smoke toward the ceiling. ''When she asked me if I wanted to take her home, I told her I was engaged and very much in love with my fiancée, but she wouldn't leave me alone.''

''You could have left.''

''I could have done a lot of things. Unfortunately, after three martinis, I wasn't exactly thinking with my brain.''

''So you took her to bed.''

He nodded. ''I woke up at three in the morning with a hangover and a naked woman lying next to me.''

''What did you do?''

''What do you think? I dropped a hundred bucks on her bureau and hightailed it out of there as fast as I could, while praying I'd never see her again.''

''I take it your wish didn't come true.''

He took another drag on the cigarette. ''Unfortunately no. At two o'clock this afternoon, the little bitch waltzes into my office, perches her ass on my desk and waves a videotape under my nose. Then, before I have a chance to ask what the hell it is, she sashays to my VCR and inserts the tape into it.'' He paused before adding, ''I'm sure you can guess who the main attraction was.''

Kate's eyes widened. "You mean she taped the two of you? In bed?"

"She must have had a camera set up in the bedroom. I bet she does that with all her johns. What a racket."

"What does she want?"

Eric met Kate's inquiring gaze. "A lot more than the hundred bucks I left her."

"How much?"

"Two hundred and fifty thousand dollars."

"*What?*"

"My feelings exactly. I tried to tell her I didn't have that kind of money. She didn't want to hear it. I have one week to get it or she'll send a copy of the tape to all the major tabloids. I can see the headlines now. Fiancé Of Multimillionaire Heiress Beds Hooker." He crushed his cigarette in the saucer and immediately lit another.

Kate felt sorry for him. He had a way of attracting trouble that was almost uncanny. Somehow he always managed to get out of it, partly because he was resourceful and partly because he was lucky. But this time, Lady Luck was nowhere in sight. And he had good reason to worry. Not about his fiancée, who might even forgive him, but about the girl's mother, the formidable and very powerful Abigail Hollbrook.

In a candid interview with the *Washington Post* a few months ago, the CEO of Hollbrook Industries had not concealed her displeasure at her daughter's choice of a husband. Like any other loving mother, however, she had bowed to Megan's wishes, given them both her blessing and promised to make Eric a junior vice president after the wedding.

Eric was terrified of her. According to Rose, Abigail had warned him that at the slightest infraction on his part, he would be out of Megan's life—and Hollbrook Industries—forever.

"Well." Kate reached for the coffeepot and topped off both mugs. "Since I assume you came here for advice, I'll give it to you. Tell Megan everything. She's your fiancée, and should hear the grisly details from you, not from some rag."

"What good would that do? Abigail would finally have an excuse to cancel a wedding she never wanted in the first place. That old broad hates me, you know. She thinks I'm nothing but a fortune hunter."

At that remark, which she let pass, Kate almost smiled. "You're marrying Megan, not her mother."

"Megan will do what her mother tells her to. She always does."

"She stood up to her when you proposed. What makes you think she won't do it again?"

"Because she's going to be devastated. I slept with another woman—a hooker no less." His voice turned whiny, like that of a spoiled child. "I'm going to lose everything, Kate—my fiancée, my job, my future at Hollbrook..."

Kate's eyes filled with contempt. How typical of him to think of himself and not the woman he had wronged. "In that case, your only other recourse is to talk to Douglas. Maybe he'll loan you the money."

"Douglas?" Eric made a derisive sound. "That bastard wouldn't raise a finger to help me if I lay in a gutter bleeding to death. After you left me last year, he wanted to throw me out. Did you know that? It took Mom three days to convince him to let me stay." He gave an emphatic shake of his head. "Trust me, my self-righteous stepfather would like nothing better than to see me being crushed like a bug. And Mom doesn't have any money of her own, so…''

He took a couple of quick, hard drags on his cigarette, then extinguished it. "You want to know how desperate I am? I tried to borrow the money from a bank. The loan officer practically laughed in my face. Apparently, without collateral, there isn't a bank in the world that will lend me that kind of money. And my upcoming marriage to one of the country's richest women didn't impress him, either. Unless, of course, I can get Megan to co-sign the loan. Isn't that a blast?''

"Well, don't look at me," Kate said as he gave her a long, intense look. "A quarter of a million dollars is hardly the kind of change I keep tucked in the cookie jar.''

He continued to look at her.

Kate raised an eyebrow. "What?''

"You have the money, Kate.''

"What are you talking about? You know perfectly well that the down payment on this house took nearly every cent I had.''

"There's Alison's trust fund. You can lend it to me. I promise I'll pay you back after I'm married to Megan.''

Whatever pity she had felt for him until now vanished. "How dare you suggest something like that? Douglas set up that trust fund for Alison's education. And you want to hand it over to a *prostitute?*''

"I said I'd pay it back.''

"With what? Do you think Megan is going to let you have two hundred and fifty thousand dollars without wanting to know where it's going?''

"I'll think of something.''

She shook her head. "God, you're even more despicable than I thought.''

"Kate, be reasonable. I have nowhere else to go. You're the only one who can get me out of this mess."

"In case I haven't made myself clear enough, the answer is no."

"If you won't do it for me, then do it for Alison. She would want you to help me."

"You bastard." She uttered the two words under her breath, finding it more and more difficult not to shout at him. "Don't you dare use my daughter as leverage."

"She's my daughter, too."

Kate was no longer listening. Brushing past him, she marched to the front door, Eric behind her, and held it open. "Good night, Eric. And next time you find yourself in trouble, do me a favor and go cry on someone else's shoulder. I have enough problems of my own without being burdened with yours."

He stood in front of her, eyes pleading again. "Kate—"

"Go." When he showed no sign of leaving, she gave him a hard shove and slammed the door shut.

Standing in the foyer, she waited until his Corvette had roared off. Then, feeling suddenly bone tired, she turned on the burglar alarm again and went upstairs.

Five

"Scotch, please. Straight."

In the dimly lit Virginia tavern some ten miles south of Washington, Eric Logan waited as a surly bartender in a dirty sweatshirt poured his drink. Then, picking up his glass, he brought it to his mouth, tilted his head back and downed the contents in one gulp.

The liquor brought tears to his eyes. He had never been much of a drinker. Even in college, when doing shots was all the rage, he had been the subject of constant ribbing about his "unmanly" drinking habits.

But tonight, he needed more than the smoothness of a good martini or the tang of an imported beer. He needed something that would not only soothe his frazzled nerves, but drown his fears, as well. He needed complete oblivion. If there was such a beast.

Before the bartender could put the bottle of Johnnie Walker away, Eric slammed his empty glass down on the counter. "Hit me again, will you? Make it a double this time."

Glass in hand, he walked across the room and sat down at a water-stained table, not bothering to remove his coat. Except for two loudmouths in cowboy hats shooting pool, the place was empty. Which suited him just fine. He was in no mood for company.

After leaving Kate's house, he had driven south with

no particular destination in mind. Then, as he had turned a bend, he had seen the sign for Joe's Tavern. The dingy bar reeked of stale tobacco and cheap liquor, but it was open, and it was next door to a motel, which might come in handy a couple of hours from now. What more could a guy in search of oblivion want?

With a sigh that sounded more like a groan, he propped his elbows on the table and pressed the heels of his hands against his eyes. How could he have been so stupid? How could he have risked all he had for a lousy, overused piece of ass?

Dragging his hands down his cheeks, he tried to imagine the look on Megan's face when she found out the truth. One thing was certain. She would never forgive him. To Megan, who had inherited her mother's pride if not her strength, the soiling of the Hollbrook name would be as unforgivable a deed as committing high treason.

His eyes on the pool players, Eric took small sips of his drink. He had met Megan at the company's fiftieth anniversary party, an event that had been attended by some of the most famous people on the East Coast.

Last May, two months into his divorce and eager for a little action, he had gone to the Four Seasons bash for only one reason—to get laid—preferably by someone sexy, free spirited and totally devoid of intelligence. He'd had it with brainy females.

As his well-practiced eye scanned the room, he had spotted, and immediately recognized, Megan Hollbrook, Abigail's twenty-seven-year-old daughter. And the only heir to the huge Hollbrook fortune.

She stood in a corner of the room, a rather plain, slender girl with shy brown eyes, ash-blond hair shaped in a chin-length bob, and a strong, square jaw that made her look more like her late father than her attractive mother. Not exactly what he would call a raving beauty, but with that kind of money, who cared about looks?

Sipping his drink, he took in the expensive designer gown, the huge emerald drops dangling from her ears and the matching choker encircling the aristocratic neck. What would it be like, he wondered, to marry into such wealth? To have unlimited funds. Every wish fulfilled. Twenty-one years ago, when his mother had married Douglas Fairchild, he had come close to finding out. But the old man had hated him on sight. Other than allowing him to live in his house and eat his food, Douglas had never done one damn thing for him.

"There won't be any free ride where you're concerned, boy," Douglas had told him the day after the wedding. "You want pocket money, you've got to earn it."

That from a man who had inherited everything he owned—the law firm, the Potomac mansion, even the house in Bermuda.

Well, maybe he wouldn't have to grovel to Douglas anymore. Maybe he had found a bigger fish....

Drink in hand, Eric approached the heiress and introduced himself. Five minutes later, they were on the dance floor, chatting like two old friends. Sensing that candor was a quality a woman like Megan Hollbrook would appreciate, he told her about his recent divorce, improvising a little as he went.

"My ex-wife was always very career-oriented," he said as they moved slowly to the music. "And I was more of a family man. The marriage began to go sour when she went to work for my stepfather. You may know him. Douglas Fairchild? Anyway," he continued as Megan shook her head, "when Kate told me she wanted a divorce, I didn't fight her." He allowed his voice to drop.

"I suppose I should have, for my little girl's sake, but I just didn't have it in me anymore, so I agreed."

Megan's gentle eyes filled with genuine sorrow. "I'm sorry," she said in her well-bred, finishing-school voice. "It must be difficult for you, being separated from your daughter."

All of a sudden, those millions Eric had thought out of reach no longer seemed so inaccessible. Unlike her mother, Megan Hollbrook had a tender heart. With a little ingenuity, he might be able to make that work in his favor.

"It still is. Do you know that this is the first social affair I've attended since my divorce? I almost didn't come." Tightening his hold around her waist, he gave her his killer smile. "Now I'm glad I did."

The blush on Megan's cheeks and the look of sheer pleasure in her eyes as she looked up told him that the old Logan charm had worked its magic once again.

Making her fall in love with him in the days that followed was easier than he'd thought. For all her millions, Megan Hollbrook was remarkably unsophisticated when it came to men. Except for a couple of boyfriends in college, she had never had a serious relationship.

Winning her mother's trust, however, was another matter. Abigail Hollbrook, who had headed her two-hundred-million-dollar company with an iron hand since her husband's death nineteen years ago, was not a woman one could fool with sweet talk alone.

"Don't mind my mother," Megan told Eric after a particularly chilly first meeting. "She tends to be overprotective at times. She'll come around."

She never had. When, a month after meeting Megan, Eric had asked her to marry him, Abigail had immediately summoned him to her office.

"For reasons I can't possibly fathom," she told him,

her sharp blue eyes piercing through him like a laser, "my daughter has fallen in love with you and wants to marry you. I, on the other hand, am very much opposed to this marriage."

Ignoring the trickle of sweat that was running down his chest, Eric held her formidable gaze. "I assure you that—"

"I've had you investigated, Eric." Her voice snapped at him like a whip. "It seems that when you told Megan about your fourteen-year marriage to Kate Logan, you conveniently forgot to mention that you cheated on her. Repeatedly."

Although the "repeatedly" part was something Kate hadn't been able to prove, it seemed pointless to deny it now. Obviously, the woman had done her homework.

"My wife and I had problems I'd rather not go into at the moment, Mrs. Hollbrook," Eric replied, trying hard to keep his voice from shaking. "Still, my behavior was inexcusable and not something I'm particularly proud of. That's why I didn't tell Megan." He paused as he tried to read the woman's face. When he couldn't, he asked, "Did you tell her?"

"Of course I told her. What would be the point of conducting an investigation if not to open my daughter's eyes? I regret to say, however, that it didn't do any good. She's naive enough to believe that adulterers can be reformed."

Eric held back a sigh of relief. He should have known he could count on Megan. "I can't speak for others, but in my case, Megan is right. I'm a new man, Mrs. Hollbrook."

Abigail didn't seem to have heard him. "Why do you want to marry my daughter, Eric? From what I hear, your tastes in women lean more toward...the exotic, well-endowed type, shall we say?''

The accuracy of her statement astounded him. How far down had that witch dug anyway? Refusing to let her intimidate him, he summoned every ounce of passion he could muster. "That may have been true at one time, but not anymore. As I said, I'm a new man. And I love Megan. It's that simple."

"Are you sure it isn't her money you love?"

"Money is of no importance to me."

The smile on Abigail's lips was chilling. "In that case, you have no objection to signing a prenuptial agreement, do you?"

He could have named half a dozen objections, starting with how damn humiliating the request was. Who the hell did that broad think she was? Megan was a grown woman. She didn't need her mother's permission to get married. Hell, she didn't even need her approval. They could elope to Las Vegas tomorrow if they wanted to and there wasn't a damn thing old Abigail could do about it.

But as much as he would have loved to tell her that, he kept his mouth shut. Megan might be of age, but she loved her mother and would never intentionally hurt her.

He met the steely, condescending gaze without flinching. "None whatsoever."

"Good." Her hands clasped in front of her, Abigail leaned across her massive antique desk. "But don't think for one moment that giving up my daughter's fortune gives you the right to do to her what you did to your ex-wife. If you hurt her or embarrass this family in any way, I'll make you regret it until the day you die. Do I make myself clear?"

Eric swallowed. "Perfectly." Sensing he should say something a little more substantial, he added, "I'll spend the rest of my life making your daughter happy, Mrs. Hollbrook. You have my word on that."

The following six months were a whirlwind of activities—wedding preparations, parties, magazine interviews and, of course, the signing of the prenuptial agreement, which was an event in itself.

"It's just a formality, darling," Megan had whispered in Eric's ear as Abigail and her attorney looked on. "A small concession to make Mother happy. She doesn't know it, but on our first wedding anniversary, I plan to tear those damned papers up. That will be my present to you."

One year. That's all that had stood between him and great wealth. At the end of that year, he would have been free to do anything he wanted—even divorce Megan—and half her fortune would have been his. Of course, he would never divorce her. He wasn't stupid. Why should he settle for half of Megan's trust fund when he stood to inherit the old woman's fortune?

"Hey, buddy." Someone nudged his arm. "We're closing."

Eric turned his head and peered at the bartender through eyes that were blurry from the alcohol. "What?"

"We're closing," the man repeated. "And your tab comes to six bucks. So pay up and get lost."

As the words slowly sank in, Eric reached into his pocket and pulled out a handful of bills. Then, dragging his chair back, he stood up, selected a ten-dollar bill and dropped it on the table. "Here you go. Keep the change."

The words almost made him laugh. Who the hell was he to be so generous? Six days from now, he would be destitute. Unless he found someone willing to part with a quarter of a million dollars.

Swaying slightly, he walked out of the tavern. A cold,

bitter wind blew across the parking lot but failed to sober him up. What he needed was a good night's sleep. Hopefully, by tomorrow, everything would be clearer.

But as he started toward the motel, he stopped. A No Vacancy sign with the *y* missing, blinked at him from the top of a pole.

He cursed under his breath. Now what? Drive home? In the condition he was in, he'd be stopped for DWI before he even reached the highway. That left him with only one option—to sleep in the car.

After a few seconds of indecision, he unlocked the Corvette and collapsed on the front seat. His last thought as he pressed the back of his head against the leather seat was that life was a real bitch.

Stepping out of his Toyota at four-fifteen on this cold, misty morning, Danny Bronson whistled happily as he walked toward The Hamptons, a turn-of-the-century building west of the Dupont Circle that had been converted into twelve luxury condominiums.

He had good reason to be happy. In less than two hours, the promotion to line supervisor he had been promised a year ago would finally be his.

The extra money sure would come in handy, especially now with the baby on the way. And he would finally be able to give up his paper route. Not that he minded the extra work. Hell, he was grateful to Mr. Hernandez for giving him the job three years ago, but getting up at three-thirty every morning so he could deliver his papers and be at the factory by six was getting to be a drag—especially during these cold winter months.

Still whistling, he threw folded copies of the *Washington Post* on each doorstep before proceeding to the next level. When he reached the fourth floor, he walked all the way to the end of the hall, where apartment 8B—his last delivery in this complex—was located.

Holding the paper like a Frisbee, he was about to toss it on the bright yellow welcome mat, then stopped, frowning.

The door to the apartment was ajar, which was unusual. Even in a nice neighborhood like this, people were cautious about leaving their doors unlocked, much less open.

Feeling slightly uneasy, he looked around, then back at the door. Maybe he should call the police. If this was a robbery, the guy might still be inside. He might even have a gun. On the other hand, if the woman who lived here was sick or hurt, prompt action on his part could save her life. She was a nice lady. And she was always generous to him at Christmastime.

After a short hesitation, he approached the apartment and peered through the door opening. He couldn't see a thing. It was pitch-black inside. And silent as a tomb, which convinced him that if a robbery had taken place, the robber was long gone.

He gave two short knocks. "Ms. Lamont? You okay?" When there was no reply, he pushed the door wider. "Ms. Lamont?" he repeated, embarrassed that his voice was shaking. "You in there?"

Although he didn't spook easily, the stillness reminded him of the house-to-house search he and three army buddies had conducted in Kuwait during the early stages of the Gulf War. His heart had been lodged in his throat at the thought of some fanatic Iraqi soldier jumping him from behind. But this was different. This time, he was alone, with no backup unit in the vicinity and no walkie-talkie to send out a distress call.

He swallowed hard and walked in, cursing softly as he

bumped into a table. At last, he located a switch and turned on the lights.

The living room, which he had seen only at Christmastime when Ms. Lamont gave him his present, was as he remembered it—elegantly furnished and orderly.

Calling out her name again, this time much louder, Danny walked around a chair and hurried down the hall. He stopped in front of an open door, searched for a light switch and flipped it.

"God Almighty."

In the middle of the room, an enormous brass bed held center stage. And on that bed, lying on her back with her arms spread out wide, was Ms. Lamont.

Reacting on sheer reflex, Danny dropped his canvas bag on the thick white carpet and ran toward her. "Ms. Lamont—" The name caught in his throat as he came to a halt.

Although there was no blood on her, he had seen enough dead people during his seven months in the Gulf to know that this one was as dead as they came. Her eyes, frozen in an expression that had turned glassy, bulged out of their sockets, and there were deep red marks at the base of her neck.

"Jesus." His heart hammering, he looked around for a phone, saw one on the nightstand and picked it up. With trembling fingers, he dialed 911.

Six

His hands in his pockets, Mitch Calhoon made a slow circuit of the room, taking in every detail—the slick black-and-white furniture, the white carpeting, already filthy from police traffic, the partially open closet crammed with expensive clothes. Finally, and with great reluctance, he let his gaze rest on the dead woman on the bed.

No matter how much he tried to distance himself from the victims, death always affected him profoundly. Especially when it involved a young woman in the prime of life, or a teenager who had thought himself invincible. When it was a child, it was even tougher.

All the dispatcher had said when he called was that the victim was female and had apparently died of strangulation.

A two-man team from the Crime Scene Unit had arrived moments before and was going about its business, quietly and methodically recording the scene and collecting evidence. Outside the apartment door, a uniformed policeman kept the gawkers, mostly neighbors, at bay.

His eyes on the woman, Mitch crossed the room and came to stand by the big brass bed. Although death had changed her dramatically, the photograph on the nightstand showed a beautiful woman with long, shiny black hair, brown eyes and the kind of cheekbones that would make a high-fashion model green with envy.

As a CSU photographer crouched to take another picture of the dead woman, Joe McCormack, the uniformed officer who had first arrived at the scene, approached, notebook in hand.

"Who found the body, Joe?" Mitch asked.

McCormack, a tall, heavyset man with twenty years on the force, nodded toward a corner of the room where a young man in jeans and a blue parka sat, watching the activity around him with a half-dazed expression. "Paperboy. Says his name is Danny Bronson. He's been delivering the *Post* to this address for the last three years." He glanced at his notes. "He found the body at approximately 4:05. Says the door was ajar. That's what alerted him something was wrong. He didn't notice it had been forced open until after he called us."

"You got anything on him?"

"Not yet. I have a call in." McCormack reached into his breast pocket and pulled out a piece of paper. "I knew you'd want to talk to the other tenants, so I took their names and apartment numbers." He handed Mitch the slip of paper. "They're all accounted for, except the woman in apartment 8A. The super says she's a flight attendant, so she's probably on a trip."

"Thanks." Mitch scanned the list before putting it in his pocket. "What about the victim?"

"D.C. driver's license identifies her as Gina Lamont. Age thirty-four. The super says she's a model, but according to our records, the lady's a hooker. She was arrested three times this year alone. Twice for solicitation and once for drug possession. Cocaine," he added in answer to Mitch's quick, questioning glance. "Looks like she was a serious user, too. Johnson's already found a stash.''

"Did you find an address book?"

McCormack pointed to a small black book on the end table. "Not too many names in it, though."

"Thanks, Joe. I'll take a look at it later. Let me know if anything else comes up."

Mitch pulled out his own notebook from his breast pocket and walked over to Danny Bronson. He was just a kid, no more than twenty-four or twenty-five with blond hair, blue eyes and pale, freckled cheeks.

"Hi," Mitch said in a low, unthreatening voice. "I'm Detective Calhoon."

The man, who had watched him approach, stood up. His eyes registered a mixture of bewilderment and fear. He nodded and threw a nervous glance toward the bed where the medical examiner was conducting a preliminary examination.

Mitch motioned toward the hallway. "Let's go in the living room." Once there he turned back to Danny. "I understand you found the body?"

"Yes, sir." In a voice that shook, Bronson told Mitch how he had discovered the body.

"Did you know the woman?"

"Yes. But not well. I mean, I only saw her once a year—around Christmas."

"Why is that?"

"She always asked me to stop by so she could give me my Christmas present."

"What kind of present?"

Danny blushed. "Fifty dollars. In cash."

Mitch held back a smile as he wrote down the information in his neat handwriting. "That's all right, son. I'm not the IRS." When he stopped writing, he looked up. "Did you ever see anyone here? Man? Woman?"

Danny shook his head. "No, sir. She was always alone."

Mitch nodded. "How come you deliver the paper so early?"

"I have another job. I'm a full-time production employee at Chesapeake Frozen Foods. In order to punch in at six, I have to start my paper route at four."

"When do you finish?"

"Five-thirty."

"Did you touch anything besides the telephone?"

"The light switch." Danny pointed behind Mitch. "That one. And the one in the bedroom. Oh, and I touched the door when I pushed it open."

"Did you see anyone coming out of the building when you entered it?"

Danny shook his head.

"Did you hear any noise from the floor below? Or the one above?"

"No. It's pretty quiet at this time of the morning."

Mitch closed his notebook. "All right, Mr. Bronson. One of the officers is going to escort you downtown—"

The man's eyes grew fearful. "What for? I told you all I know." His face turned white. "Jesus, you can't think I killed her." He shook his head. "I didn't. I swear—"

"Take it easy, Danny," Mitch said, hoping the use of the kid's first name would calm him down. "I don't think you killed her. But you discovered the body, which means we need a signed statement from you. After you've given it, you'll be free to go."

Mitch motioned to the patrolman at the door and gave him his instructions, then, as he returned to the bedroom, he saw the M.E. remove his glasses and wipe them with a tissue. Mitch walked over to him. "What's the scoop, Abe?"

Abel Moskowitz, a diminutive man with a bald head and squinty eyes, slid his glasses into his jacket pocket. "Looks like the cricoid was crushed, so it's pretty safe to assume she died from strangulation. Judging by the marks on her neck, I would guess the murderer, most likely a man, had very large, very strong hands."

"Approximate time of death?"

"Somewhere between midnight and 2:00 a.m. I'll have a more accurate time after the autopsy." His voice was impersonal, almost monotonous.

"Was she raped?"

"No. But she put up quite a fight." He pointed at half a dozen lacerations across her neck. "These are fingernail scratches, probably her own as she attempted to free herself." He removed his disposable gloves and dropped them into a paper bag. "I'm done here, Mitch. Send her down whenever you're ready." Snapping his bag shut, he gave Mitch a cursory nod and left.

Two ambulance attendants stood nearby, waiting for instructions. "Bag her," Mitch told them. "The bedding, too." He watched as the body was wrapped in the black satin sheets and deposited in a body pouch.

"Hey, Mitch."

He turned around to see his identification technician, Roy Johnson, motion to him. Mitch pulled out a pair of latex gloves from his pocket and drew them on as he walked across the room. "What have you got, Roy?"

Johnson pointed at a video camera on the dresser. "I found this baby tucked into that air return up there." He nodded toward a rectangular opening above the bedroom closet. "And then I found this. It was taped under the bottom dresser drawer." He handed Mitch a videotape.

Mitch tilted his head to read the side label. The letters E.L. were written in a slanted, feminine scrawl. "Dust it, will you, Roy? Then maybe I should take a look at it."

Mitch watched as Johnson examined the tape with a flashlight, covering every inch of it. Then he dipped the tip of a large fiberglass brush into the powder and very gently dabbed it all over the tape.

"You getting anything?"

"Only a couple of prints," Johnson replied without looking up. "But they look pretty clean." He pressed a strip of special pressure tape on the dusted surface and lifted it in one quick motion. Then, with a speed and dexterity that explained why he was considered one of the best ident technicians on the East Coast, he pressed the tape to the edge of a lifting card, snipped it from the roll and immediately labeled the card. The whole process hadn't taken more than two minutes.

He handed the videotape back to Mitch. "It's all yours."

Having already spotted a sophisticated entertainment center across from the bed, Mitch walked over to it and slid the tape into the VCR. As the image of a naked couple lying on a big brass bed came into focus, Joe, who had sneaked up behind Mitch, chuckled. "Hey, that's the lady of the house. Looks like she was into home movies, huh?"

"Guess so." As the woman rolled on top of her partner, the man's face suddenly came into view. "Well, I'll be damned," Mitch murmured.

"What?" Joe edged a little closer. "You know the guy?"

"That's Eric Logan. Megan Hollbrook's fiancée."

Joe gave a low whistle. "Eric Logan. Sure, I recognize him now. He was married to that attorney, wasn't he? The one who defended Fuente in that last case you investigated? What's her name?''

''Kate Logan.''

''Right.'' McCormack's gaze, as if pulled by a magnet, returned to the screen where the action was definitely heating up. The officer chuckled again. ''Could it be that our little filmmaker was also into blackmail?''

''Somebody say the word 'blackmail'?''

At the sound of the thin, nasal voice, Mitch's jaw tightened. He shut the VCR off, removed the tape and handed it back to Johnson. Although a close relationship between the police and the press was considered essential, Eddy Povich was an exception. A crime reporter for the *Washington Chronicle,* Povich was a weasel of a man in every sense of the word. Skinny as a rat and no taller than five feet, he would stoop to any level for a story. The fact that he was a cousin of the U.S. attorney and had access to information no one else had made him even more despicable. Cops in the District and beyond ran over each other for the privilege of avoiding him.

''Get out of here, Povich. You know better than to enter a crime scene during a preliminary investigation.''

''Stop treating me like a rookie, Calhoon. I know the drill.'' Povich's beady eyes shot back to the now dark screen. ''What happened? The hooker was blackmailing one of her johns, so he iced her?''

Mitch was having difficulty holding back his temper. ''I'm warning you, Povich. If you print a single unsubstantiated word the way you did with the Gallagher case, I'll come after you personally.''

But the reporter wasn't a man who was easily intimidated. ''The public has a right to be informed, Detective.''

''Then inform them that a woman was murdered. Nothing more.''

"At least give me her name."

"Not until her next of kin has been notified."

"What about her john? I can tell you know him. Who is he? Some political bigwig?" Povich grinned, exposing small yellow teeth. "The president maybe?"

"That information is confidential."

"You know I'm going to find out anyway. All I have to do is pick up the phone and call my cousin."

"Then why don't you do that and get the hell out of my way?"

"Because I prefer to get my stories from the horse's mouth." His irritating smile grew wider. "I'll even spell your name right this time."

Mitch had about all he could stomach. He nodded to McCormack, who immediately took the reporter by the arm and escorted him out of the apartment, deaf to the man's protests.

When the reporter was safely out of the way, Mitch removed his gloves, threw them into a paper bag and used his cell phone to call headquarters.

"I need an address for one Eric Logan," he said when Officer Devane in Records answered. "That's Eric with a *c* and Logan, *L-o-g-a-n.*"

Mitch could hear the click of computer keys as Devane began searching the Washington Area Law Enforcement System database, known as WALES. A few seconds later, he was back.

"It's 1035 Norton Lane in Potomac, Maryland."

"Thanks, Pete."

The pounding inside his head woke him up. Moaning, Eric opened one eye, then the other. It took him a moment to realize he was in the Corvette, curled up in the front seat in a fetal position. And that he was freezing.

Gripping the steering wheel with his left hand, he pulled himself up slowly. Little by little, the fog lifted from his brain and he remembered. He had been too drunk to drive home, which explained the splitting headache, and there had been no vacancy at the motel next door.

Peering through the windshield, he surveyed the small parking lot. Christ, he could have been mugged. Or even killed. And the bitch of it was, the binge had been a complete waste of effort. His problem hadn't gone away. It was still there, as insolvable as before.

Shivering from the cold, he turned on the ignition and cranked up the heat. As the powerful engine roared to life, the radio, which he had tuned to a twenty-four-hour news station, came on.

The broadcaster's first words hit him like an iced dagger.

"A Dupont Circle woman, who has been identified as Gina Lamont, was found strangled to death in her home early this morning. Although no arrest has yet been made, a full-scale investigation is under way to locate Eric Logan of Potomac, Maryland. According to several witnesses, Logan, who is engaged to industrial heiress, Megan Hollbrook, was seen leaving a Georgetown party on Saturday night in the company of the victim. Ms. Hollbrook could not be reached for comment. On Capitol Hill, Speaker Gingrich threatened to shut down the government again unless..."

Totally sobered up, Eric fell back against his seat. *Gina dead.* The words kept bouncing in his head as he tried to make sense out of them. How could she be dead when she had been in his office only yesterday? And why the hell were they looking for him? What did *he* have to do with anything?

In spite of his rising panic, he tried to think rationally.

There was nothing to be afraid of. He hadn't killed anybody. How could he? He had been right here in his car most of the night. And in that crummy tavern before that.

With fingers that shook, he turned the radio dial in search of another news flash. When he found it, the announcement was basically the same. Gina Lamont was dead and the police were looking for him.

His first impulse was to drive back to Washington and tell the cops everything he knew. Well, not quite everything. He would be a fool to tell them about Gina's little blackmailing scheme, or that he had slept with her. But how much harm could there be in admitting that he had talked to her at Lyle's party and that he had walked her to her car?

He rejected the idea almost immediately. The newscasts hadn't given the time of death, only that Gina had been found dead early this morning. How early? What if she was killed *after* he'd left Joe's Tavern? Would the cops believe he had spent the night passed out in his car? Or would they haul him to jail and book him for murder?

He swallowed to get rid of the dryness in his throat. Before he handed himself over to the wolves, he had to find out the time of death. If he was in the clear, he'd go back. If not...

Christ. He had no idea what he would do then.

He waited until his breathing had returned to normal before putting the Corvette into Reverse. Then, after a last look around, he drove out of the parking lot and headed for the highway.

Seven

When Alison came down for breakfast on Tuesday morning, one of the first things she saw was the mismatched saucer on the kitchen counter. "Was Daddy here?" she asked.

Following her gaze, Kate cursed herself for not having thrown out those cigarette butts before going to bed. "He stopped by for a few minutes last night," she said, ladling pancake batter onto the hot griddle.

"What did he want?"

"Nothing important." Anxious to change the subject, Kate opened the refrigerator. "Do you want Aunt Jemima Light or should we live dangerously and try that sinfully rich maple syrup Grandma brought back from Vermont last month?"

"I don't care." Alison came to stand beside Kate. "It *must* have been important for him to come all the way here." Her gaze drifted back to the saucer. "And to smoke so much. He always chain-smokes when something's on his mind."

Kate held back a sigh. For a thirteen-year-old, Alison's powers of observation were uncanny. She would make an excellent attorney some day—although the way things were going between them, it was doubtful that she was still interested in following in her mother's footsteps.

For a moment, Kate was tempted to make up a story,

then changed her mind. Maybe Douglas was right. How was Alison ever going to realize that Eric wasn't perfect if Kate kept covering up for him? "If you must know, he came here to borrow money."

Alison raised an eyebrow. "You gave it to him, didn't you?"

Kate flipped two pancakes onto a plate and took them to the kitchen table by the bay window. "No, Alison, I didn't give it to him. I'm not a bank, you know. And I'm certainly not rich."

"How much did he want?"

"Two hundred and fifty thousand dollars."

"Wow." Alison's eyes gleamed with curiosity. "What did he need all that money for?"

This time, a slight deviation from the truth was necessary. No matter how upset Kate was with Eric, she couldn't allow his daughter to see how low he had sunk. "A business venture," she improvised as she took her own plate to the table. "Something I thought was quite risky."

"But I don't understand why he came to you. He knows you don't have that kind of money."

Encouraged by Alison's calm reasoning, Kate met her gaze. "He was hoping I would let him borrow your trust fund."

Too late, Kate realized her mistake. Rather than be outraged at Eric's gall, Alison turned on her, eyes flashing. "And you told him no? Without asking me?"

"Of course I told him no. That money is for your education, Alison. I wouldn't touch a penny of it myself, no matter how badly I needed it, much less risk it on some crazy venture."

"It's *my* trust fund, isn't it? Which means I have the

right to do what I want with it. And I want Daddy to have it.''

"Not as long as I'm the trustee. When you turn twenty-one and the trust reverts to you, you'll be free to do what you want with it. Not before.''

Alison's body was rigid. "You are so mean, Mom. And so unfair. You'd think Daddy had asked you for the moon. It's only money, you know. *My* money," she emphasized.

In a rare display of frustration, Kate hit the table with the palm of her hand, causing the plates to rattle. "Dammit, Alison, why do you always have to take his side? Why can't you see things my way for a change? I'm only trying to protect you, to do what's best for you.''

Flipping her hair behind her shoulder, Alison gathered her schoolbooks. "Yeah, right.''

"Where are you going?''

"School. Where else?''

"You haven't touched your pancakes—''

"You eat them. I lost my appetite." She scooped up her lunch money from the island in the center of the room. When she turned around again, her eyes were flat. "I want to move back into Grandpa's house," she said in that defiant tone that had become so familiar. "And after Dad is married, I want to live with him and Megan. They said I could.''

Kate's heart sank. Although Alison had made no secret that she was unhappy with the move to Cleveland Park, she had never come right out and said she wanted to leave. "You don't want to do that," she said, rising from her chair.

"Yes, I do.''

Then, without bothering to say goodbye, Alison stalked out of the room.

Kate started to go after her, but it was too late. The front door had already slammed shut.

Kate was putting the breakfast dishes into the dishwasher when the phone rang. Reaching for the extension on the wall, she picked it up. "Hello?"

"Kate. Thank God you're there." Eric's voice was strained, shaky.

Kate briefly closed her eyes. "Eric, what in God's name is it going to take for you to understand—"

"Gina is dead."

"Who?"

"Gina! The woman who was blackmailing me. She was strangled. And the police think I did it. Christ, haven't you heard the morning news? It's on every radio and television station."

As the first wave of shock receded, Kate leaned against the wall. "Where are you?"

"Never mind that. I didn't do it, Kate. You've got to believe me. I wasn't even in Washington when she was killed."

"Where were you?"

His voice dropped. "Passed out in my car. I felt sorry for myself after I left your house last night, so I tied one on. I didn't wake up until seven-thirty this morning. That's when I heard the news. And before you ask, no, I have no witness. My only alibi is for the time I spent in a bar between eleven-thirty and midnight."

The attorney in Kate took over. "Have they established the time of death yet?"

"I don't know. That's why I'm calling. You've got to find out, Kate."

"No, Eric. I'm not getting involved in this."

"Kate, for God's sake, I'm not asking you to get involved. All I want is for you to call someone at Metro P.D. and find out when Gina was killed. Is that really too much to ask?''

The desperation in his voice struck a chord. Why did she always have to be such a sucker for people in trouble? ''How do I get back to you?''

She heard his sigh of relief. ''I'll call you. How long do you think it'll take? Five minutes? Ten?''

''Give me fifteen.''

''Okay.'' There was a short pause. ''Thanks, Kate. Thanks a lot.'' He hung up.

Preferring to deal with someone Kate knew she could trust, she called the medical examiner directly. What Abe Moskowitz told her, however, wasn't very reassuring.

No sooner had she hung up than her phone rang again. ''I couldn't stand it,'' Eric said when she answered. ''Did you find out anything?''

''I'm afraid the news isn't good, Eric. According to the medical examiner, Gina died between one and one-fifteen in the morning. So unless you were too far away to make it back to her apartment by that time and can prove it, you're in trouble.''

''I was less than twenty minutes away,'' Eric said in a leaden tone.

''Are you sure no one saw you while you were in your car?''

''Yeah, I'm sure. The parking lot was empty when I came out of the tavern and it was empty when I woke up this morning. The owner must have parked in the back, so chances are he never saw me.'' Then in a pitiful voice, he added, ''I didn't kill her, Kate. I swear I didn't.''

Outside Kate's kitchen window, the morning sky was heavy with rain clouds, making the situation seem even more ominous. Even if she wanted to, which of course, she didn't, she wouldn't be able to get him out of this one. "Do the police know Gina was blackmailing you?"

"No, thank God. But they know she and I left Lyle's party together. And half a dozen people must have seen her at Hollbrook Industries yesterday afternoon. They're going to want to know what she was doing there."

She heard him groan. "What is it?"

"Turn on your TV. Channel 2."

Reaching for the small set under the kitchen cabinet, Kate turned a knob. As the image slowly came into focus, she saw a snapshot of Eric in the upper right-hand corner of the screen. A blond newscaster with a grave expression on her face was speaking into the camera.

"The Metropolitan Police Department has been unsuccessful in locating Eric Logan, who is wanted for questioning in connection with the murder of a Washington call girl. Unconfirmed at this time is the finding of an incriminating videotape in the victim's apartment and the possibility that blackmail may have been a motive."

"They found the tape," Eric said, his voice barely audible. "I'm dead."

Kate turned off the TV set. "Eric, listen to me. You've got to turn yourself in."

"That's brilliant, Kate. Why don't you ask me to sign my own death warrant while you're at it?"

"You're making things worse by running away."

"Worse?" He laughed. "A roomful of people saw me leaving Lyle's party on Saturday night with Gina, my fingerprints are all over her apartment, and the cops just found a tape that will make me a prime suspect, possibly the *only* suspect. How much worse can things get?"

"I know it looks bad for you, but you can't just keep on running. The longer you stay away, the worse it'll be.

And anyway, with that red Corvette of yours, you might as well be waving a flag."

"I'll get rid of the Corvette." She heard him take a deep breath and exhale it slowly. "Help me, Kate. I know I'm the last person in the world you wanted to hear from this morning, but I'm desperate."

"I can't help you unless you turn yourself in."

"Bull. You can do anything you want, whether the suspect is in custody or not."

"I'm an officer of the court, Eric. I can't afford to—"

"Talk to Gina's neighbors," he said as if he hadn't heard her. "Talk to the guy who brought her to the party. His name is Brad Carpenter. Talk to her pimp. Maybe *he* killed her."

"Call girls don't have pimps."

"I don't care! Somebody killed her, and it wasn't me." His voice had turned pleading again. "You know I'm not capable of murder, don't you, Kate? Hell, I don't even like to squash bugs."

It was true. Eric was many things, but he wasn't a murderer.

"Oh, Christ," he said suddenly. "A cruiser just pulled in. I've got to split. I'll call you later."

"Pulled in where? Eric, tell me where you—"

He had already hung up.

Kate slammed the phone down. Damn him. Why had he come to her with this? Why hadn't he called the Fairchilds' family lawyer and laid all that crap on *him?* Didn't she have enough problems with Alison...?

Her blood turned cold. Alison. Dear God. If the news was on television, then the entire school could have heard by now. What if Alison found out that her father was wanted for murder from a classmate? Or worse, from a nosy reporter camped outside her school? Prostitutes, even dead ones, didn't normally generate a lot of press, but this was no simple murder. The suspect was engaged to one of the richest women in the country. The media would pounce on the story like a pack of hungry dogs.

She had to get to Alison before they did.

Scooping up her car keys from a ceramic dish on the kitchen counter, Kate ran out of the house.

She was only a block from Alison's school when her car phone rang. For an instant, she considered not answering it. Sooner or later, Eric would have to understand that she wanted no part of his problems. But on the third ring, she sighed and picked it up. It was Douglas.

There was no greeting, no small talk. He had obviously heard the news about Eric and was understandably upset. "Have you heard?" he asked.

She wondered what he would say if she told him that not only had she heard about the murder, but she had heard it from Eric. "A few minutes ago." Then, remembering Douglas had left for Bermuda the day before, she asked, "Where are you?"

"At the airport. Rose and I chartered a plane back home as soon as we heard. Apparently, the police showed up on our doorstep at five-thirty this morning, looking for Eric." As an afterthought, he added, "Where's Alison?"

"In school. I'm on my way to pick her up now. I thought it would be best to keep her out of the limelight for a while."

"Good idea."

"Douglas," she said, choosing her words carefully. "You know Eric didn't do this, don't you? He's incapable—"

"Rose and I are calling a family meeting," he said

curtly. "I asked Megan and Abigail Hollbrook to join us. I would appreciate it if you came, too."

She didn't like his gruff tone. But these were trying times for all of them. "Are we meeting at your house?"

"Yes. At ten-thirty." As if he'd read her thoughts, his voice softened. "Thank you, Kate."

"Baby, I know how upset you must be, but we'll get through this. I swear we will."

They were in Kate's car, heading back toward the house. The school principal, who had already heard the news by the time Kate walked into her office, had agreed that Alison's interests would best be served by staying out of the public eye for a few days.

Sitting in her red Saab in the school parking lot, Kate had broken the news to her daughter as gently as possible. It wasn't until an Action News van had come up the road that she had put the car in gear and headed for home.

Casting a quick glance in Alison's direction as she drove, Kate reached for her hand, which lay limply on the girl's lap, and squeezed it. "I'm going to keep you home for a few days. I've already talked to Maria. Between the two of us, we should be able to keep the press away."

"They can't think Daddy killed that woman," Alison said in a small, trembling voice. "They just can't."

"He's not helping things by hiding from the police."

Alison yanked her hand away. Her eyes took on that angry, rebellious look again. "He's scared, Mom. Can't you see that? He has no one to turn to, no one who will believe him. You would run, too, if you were in his shoes."

Kate stopped for a red light. A pelting rain had turned the streets of Washington slick and gray. Outside a store-front window, a homeless man huddled in a green plastic sheet sat on the soaked sidewalk, his hand extended. "No, I wouldn't," she said, returning her gaze to Alison. "I would do everything in my power to clear my name. No matter how scared I was, I wouldn't compound the problem by becoming a fugitive."

"Right." Crossing her arms against her chest, Alison stared out the passenger window. "You're so much smarter than the rest of us."

The words stung, but Kate decided to ignore them. Now was not the time for self-pity. "No, I'm not," she said softly. "I just know about those things. It's my job."

The light changed and Kate pressed on the gas, moving through the heavy morning traffic. From time to time, she glanced at Alison, hoping to make eye contact, but all she could see was the girl's tight, angry profile.

Five minutes later, she was pulling the Saab into her driveway, grateful that no reporters were waiting for them. She was reaching for the door handle when Alison turned to face her.

"You're going to help him, aren't you, Mom?" Her daughter's huge gray eyes searched hers. The resentment was gone, replaced by sheer anguish—and something else. Something Kate hadn't seen in her daughter's eyes for a long time. Trust.

That look went right through her, momentarily dulling her thoughts. "Alison, I—"

"You have to, Mom." Alison's hand closed on Kate's wrist as her eyes bore into hers. "I wouldn't be asking you to help him if I thought he had killed that woman. But I don't. And you don't, either."

At the look of despair in Alison's eyes, Kate felt her heart break. "No," she said at last, "I don't."

"Then help him. Find out who killed Gina Lamont." Fat tears formed at the corners of Alison's eyes and hung on the edge of her lashes before spilling onto her cheeks. This time when she spoke, her voice was trembling with pent-up emotion. "I'm so afraid for him, Mom. He's out there all alone. He needs to know we're on his side."

Despite her earlier resolution not to get involved, Kate's resistance began to falter. As much as she believed in, and supported, the justice system, there were times when she felt it failed—as it had for Tony. But there was another reason for her change of heart. How could she, in all conscience, turn her back on Eric and not feel she was turning her back on her daughter, as well?

Alison's grip on Kate's wrist tightened. "Mom, please, say you'll help him. Say you won't let him go to prison."

"No," Kate whispered, drawing the frightened child into her arms, "I won't let him go to prison."

Eight

The Fairchilds' home was a magnificent estate in Potomac, Maryland, set amid eighteen acres of lush, perfectly manicured grounds. Being there again brought back a wave of memories for Kate—some happy, some she would have preferred to forget.

As Joseph, the Fairchilds' longtime butler, ushered her down the long hallway where portraits of Douglas's famous ancestors were prominently displayed, it dawned on her that although she had spent thirteen years of her life in this house, it had never truly felt like home.

Now, standing in the doorway of the elegant green-and-ivory drawing room, she waited as her ex-mother-in-law, a small, plump woman in a gray pin-striped suit rushed toward her, hands extended.

"I'm so glad you're here, Kate." Rose pressed her cheek against Kate's and spoke in a trembling whisper. "At least I know *you* won't jump to conclusions."

Then, taking Kate's hand, she led her toward the sofa where Megan and Abigail Hollbrook were sitting and made the introductions.

Up close, Megan Hollbrook seemed younger than her twenty-seven years and much more vulnerable than the poised, elegant woman whose photographs often appeared in the society pages of countless magazines. Her eyes were red and swollen from crying, and although she gave

Kate a timid smile, her expression was that of a devastated young woman.

By contrast, Abigail Hollbrook, who sat next to her daughter, projected a picture of great strength and self-control. At sixty-two, the head of Hollbrook Industries was still an attractive woman with snow-white hair pulled back in an elegant chignon, assessing green eyes and a thin, unsmiling mouth.

Douglas stood by the fireplace where a bright, cheery fire crackled, contrasting sharply with the somber mood of the room. As he cleared his throat, Rose took her place by his side and all eyes turned toward him.

"I've called this meeting," he began in a voice that was just a shade too dramatic, "in order to decide how we can help Eric, who seems to have vanished into thin air."

As if on cue, Megan lowered her head into her hands and began sobbing softly. Instantly maternal, Abigail draped a comforting arm around her daughter's shoulders. "Have you heard anything new, Douglas?" she asked.

"I have. Detective Calhoon, who's in charge of the case, was here earlier."

Mitch Calhoon, Kate thought. So she would have to deal with him again. She couldn't decide whether the thought pleased or irritated her.

"He's traced Eric as far as a tavern in Brookville, Virginia," Douglas continued. "The bartender there says that Eric came in at approximately eleven-thirty last night and left a few minutes before midnight. And since Gina Lamont was killed around one, the police concluded that Eric had ample time to drive from Brookville to Washington."

"Assuming," Kate interjected, "that he was in a condition to drive."

"It would seem that he was. According to the bartender, Eric never finished his third Scotch."

"That may be, but we all know how badly Eric holds his liquor. Three drinks, or even slightly less than that, may not be much for an average drinker, but it's enough to put Eric out of commission."

Douglas's expressionless eyes stayed on her. "Unfortunately for him, whether or not he was intoxicated isn't going to be much of an issue."

"What do you mean by that?" Abigail asked.

"One set of fingerprints found in Gina's apartment has been identified as Eric's. And while the fingerprints alone don't prove that he killed her, they do prove that he was there."

Kate glanced sharply at Rose. "I didn't know Eric's prints were on file."

Rose lifted helpless shoulders. "Neither did I."

"I can explain that," Abigail said, her arm still around her daughter. "Every Hollbrook employee is required to provide a complete set of fingerprints. It's a policy we have enforced for quite some time now, ever since one of our designers was arrested a few years ago for industrial espionage."

"In addition to Eric's fingerprints," Douglas continued, "the police found a videotape that was apparently made by Gina Lamont the night Eric took her home. It shows Eric in a—" pausing, he rubbed an index finger across his bottom lip "—shall we say, compromising situation."

As Douglas turned to look at her, Kate found it difficult to hold his gaze for more than a couple of seconds. She hated to lie to him, to pretend that she only knew w' he knew. In spite of his dislike for Eric, Douglas had always treated her fairly and kindly. More than a father figure, he had been a teacher, a mentor whose trust she had never betrayed. Until now.

Sooner or later, she would have to tell him the truth, but not now. If he knew that Eric had called her, he would immediately tell the police. They, in turn, would insist on monitoring her phone with one of their sophisticated tracking instruments. Eric wouldn't stand a chance. And Alison would never forgive her for allowing her father to be caught.

Bracing herself for a possible confrontation, she rallied to Eric's defense. "That tape could have been made for a number of reasons," she pointed out. "Including Ms. Lamont's personal enjoyment. I don't profess to be an expert on the subject of call girls, but isn't it common knowledge that women in her profession often resort to outside stimulation to get themselves...in the mood?"

"Kate is right," Rose said quickly. "Besides, judging from the woman's address, she doesn't look to me as if she was in need of money."

Douglas's tone turned patronizing. "Appearances can be deceiving, Rose."

Why was he doing this? Kate wondered. Why was he being so hard on Eric without having heard his side of the story? Granted, the two men had had their differences in the past, but didn't he owe Eric at least the benefit of the doubt? For Rose's sake?

On a small console, a phone rang. Before one of the servants could answer it, Douglas picked up the receiver and snapped, "Douglas Fairchild." He handed it to Abigail. "It's for you," he said in a softer tone. "Your office."

All eyes remained on Abigail as she listened for a full minute. When she spoke at last, her voice was calm. "You did the right thing calling me first, Deborah. No, don't call the police. I'll handle it. And please, don't discuss this with anyone, and that includes your co-workers. Is that clear?''

She handed the phone back to Douglas. "That was Deborah Manning in marketing. She saw a photograph of Gina Lamont on the morning news and says the same woman came to see Eric yesterday afternoon."

"What did she want?" Douglas asked.

"Deborah doesn't know. She said the woman was very rude. She didn't have an appointment and refused to make one. She didn't even wait for Deborah to announce her. She just walked into Eric's office and slammed the door behind her. She wasn't there much more than ten minutes. Eric came out shortly after that, looking pale and distraught. That's the last Deborah saw of him." Abigail turned to look at Kate, her gaze mildly triumphant. "Does that change your opinion on the blackmail issue, Mrs. Logan?"

It was obvious from her smug tone that she considered this latest development an indisputable victory. "I was taught to never take circumstantial evidence as proof of guilt, Mrs. Hollbrook." This time, she met her former father-in-law's gaze without flinching. "Isn't that right, Douglas?"

Because he had always been a strong advocate of that doctrine, Douglas acknowledged the remark with a slight bow of his head. "Kate is right. We shouldn't jump to conclusions too quickly. And we must not lose focus of our main goal—to help Eric."

"But how can we do that?" Rose asked, her voice trembling with emotion. "When we don't even know where he is."

Wrapping an arm around his wife's shoulders, Douglas drew her close. "To begin with," he said in that patrician tone Kate knew so well, "we will remain united. As a family should. There will be no statements made to the press, no interviews of any kind, nothing that could aggravate Eric's situation." He glanced first at Megan, then at Kate. "However, if he should contact one of us and ask for help, it will be that person's responsibility to convince Eric to turn himself in. Or to find out where he's hiding so that we can bring an end to this nonsense."

Megan looked up at him. "You mean…we should turn him in? Tell the police where he is?"

"I know that sounds cruel, Megan, but believe me, he's only making things worse for himself by running away."

With a strangled sob, Megan sprang from the sofa and hurried out of the room.

Kate was halfway to her car when she heard someone running behind her. "Mrs. Logan!"

Turning around, she watched as Megan Hollbrook caught up with her. This time, her smile was apologetic.

"I'm sorry I made such a spectacle of myself in there," she said, her voice much more steady than it had been earlier.

Kate brushed off the apology with a wave of her hand. "You're under a lot of stress. I can certainly understand that."

"I didn't want to leave without telling you how grateful I am that you came to Eric's defense. I don't know too many people who would have stood up to Douglas and my mother the way you did." Her mouth curved into a lovely smile. "They make a rather formidable pair, don't they?"

"They certainly do. The trick is to make them think you're even more formidable."

"That's easy for you to say."

"It helps if you feel strongly enough about something. Believe me, I wouldn't have fought as hard as I did if I thought Eric was guilty."

Soft brown eyes looked at her. "You've heard from him, haven't you?"

Denying it would have been pointless. Megan was apparently much too smart and much too intuitive to fall for a lie. "Yes, I have."

"When?"

"He called me this morning when he found out the police were looking for him."

"Do you know where he is?"

Kate shook her head. "He wouldn't tell me. And he won't turn himself in, either."

"Why not, if he's innocent?"

"He's afraid that with the kind of evidence the police have, they won't bother to look for another suspect."

"Is that what you think?"

As a movement caught her eye, Kate glanced toward the house. At one of the tall Palladian windows, a curtain fell back. Someone had been watching them. Her bet was that it was either Douglas or Abigail. Perhaps both.

"I think Eric is in serious trouble," she said, returning her gaze to Megan.

"But you're going to help him, aren't you? You're going to find out who killed Gina Lamont."

The hope and trust Kate saw in the young woman's eyes reminded her of Alison. How in the world was she going to live up to all these expectations? "I'm going to try, Megan. That's all I can promise right now."

"That's all I'm asking," Megan replied quietly. "Thank you, Mrs. Logan."

"Please call me Kate."

"All right." As if afraid that someone might be listening, she moved closer to Kate. "If you should hear from Eric again, would you...would you ask him to call me?"

"Of course."

As Kate walked back to her car, she wondered if the girl wouldn't be better off if she never heard from Eric again. Even if he were to be cleared of all charges, with his track record, it wouldn't be long until he was up to his old tricks again. One way or another, he'd end up breaking her heart.

The huge house was quiet again, and Rose was finally alone. Sitting on the same sofa Abigail had occupied earlier, she pressed a lacy white handkerchief to her eyes. Except for Kate, who had been such a comfort, and Megan, who loved Eric almost as much as Rose did, no one understood the fear that gripped her heart, or how badly she wanted to help her son.

Moving to the well-stocked bar, she poured herself a glass of Evian and sipped slowly. Douglas had never understood the special relationship that existed between a parent and a child. How could he when he had never been a parent himself?

She had hoped to change that by giving him a child of his own, but on the eve of their wedding, Douglas had told her he didn't care for children and didn't wish to have any. He had even pressured her to put Eric in a boarding school, but she had refused, certain that Douglas would eventually warm up to the boy. He hadn't.

Considering what Rose knew about Douglas's strict childhood, she hadn't found his lack of compassion for her son terribly surprising. An only child, Douglas had tried desperately to live up to his father's expectations. But nothing he did, including running the law firm Aaron Fairchild had founded, was ever good enough. It wasn't until Aaron had died, twelve years ago, that Douglas had finally felt free of his father's tyranny.

But the stand he had taken against his stepson today was much too harsh, even for a man like Douglas.

As Rose continued to sip her water, her gaze drifted to the phone. She hadn't ruled out the possibility that Eric would eventually call her. And when he did, she would not turn him in as Douglas had suggested, but do whatever was necessary to keep him safe. How could anyone in his right mind expect any less from her?

Brad Carpenter's photo studio on N Street was one of Georgetown's oldest brick structures and still featured a rooftop widow's walk, once used to keep a lookout for returning ships. A simple plaque with the inscription Photography hung on the front door.

Kate had gotten the photographer's name and address from Lyle Wanamaker. As she'd expected, the playboy had already told the police that Eric and Gina had met at his house.

"Brad is an old friend of mine," Lyle had explained as he handed her one of Carpenter's business cards. "Whenever I need someone to photograph parties, I call him. It's not exactly his line of work, but like I said, we're buddies. I must warn you, though. He is—was—a close friend of Gina Lamont, and once he realizes that you're Eric's ex, he'll probably slam the door in your face."

Lyle had always had a way with words.

Brad Carpenter opened the door himself. In his early forties, he had a deep coppery complexion, strong Native American features and ink black hair that hung over his shoulders. He wore black pants and a black T-shirt with the sleeves cut high enough to reveal impressive biceps.

"Good morning," Kate said, flashing her best smile. "Are you Brad Carpenter?"

The slanted dark eyes watched her dispassionately. "Who wants to know?"

"My name is Kate Logan. I'm an attorney." Knowing a skeptic when she saw one, she pulled out one of her cards and handed it to him.

He glanced at it. "Are you Eric Logan's wife?"

"*Ex*-wife."

The emphasis on the "ex" failed to mellow him. "So what do you want?"

"To ask you a few questions regarding Gina's murder."

"I've already told the cops all I know."

Although he wasn't making it easy, she kept the smile on. "It's been my experience that the police and I seldom ask the same questions, Mr. Carpenter." From behind her came the sound of a car door being shut. "Would you mind terribly if I came in?" she asked. "I'd rather not have this conversation on your front step."

With an indifferent shrug, Carpenter turned his back on her and started walking down the hall, leaving her in charge of closing the door.

The room where he led her was large and featured several scenic backdrops ranging from a fake sandy beach to a snowcapped mountain. A tripod camera and two umbrella diffusers angled toward what looked like an exact replica of the Golden Gate Bridge completed the decor.

As if she wasn't even there, Brad walked over to the camera, removed a roll of film from the film chamber and replaced it with a new one.

Kate positioned herself near a small console so she could observe him. "Lyle tells me you were a good friend of Gina's."

"I was. I met her when she first arrived in Washington."

"How long ago was that?"

He shrugged. "Can't remember. Eighteen years. Maybe more." He turned to look at her, his gaze hostile. "Why did he do it? Why did your ex-husband have to kill her?"

"He didn't, Mr. Carpenter. That's why I'm here."

"The police say he did. They say he got scared and split."

She doubted Mitch Calhoon had phrased it quite that way, but then, what did she know about the detective's interviewing techniques? "The police are wrong. Someone else killed Gina, and with your help, I might just find out who that someone is."

He kept staring at her. It was obvious from the expression in his eyes that he didn't entirely trust her, but he surprised her by nodding. "All right." He returned his attention to the camera and checked its focus. "What do you want to know?"

"My theory is that Gina's death was connected to her life as a call girl, so whatever you can tell me about her profession and the people she was seeing would be very helpful."

He shook his head. "You came to the wrong guy. I don't know anything about her job. Or close to nothing."

"You said you were her friend."

"I was. But I didn't approve of what she did for a living, and she knew it. So we never talked about it. That's how we stayed friends."

Kate tried to conceal her disappointment. "All right then, tell me about the night of Lyle's party. I understand you took Gina with you."

"That's right. Gina loved parties, especially the kind

where the champagne flowed. When Lyle said I could bring a guest, I asked her.''

''Who did she talk to while she was there?''

''A number of people, although I couldn't tell you who they were. Gina was very social, never at a loss for words. And of course, she was very beautiful. That alone made her a hit.'' He slanted her another glance. ''Just ask your ex-husband.''

''Eric says she came on to him.''

Brad laughed. ''Yeah, well… Nobody held a gun to his head.''

''No.'' She glanced around the room. ''Gina told Eric that she was a model. Is that true?''

''She was a model when I first met her, before she changed professions. Then, a few months ago, she came to see me and said she wanted to start modeling again.''

''Why did she need to model all of a sudden? Wasn't she earning good money as a call girl?''

Brad turned around to face her again. ''She was. Until they fired her.''

''They?'' Kate snapped to attention. Finally, a clue she could hang on to. ''You mean…she worked for someone? Like an organized ring?''

''That's what I understood.''

''Do you know who ran that ring?''

He shook his head. ''No idea.''

''Why was she fired?'' Brad's expression changed and he turned away from her, pretending to be fussing with the camera again. Surprised by his sudden silence, Kate came to stand beside him. ''Brad? If you know something, please tell me. It could make the difference between finding her real killer and letting an innocent man go to prison.''

His eyes shut briefly, as if he was in deep pain. It was

another two or three seconds before he spoke again. "She was doing drugs."

"Heroin?"

"Cocaine. She tried it at a party a couple of years ago and she got hooked real bad." His expression turned grim. "I tried to tell her that the stuff was deadly, that it would drain her financially, but she wouldn't listen. She said she had it under control, that she was just doing it for fun, not because she was hooked." He let out a small, mournful sigh. "She was just kidding herself."

"And that's why they let her go?"

Brad nodded. "Those bastards. They could have tried to send her to a rehab center, but instead they told her to hit the road."

"Do you have any idea who her supplier was?"

Carpenter's jaw tightened and his eyes flashed. "I wish to God I did. If I'd known who he was, I would have gladly punched the life out of that snake." He raked his long hair back. "After a few months on the stuff, she was broke. That's when I started arranging for her to do some modeling, but she never really got into it."

"Didn't she have parents she could turn to? Siblings?"

"She had no one. She lost her parents when she was just a little kid. Her aunt raised her, but the old bat didn't give a damn about her. On her thirteenth birthday, Gina ran away from home. She's been on her own ever since."

Since he had begun to warm up to her, Kate decided to push it one notch further. "Had she ever tried to blackmail anyone else besides Eric?"

"I don't know. But I can tell you this. She was about to get a bundle."

"How do you know that?"

"Because the night she was killed, she called me and

asked me to cancel the shoot I had scheduled for her the following afternoon.''

"How come?"

"She said she had just hit the jackpot—a big one—and that she would never have to work another day in her life. Given her age, her lifestyle and her drug habit, she had to be talking about a lot of money."

"How much, would you say?"

He shrugged. "A couple of million. At least."

A couple of million? Far more than what she had expected to get from Eric.

He glanced at his watch. "I've got a shoot in about ten minutes."

Kate took the hint. "I'll be on my way. But before I go, could you give me a picture of Gina?"

Quietly, Brad walked out of the room and returned a few moments later with an eight-by-ten photograph. "Here you go."

The girl was truly stunning, Kate thought as she studied the black-and-white shoulder shot. A cross between Cindy Crawford and Cher. "Thank you." She nodded at the card he had laid on the console. "If you think of anything else that might be useful, will you call me?"

He shrugged. "Sure." When it became clear that he wasn't going to walk her to the door, Kate left.

Nine

"How did it go with Brad Carpenter?" Kate's secretary asked when Kate returned to the office shortly before three that afternoon.

Although she couldn't be called pretty, Francine Morgano, better known as Frankie, definitely commanded attention. Petite and perky, she had lustrous black hair she always wore in a tight French braid, and thin, outrageously arched eyebrows over large, round eyes that made her look like a Kewpie doll.

Twice divorced, she claimed to have only two passions—her work and men. Her affairs could be monitored through the photo cube on her desk, the contents of which changed with alarming frequency. This month, the featured hunk was a dark-complected Cuban by the name of Roméro.

Frankie had been Kate's devoted secretary and close friend for eight years, five of which had been in the U.S. attorney's office. She was trustworthy, opinionated and honest to the point of being blunt. At first, Douglas had been reluctant to hire her, not because he doubted her capabilities, but because he didn't think she fitted the firm's highly sophisticated image.

Kate had held her ground, insisting that she and Frankie were a package deal. In the end, Douglas had capitulated.

"Not bad," Kate replied in answer to Frankie's question. "He gave me my first clue."

"Do tell." Frankie perched herself on the corner of Kate's desk and crossed her shapely legs.

"Do you remember that drug dealer who used to operate around the Dupont Circle? The one you said had cute buns?"

Frankie giggled. "As if I could forget. If he hadn't been so revolting in every other way, I would have tried to reform him." Pretending to be holding a cigar in front of her mouth, she wiggled her eyebrows in a fairly good imitation of Groucho Marx. "If you know what I mean."

"Do you remember his name?"

"Pete something or other. Farley? Finley? That's it. Pete Finley. What do you want with him, Boss?"

"Brad Carpenter told me that Gina Lamont was a cocaine junkie. If she was buying her drugs close to home, it's possible Finley was her supplier." She leaned back in her chair. "You wouldn't happen to know where I could find him, would you?"

"What am I? A listing for two-bit hoodlums?"

Kate fought back a smile. "No, but since you were dating the officer who busted Finley three months ago, maybe you could find out?"

"I guess I could." Frankie wiggled her eyebrows again. "Or you could ask that hunk in homicide. I have a hunch he'd do just about anything for you."

Feeling color rise to her cheeks, Kate opened her briefcase and pulled out Tony's case file. "Don't be silly."

"Oh, don't tell me you didn't notice." Frankie chuckled. "Calhoon's got the hots for you, Boss. It's written all over that handsome puss of his."

"You're reading too many romance novels."

"What can I say? I'm a romantic gal. And I can tell love in bloom when I see it."

Kate shook her head. "You won't see any blooms over here, Frankie. I swore off romance forever, remember? One disastrous relationship is enough for me."

"Never give up on love, Boss. That's my motto."

Winking at her, Frankie slid down from Kate's desk and walked back into her office.

Mitch brought his Ford to a stop in front of Kate Logan's house and just sat there, looking at it for a moment. He had been here a couple of times before, during his investigation of Lilly Moore's murder. Kate hadn't been very friendly then, and he didn't expect her to be any different now. But he was willing to give it a shot. Partly because he had a hunch Eric Logan had contacted his former wife and partly because he had been looking for an excuse to see her again.

That last thought brought a smile to his lips. Was his physical attraction to Kate Logan that powerful? Or was it more than that? Either way, he ought to know better. Involvement of any kind between a cop and a defense counsel had always been frowned upon. When that defense counsel also happened to be the ex-wife of a prime murder suspect, the ramifications could be disastrous.

Stepping out of the car, Mitch glanced up and down the quiet street. Houses of all sizes and shapes, many of them decorated for the Christmas holiday, twinkled with hundreds of lights. It was a picture-perfect scene, almost impossible to associate with the violence that took place every minute of the day in other parts of the city.

Kate's house was just as festive, with miniature ligh strung through the shrubs and a gigantic wreath hanging on the door.

Whistling lightly to the tune of "Oh, Tannenbaum," Mitch walked up the path to the front door and rang the bell. Kate answered it after the second ring.

In her faded jeans and red sweatshirt, she didn't look anything like the sophisticated attorney he had seen in the courtroom only yesterday. Her shaggy red hair was in disarray and looked inviting enough for him to want to run his fingers through it. That same light scent he had noticed before enveloped him. One of these days, he'd have to find out the name of that perfume and why it was having such an effect on him.

"Good evening, Mrs. Logan."

"What is it now, Detective? Another riot brewing?"

He thought he saw the hint of a smile cross her face, but couldn't be sure. "None that I can see. But I'd like to ask you a few questions—if you don't mind."

"At eight o'clock in the evening?"

He shrugged. "I was in the neighborhood, so I thought I'd save myself a trip in the morning." Before she could reply, he leaned forward, hands in his pockets. "You mind if I come in?"

For a moment, Kate just looked at him, taking in the friendly, unthreatening blue eyes, the light brown hair with a stubborn strand falling over his forehead, the navy blazer over a cream turtleneck, the 501 jeans. Douglas had labeled him, not without some scorn, one of the new breed of detectives, hip and undisciplined. It was easy to see why Frankie, who had quite an eye for men, had turned to mush the moment she had seen him.

Reluctantly, Kate pulled the door open and moved aside let him in. She had known that sooner or later he would want to talk to her. She might as well answer his questions now and get it over with. "All right, but please make it short. I brought work home and I'd like to get back to it."

Mitch followed her across the foyer and into a cheery blue-and-white kitchen. A butcher-block island with a circular rack of gleaming copper pots hanging over it dominated the room. To his left, a cosy nook with a round table, piled high with files, and four chairs overlooked a large backyard.

Mitch tried to imagine Kate in these surroundings, performing a variety of domestic chores, looking relaxed and happy instead of tense and on guard as she was now.

She leaned against the counter, her arms folded across her chest. "So what was so important that it couldn't wait until tomorrow morning?"

Mitch eased a hip onto a kitchen stool. "I was wondering if you had heard from your ex-husband."

Although Kate had expected the question, had even prepared herself for it, the intensity of his gaze as he asked it threw her off. "No," she replied, trying to compensate her slight hesitation with a firm shake of her head. "Why would I?"

"Because you're an attorney. And the mother of his child. And because, according to your ex-father-in-law, you're probably the only person on earth Eric truly trusts."

This time, she was able to manage a small laugh. "I'm afraid Douglas is overestimating Eric's opinion of me. The truth is, my ex-husband and I are barely civil to each other. If it wasn't for our daughter, we wouldn't be talking at all."

"When did you hear from him last?" he asked.

"I couldn't say exactly." Conscious of his eyes on her, she picked up a glass from the counter and put it in the dishwasher. "Weeks."

"Do you have any idea where he might have gone?"

"None whatsoever," she replied lightly.

"Does he have any close friends? Someone who might be willing to hide him for a while?"

"Eric has lots of friends, all as shallow as he is. I doubt any of them would take such a risk."

He watched her hand as she closed the dishwasher. "Yet he's managed to elude an entire police force for the past seventeen hours."

"Believe me, Detective, no one is more surprised by that than I. I never thought of Eric as a man with strong survival instincts."

"Desperation can be a powerful motive."

Kate's eyes narrowed as she measured the man across from her. He was a tough cop, and a smart one. Did he really believe Eric was guilty, or was he just fishing? "You're barking up the wrong tree, Detective. Eric is no criminal. Except for a few traffic tickets, he's never done anything even remotely unlawful."

Mitch's lips twitched in a wry smile. "Your loyalty is admirable, Mrs. Logan, but the fact remains that the evidence against him is staggering. Unless of course, you don't consider blackmail a reason for murder."

"That's assuming he was being blackmailed."

His laugh came easily. "Come on, Counselor. Gina Lamont didn't record their little interlude out of sentimentality. And she didn't come to Eric's office two days later to discuss the marketing of semiconductors."

So Abigail hadn't wasted any time in notifying the police about Gina's visit to Hollbrook Industries, Kate thought. "That's circumstantial evidence, and you know it," she stated. "It will never stand up in court."

"You sound as if you were planning to represent Eric."

"I *am* representing him, Detective." She folded her arms. "Is that a problem for you?"

"Nope." He continued to scrutinize her with unnerving intensity. "Tell me something, though. If he's innocent as you claim, why isn't he coming forward to defend himself instead of hiding?"

"You would have to know Eric to understand that. He doesn't handle problems well. Faced with a difficult choice, he'll invariably choose the easiest option rather than the wisest. In his mind, staying in hiding while I solve his problem seems like the perfect solution."

Although she sounded sincere enough, something about the way she had averted her eyes earlier told Mitch his hunch had been right after all. She had heard from Eric. She might even know where he was. He could have pushed her, thrown his weight around a little, but he didn't. She was an attorney. She knew the risks of protecting a fugitive as well as he did. And besides, he wasn't all that certain that Logan was his man.

An angry voice ripping through the air jolted him out of his thoughts.

"What's *he* doing here?"

He turned around to see Kate's daughter glaring at him.

"Alison!" Kate's voice rang just as sharp and accusing. But Alison was in no mood to listen. Her eyes bright with fury, she stomped into the kitchen, one angry fist on her hip.

"Haven't you done enough harm?" she snapped at Mitch. "You already sent one innocent man to prison. Now you want to do the same to my dad?"

"Alison, that's enough."

Alison's eyes brimmed with tears as she turned to h mother. "I thought you were on Daddy's side. I thought you were going to help him."

"I *am* helping him. I've done nothing since this morning but try to sort through the mess he left behind."

"And that's how you do it?" Alison cried, emotion cracking her youthful voice. "By talking to *him?* By letting him in our house?"

Devastated by the child's anguish, Kate went to her. "Darling, Detective Calhoon is conducting an investigation. I was merely answering his questions—"

Before Kate could finish her sentence, Alison let out a small cry of frustration and fled the room.

It took Kate a few moments to collect herself and a few more to realize that the door Alison had just slammed was not to her bedroom, but the front door.

Alarmed, she ran into the foyer. "Alison!" Her eyes darted toward the coatrack where Alison's red coat always hung. It was gone. Mitch right behind her, Kate threw the door open and ran the few steps to the sidewalk. Alison was nowhere in sight. "Oh, my God."

"She can't be far," Mitch said in a voice that was instantly calming. "Take your car and ride around that block." He pointed toward the left. "I'll go the other way." He squeezed her arm. "We'll find her."

As Kate ran back inside the house to get her car keys, a dozen terrifying thoughts bounced in her head. Where could Alison have gone? What if they didn't find her? What if someone took her? She was only thirteen. Anything could happen to a young girl these days. Even in this neighborhood.

By the time she reached her car, Mitch was already gone.

Her heart pounding, Kate jumped into the Saab and drove around the familiar streets, peering through the windshield and into the night, hoping to see Alison's red coat. She even got out of the car a few times to knock at her neighbors' doors. But no one had seen Alison. Yes, they would call if they heard anything.

Ten agonizing minutes later, having searched every nook and cranny of Cleveland Park, including the Forest Hill playground where kids sometimes gathered, she drove back to the house. Mitch was already there, standing by his car and talking on a cellular phone.

She kept her eyes riveted to him as he gave the police dispatcher a thorough description of Alison, grateful for his extraordinary memory.

When he was finished, he hung up and looked at Kate. "Did she have any money? Enough to take a cab?"

Not trusting her voice, Kate nodded.

"Let me have your phone book," he said as they hurried back toward the house.

In the kitchen, he took the heavy yellow pages she handed him, laid it on top of the island and started flipping through it. Once he had located the listing for local cab companies, he dialed each one, explaining who he was and why he was calling.

"They're going to check with all their drivers," he said when he was finished.

Kate sank into a chair. "I'm scared." She couldn't remember the last time she had admitted that to anyone.

Mitch crouched down in front of her and took her hands in his. "I know, Kate. Just hang in there."

Her heart continued to pound furiously as she imagined the worst—Alison hurt, bleeding, calling for her. "What if someone drove by and saw her and...took her?"

"We were right behind her, Kate. We would have heard something." He remembered the girl's violent outburst earlier. "She wouldn't have gone quietly."

The words, although spoken with a great deal of faith,
failed to reassure her. Unable to hold back her tears, she
buried her head in her hands and cried helplessly.

Ten

Huddled in an empty stall and surrounded by nothing but darkness and hay, Alison shivered. Taking a cab to her grandfather's house and then hiding in one of the stalls had seemed like a good idea at first, but now she wasn't so sure.

She pulled her coat collar around her face and tucked her cold hands into the woolly fabric. God, it must be zero degrees in here. If she had realized it would be that cold, she would have worn an extra sweater. And gloves.

But there had been no time to think. She had been too mad. Mad at that detective for coming to her house, and mad at her mother for talking to him as if he was her new best friend. Couldn't she see that he was only pretending to be nice? So he could trick her into saying something about her dad.

And she didn't like the way he looked at Kate, either. Nobody thought she noticed those things, but she did. She wasn't stupid.

What really annoyed her was that she had liked him at first. He wasn't like other policemen she knew. He was friendly and good-looking. And with his easy manner and crooked little smile, he reminded her a little of Kevin Costner. She had even believed that he was trying to help Tony when all along he had been planning to throw him in jail. What a joke.

In the next stall, Prince, her grandfather's high-strung Arabian, was getting restless. She could hear him snorting and shifting around in the confined space.

How long had she been here? She had no idea. At least an hour. She didn't want to freeze to death, but she didn't want to go back too soon, either.

If she had any guts at all, she would *really* run away from home, the way Cathy Forrester had after her mother brought their new baby home from the hospital. But Cathy hadn't gotten very far. The police had found her an hour later, sitting in a bus terminal, trying to figure out what to do next. Her short escapade hadn't really changed things, but it had helped, and the baby was no longer getting all the attention. Cathy had felt pretty smug after that.

The sound of footsteps made her jump. Heart pounding, she sank deeper into the hay, terrified it might be a prowler. To her relief, she recognized Billy's voice. He was talking to Prince.

"What's the matter, big guy?" the stable boy asked. "Something spooked you? Okay, okay, I'll check it out. Keep your shirt on."

Billy's footsteps started again, this time in the direction of Alison's stall. She held her breath. She couldn't be found yet. It was too soon. Her mother hadn't worried enough. Still, at the same time, she was glad to have another human being so close by.

An overhead light came on, nearly blinding her. "Who's there?" Billy asked.

How did he know someone was here? Had she left a trail or something?

"Suit yourself," Billy continued. "But you're going to be howling when I start poking through that pile of hay with my pitchfork."

"Don't!" Alison jumped up, bits of straw sticking to her coat and hair. "It's me, Alison!"

Billy lowered the pitchfork. In his hands was a red-and-white wool scarf. Her scarf. She hadn't even realized she had dropped it.

"Alison! What in God's name are you doing here? Don't you know that everyone is looking for you?"

When she didn't answer, he walked out and went to pick up a wall phone hooked outside the stall. He dialed, his eyes fixed on Alison.

"It's Billy at the stables," he said when someone at the main house answered. "I found Alison. Yeah, she's fine."

"Here you are, dear," Rose said gently as she handed Kate a steaming cup of tea. "This will make you feel better. Douglas," she added, glancing at her husband who stood by the fireplace. "Would you care for some tea?"

"No, thank you."

Still distraught from the recent ordeal, Kate held her cup with trembling hands. The call that Alison was safe had come a little less than an hour ago. Mitch, who had stayed with her until that time, had left, and she had come straight to Potomac, ready to ground Alison for a year. But the moment she saw her, huddled in one of her grand-mother's quilts, sipping hot chocolate, Kate's anger had melted away.

She had tried to talk to her after that, but Alison had claimed she was too tired. She wanted to go upstairs to her old room and sleep. As Kate, anxious to take her daughter home, started to object, Rose had given an im-perceptible shake of her head. Seeing the wisdom of th silent message, Kate had let Alison go.

Rose waited until Kate had taken a sip of her tea before

speaking again. "About Alison," she said softly. "Maybe it would be best if she stayed with us for a while. The separation might do you both some good."

Kate's head shot up. "You want me to let her live here?"

"It would only be for a short time."

"Oh, Rose, I couldn't." Kate's voice was low, breaking as she spoke. "She's my daughter. I would be lost without her." She gazed into her tea. "And there's already such a wall between us. A separation, however short, could make things worse."

Rose reached across the sofa to touch Kate's hand. "I know things have been rough between you two since the divorce, but deep down Alison loves you very much. Being away from you for a while might just make her realize that."

Her heart heavy with sadness and indecision, Kate remained silent. How could she have let it come this far? And what would become of them if she allowed Alison to have her way? What if she *never* wanted to come home? The thought was so unbearable that her hands began to shake again and she had to put her cup down.

Of course, she didn't have to listen to anybody. She could simply exercise her rights as a parent and take Alison home. No one would blame her.

Except Alison.

"What about school?" she asked at last. "I was planning to let her return to class in a day or two."

"I can talk to Flora Cornfield and see if she can arrange for Alison to go back to Sawmill Academy on a temporary basis. I'm sure Flora won't have any objections—under the circumstances. And she's always been fond of Alison."

"Rose is right." Douglas walked toward them, a

brandy snifter in his hand. Dressed in tan gabardine pants, a white shirt open at the neck and a navy cardigan, he looked very much the lord of the manor. "The change will do the girl good," he continued. "It'll give her a chance to see things from a different perspective."

How sensible they were, Kate thought, feeling suddenly very inadequate. No wonder Alison loved it here. There was no chaos, no pressure, no arguments. Only common sense.

The separation would only be for a short while, she reminded herself. As soon as this mess with Eric was cleared up, Alison would come home. They would celebrate in style, go to Disney World perhaps, or to Aspen. How long had it been since they had gone skiing together?

"I guess you're right." Trying not to think of how lonely the house would be without her daughter, Kate stood up. "I'll stop by in the morning with some of her clothes. Maybe she'll be ready to talk to me by then."

Rose linked her arm with Kate's and together they walked toward the door. "I'm sure she will, dear. Meanwhile, don't worry about your little girl. We'll take good care of her."

Not sure if Alison was still awake, Rose tiptoed to her room, peering through the partially open door.

"Hi, Grandma."

"I thought you were asleep." Smiling, Rose walked in and came to sit on the bed with its lacy pillows and pink comforter.

The small night lamp on the bureau cast a gentle glow over the room. Rose hadn't changed a thing. The stuff animals that had delighted Alison's childhood were still displayed on a shelf, and her favorite doll, an Orphan

Annie with a missing eye, still held the place of honor on a chintz-covered chair.

"How are you, pumpkin?" Rose pushed a strand of golden hair from the child's smooth forehead. "All recovered from your little adventure?"

Under the comforter, Alison shrugged. "I guess so."

"You scared your mother half to death, you know. She was imagining all sorts of terrible things—"

"No, she wasn't. She doesn't care about me." That familiar rebellious look Alison had adopted of late was back. "If she did, she wouldn't have divorced Daddy."

Rose felt a small twist of pain. She had no idea the girl still harbored such deep resentment toward her mother. "You're wrong, Alison. Your mother cares very much. And she thought long and hard before divorcing your father. But she had no choice, you see. She wasn't happy anymore."

"Why didn't she tell him that and talk it over with him, the way she does with me all the time?"

"They did talk it over, pumpkin. But eventually they reached a point where splitting up seemed like the only thing to do. Just as Eric's father and I did when we realized we couldn't live together anymore."

"That's different," Alison argued. "Daddy was already sixteen when you divorced my other grandpa. And right after that, he moved into this great big house where he could do all sorts of fun things. Mom and I moved to Cleveland Park." She made a contemptuous sound. "We don't even have a garage. And Mom is always bugging me to turn my music down."

Rose smiled. "You had to do that here, too."

Alison made a pout. "It wasn't the same. Nothing is the same."

"Things will get better, Alison, I promise. You just

have to give your mother a chance. You have to stop being so angry with her. That's the root of all your problems.''

"I hate it when she talks to that detective Mitch Calhoon.''

"Why is that?''

"He's in love with her.''

Startled by that unexpected reply, Rose raised an eyebrow. "What makes you think that?''

"The way he looked at her when he was investigating Lilly's murder. And the way he talked to her. It was different than when he talked to Maria.''

"Well, I wouldn't know about that, but I can't say I'm surprised. Your mother is a beautiful woman. She is also smart, warm and generous. I can see why a man would be interested in her.'' She cocked her head to the side and smiled. "Don't you?''

Rose's gently teasing tone had no effect on Alison. "Not him,'' she said stubbornly. "I hate him. He wants to put Daddy in jail.''

Rose sighed. She couldn't offer much of an argument there. Almost everyone, it seemed, wanted to put Eric in jail. "Your mother isn't going to let that happen, pumpkin,'' she whispered as she bent to kiss her granddaughter's cheek. "You can count on that.''

But she could tell by Alison's sullen expression that she didn't entirely believe her. Rose sat with her a moment longer, holding her hand, watching her lovingly as the girl's eyelids began to droop. When she was certain Alison was asleep, she stood up and tiptoed out of the room.

The bitter cold front that had plagued the East Coast for more than a week had finally ended, leaving behind crisp blue skies and rather mild temperatures.

Carrying a small suitcase filled with a few of Alison's clothes, Kate walked out of the house at seven-thirty that morning and collided with Mitch Calhoon. As she stumbled, he caught her, holding her a moment too long. The contact sent a flutter through her she would neither name nor acknowledge.

Remembering, however, that he was the reason she had remained relatively sane the night before, she didn't yank her arm free as she had done in front of the courthouse. Instead, she smiled, finding it surprisingly easy to do so. "Did you happen to be in the neighborhood again, Detective?"

Amusement danced in his eyes. "No. This time, the trip was intentional. I feel somewhat responsible for what happened last night and I wanted to make sure your daughter was all right."

Kate closed the door behind her and started toward her Saab, Mitch at her side. "Alison wasn't angry with you, Detective. She was angry with me. She ran away to punish me."

"Because you were talking to me?"

Kate nodded. "She adores her father. The thought that he might be arrested and put in jail frightens her very much."

"Where is she now?"

"At her grandparents' house. She'll be staying there for a while. And in case you thought I was skipping town," she added with a small smile as she held out the suitcase, "I'm not. These are Alison's clothes."

She didn't tell him that she had spent half the night wondering if Alison would ever want to live with her again. It was bad enough that she thought about it constantly, she didn't want to hear herself say it out loud.

"And I bet you miss her already." His voice was gentle, as though he understood what she was going through.

"More than she'll ever know." She looked up at him, squinting against the morning sun. "Is there anything new on the murder?"

"They found Eric's car."

Kate arched a brow. "Really? Where?"

"One mile south of Fredericksburg, Virginia."

"Any sign of Eric?"

"No, but a desk clerk at a nearby motel remembers him. He checked in at about eight o'clock on Tuesday morning, paid cash for the room and left it a few hours later. Another witness saw him hitch a ride."

"In which direction?"

"South on I-95."

"Well, Alison will be happy to hear that he's all right. She's been very worried about him."

Inside the house, the phone began to ring. Kate ignored it and opened her car, tossing the suitcase on the passenger seat.

"Aren't you going to answer that?" Mitch asked.

"The machine will pick it up. I've got to go."

She was sliding behind the wheel when her car phone started ringing.

"Somebody wants you pretty bad." Although Mitch's tone was light, he was watching her intently. Because she didn't want to give him a reason to be more suspicious than he already was, she picked up the receiver. And instantly regretted it.

"Kate, it's me. Eric."

She glanced at Mitch, who was still watching her. "Hello, Frankie."

"Frankie?" Eric paused. "What's the matter? Can't you talk?"

She brushed an imaginary crumb from her camel-hair coat and tried to keep her voice level. "No, I haven't forgotten about my appointment with William Fox. I'll drop off Alison's clothes and go to the police station from there. Detective Calhoon stopped by. That's why I'm running a little late."

"The cops." There was a low groan, then a click. Eric had hung up.

"My secretary." Kate put on a smile she hoped wasn't too phony and snapped the receiver back in place. "I don't know what I would do without her." She wondered if he bought the act. She hoped so. Any suspicion on the part of the police and they'd have the house wired in a heartbeat.

"I see you're in a hurry, so I won't keep you." Mitch regarded her for another few unsettling seconds before adding, "By the way, if you need to take a look at Gina's apartment, my team is all done there."

The tension eased off Kate's shoulders. "I'd like that very much. Thank you."

"No problem. I'll call the super and let him know you'll be stopping by."

"I hope your people left something for me to find," she said in a playful tone.

A smile curved his mouth, creating a small groove at one corner. "Don't count on it."

She closed her door and rolled down the window. "Since you're in such a generous mood, you wouldn't happen to have the crime-lab results, too, would you? And be willing to share them? It would save me a call to Rencheck's office."

Mitch laughed. "What would it be worth to you if I did?"

She met his gaze. "I suppose I could return the favor—at some point."

He stuck his head through the window, coming close enough for her to notice the fine lines around his blue eyes and how they deepened when he smiled. "I have a confession to make, Counselor. I'm a greedy sort of guy. I like to collect my rewards right away. How about dinner tonight and we'll call it even?"

Kate laughed. "It's more than I've paid for a favor in a long time."

"Then I'll appreciate it even more."

For a moment, she was tempted to say yes. When was the last time she had been out with a handsome, attentive man? Had felt attractive? And wanted. Reluctantly, she pushed the thought out of her mind. There was Alison to consider. Until the two of them had made some kind of truce, she didn't want to do anything that would upset her further.

"I'm afraid I can't," she said without offering an explanation. "Maybe another time?"

To his credit, he didn't push her. "All right, Counselor. I'll hold you to that promise."

She leaned back against her seat. "About the lab results?"

"Ah, yes, the lab results." Serious again, Mitch glanced up and down the street. "The autopsy confirmed what we already knew. Gina Lamont died of strangulation. There were scratches on her neck, but they came from her own fingernails as she tried to loosen her killer's grip."

Kate felt a surge of pity for the woman. No one deserved to die that way. "Any skin residue under her fingernails?"

Mitch shook his head. "Just her own."

"Any fibers? On her body? Her bedding?"

"A few. All were of some black cotton fabric. It'll be a few days before its origin can be determined."

"Eric wasn't wearing black the night of the murder."

His glance was quick and sharp. "How do you know?"

Heat rushed to her cheeks. Stupid, she thought, biting her bottom lip. Stupid, stupid, stupid.

"He came to see you that night, didn't he?" The playfulness was gone from the detective's voice. He was all business now. "Eric was here."

It was another few seconds before she could speak. "Yes," she admitted, turning to look at him. "But I never saw him again after that."

"What time was he here?"

"Ten-fifteen."

"Why didn't you mention it before?"

"Because I didn't want to subject myself to the kind of interrogation I'm being subjected to now." She held his hard blue stare as long as she could, then turned her head away.

"What did he want, Kate?"

She expelled a long breath. Either she told him the truth and hoped he believed her, or he would have no choice but take her in for questioning. Deciding to follow her instincts, she opted for the truth. "He came hoping to borrow Alison's trust fund. Gina wanted two hundred and fifty thousand dollars in exchange for the tape."

"I take it you turned him down."

She nodded.

"Then what did he do?"

"He left."

His eyes, always watchful, followed a school bus as it drove by. "Was he angry?" he asked, returning his attention to her. "Did he threaten anyone?"

"Eric doesn't get angry, Detective. Eric whines, he begs, he cajoles, but he doesn't get angry. And he never threatens."

"Have you heard from him since?"

On the steering wheel, her knuckles turned white. She forced herself to relax her grip. "No. And I don't expect to." She hated that she was getting so good at lying. But what else could she do? If Mitch knew Eric had contacted her a second time, he would have no choice but to tap her phone.

Rather than give him a chance to decide if she was lying or telling the truth, she changed the subject. "By the way, I can't remember if I thanked you for all your help last night, but in case I didn't, I'd like to do it now." She gave him an apologetic smile. "I don't usually come unglued the way I did, but the thought that Alison was alone on the streets was more than I could handle. I guess you would have to be a parent to understand that kind of fear."

An expression she couldn't quite define flashed in his eyes. In the time it took her to see it, it was gone.

"I'm glad I was there."

Kate glanced at the dashboard clock. "I'd better get going. I have just enough time to make it to Potomac before Alison leaves for school."

"Right."

She waited until Mitch had reached his Ford before pulling away from the curb. As she passed him, she touched her horn and drove off.

Eleven

"Mr. Fox," Kate said gently as she and her new client sat facing each other in an interview room, "you hired me to do a job, but unless you cooperate with me, I won't be able to do that job well. And I certainly won't be able to get you out on bail."

William J. Fox, a small, nervous man with a twitch above his right eye, gave her a look of alarm. "Why not? This isn't premeditated murder. It isn't even murder. I killed Ben in self-defense."

"I know you did, but the U.S. attorney doesn't see it that way. His theory is that you panicked when your boss confronted you about the missing funds and you killed him. The money, which you claim you don't have, makes you a high flight risk. And high flight risks seldom get bail."

Fox's nervous twitch began working double-time as he glanced from Kate to the uniformed guard standing at the door. Although his stubbornness about the money was making Kate's job more difficult, she couldn't help feeling sorry for the man. Accused of killing his boss and of embezzling $1.3 million, the president of Vanco Labs hadn't had more than a couple hours' sleep since his arrest twenty-four hours ago. Unshaven and exhausted, he looked ten years older than his forty-eight years.

"That money is mine," Fox protested, more or less

admitting for the first time that he'd taken it. "I was supposed to get it as a bonus over a period of ten years and never did."

Grateful for this small progress, Kate leaned forward. "I understand that." She talked softly, unthreateningly. "But holding on to it is going to do you more harm than good."

"Can you guarantee me an acquittal if I return it?"

"No, but your chances would be much greater if you did. No jury in the world is going to sympathize with a man who stole $1.3 million from his company."

After what seemed like an eternity, Fox's thin shoulders sagged. "All right," he whispered, falling back against his chair. "I guess I don't have much of a choice." He looked up, his eye giving one final twitch. "But I'm sticking to my original plea. Not guilty by reason of self-defense. Ben charged me like a bull. I had to stop him or he would have killed me."

Before Kate could breathe a sigh of relief, her cellular phone rang. Excusing herself, she pulled it out of her open briefcase and took the call. It was from Rose.

"Kate, I know this is short notice, but can you meet me for lunch? I need to discuss something with you."

Kate was filled with sudden anxiety. Had Alison decided to stay with the Fairchilds on a permanent basis and sent Rose to deliver the news? She hadn't said anything when Kate had dropped off her clothes earlier. In fact, Alison had been almost friendly and very excited at the prospect of returning to Sawmill Academy.

Not wanting to hear the bad news in front of her client, Kate resisted the urge to question Rose further. "Lunch would be difficult today," she replied, trying to sound calm. "But I could meet you for a quick cup of coffee at Union Station. Say in about an hour?"

"That's perfect."

Kate tucked the phone back in her briefcase and stood up. "I'll contact the U.S. attorney right away," she told Fox as he pushed his chair back. "With a little luck, I'll be able to schedule a bail hearing before the end of the day." She nodded at the guard, indicating she was ready to leave. "I'll let you know what happens as soon as I hear something." Catching her client's worried gaze, she added, "You made the right decision, Mr. Fox. Now why don't you try to get some rest."

She left the jail wishing that all her cases were that simple.

It was exactly ten-thirty when Rose, looking lovely in a red wool suit, walked into the International Café in Union Station and made her way toward Kate's booth.

"I'm so glad you could meet me," she said, removing her black leather gloves and setting them on the table. "I would have talked to you earlier, but with Douglas there when you arrived, and Alison, and all the servants..." She rolled her eyes toward the ceiling. "We wouldn't have had any privacy anyway."

"Alison isn't giving you any trouble, is she?" Kate watched Rose closely, almost hoping for an affirmative answer.

But Rose smiled and shook her head. "Oh, no. She's no problem at all. By the way, Flora is thrilled to have her back at Sawmill Academy. She'd always thought highly of Alison."

Kate tried to hide her disappointment. "I'm glad. I know she has a way of getting on Douglas's nerves at times."

Rose picked up the mug of cappuccino Kate had ordered ahead of time and took a small sip of the fragrant concoction. "Well, you needn't worry. She's been the perfect little granddaughter."

Kate braced herself for the worst. "Then you didn't call me here to complain about her."

"No." Rose took another sip of her coffee, watching Kate over the rim of her cup. "Alison told me something rather interesting when I went to tuck her in last night."

"Oh."

"She said that Detective Calhoon is in love with you."

Startled, Kate stared at the older woman. "Where did she get an idea like that?"

"Watching, listening. You know what a keen observer she is, especially when it comes to grown-ups."

"Dear God, is that why she was so upset with me?"

"It's one of the reasons."

"What else did she say?"

"Oh, the usual, that you shouldn't have divorced Eric and that everything used to be better. And as you can imagine, she didn't hide her feelings about Mitch Calhoon. To quote her own words, she hates him."

"I'll have to talk to her, then. The poor child. No wonder she was so confused last night."

"Oh, she'll be all right, dear. And anyway, it's not Alison's feelings that I came to discuss. It's yours."

"Mine?" Kate laughed. "Feelings about what?"

"Detective Calhoon, of course." Rose's eyes twinkled again. She was definitely enjoying this. "He's a very handsome man, isn't he?"

Oh, no, Kate thought. First Frankie, now Rose. Didn't they think she knew what she was doing with her life? "Rose, you know that I have no intention of becoming involved again."

"Because of Alison?"

"Because of a lot of things, but yes, Alison is the main

reason. How could I even think of having a relationship with a man she hates?''

"Oh, in time, Alison would get used to it. I think you're the one who's afraid of getting involved. I know it wasn't easy being married to Eric,'' she added when Kate remained silent. "But don't let one bad experience ruin your life, Kate. Alison is thirteen years old. In a few years, she'll be going to college, starting a life of her own. What will you do then?''

"I have my career.''

"It won't be enough, dear. A career, no matter how rewarding, doesn't keep you warm at night. It doesn't make you laugh, and it doesn't have a strong, comforting shoulder to lean on when things get rough.''

Kate couldn't hold back a smile. "Rose, are you telling me to have an affair with Detective Calhoon?''

Rose chuckled. "Wouldn't Douglas fly into a raging fit if he heard that?'' She shook her head, serious again. "No, dear, I didn't come here to tell you to have an affair with Detective Calhoon. I came to tell you to live your life for yourself and not for those around you. I almost let a second chance pass me by once, and if it hadn't been for my sister who put some sense into my head, I never would have married Douglas.''

"I didn't know that.''

"Not too many people do.'' She laughed, a happy, almost girlish laugh. "Douglas likes to think he swept me off my feet, but the truth is, I thought he was overbearing and a tad too full of himself. He still is, of course.'' Her eyes filled with tenderness. "But now I love him too much to let it matter.''

Kate was relieved that they were no longer discussing Mitch Calhoon. It was bad enough that he kept jumping into her thoughts at the most inopportune times; she didn't need well-meaning friends and colleagues to push her into something she wasn't ready for.

Something she would probably never be ready for.

"Megan, darling," Abigail Hollbrook said in a gently chiding voice, "if you don't start eating, you'll wither away like an old prune. You don't want that, do you?"

Megan stood looking out her bedroom window, her arms folded beneath her breasts, her beige silk robe tightly cinched around her slender waist. She didn't care if she withered away. She didn't care about anything now that Eric was gone.

"I know what you're thinking." Abigail's voice softened as she came to stand beside her daughter. "You think that I don't understand what you're going through. But you're wrong, darling. I know how painful love can be. I was young once, too."

Megan wanted to laugh. How could her mother possibly understand about love and pain when she had never experienced either? Abigail Hollbrook came from a long line of strong, independent women—women who had carved their place in history without the help of any man. Oh, there had been marriages, but each one of them had been a well-orchestrated business deal, a transaction meant to link one great family fortune to another.

"This seclusion on your part isn't doing anyone any good." This time, there was a slight trace of impatience in Abigail's voice. "Life must go on, Megan, whether you want it to or not."

Megan felt a sob rise in her throat and held it back. How could she go on when she had that awful cold ache in her heart? When she felt like bursting into tears at the mere mention of Eric's name?

"Tess made a mushroom quiche for lunch," Abigail coaxed. "It's your favorite, isn't it?"

"I'm not hungry." Megan's gaze remained fixed on the same barren oak she had been staring at for the past ten minutes.

"Why don't we go for a nice long ride, then? I'm sure Salomé would love it." Abigail laughed. "That poor mare is beginning to get cabin fever."

For a moment, Megan considered the suggestion. Galloping through the countryside with the wind in her face had always helped clear her head. But if she went out, she might miss the call she was hoping for. "I don't think so, Mother."

Abigail's self-control finally snapped. "If you think that spending all your time in this bedroom, waiting for the phone to ring, is going to make it happen, you are deluding yourself. Eric Logan isn't going to call. And he's not coming back."

"You don't know that!" Megan spun around, her blond hair flying. "And stop hoping I'll give up on him because I never will. You wouldn't, either, if you knew him the way I do. But you've never even tried to do that, have you? You've never wanted to look beneath the surface."

"Oh, Megan." Abigail's sigh of despair seemed to rise from her very soul. "How can you be so blind? The man betrayed you. He went to bed with another woman, a *prostitute*. How can you still defend him after that?"

"I love him," Megan said simply.

"Well, he certainly doesn't love you. If he did, he wouldn't have taken off with the lowest form of human life and slept with her."

"That was a mistake. He was drunk."

Abigail's laugh was brittle. "Not that drunk, I'm told.

He knew exactly where he was going that night and with whom."

Megan gave her a startled look. "How do you know that?" When Abigail looked away, Megan's eyes widened in shock. "My God, you were having him watched, weren't you? You hired a private investigator."

Abigail lifted a proud chin. "Don't make it sound as though I committed a sin. I did it for your own good."

"How many times have I told you that I don't need anyone to look after me? I'm twenty-seven years old and perfectly capable of taking care of myself." The anger and frustration Megan had kept bottled up for the past forty-eight hours began to unravel. "How long have you had Eric watched?"

With a hand that would have been steady under the most trying circumstances, Abigail lightly touched her pearl choker. "Since the day you told me you were going to marry him."

"*Seven months?* You've had Eric watched and followed for seven whole months? Why, Mother?"

"Because I never trusted him! And for good reason, wouldn't you say?"

"How could you?" Megan shot at her. "Wasn't it enough that you had him investigated, that every moment of his life, every mistake he'd ever made was laid out for the whole world to see? You had to have him watched, too?" She shook her head in disbelief. "*That's* low, Mother."

"I did it for you," Abigail repeated. "You may hate me for it now, but someday, when you have children of your own, you'll understand."

As a thought suddenly dawned on her, Megan frowned. "Wait a minute. If your private investigator was watching

Eric twenty-four hours a day, then he must know where he was the night of the murder.''

"Monroe was no longer watching him by then."

"But you said—"

"After Monroe told me Sunday morning that Eric had spent the night with that woman, I no longer had any need for his services. I had what I wanted."

"Why didn't you say something to me then? That was your plan, wasn't it?"

"Of course. I had intended to confront Eric in front of you that very morning, but as you recall, the two of you went skiing that day, and on Monday I was tied up in a series of meetings. By the time I was finally free, Eric had disappeared."

Megan laughed, a small, muffled laugh that sounded perilously like a sob. "You must have been thrilled when Monroe called you with the news. That's exactly what you had been praying for, wasn't it?" Normally, the stern look on her mother's face would have been enough to silence her, but not this time. "And what if he hadn't strayed?" she asked, her tone sharp and defiant. "Would you have gone so far as to set the stage for him? Would you have put a woman in his path in order to tempt him?"

"Dear God, Megan, what's gotten into you?"

"I'm right, aren't I? Don't try to deny it. There is only one thing in this world you hate more than Eric, and that's the thought of me marrying him. You would do anything for that not to happen." Her eyes remained riveted to her mother. "Perhaps even having Eric framed for murder."

"Megan!"

"Oh, don't look so shocked, Mother. We both know that you're clever enough to think of it and well connected enough to carry it out."

"I won't even dignify that comment with a reply."

With those words, Abigail Hollbrook pulled herself erect and stalked out of the room.

Twelve

Dressed in a leopard-trimmed black suit Eric loved, Megan stood in the elegant reception room of Warwick Investigations, waiting for Monroe Warwick, the owner of the agency and one of her mother's oldest friends, to come out and greet her.

Although she hadn't mentioned her visit, she had no doubt that Abigail already knew about it. One of the reasons her mother's friends remained her friends was that they were blindly loyal to her.

"Megan, my dear!"

Monroe Warwick walked quickly across the thick cream carpet, both hands extended. He was an average-size man with brown hair, brown eyes and no distinguishing features of any kind, a characteristic that allowed him to observe others without ever being noticed. Or remembered.

"You look lovely." After kissing her cheek, he wrapped an arm around her waist and led her to his office, a well-appointed room overlooking the Washington Monument. "Would you care for some coffee, or—"

She shook her head and sat down. "Nothing, thank you." She set her purse on her lap and clasped it tightly. "Actually, I'm in a bit of a hurry and would appreciate it if you could answer just one question for me."

"Surely." His face remained neutral. No doubt he had his orders, but she would know if he was lying.

"I just learned you've been watching Eric for many months," she said, keeping her voice free of emotion. "What I need to know is what day you stopped watching him."

He sighed. "Your mother told me that you'd probably be stopping by *and* what question you would be asking."

His honesty surprised her. "Did she also tell you what answer to give me?"

Warwick laughed. "No, she didn't." Folding his hands, he clasped them lightly and rested them on his desk. "I'm sorry for all the heartache you're going through, Megan. And I'm sorry that I can't tell you what you so badly want to hear. But the truth is, my surveillance of your fiancé ended when I gave your mother my report on Sunday morning. That's the God's truth. I wouldn't lie to you about something like that. And neither would your mother."

She believed him. She had suspected she would. Monroe Warwick was one of those rare persons who, although he possessed a great deal of money, was unaffected by it. He was also the only man she knew who could stand up to Abigail.

As the flimsy hope she had held on to until now began to evaporate, she felt a deep sense of loss. Anxious to be alone, she stood up. "Thank you, Monroe."

"I'm sorry," he said again as he rose from behind his desk. "If there's anything I can do…"

She nodded, tears of disappointment stinging her eyes. "I'll let you know."

In a motel room on the outskirts of Goshen, Virginia, Eric stood by the window, nervously watching the parking lot as he ate the stale cheese sandwich he had bought from a vending machine.

Fortunately, the lot was relatively empty at this time of year. He counted three cars, two eighteen-wheelers and an RV with Nevada plates. Yet he knew that at any given moment, the cops could show up, alerted by someone who had recognized him from the photograph TV stations kept showing during their newscasts.

His left hand went to his face, cupped his jaw and rubbed it gently. Not that he could be so easily recognized. Four days' growth of beard dyed the same dark gray as his new hair color covered most of his face. The Ralph Lauren jogging suit Megan had bought him for his last birthday had been replaced by baggy khakis and a denim shirt he had bought at a navy surplus store. A black canvas bag containing the bare essentials—a change of clothes, toiletries and thermal underwear—stood on a chair.

Afraid to travel the major highways, he had stuck to small roads, not really caring where he went as long as it was far from Washington. In Fredericksburg, where he'd abandoned the Corvette, he had hitched a ride from a chicken farmer who'd brought him all the way to Goshen. But he wouldn't do that again. Those people were too damned nosy. In exchange for a free ride, he was expected to tell his life story.

Money, or rather the lack of it, worried him almost as much as the cops. The two hundred and fifty dollars he had withdrawn from the automated teller machine in Brookville was disappearing fast. If he tried using the ATM again, the police would concentrate their search in this area. He couldn't risk that.

He took another bite of his sandwich and chewed slowly. He could remember the days when two hundred and fifty dollars had seemed like a fortune. It sure wasn't a fortune now. Thank God he had found this shabby, out-of-the-way motel. At $19.95 a night, he could afford to stay here a few more days. But what the hell would he do once the money ran out?

One thing was certain, though. He couldn't call Kate again. It was too risky. The thought that the police had been there when he called earlier tied his stomach in knots. What did they want with her? Did they suspect he had contacted her? Had they tapped her phone? Lucky for him she hadn't given him away, but from now on, no more calls. If he wanted news, he would have to get it from the TV.

He finished off his sandwich, rubbed his hands to get rid of the crumbs and walked to the bathroom for a glass of water, wishing it was a cold draft instead. As he passed the small, cracked mirror over the dresser, he glanced at his reflection. His lips twitched in a small smile.

What was he worried about? In this getup, even his own mother wouldn't recognize him.

The superintendent of The Hamptons condominium, a strong, silent type in blue overalls and a denim jacket, unlocked the door to Gina Lamont's condo and moved aside to let Kate in. "There you go. Just holler when you're done and I'll come and lock up."

The apartment, which as usual the police had left in a mess, consisted of a spacious living room, a bedroom with a stripped, king-size brass bed in the center, a bathroom and a state-of-the-art kitchen.

Kate took her time, opening drawers, checking closets, hoping to find one piece of evidence, however small, that Mitch and his men might have missed.

Thirty minutes later, she had concluded that Gina Lamont liked expensive clothes, only drank French wine and, judging from the impressive selection of Lean Cuisine entrées in her freezer, was a consummate dieter.

But she hadn't found a single clue as to who might have killed her.

After one last look at the living room, she closed the door and was about to go look for the super when an attractive young woman in a flight attendant's uniform came out of the elevator, pulling a small black suitcase behind her.

Kate watched her as she headed toward the apartment across from Gina's—8A. "Hello there."

The woman looked up. "Good afternoon. I mean good morning. It *is* morning here, isn't it?"

Kate laughed with her. "For another hour or so." She glanced at the wings on the woman's jacket. "Long flight?"

"The longest. Hong Kong. I've been gone since Saturday afternoon."

Saturday. Which meant she hadn't been home at the time of Gina's murder. But even more significant, she hadn't been questioned by Mitch Calhoon. Kate walked toward her. "I know you must be tired, but would you mind very much if I asked you a couple of questions?"

The woman's friendly smile faded. "What kind of questions? Who are you?"

"My name is Kate Logan." Kate took one of her cards from her purse and handed it to her. "I'm an attorney."

The resident of apartment 8A chuckled as she read the card. "Is Gina in some kind of trouble?"

"You knew her, Miss...?"

"Jacob. Shirley Jacob." She looked up. "You said 'knew.' Does that mean... Did something happen to Gina?"

"She was murdered, Miss Jacob."

Shirley's hand flew to her breast as she let go of her suitcase. "Oh, my God! That's awful." She shook her head as if in denial. "How? When?"

"She was strangled." There was no point in mincing words. Neighbors often had a way of clamming up when questioned by the police or by an attorney. Fear, on the other hand, had a way of turning the most reluctant of witnesses into a fountain of information.

"How horrible." Shirley threw a nervous glance around her. "Was the murderer caught?"

"Not yet." Kate chose not to tell her about Eric. What mattered now was to get as much information from this woman as possible.

"I should have listened to my mother," Shirley Jacob said. "When I told her what Gina did for a living, she wanted me to move. She said that living across the hall from a hooker could only bring trouble. But I'd just bought the condo, and Gina's lifestyle didn't bother me all that much. Half the time, I was away on a trip."

"How did you know she was a hooker?"

"Are you kidding? With all those men coming in and out of her apartment at all hours of the night, it wasn't too difficult to figure out. Although I must say, in the past year or so, the activity had decreased considerably."

"Did you know any of the men who came to see her?"

"Good heavens, no. And don't ask me to describe them because I couldn't. I made a point to avoid all eye contact with anyone coming out of Gina's apartment. Except..." She looked at Kate, her gaze suddenly more intense. "Except that one time. When I saw the girl."

"What girl?"

"It was about six months ago. I was getting ready for a trip to Montreal. As I was coming out of my apartment,

Gina's door opened and a young woman came out. They were having a rather heated discussion. When they saw me, they stopped.''

A break, Kate thought as her excitement mounted. Finally. ''Can you describe the woman?''

''Sure. She was pretty, with short, curly black hair, a dark complexion and beautiful eyes. I particularly remember the eyes because they were such an unusual color, at least for a Hispanic woman. They were the most incredible limpid blue. Oh, and she had a beauty mark above her upper lip. On the right side, I believe.''

Kate went still.

Shirley Jacob had just described Lilly Moore.

Thirteen

William Fox's bail hearing, which had been scheduled for two o'clock that afternoon, was a major victory for Kate. Following the recovery of $1.3 million in a locker at National Airport, Kate had convinced the assistant U.S. attorney to reduce the charges from first to second degree murder. The judge, one of the most impartial in the district, had released Fox on two hundred thousand dollars bail.

From the courthouse, Kate had gone directly to the district jail where Tony had been held since being arrested on June 6. He looked even thinner now than he had last Monday, Kate noted as he was escorted into the visiting room. There were dark circles under his eyes, and although he attempted a smile when he saw her, there was a defeated look about him that hadn't been there before.

"How are you, Tony?" She sat on the other side of the wooden table while the guard positioned himself by the door.

He shrugged. "Hanging in there." Then, realizing her visit could be significant, his expression brightened. "You found out something?"

Not wanting to raise his hopes too high, Kate chose her words carefully. "I came across an interesting piece of information, although I'm not sure what it means. Yet." Reaching into her purse, she pulled out the photo Brad

Carpenter had given her and laid it on the table, turning it around so Tony could see it. "Do you know this woman?"

Tony glanced at the photo of Gina Lamont. "No, why?" His tone was mildly sarcastic. "Am I supposed to have killed her, too?"

Kate ignored the remark. He was entitled to some bitterness. "No. My ex-husband is."

"Come again?"

"Her name is Gina Lamont. She was found dead in her condo on Tuesday morning and the police believe Eric killed her."

"Did he?"

"No, but he's on the run, which isn't helping him any."

"Who's the woman?"

"A call girl Eric met at a party." She left the photo where it was. "Did Lilly ever mention Gina's name?"

He let out a dry chuckle. "Why would Lilly even know a call girl?"

Kate repeated what the flight attendant in apartment 8A had told her.

Tony slowly shook his head. "That doesn't make sense, Kate. Lilly didn't have many friends, you know that. All she lived for was law school and her part-time job at Fairchild Baxter."

It was true. Lilly had been so wrapped up in her studies that she barely had time to do anything else. Her encounter with Tony had been the product of sheer fate. Early one evening, he had stopped at Kate's house to pick up his mother just as Lilly, who was delivering a file Kate needed for court the next morning, was arriving. For the handsome youth, it was love at first sight. Lilly, on the other hand, although clearly attracted to Tony, had been more reluctant to commit herself to a relationship that might take time from her studies. But Tony was persistent, and in the end, he had managed to break down the young woman's resistance.

"Of course," Tony added, his expression thoughtful, "she could have been doing something specific for one of the partners."

"I questioned everyone at the firm at the time of your arrest. Lilly was doing some background check in that arson case Ian Baxter defended, but it had nothing whatsoever to do with Gina Lamont."

Tony's shoulders sagged and he fell back against his chair. "I knew it was too good to be true."

"Don't give up yet, Tony." She leaned forward, hoping some of her confidence would rub off on him. "This is the first big break we've had. If there's a connection between Lilly and Gina Lamont's murder, I'll find it. Until then, you keep your chin up, okay?"

"Sure, Kate."

But she could tell by the way he walked away, with his shoulders hunched low, that he wasn't holding much hope.

Back in the car, she called Frankie for messages. "I've got some news about that drug dealer you wanted me to check out," Frankie said after she'd read Kate's three messages. "But you're not going to like it."

"Tell me anyway."

"The creep checked himself into a drug rehabilitation center three weeks ago."

"Are you sure?"

"Positive. I called my former boyfriend, who called Pete's parole officer. After being released from prison, Finley said he was through with the drug scene and had decided to go clean."

"Could he have been there as an outpatient?"

"No. Pete Finley was admitted as an inpatient. According to the staff, there's no way he could have gotten out of that place without someone knowing about it." She paused. "I'm sorry, Boss. I know you were counting on that drug connection."

Although disappointed, Kate didn't dwell on the bad news too long. As she had pointed out to Tony earlier, the revelation that Gina Lamont and Lilly had known each other was significant. She couldn't explain it yet, but it was definitely a step forward.

As soon as Kate returned to the office, Frankie came in.

"So," she said, making herself at home on the edge of Kate's desk, "did Tony recognize Gina?"

"He's never seen her before, and Lilly never mentioned her."

"Bummer."

"Oh, I don't know, Frankie. It's the first real clue we've had so far. And I intend to take full advantage of it."

"Well, I always say, if anyone can do the impossible, it's you, Boss."

Kate smiled. "Thanks for the faith, Frankie."

"What's your game plan?"

Leaning back in her chair, Kate began to swing side to side. "Well, since I seem to have missed something vital during my initial investigation of Lilly's murder, it's only fitting that I reinvestigate the case, don't you think? From the beginning." She gave Frankie a wicked grin. "And what better place to start than with Chuck Winslow."

Frankie made a disapproving sound with her tongue. "The partners aren't going to like it."

"I'll handle the partners." She glanced at her watch. "Right now, as a matter of fact. Douglas in?"

"I believe so."

"Good." She stood up. "Buzz him and tell him I'm on my way to see him, will you?"

Douglas rose the moment Kate entered his plush, green-carpeted office. "How did the bail hearing go?" he asked before she even had a chance to sit down.

"Pretty much as I expected. Fox was released on two hundred thousand dollars bail and the case goes to the grand jury tomorrow."

"What's your gut feeling on this?"

"I'm almost certain he'll be indicted. But a trial date can't possibly be set until March or April of next year. That will give me ample time to prepare his case." She smiled. "And win it."

Douglas looked pleased. "That's the spirit."

As he continued to look at her, Kate felt herself falter. Despite the fact she had known him for almost fifteen years, his rigid ways and low tolerance for human failure often made him intimidating. Yet she could no longer continue to lie to him. She was surprised that she had kept up with the deception as long as she had.

"I didn't come here to discuss the Fox case," she said at last.

"You didn't?"

"No." She took a deep breath. "I heard from Eric." She said it quickly, and without flinching.

Except for a slight tightening of his lips, there was no change in his expression. "When?"

"The morning of the murder and again yesterday."

"Do the police know?"

"No." There was no need to tell him about the possible alliance she had formed with Detective Calhoon.

"My God, Kate, do you realize what you're doing? You're aiding and abetting a fugitive. That's a felony. You could be disbarred."

"I'm not aiding and abetting anyone! I only agreed to look into the circumstances of Gina's death, that's all."

"You shouldn't even have done that."

"What else could I do?" she flung at him, relieved that the deception was over. "You saw how devastated Alison was, how upset she was when she thought I wasn't helping her father. What was I supposed to tell her when she asked me to help him? No, I won't because I may be disbarred?"

"You're not helping him by keeping his whereabouts from the police."

"I'm not keeping his whereabouts from the police. I have no idea where Eric is. He wouldn't tell me."

"So why didn't you tell Calhoon that he called?"

"Because if I had, he would have put a tap on my phone." She leaned forward, her features taut with tension. "The reason I'm telling you this is that I can't stand to keep the truth from you any longer." Afraid he might bypass Mitch and go straight to the chief of police, whom he knew well, she added, "but I warn you, Douglas, if you breathe one word of this to the police, Alison will never forgive you." She squared her shoulders. "And neither will I."

"Does that mean you intend to represent Eric?"

"Yes."

Douglas remained silent, his arms folded and his index finger curled around his mouth. As always, it was impossible to guess what he was thinking. When he finally spoke, his voice was strained. "He doesn't deserve what you're doing for him, Kate. Or what you're risking."

"That's my choice to make." She swallowed, readying herself for another outburst. "And you might as well know that I'm also planning to reinvestigate Lilly's murder. From the beginning."

His jaw tightened. "Whatever for?"

Once again, she repeated her conversation with Shirley Jacob.

Douglas stared at her in disbelief. "Those two women had nothing whatsoever in common. That flight attendant must be mistaken."

"She's not. I had Frankie pull Lilly's picture from our files and take it to Ms. Jacob's apartment. She identified her without a moment's hesitation."

Douglas picked up a pencil and began to drum it against the edge of his desk. "You said you were going to reinvestigate that case from the beginning. What did you mean by that?"

"I'm going to question Chuck Winslow again."

This time, Douglas nearly jumped out of his chair. "That's insane! You'll leave yourself wide open for a harassment suit."

"Not if I proceed cautiously."

"Where will you find the time to investigate two murders and prepare for William Fox's trial, as well?"

"I can handle it. I'll work night and day if I have to."

Douglas's expression remained implacable. "When did you become so stubborn, Kate? So damned unreasonable?"

"Isn't that why you hired me, Douglas? Because I never give up?" She smiled. "I believe at the time you called it my 'pit bull determination.'"

For several seconds, they held each other's gaze, two

old friends who were suddenly on opposite sides. After a while, Douglas nodded, but his expression was still somber. "Very well, then. I guess I can't stop you from doing what you think is right. But be careful with Winslow, will you? I was just informed that I'm one of this year's recipients for the Washingtonian of the Year Award and—"

"Douglas!" Kate beamed, genuinely pleased. "How wonderful." The annual award, sponsored by the monthly magazine, *The Washingtonian*, was presented each year to fifteen men and women who had spent time and money to make the capital a better and safer place. Douglas, whose neighbor had been paralyzed following a riding accident, had contributed large sums of money to the rehabilitation of paraplegics and quadriplegics throughout the District. "I'm so glad for you," she added. "I can't think of anyone more deserving."

Douglas allowed himself a small smile. "Thank you, Kate. But I didn't mean to brag. What I was going to say was that a lawsuit at this time would be embarrassing, not only for me but for the firm."

"There won't be a lawsuit, Douglas. I'll question Winslow with such a light hand, he won't even know what I'm doing. And if I need to push a little harder, I'll hire a private investigator and let him do the dirty work."

"All right." He stood up, indicating the meeting was over. "Go for it, then, but keep me informed, will you?"

"Of course."

She had hoped for a little more encouragement, maybe even a word of praise for her tenacity, which he had always admired. It disappointed her that all he had seemed to care about was the firm.

The Winslows lived on 15th Street, in a four-story building that was sandwiched between a flower shop and a Thai restaurant. As usual, the elevator was out of order and Kate had to climb the three flights of stairs. At the door bearing the Winslows' name, she knocked, waited a few seconds and then knocked again.

"They ain't here no more."

Kate turned around. Across the hall, a gray-haired woman with a deeply lined face and granny glasses held her door as far back as the safety chain would allow.

Kate's heart gave an extra beat. "Not here anymore? Why? Where did they go?"

"Myrtle Beach, South Carolina. They packed everything they owned into a U-Haul and just took off."

"When did that happen?"

"Monday."

Monday. The day the jury had brought back Tony's verdict. "Did they leave a forwarding address?"

The woman scrunched her nose. "Why do you want to know? Who are you?"

Knowing she would never get anywhere if she admitted to being an attorney, Kate went into one of the routines she had learned from a private investigator she knew. "I'm with Lifetime Insurance, ma'am. Mrs. Winslow bought a policy from us a couple of weeks ago, but she forgot to sign one of the forms."

"She didn't tell you she was moving?"

"I'm sure it was an oversight." She took a few steps toward the other apartment, being careful to keep enough distance between her and the woman so as not to frighten her. "Did she leave you a forwarding address?"

"Of course she did. Cora and I were friends."

"It would save me a lot of time if you gave it to me. That way, Mrs. Winslow's policy wouldn't have to be delayed unnecessarily."

"Well..." The woman gave Kate another scrutinizing

look. Then, having made up her mind, she shrugged. "I guess Cora won't mind, seeing as the two of you are doing business an' all."

Leaving the door ajar, she walked back into her apartment. A few moments later, she returned. Through the opening, she handed Kate a small piece of brown paper on which she had scribbled an address.

Kate thanked her and left. When she reached her car, she dialed the travel agency she had been using for years and booked a round-trip flight to Myrtle Beach, South Carolina, for the next morning.

"Do you have everything you need, baby? Have I brought you enough clothes?" Trying not to sound too mushy, Kate smiled at her daughter as they both sat in Rose's elegant drawing room.

Alison gave a careless shrug. "You forgot my Calvins, but that's okay. Grandma is taking me shopping on Sunday."

"I'd be glad to take you." Kate's voice rose with hope. "Tonight if you'd like."

"Thanks, but..." Alison flipped her hair back. "I'd rather go with Grandma." She waited a beat before adding, "You don't mind, do you?"

Kate's heart sank. Shopping was one of Alison's passions, one she had always enjoyed sharing with her mother—until now. Concealing her disappointment, Kate smiled bravely. "Of course not. You and I can go another time. Next week maybe? We'll make a day of it." She laughed. "We'll raid the town."

"That sounds good." Alison stretched her legs and contemplated her sneakers for a moment. When she looked up again, there was a trace of challenge in her eyes. "Are you making progress on Daddy's case?"

Glad that they still had something in common, Kate nodded. "As a matter of fact, I am. It's nothing I can discuss at the moment, but I can say this—the prosecution's case doesn't look nearly as strong now as it did a couple of days ago."

Alison's mood perked up considerably. "Oh, Mom, tell me what you found out. Please? I won't tell anyone, I swear."

Enjoying the game, Kate laughed and shook her head. "I can't, darling. Professional ethics and all that. But the moment I can tell you, I will. That's a promise."

"Okay." Alison's gaze drifted toward the telephone. "I just wish Daddy would call. I haven't talked to him in so long." As if on cue, the phone rang. Alison lunged at it, her eyes wide with expectation as she said hello. Then, almost immediately, her shoulders sagged. "It's Melissa," she said, turning to Kate.

Knowing how much Alison treasured her privacy, Kate rose and hugged her daughter. "I'll see you tomorrow night, baby. Be good."

Then, rather pleased with the way this visit had turned out, Kate left.

The temperature in Myrtle Beach was a pleasant sixty-four degrees when Kate's cab dropped her off at 1145 Bridgen Road the following morning.

Her coat draped over her arm, she gazed at the modest blue ranch house with its white shutters and small, fenced-in yard. The old pickup was there, parked along the curb, and the front door was open to let in the warm ocean breeze. Only the screen door was closed.

Kate rapped lightly on the frame and waited. Within moments, Cora Winslow, looking the same as she had six months ago, appeared, wearing one of her flowered house-dresses.

Everything about her was gray and lifeless—gray hair as coarse and dry as steel wool, a gray complexion and gray teeth. She was a quiet, unsmiling woman, who seemed perfectly content to go through life in her husband's shadow.

"Mrs. Winslow?" Kate put on her friendliest smile. "Do you remember me? Kate Logan. I'm Tony Fuente's attorney."

Cora Winslow looked neither surprised nor upset to see her. She didn't even ask how Kate had found them. "I remember you. What do you want?" She sounded tired, as if the long trip had been too much for her.

"May I come in?"

Cora hesitated, then, with a shrug, she pulled the screen door open and took a step back.

A threadbare rug, a couch, two easy chairs and a television set were already in place in the living room. Scattered across the floor were a dozen packing boxes, some open, others still taped shut. There were no luxuries here, just the bare essentials.

"I'm sorry to intrude at such a busy time," Kate said. "But this is important—"

"What do you want, Mrs. Logan?"

Apparently, the past six months hadn't improved Cora Winslow's sour disposition. "I'd like to talk to your husband for a few minutes." She threw a casual glance around the room. "Is he home?"

The lifeless gray eyes continued to watch Kate without a change of expression. Then, a small sigh escaped from Cora's pale, dry lips. "No, he ain't, Mrs. Logan. My husband's dead."

Fourteen

"Calhoon!" Lieutenant Jarvis strode past Mitch's desk without looking at him. "In my office. Now."

Pushing his chair back, Mitch stood up and made his way through the busy squad room. No one bothered to look up. Jarvis's temper and callous disregard for people's feelings were legendary. Except for a few rookies, who feared him like the plague, the rest of the department had learned to live with his tantrums.

"Close the door," Jarvis instructed as Mitch walked in.

Lieutenant Frank Jarvis was a big man with a barrel chest, a big, bulbous nose and hair so black it could only have come from a bottle. He had been on the D.C. force for twenty-eight years. He held two commendations, had been praised by three presidents and had escaped death too many times to count. He had been a newly appointed detective when Mitch had first joined the force nineteen years ago and had risen through the ranks quickly. Some said too quickly. But, although his meteoric climb to the top had raised a few eyebrows, nothing about his behavior had ever suggested that he was anything but a tough, honest, dedicated cop.

Sitting behind his desk, Jarvis gestured impatiently toward a chair. Then, without preamble, he asked, "What's the latest on Logan?"

"We've recovered his car, sir. It was abandoned just outside Fredericksburg."

"What about Logan? Where the hell is he?"

"He checked in at a nearby motel, but was gone a few hours later. He hasn't been seen since."

"So what you're telling me," Jarvis said, his voice heavy with sarcasm, "is that the man performed a vanishing act."

"Simply put…yes. The Fredericksburg Sheriff's Department is canvassing the area, but I'm not holding out much hope. He could be anywhere by now and looking nothing like the Eric Logan we know."

"What about his ex-wife? She heard from him?"

For reasons he didn't fully understand, Mitch shook his head. "No, she hasn't."

"That's great." Jarvis stood up and began to pace the floor like a caged animal. "Just great. The eyes of the entire country are on us and what do we do? We let the prime suspect slip through our fingers." He stopped in front of Mitch. "You know what that's going to make us look like? A bunch of jackasses."

Propping an ankle on his knee, Mitch made it a point to remain calm. "Actually, I'm not so sure Logan is our man, Lieutenant. Just because he spent the night with Gina Lamont the Saturday prior to the murder doesn't mean he killed her."

Jarvis's face turned an angry shade of red. "Who the hell's side are you on, Calhoon? Of course Logan is our man. You only have to look at the evidence to know that."

"The woman was a hooker, Lieutenant. And it stands to reason that if she was blackmailing one man, she could have blackmailed others."

"But it's Logan's bare ass that ended up on an X-rated

video. And it's Logan's fingerprints we found all over Gina's apartment. And it's Logan who's on the run."

"The guy is scared. He figures with Douglas Fairchild and Abigail Hollbrook putting on so much pressure to have him captured, he doesn't have a chance."

Jarvis put up a hand to stop him. "Do me a favor, will you? Spare me that psychology shit. I'm not in the mood for it. The bottom line is, I want Logan behind bars. And so does the U.S. attorney. Even the mayor is calling for regular updates."

Mitch made a derisive sound. "The only reason the mayor is so interested in this case is because Abigail Hollbrook is one of his largest political contributors. He's got to keep her happy."

"I don't give a fuck what his reason is! He's still the mayor and what he says goes. So don't give me speeches, okay, Calhoon? Give me results. It's my ass that'll fry if you screw up."

Trying to reason with him when he was that wound up would have been pointless. Maybe in a day or two, when Mitch had something more concrete, he'd be in a better position to talk to Jarvis.

He had just reached his desk when his phone rang. It was Jim Faber, a retired Washington cop who had turned private investigator. Following his earlier suspicion that Winslow's testimony had been tainted, Mitch had hired Jim at his own expense and asked him to keep a twenty-four-hour watch on the ex-janitor. When the investigator had called earlier this week to report that the Winslows had moved to South Carolina, Mitch had asked Jim to follow them.

"What do you have for me, Jimbo?"

"Bad news, Mitch. Winslow got himself killed last night."

"You're kidding. What happened?"

"Some nut in a parking lot pumped five bullets into his chest and then drove off."

"The cops have any clues?"

"Not a one. I'm on my way to the police station to see what I can find out. I'll call you as soon as I hear something."

"Thanks, Jim. And keep an eye on Chuck's widow, will you? Who knows? She might find a bundle hidden in the mattress. If she does and she starts spending it, let me know."

After he hung up, Mitch leaned back in his chair and tapped the end of his pencil against his mouth. Now wasn't that an odd twist to an otherwise uncomplicated case? An apparently harmless man gunned down in a parking lot. It had all the characteristics of a mob hit. Or maybe someone only wanted it to *look* like a mob hit. Someone who no longer had any use for Chuck Winslow....

"Gunned down?" Douglas, who had been stuffing papers into his briefcase in preparation for a court appearance, stopped and gave Kate a bewildered look. "Are you serious?"

"Very. I talked to the detective who's handling the case. According to an eyewitness, Chuck Winslow was killed in the Farmington Shopping Center at 9:00 p.m. last night as he was walking toward his truck. The shots, five of them, came from a car parked next to Winslow's pickup."

"Has the killer been apprehended?"

"Not yet. The car took off at high speed before the witness could identify it, or the driver."

Douglas snapped his briefcase shut. "That poor bastard.

He probably moved south to escape the craziness of this city and he got himself killed the first week he was there." He shook his head. "Talk about bad luck."

"Bad luck has nothing to do with what happened," Kate replied. "This was deliberate. Someone was lying in wait for him."

Douglas gave her a quizzical look. "Is that the police theory?"

"No," Kate admitted grudgingly. "Detective Sanford thinks the shooting is either mob related—which doesn't fit Winslow's profile at all—or a case of mistaken identity, or one of those senseless drive-by shootings so popular nowadays."

"All valid assumptions, Kate."

"Except that I'm not buying any of them. I find it just a little too coincidental that Winslow would get killed just as I was about to question him again."

"Did you tell anyone you were going to Myrtle Beach?"

"Only Frankie. I didn't even tell Maria for fear of disappointing her if I struck out."

"Then why would anyone want to kill him?"

"I don't know, Douglas. Maybe his death had nothing to do with me. Maybe Winslow had outlived his usefulness and that's the reason he was killed."

Douglas gave her a long, thoughtful look, but said nothing.

"You believe it, too, don't you, Douglas?" Kate watched him intently as she tried to read his thoughts. "Dammit, say it. Someone killed Winslow because they were through with him. That was the plan all along."

Briefcase in hand, Douglas circled his desk and came to stand in front of her. "All right, yes, foul play could be a possibility, but what truly worries me is that you, Kate, are right in the thick of it.''

"It wouldn't be the first time."

"This is different. And much too dangerous.'' He squared his shoulders. "Drop the case, Kate.''

"You know I can't do that—"

He raised a finger to silence her protest. "If what you say is true—and I'm not a hundred percent convinced it is—then, if you get in his way, whoever killed Winslow won't hesitate to kill you, too. Is that what you want, Kate? To find yourself in some back alley with five bullets in your chest?''

"Of course not."

"Then drop the case. If you won't do it for yourself, then do it for Alison. You've been the one constant factor in her life, the one person she knows she can count on. Don't take that away from her by making yourself a target for some killer.''

He gave her arm a gentle squeeze. "I've got to go. Think about what I said.''

She walked with him as far as his office door, which he always left open, and watched him as he hurried toward the elevators. What if he was right? she wondered, aware that a mild fear had lodged itself in the pit of her stomach and didn't want to let go. What if the man, or woman, who had killed Chuck Winslow came after her next?

But as she walked back to her office, the fear began to ebb. As a prosecutor, she had gone after the scum of the earth—drug pushers, rapists, even serial killers. Not a single one had ever come after her. Oh, there had been a few threats, but what prosecutor hadn't had his or her share of them?

She would have to be more careful, that's all, pay more

attention to small details—like locking her door immediately after entering her car, and being wary of anything, or anyone, who looked even mildly suspicious.

Thank God Alison was tucked away in a secure house, she thought as she sat behind her desk. As much as she hated to be separated from her daughter, it was a relief to know she didn't have to worry about her.

"Tony looked so thin," Alison said in a small, sad voice. "Even more than he did the last time I saw him."

Kate and her daughter were having lunch at K-Paul in Georgetown, one of Alison's favorite restaurants. It had taken a little imaginative bribing on Kate's part—a visit to Tony and a new pair of boots—to get Alison to agree to this Saturday tête-à-tête. Although Kate had seen Alison every day since she'd run away, every attempt she had made to spend time with her daughter had been met with a flat no.

"The first few days after a conviction are always the hardest," Kate replied. "It gets easier after a while."

Alison's eyes were heavy with reproach. "Tony doesn't want it to get easier, Mom. He wants to get out. He wants to be free."

"That's what we all want, baby, but it's not going to happen overnight. Appealing a conviction is a long, tedious process."

"What about Daddy? Are you trying to find out who killed Gina Lamont? You said you would."

Obviously, the child was determined to start a fight, if not about one subject, then another. "I'm working very hard to do just that, Alison," she said gently. "But I have other clients, people who depend on me. As much as I would like to, I can't just drop everything and concentrate on those two cases. You understand that, don't you?"

The gentle tone had more effect than Kate had expected. Her cheeks reddening, Alison lowered her head. Kate felt an instant surge of guilt. What was the matter with her? Here she was, with an opportunity to impress her daughter with her talent and goodwill, and she was blowing it by giving her a lecture.

Quickly, she reached across the table to cover her daughter's hand with hers. Surprisingly, Alison didn't withdraw hers. "Why don't you tell me about that Christmas play you're auditioning for?" she asked cheerfully. "It's an original script, isn't it? Something your English teacher wrote?"

Because acting had always held a great fascination for Alison, her dark mood vanished instantly. "Oh, Mom, it's such a neat play." Her eyes gleamed with excitement. "It's the story of a young girl, Elena, whose mother abandoned her on Christmas Eve when she was just a baby. Fifteen years later, on another Christmas Eve, they meet again. There are lots of other characters—the girl's adoptive mother, a father and a postman. There's even a nosy neighbor." She wrinkled her nose. "She reminds me of Mrs. Lieberman."

"It sounds like a lot of fun. Which role are you auditioning for?"

"All of them, but Melissa says I'm a shoo-in for the lead because I look so much older than the other girls."

Kate smiled. Like many girls who entered their teens, herself included, looking older had always been one of Alison's major preoccupations. "When is the audition?"

"Three o'clock on Monday afternoon. I'll call you to let you know how it went."

Kate's hopes soared. Before she'd left Eric, Alison used to call her at work almost every afternoon, eager to talk about her day. But in the past twelve months, the calls had decreased dramatically, and it was usually Kate who did the calling.

"I'd like that." Kate gazed fondly at her daughter. "And I'll be expecting a front-row seat."

"Sure." In a much better mood now, Alison took a healthy bite of her hamburger. After a while, she looked up, her expression serious again. "Mom, have you ever thought of remarrying?" she asked.

Although startled by the directness of the question, Kate welcomed it. Maybe now, the two of them could clear the air about what was truly bothering Alison. "Remarrying?" she repeated in a light tone. "No, I haven't. Why do you ask?"

"Is that because deep down you still love Daddy?"

Oh, God, she should have seen that one coming. There had been many hints in the past year, but nothing quite as forward as this, at least not since Eric had announced his engagement to Megan. It wasn't Mitch Calhoon personally Alison was worried about, it was any man who threatened a possible reconciliation between Kate and Eric.

"Do you still love him?" Alison pressed.

Remembering her numerous lectures about always telling the truth, Kate knew that a tactful but honest answer was the best way to handle this question. "A part of me will always love your father, Alison. For the simple reason that he *is* your father. But if by loving him you mean the way a woman should love a man, then no, I don't. Not anymore."

The gray eyes filled with disappointment. "What if he still loves you?"

"He doesn't. He's engaged to Megan now and I'm sure they'll be very happy together."

"But what if Megan doesn't want him anymore?"

"That's something they'll have to work out together, darling, without outside interference, without anyone telling them what to do."

Alison picked up a French fry and looked at it. "By anyone, you mean Abigail?"

Kate smiled. "Yes, I mean Abigail."

For the first time since their outing had begun, Alison laughed. "She's kind of scary, isn't she?"

"She can be." Kate remembered the way she and Abigail had clashed at Douglas's house. "If you let her."

Suddenly, Alison turned in her chair and glanced around the crowded room.

Kate followed her gaze. "What is it, baby? Did you see someone you know?"

Alison shook her head. "No, but..." Looking puzzled, she shot a quick glance at the door, which had just closed. "I could swear someone was watching me."

Kate put her fork down. Suddenly uneasy, she let her gaze sweep over the room. No one seemed to be paying any attention to them. A quick glance out the window and into the street revealed nothing out of the ordinary. "Did you actually see someone?" she asked, trying not to let Alison sense her fear.

"I'm not sure. It was more like a feeling." Shrugging with the insouciance of the young, she turned to face Kate again. "I guess I was wrong." She laughed. "Maybe that horror movie Melissa and I watched together the other night is still on my mind. It had this thing—part man and part beast—stalking young girls and—"

"Alison," Kate said sternly, "you know I don't want you to watch those films. They give you nightmares."

"Oh, Mom. I don't have nightmares anymore. I'm thirteen."

Kate glanced around the room again. Had someone really been here, watching them? Or was Alison's reaction simply the product of a young girl's fertile imagination?

Her first impulse was to take her daughter back to Potomac, to the safety of Douglas's well-protected home. But if she gave in to her fears, she would be disappointing Alison, who expected to go shopping for new boots after lunch. She couldn't do that to her. Not when they were finally starting to get along.

After taking Alison back to the Fairchilds' at four o'clock that afternoon, Kate made a small detour and stopped at the police department, hoping Mitch Calhoon was on duty.

As usual, the place was like a zoo, with phones ringing off the hooks, detectives scrambling to answer calls, and suspects being brought in, sometimes against their will, for questioning.

Mitch sat at his desk, talking on the phone while he shuffled through a file. The sleeves of his dark blue shirt were rolled up to the elbows, revealing sinewy forearms Kate tried hard to ignore. She had barely pulled her gaze away when he looked up. He grinned and waved her in.

By the time she reached his desk, he had hung up the phone and was standing. "Kate. What a pleasant surprise. Please sit down. Can I get you anything? Coffee? A soft drink?"

"Nothing, thank you. I can't stay long." She came straight to the point. "Did you know that Chuck Winslow was killed last night?"

He shot her a quick glance. "How did you find out about that?"

"I tracked him down in Myrtle Beach and found Cora preparing for his funeral."

"Any particular reason you wanted to see him?"

She told him about Gina and Lilly knowing each other, something he would find out as soon as he interviewed Shirley Jacob.

"Are you sure it's Lilly she saw?"

"She made a positive ID from a picture we had on file."

"In that case, I'd better get a statement from Miss Jacob." Reaching across his desk, he wrote something on his daily calendar. "Gina and Lilly," he mused. "What could those two possibly have in common?"

"That's what I intend to find out."

He threw his pen back on the desk. "Don't do anything foolish, Kate. Winslow was brutally killed last night. If his death is connected to Lilly's murder, anyone poking his or her nose into the matter could become a statistic, as well."

"What choice do I have if the police won't do anything?"

"Detective Sanford is following every lead."

"Detective Sanford won't find anything in Myrtle Beach. You know as well as I do that Winslow's killer is right here. In Washington."

"I wish I could do something," Mitch said, looking genuinely sorry that he couldn't. "But Winslow's murder isn't my case. And it's certainly not my jurisdiction. However, if Sanford's investigation leads him to Washington, I'll do whatever I can to help him. Until then—" he shrugged "—my hands are tied."

He was right, Kate thought. Fighting for Tony's appeal was her job, not his. His was over. She wasn't even sure why she had come here, what she had expected him to do, unless... A sudden flush rose to her cheeks. Unless she had been looking for an excuse to see him.

Mortified at the thought that Mitch may have arrived

at the same conclusion, she stood up. "I just wanted to make sure you knew about Winslow's death," she said as much for her benefit as for his. "That's all." She hooked the strap of her purse over her shoulder. "Let me know if you hear from Detective Sanford."

She was halfway across the room when Mitch called her name.

She turned around. "Yes?"

"Gina Lamont's funeral will be held on Monday. Prospect Hill Cemetery at ten o'clock. I thought you'd want to know."

She smiled. "I do. Thank you."

Fifteen

Today was his daughter's birthday. Gabrielle Marie Calhoon would have been ten years old. It was hard to believe the child who was still so alive in Mitch's heart had been dead for three years.

Mitch picked up the photograph of his daughter from the end table. A knot in his throat, he ran a finger over the glassed-in likeness, the laughing blue eyes, the blond hair so soft and light it seemed to float around her face, the yellow dress he had helped her choose for that picture.

Sometimes, when he allowed it, the loss was almost palpable. They had been so close, so alike. "Two peas in a pod," his mother used to say.

He blamed no one for Gabrielle's death but himself. For all his experience and know-how, he had committed the greatest sin of all—he had acted on impulse. It would have been easy to put some of the blame on Ava, but he tried not to do that. At times, he even thought he should have been more patient with her, more understanding. If he had, they might have stayed married and this senseless tragedy would have never happened.

But Ava had a restless soul. And she liked expensive baubles—baubles Mitch couldn't afford on his detective's salary. And so, when his friend, Randy Vargas, had approached him with an offer to join his private investigative agency, Mitch hadn't been able to turn it down.

Vargas World Wide Investigations was based in Laurel, Maryland, and specialized in locating and rescuing kidnapped children all over the world. It was a risky, high-paying job that required guts, expertise and long absences from home. That's the part Mitch hadn't been fond of, especially after Gabrielle was born. Ava didn't seem to mind. Between her daily gym classes, her hair appointments and shopping, she had kept herself busy.

It wasn't until he came back from an assignment earlier than expected one day and found Ava in the arms of another man, right there in their own house, that Mitch realized what a sham his marriage was.

Ignoring his wife's pleas for another chance, he had filed for divorce immediately.

Because of his frequent absences from home, the court had awarded custody of Gabrielle to Ava, a decision Mitch had appealed to no avail. Two months after the divorce was finalized, Ava married some thug, a man Mitch was certain had ties with the mob, and moved to California.

Mitch had tried to fight the move, claiming the three-thousand-mile distance made it impossible for him to visit his daughter on a regular basis. But when Ava had showed up in court with three of the country's most powerful attorneys, he hadn't stood a chance.

At first, judging from Gabrielle's letters and phone calls, the child seemed happy. Then one day, she called him. At the sound of her frightened voice, a chill went through him. When she told him that Paul was mean to her and sometimes hit her and locked her in a dark closet, he had wanted to kill the bastard.

He had done something very stupid then, something he had been trained never to do, something he would regret for as long as he lived. He had taken off, alone and without a specific plan, to rescue his daughter.

The house where Paul, Ava and Gabrielle lived was perched on the top of a mountain outside San Luis Obispo and was built like a fortress. But that didn't stop Mitch. There wasn't a house in the world he couldn't enter.

After a two-hour climb through a thickly wooded area, he finally reached the property. With the aid of special infrared glasses, he was able to get through the perimeter security system undetected. Then, using a rope he had tied to a tree, he climbed over the stone wall and dropped into Paul's backyard.

A big security guard carrying an Uzi stood under a sequoia tree, lighting a cigarette. Without a sound, Mitch attacked him from behind. Momentarily dazed, the guard went down, but not before spraying a round of bullets into the gravel walk.

The racket brought everyone who was inside the house out to the yard. As Mitch scooped up the Uzi, he saw his daughter, and his heart jumped into his throat. He had no idea how she had managed to slip away from her nanny, but there she was, hiding behind her mother, looking small and frightened.

As Paul started to reach for his own gun, Mitch took aim and hit him in the arm. Then, taking advantage of the chaos the incident created, he scooped up his daughter, unaware that a second armed guard was coming around the corner.

As Mitch hoisted his precious cargo over the wall, another shot rang out.

And hit Gabrielle in the back, killing her instantly.

Crazy with grief and rage, Mitch charged his daughter's killer like a mad bull, taking him down and nearly beating him to a pulp. It had taken Paul and the other guard more than five minutes to pull him off.

Nothing had mattered after that—not the conviction of Paul's bodyguard for the murder of his daughter, and not the fact that the police had found a kilo of cocaine in the house and arrested Paul.

Mitch had faced some serious charges himself—breaking and entering, assault with a deadly weapon and attempted kidnapping. Fortunately, the San Luis Obispo's D.A., who had been investigating Paul for years, but had never been able to make any charge against him stick, had been grateful enough to let Mitch go.

Two weeks later, despite Randy's protests, Mitch had resigned from Vargas World Wide, convinced he was no longer qualified to save and protect children. He had, in his own words, become a liability.

Gabrielle's birthdays were the hardest, for him and for his mother, who now lived in Florida. Knowing she was expecting his call, he put his daughter's photograph back on the table and picked up the phone.

"...though I walk through the valley of the shadow of death..."

A pale December sun had broken through the thick gray clouds, wrapping the cemetery in a light that was as dismal as the day itself.

Gazing at the plain, unadorned casket that stood beside the freshly dug grave, Kate listened as the preacher spoke of eternal life.

Although she hadn't known Gina Lamont, she felt an inexplicable sadness for the woman. Except for herself and Mitch, who stood beside her, only two people had come to say their final goodbyes—Brad Carpenter and a woman dressed in black. No one else was here for her—no family, no lover, certainly not any of the men whose lives Gina Lamont had touched.

Kate's gaze came to rest on the woman. She was in her early to mid-forties, pleasantly round and relatively attractive from what Kate could see. She had brassy blond hair she wore in a dated Farrah Fawcett do and a generous mouth painted a vivid shade of red. Oversize sunglasses concealed the rest of her face.

Kate leaned toward Mitch and spoke in a hushed tone. "Who's the woman?"

Hands folded in front of him, Mitch followed her gaze. "Her name is LuAnn Chester."

"Friend of Gina's?"

"She used to be—years ago."

"How come you know about her and I don't?"

He gave her a smile. "Cops have connections, too, you know." He returned his attention to the minister. "Actually, she was one of the few names in Gina's address book, along with Brad's, and a few others who lost track of Gina years ago."

"Was LuAnn Chester helpful?"

"Not particularly. She claims she hasn't had any contact with Gina in a long time and has no idea who would want to kill her."

"You don't sound like you believe her."

"I don't. My gut feeling tells me she knows more than she lets on and is holding back, either out of some hooker's code of ethics or out of fear. My bet is on the latter."

Kate's interest deepened. Fear. Of course. Why hadn't she noticed it before? Everything about the woman's demeanor suggested that—from the unnecessary dark glasses to the way she kept glancing over her shoulder as if she expected someone to suddenly jump out and say "boo."

As the sun disappeared behind a cloud, Brad leaned toward LuAnn and whispered something in her ear. Although Kate couldn't see the woman's eyes, she felt them bore through her with unnerving intensity.

"I guess she's as curious about you as you are about her," Mitch whispered.

"I noticed that." Kate made a mental note to approach her after the funeral. If Mitch was right and she knew something, she might be more open with a woman questioning her.

As soon as the service ended, Kate walked over to Brad to offer her condolences. Then, turning to LuAnn Chester, she introduced herself and handed her a business card.

"You're wasting your time talking to me, Mrs. Logan," LuAnn said, reading the card. "I already told that cop over there—" she nodded toward Mitch who stood a few feet away "—that I don't know anything." Her voice was low and raspy, like that of a heavy smoker.

"I thought Gina was a friend of yours."

"We weren't what you'd call close."

Kate kept her voice soft, unthreatening. "Yet you came to her funeral."

LuAnn glanced over her shoulder, toward the road, and remained silent.

Mitch was right. The woman was afraid. But of what? Or whom? Pulling her aside so their conversation wouldn't be overheard, Kate spoke in a whisper. "I'm trying to find out who killed Gina, Miss Chester. If you could give me just a few minutes—"

"Brad said your ex-husband killed her."

Turning her head, Kate saw Brad looking at her, his expression neutral. So her attempts to convince him that

Eric was innocent had been a waste of time after all. "He
didn't," she replied, bringing her gaze back to LuAnn.
"But with a little cooperation from Gina's friends, I might
find out who did."

LuAnn's hand went to her glasses. "Talking to you
could get me in a lot of trouble."

"I can meet you anywhere you say." Kate paused,
wondering which approach would work best. Taking a
gamble that a prostitute her age might be in need of cash,
she added, "I'll make it worth your while."

This time, there seemed to be a spark of interest. "I'll
let you know, okay?" Then, without bothering to say
goodbye, LuAnn went to join Brad and walked with him
toward a waiting taxi.

Kate followed from a distance. The wind had picked
up again, scattering dead leaves around her feet as she
walked. Mitch was waiting by the Saab, one arm resting
on the roof.

"Any luck?" he asked.

"I'm not sure." Kate unlocked her car door. "We'll
just have to wait and see. You were right, though. She's
a very frightened woman."

Mitch watched the couple step into the cab. "Be careful, will you? We don't know whom we're dealing with
here."

Without being sure why, his concern pleased her. "I'm
always careful, Detective."

Mitch held the door open as she slid behind the wheel.
"Don't you think it's about time you called me Mitch?"

"Hmm." She threw him an amused glance. "I'll give
it some thought."

As she drove away, she glanced in the rearview mirror.
Mitch was still standing at the curb, hands in his pockets,
watching her.

It was half past two when Frankie buzzed Kate. Her voice was low and excited. "I think this is the call you've been expecting, Boss. It's a woman and she wouldn't give her name. Said you'd know who it was."

"Put her through, Frankie." Kate waited until she was connected, then said, "This is Kate Logan."

LuAnn Chester didn't waste any time. "You said something about making it worth my while?"

"I'm willing to offer you a thousand dollars for whatever information you may have on Gina Lamont."

LuAnn hesitated, but not for long. "I can meet you in half an hour at the Museum of Natural History. Can you make it?"

"Yes."

"I'll be in the dinosaur exhibit."

"All right."

About thirty children from a local elementary school were gathered around the skeleton of a huge *Brontosaurus* when Kate walked into the exhibit room at three o'clock.

Partially hidden behind a reptile display case, LuAnn tried to look inconspicuous as she flipped through a brochure. Up close she looked older than she had at the cemetery. The skin around her jaw was thick and slack, and without the protection of her sunglasses, the heavy bags under her eyes were clearly visible.

"Thanks for meeting me," Kate said.

LuAnn cast a quick glance around her. "Look casual," she instructed. "I don't think anyone followed me here, but you can never be too careful. As far as anybody's concerned, we're just two old pals soaking up a little culture."

"All right." Leaning toward the descriptive plaque,

Kate pretended to read it. "I'm curious, though. Why here?"

LuAnn shrugged. "It's smaller and darker than other exhibits. And I know my way around it. My little grandson and I come here a lot when he's in town. His name is Brian and he's crazy about dinosaurs." She chuckled. "Ever since he saw *Jurassic Park*, he can't get enough of them."

"You have a grandson?" Kate looked at her with renewed interest.

LuAnn's ruby red lips curved into a small, ironic smile. "What's the matter? You don't think hookers have lives of their own? Families to care for?"

"I guess I never thought about it."

"Nobody ever does. But the truth is, we're just like other folks. For many of us, turning tricks is just a job, a way to pay the bills, put food on the table, send the kids to college."

Kate was beginning to like this woman. "How old is Brian?"

"Seven. You want to see a picture?"

"I'd love to." She was much too grateful to deny her this small pleasure. She watched the woman take a brown leather wallet out of her purse.

"That's him." LuAnn proudly held the wallet open. Tucked into a plastic insert was the picture of an attractive young woman with a young boy on her lap. He had brown hair, blue eyes and a mischievous smile.

"He's very handsome." Kate looked up. "He has your eyes."

LuAnn flushed with pleasure. "You think so? A couple of people have told me that." She pointed at the young woman. "That's my Holly. She's a marine biologist at the Baltimore Aquarium."

"She's beautiful. You must be very proud of her."

"I am." They moved to the next display, mingling with the crowd, chatting like two old friends.

When they were out of earshot, Kate asked, "How long had you known Gina?"

"I met her when she first came to D.C. She was just a kid then, an aspiring model who thought she was going to set the fashion world on fire." LuAnn's smile was wistful. "Poor kid. Who would have thought she'd end up that way, huh?"

"Tell me about that call-girl ring she worked for."

LuAnn's gaze shifted toward the entrance where a man in a trench coat stood. It wasn't until he waved at a teenage boy that she relaxed. "You won't tell anyone where the information came from, will you?"

"Not a soul, LuAnn. You have my word on that."

"All right." She took a deep breath as if she was trying to gather up courage. "A few years ago, a leak got out that a woman by the name of Maddy Mays ran the ring, but nothing was ever proven."

"Maddy Mays?" Kate was stunned. "The owner of the Europa Hotel?"

LuAnn nodded.

Kate could hardly believe it. The woman was an icon, a champion of good causes, a shining example for fallen women everywhere. A former call girl herself, she had given up her line of work when she married millionaire toy manufacturer, Henry Mays. In 1978, after Henry died of a massive heart attack, Maddy found herself a widow—a very rich widow.

Ignoring her accountant's cautious advice to keep her money in Fortune 500 stocks, she invested a large part of her inheritance in a run-down, eight-story hotel on Massachusetts Avenue. By the end of the following day, she had hired the best decorators money could buy, a New York firm to do PR work and a hotel manager she had coaxed away from the Hay-Adams for an obscene amount of money.

When the Italian-inspired Europa Hotel reopened its doors six months later, the press dubbed it the capital's "newest jewel," a place where, for a price, one could be pampered and coddled like royalty.

Rather than keep her past a secret, Maddy Mays told her life story to whoever wanted to listen to it. When a publisher approached her, suggesting she write an auto- biography, Maddy had embraced the idea with great en- thusiasm. "If I can bring hope to just one young woman," she told a reporter on the eve of the book's much publi- cized release, "everything I went through will have been worth it."

The thought that a woman who had donated millions to charity ran a call-girl ring was beyond the imagination. "Did Gina tell you she worked for Maddy?" Kate asked.

"Are you kidding? In this business, you talk, you're dead."

"Then how do you know?"

"Six or seven years ago, Gina tried to recruit me. I turned her down, but not without a heavy heart, let me tell you, especially since I knew she was making five thousand dollars a week. I was lucky if I made half that in a month."

"Why did you turn her down?"

"I didn't like the idea of having some high-class mad- am telling me what to do. I like to pick my own johns. And I don't go for all that kinky stuff—whips and hand- cuffs." She made a face. "That's not for me."

"If you turned Gina down, how can you be sure that Maddy was the one who ran that ring?"

"Shortly after that, the word on the street was that the police were investigating Maddy, but nothing ever came of it. After a few days, the investigation sort of fizzled out."

Kate waited until the group of schoolchildren surrounded them again before pulling out the sketch of the man Tony had seen outside Lilly's apartment building the night she was killed. "Have you ever seen this man?" She handed LuAnn the drawing. "He's about six foot four and weighs approximately two hundred and fifty pounds."

LuAnn studied the sketch. "Can't say I do." She looked up. "Who is he?"

"Maybe the killer."

LuAnn shivered. "I wouldn't want to meet him in some dark alley." As they reached the last display, she glanced at her watch. "I've got a four o'clock appointment, so if you're finished, I should go." She gave Kate a sheepish smile. "Time is money as they say."

The envelope with the one thousand dollars in it was already out of Kate's purse. Discreetly, she slipped it into LuAnn's hand. "Thanks for all your help. I appreciate it."

"Just don't make me regret it, okay?" LuAnn tucked the envelope into a black tote bag. "I wouldn't want to wake up in the middle of the night with some big ugly goon's hands wrapped around my neck."

Kate waited until LuAnn was out of sight before heading for the exit herself. By the time she reached her car, she had already decided how to approach Maddy Mays.

Sixteen

If Kate had had any preconceived ideas of what a former hooker looked like, they would have disappeared the moment she laid eyes on Maddy Mays.

Although the woman was about fifty pounds overweight and in her early sixties, she was still stunning. She had expressive blue eyes, full lips colored a rich shade of rust and thick brown hair that framed her face in a fluff of natural curls. The black-trimmed pink suit was unmistakably Chanel, the white blouse pure silk and the cream alligator pumps worth at least a week's salary. Except for diamond studs and a gold watch, she wore no jewelry. Her scent was subtle. And expensive.

"Please sit down, Mrs. Logan." Smiling warmly, Maddy pointed at one of the twin gold brocade chairs that faced her desk. "Your name is vaguely familiar. Have we met?"

"No." Kate returned the woman's smile and sat down. "But you may have heard my name in conjunction with a case I'm working on."

A perfectly shaped eyebrow went up a fraction. "Case?"

"A murder case. I'm a criminal attorney, Mrs. Mays."

"I see." Looking mildly interested, Maddy leaned back in her chair, both hands on the armrests. "How can I help you?"

Kate took Gina's picture from her briefcase and laid it on Maddy's desk. She didn't expect the woman to come right out and admit that the call girl had worked for her, but it would be interesting to watch her reaction. "I understand you knew this woman."

Picking up a pair of glasses that lay on her desk, Maddy slipped them on and leaned forward to inspect the photograph. "Stunning young woman."

"Yes, she was."

Maddy looked up. "Was?"

"Gina Lamont is dead, Mrs. Mays. She was murdered."

"Oh, dear." Maddy shook her head as she glanced at the photo again. "What a terrible waste."

"You weren't aware she had died?"

Surprise flickered through the blue eyes. "Should I be?"

"I was told Gina worked for you at one time."

"Who told you that?"

Kate smiled. "I never reveal my sources." She paused, expecting Maddy to make some additional comment. She didn't. "Did she?" Kate asked. "Work for you, I mean."

Maddy shook her head. "I've never seen this woman in my life." Calmly, she removed her glasses and set them down. "May I ask in what area of the hotel she was supposed to have worked? Secretarial? Reception desk? Housekeeping?"

"She wouldn't have worked in the hotel, Mrs. Mays. Gina Lamont was a call girl."

"A call girl?" This time, Maddy's reaction was one of pure amusement. "My dear Mrs. Logan, I'm afraid your sources are not as reliable as you may think. I used to be a call girl myself, as I'm sure you know, but for someone to imply that I'm back in that line of business, and as a madam no less, is simply ludicrous."

Kate was impressed. If the woman was acting, she was doing a damn good job. "Could she have worked the hotel without your knowledge?"

"I suppose that's possible, but highly unlikely. You see, I'm a hands-on type of owner, Mrs. Logan. I spend a great deal of time in the hotel. If a call girl was using my establishment to pick up customers, believe me, I would have spotted her a mile away."

"I wonder..." Kate kept her gaze level. "Would you have any objections to my questioning some of your staff?"

"Not at all. But I would have to insist that it be done discreetly, here, in my office."

"That would be fine. Thank you."

Minutes later, five employees were ushered into Maddy's office—the desk clerk who had greeted Kate in the lobby, two bellboys, a bartender, a waitress and the hotel detective. All of them had worked at the hotel for more than four years. Kate couldn't have made a better selection herself.

Standing nearly at attention, they took turns looking at Gina's picture. Kate watched closely for a sign of recognition, or any sort of reaction. There was none.

After a while, they all shook their heads. They had never seen the woman, in or out of the hotel.

When they were gone, Maddy leaned comfortably in her chair. "I trust you are convinced that what you heard about me was nothing more than a malicious rumor meant to discredit me."

"Why would anyone want to do that? You give hundreds of thousands of dollars to charity every year, you've built a halfway house for runaway girls and you own one of the classiest hotels in town. People adore you.''

''Jealousy, Mrs. Logan. Sometimes the more you do, the more you are despised.'' The blue eyes softened. ''But thank you for the compliment. It's always nice to know that your work is appreciated.'' She was cool enough to look almost disappointed when Kate rose to leave. ''I'm sorry I was unable to help you, Mrs. Logan. If there is anything else I can do for you, arranging an elegant luncheon or a romantic stay for two in one of our suites, please don't hesitate to call me. I'll give it my very special attention.''

''That's kind of you, Mrs. Mays. Thank you.''

''Not at all.'' Maddy stood up. ''May I call you a cab?''

''That won't be necessary. I drove.''

As Kate walked across the antique Aubusson rug, she could almost feel Maddy Mays's gaze burning into her.

Reclining in his chair, Mitch listened patiently to a hardware salesman in Thaxton, Virginia, telling him he had just spotted Eric Logan on a Greyhound bus bound for Clay Ridge, West Virginia. After a while, he thanked him and hung up.

There had been dozens of such calls in the past eight days, and although none of them had led him to Eric, he'd had to check each one as thoroughly as he would have any other.

Fortunately for him, the sheriff in Clay Ridge turned out to be a jovial kind of guy who listened attentively as Mitch reported the sighting. ''I'd appreciate if you could check the motels in your area, Sheriff,'' Mitch said after giving him Eric's description. ''And the restaurants.''

Sheriff Mercer seemed to find the request amusing. ''We ain't got no motels here, son,'' he said in a slow, lazy drawl. "And the only restaurant, if you want to call it that, is Betty Jo's truck stop on Route 9. This here town ain't nothing but a crossroad. You blink and you missed it." He laughed, a big belly laugh that brought a smile to Mitch's lips. "Tell you what, though," he added when his laughter had subsided. "I'll check with the sheriff in Waneta. He's a buddy of mine. Maybe he seen something."

"Thanks, Sheriff. I'll be sure to put you on my Christmas mailing list."

"You do that. And don't you send me none of them sissy cheese baskets you city folks fancy so much, you hear? This here is man country, son. We celebrate the holidays with Brother Jack. Jack Daniel's, that is."

"Sheriff, you get Eric Logan back to me, and I'll send you a case of the stuff."

No sooner had he hung up than his phone rang again. This time, it was Brad Carpenter whom he hadn't seen since the funeral.

"I came across something you might want to take a look at," the photographer told him.

Mitch was instantly alert. "What is it?"

"I'd rather not discuss it over the phone."

"I'll be there as soon as I can."

Brad met him at the door and shook Mitch's hand. As soon as they were inside the small room Brad used as an office, the photographer opened a desk drawer, took out a small black book and handed it to Mitch. "I found this in Gina's bag."

"What bag?"

Brad produced a black canvas backpack with the word "Lancôme" printed on it. "The girls like to keep a change of clothes and some toiletries in the dressing room. I didn't remember that until after the funeral."

The palm-size notepad contained detailed household expenses Gina had incurred during the last six months of her life. According to her figures, she was behind in almost all of her bills, from the mortgage payments to her hairdresser. But it was the entry a few pages farther on that held Mitch's attention.

There were three names, three *first* names. Next to each name was a dollar sign followed by a number and a date. The fourth name, however, only had a question mark after it.

Mitch read aloud, "James: $2,000, August 8. Duncan: $850, September 15. Jason: $1,500, October 30. Sander: question mark." He looked up. "You know any of those men?"

"Never heard of them."

Mitch searched quickly through the backpack. It contained a hairbrush, a tube of lipstick in a brilliant shade of red and a pair of black lacy underwear. "Gina never mentioned them to you?"

He shook his head. "I told you the other day that Gina and I didn't talk about her johns."

Mitch glanced at the feminine handwriting once again. "They could be people Gina owed money to," he reflected. "Or the names of some of her customers. And then again..." He looked up, his eyes watchful. "They could be the names of men she was blackmailing."

"Could be." Brad folded his powerful arms across his chest. "Gina was very resourceful when she needed money."

"What about you, Brad?" Mitch kept his tone casual. "Did she ever try to get money from you?"

The photographer's expression didn't change. "Yes, I gave her money from time to time. But not because she had anything on me if that's what you're driving at. I told you, Gina and I were friends, nothing more.''

"You don't seem surprised that she may have been blackmailing her customers.''

"I'm not. In fact, I suspected it, and I was worried one of her johns would turn on her. She didn't listen, though." His tone turned mournful. "She never listened. She was the most stubborn woman I knew.''

Mitch tapped the book with the back of his hand. "Those amounts are chicken feed, Brad. Hardly the kind of money she needed to keep up her lifestyle. There had to be others. Men with money, men who would have paid anything, done anything, even murder, to keep her quiet.''

"If there were, she never told me.''

Mitch snapped the notepad shut and slipped it into his jacket pocket before picking up the backpack. "Thanks for the call, Brad.''

"Don't thank me. Find Gina's killer." He walked to the door with Mitch. "She was a good person, Detective. A little misguided perhaps, but a good person. Her killer should be punished.''

Back in his car, Mitch sat behind the wheel for a few minutes. The first three names in Gina's book were fairly common, which would make finding their owners a near impossible task. Sander, on the other hand, was not common at all. To his knowledge, there was only one prominent man in the District bearing that name: U.S. Senator Sander McKackney, a wealthy, influential politician whose son had once been brought up on rape charges. Glancing in the rearview mirror, Mitch made a quick U-turn and headed for the police station.

"You son of a gun!" Randy Vargas exclaimed when his secretary put Mitch through. "I was beginning to think you had forgotten me."

Mitch laughed. "How could I forget a prince of a guy like you?"

"You were supposed to call me weeks ago."

"I've been busy. Some of us aren't as fortunate as you are, you know. We actually have to work for a living."

"Hey, you say the word and you'll be enjoying the same perks by month's end. That partnership offer we discussed a few months ago is still on the table."

"I appreciate it, Randy, but—"

"It's too soon. I know, I know." Randy sighed. "Just thought I'd mention it."

Mitch hated to let Randy down. The two of them went back a long way, before Mitch had even joined the force. Randy, twenty-two years his senior, had been part of the elite SWAT team at the time and a close friend of Mitch's father. In 1980, Randy had resigned from the force and started Vargas World Wide Investigations. For a man with a penchant for adventure and danger, the job was tailor-made for him. But he was a grandfather now and he wanted more time to spend with the kids. When his partner retired a few months ago, Randy had made Mitch an offer most men would have found difficult to refuse. But Mitch had turned him down. Money wasn't important to him. Not anymore.

"So, kid," Randy said with his usual straightforwardness, "what's up?"

"I need some information, Randy."

"Shoot."

"You remember that rape case Senator McKackney's son was involved in sixteen years ago?"

"How could I forget? The victim was my daughter's

best friend, and Detective Jarvis, now Lieutenant Jarvis, was the arresting officer.''

"Give me your recollection of the case, will you?"

"It's all in the files, Mitch."

"I know. I read them. Now I want your personal input."

"Okay, let's see." Mitch could picture the wiry, gray-haired former police sergeant leaning back in his swivel chair, eyes on the ceiling. "Sean McKackney had just graduated from med school and was doing his residency at Washington General. Peggy Bertram was a senior at Mount Vernon College. One night, the two of them went out on a date. Sean got a little fresh and Peggy quickly set him straight—no sex. So he raped her. They didn't call it date rape in those days, but that's exactly what it was."

"Why did she wait twenty-four hours to report the crime?"

"That was a bad move on her part. But you've got to understand, the kid was embarrassed, and scared the police would say it was her fault, that she had led Sean on. And the McKackneys intimidated the hell out of her. If it wasn't for my daughter, Suzan, Peggy might not have gone to the cops at all. As it turned out, she went through all that humiliation for nothing. An hour after Sean McKackney was picked up, his lawyer showed up with a girl who gave Sean an airtight alibi."

Mitch glanced at the file spread out on his desk and read the name of Sean's attorney—Douglas Fairchild. "Tell me about the girl."

"Her name was Mary Sweeney. She was a model with some hotshot agency in town."

"The Carteris Agency."

"Right. But when she showed up that day, she looked

more like the girl next door than a sexy, sophisticated model. She was beautiful, clean-cut and so soft-spoken you had to strain to hear her. I don't know if that was an act or not, but it sure worked. When she told Jarvis that on the night Sean was supposed to have raped Peggy, he was in bed with her, the poor bastard actually blushed.''

"And he let McKackney go.''

"Yup. My daughter tried to convince Peggy she should still press charges, but she didn't want to. I even offered to do some investigating for her on my own time. She turned me down. The poor kid just wanted to forget the whole thing. Shortly after the incident, she transferred to a small college in Alabama and Suzan lost track of her.''

"What was your impression of McKackney?''

"Sean?'' Randy chuckled. "He was a sleazy little bastard. A rich boy who thought the world owed him a big favor for just being part of it.''

"You think the girlfriend was a phony? Someone Sean paid to lie for him?''

"Not Sean. His father. Sander McKackney. He was the one who came up with that girl, I'm sure of it. I can't prove it. But he did it, Mitch. I'd wager a year's salary on it.''

"If you knew the alibi was a phony, why couldn't Jarvis see it, too?''

"Jarvis was under a lot of pressure in those days. Imagine, a junior detective having to deal with the great and powerful Senator McKackney. He might have acted differently if Peggy hadn't dropped the charges, but once she did, everyone figured she had made up the whole thing.''

"You're the only one who believed her?''

"That's right. I was at the station the night Sean was brought in and I saw how smug he looked when he walked out an hour later. And I saw the look he gave

Peggy. I could have smashed my fist into that arrogant face of his. I was even more convinced of his guilt a few days later when I found out he and Mary Sweeney were no longer an item.''

"What do you mean?"

"They broke up. I talked to a couple of his friends, trying to find out what happened, but they claimed they didn't know anything."

"Maybe this whole thing was just too much for her."

Randy laughed. "Yeah. And maybe the moon is made of green cheese."

"Why don't you describe Mary Sweeney for me?"

"Sure. She was tall and slim, with long blond hair and beautiful eyes. And she was so damned believable. Except for me, I don't think there was a cop in that room who didn't believe she and Sean had spent the night together."

"Thanks, Randy. You've been a big help."

"What's this about anyway? You're not thinking of reopening that old case, are you?"

"I might have to."

Randy groaned. "Don't go down that road, Mitch. Don't get yourself tangled up with McKackney. The guy's a powerhouse."

"Maybe so, but I'm not Jarvis. I don't cave in under pressure."

After Mitch ended the call, he sat at his desk and stared at the chart he had sketched while he talked to Randy. In the center of the page was Sean McKackney's name. Connected to it were three other names—Peggy Bertram, the girl Sean had allegedly raped, Mary Sweeney, who had provided Sean's alibi, and Sander McKackney, who, according to Randy, had paid Mary Sweeney to lie. Over to the right, he had scrawled Gina Lamont's name.

His eyes still on the chart, Mitch picked up his pencil and slowly drew a connecting line between Sander McKackney and Gina Lamont. Somehow those two had known each other, or the senator's name wouldn't have been in Gina's book with a question mark next to it. Had the call girl planned to blackmail him next? And if so, for what reason?

One possibility was that Sander was a client and Gina had a tape to prove it. Another possibility—and by far his favorite—was that she knew about the phony alibi. At this point, there was no reason to suspect that Gina and Mary Sweeney knew each other, but the thought nagged him. Both had been models at the time of the alleged rape. Why couldn't they have been friends? Maybe even close friends. Gina Lamont was in no position to confirm his suspicion, but Mary Sweeney was.

Provided he could find her.

His pencil stuck in his mouth, he pulled the Washington phone book toward him and started flipping through the pages. When he found the Carteris Modeling Agency, he smiled, wrote down the address on a piece of paper and stood up.

It was time to put his theory to the test.

The Carteris Modeling Agency, where Mary Sweeney claimed to have worked at the time Sean McKackney was arrested, was in a turn-of-the-century building on Connecticut Avenue, had a green canopied entrance and a uniformed doorman who informed Mitch that Carteris was located on the top floor. An elevator whisked him to his destination in six seconds flat.

The receptionist, a perfectly groomed brunette with a British accent, told Mitch that Beatrice Carteris, the agency's director, would be with him shortly.

He spent the next few minutes admiring the walls, which were covered with oversize photographs of some of the most beautiful women Mitch had ever laid eyes on.

"Detective Calhoon?"

Beatrice Carteris was in her late fifties, trim and attractive. Dressed in a red power suit and matching four-inch pumps, she walked quickly toward him, a welcoming smile on her lips.

"I'm sorry you had to wait," she said, offering her hand. "I had an unexpected crisis."

"No problem." He waved at the walls. "I kept myself entertained."

She gave a low, throaty laugh. "Beautiful, aren't they? They're my greatest achievement. All the young women you see here went on to become supermodels. I'm very proud of them."

Mitch followed her down a long, yellow-carpeted corridor and into an elegant office decorated in the same buttercup shade. An antique white-and-gold desk stood in the center of the room. On it were a dozen yellow roses in a crystal vase, a telephone and several head shots of more beautiful women.

After they were comfortably settled on a sofa, Beatrice Carteris folded her hands on her lap. "Now, what can I do for you, Detective?"

"I'm looking for a young woman who worked for you in 1979. Her name was Mary Sweeney. I don't have a picture, but she was tall, slender and blond."

The agency director smiled. "Isn't that odd? You're the second person in the past six months to inquire about her."

"Really. Who was the first?"

"A young law student whose name I have forgotten."

"Male or female?"

"Female. She was a pretty girl with exceptional blue eyes and a beauty mark above her lip. She had the kind of face that would have photographed well, and I told her so, but she wasn't interested in modeling."

Lilly Moore again, Mitch thought. The girl had covered a lot of territory in a very short time. First Gina, now Mary Sweeney. "Were you able to help her?"

"Not at first. You see, many of our girls take on pseudonyms, using them only for modeling purposes to start with, then adopting them as their legal names later on. That's what Mary Sweeney did. She hated her name. Anyway, it took me some time, but I eventually found her file."

"May I see it?"

"Certainly." Beatrice Carteris walked over to an armoire and opened it up. "I don't normally keep such old files in my office," she said, opening a drawer and flipping through it, "but when that young girl told me she'd be back, I decided to keep this one handy. I never saw her again, however. Ah, here it is."

She came back to the sofa and handed Mitch a gold folder. "As soon as I saw her picture, I remembered her right away." She opened the file, took an eight-by-ten color photo from it and handed it to Mitch. "She came to us from another agency, although I don't remember which one. I had such great hopes for her, but at the end of her first year's contract, she said she didn't want to model anymore and left us."

Mitch was no longer listening.

His attention was riveted—not on the girl's beautiful face, but on the name under the picture—the name she had adopted. It stared back at him in big block letters.

Gina Lamont.

Seventeen

There was no doubt about it, Mitch thought as he stared at the photograph. The hair color was different, but the wide brown eyes and those cheekbones hadn't changed. Mary Sweeney and Gina Lamont were one and the same.

As he rode the elevator down to the lobby, Mitch decided to drive up to Baltimore to question Sean McKackney. Randy Vargas's theory that Senator McKackney had bought his son an alibi didn't seem so far-fetched anymore.

At Baltimore General where Sean McKackney was now chief of surgery, Mitch walked directly to the front desk, flashed his shield and asked to see the doctor. The nurse on duty told him pointedly that Dr. McKackney was in an important meeting and couldn't be disturbed.

"I suggest you tell Dr. McKackney that he can either talk to me here, right now, or at the police station in Washington, at my convenience. The choice is up to him."

Less than a minute later, Mitch was shown into Sean McKackney's office, where the doctor, looking very professional in an immaculate white coat with a stethoscope around his neck, was already waiting. Although Mitch had never met the senator's son, he would have recognized him anywhere. He had his father's imposing height, the same aquiline nose and that same arrogant way of looking at people he felt were beneath him.

"You're a hard man to pin down, Doctor."

"Sorry about that." McKackney ran a hand down his tie and waited until Mitch was seated before doing the same. "I wasn't trying to be difficult. It's just that our nursing staff is about to go on strike and things are a little hectic around here." He smiled. "Now, Detective, what is this all about? Have I neglected to pay a parking ticket the last time I was in our capital?"

Mitch ignored the sarcastic question. "Do you keep up with your hometown news, Doctor?"

"Not as much as I'd like."

"Then you may not know that a few days ago, a Washington call girl by the name of Gina Lamont was found murdered in her apartment."

One corner of McKackney's mouth lifted in a lofty smile. "I'm afraid that's not exactly the kind of news that would catch my attention."

"What about Mary Sweeney?" Mitch asked mildly. "Would that name catch your attention?"

The smile slipped a notch.

"She was your girlfriend at one time, wasn't she? Pretty girl? A model?"

"I remember Mary, Detective. What I don't understand is why we're discussing her. That relationship ended a long time ago."

"I realize that. In fact, I'm told that it was a very short-lived relationship."

The doctor's eyes hardened. "What are you driving at, Detective?"

"While investigating Gina Lamont's murder, I learned that Gina's real name, the name she was known under sixteen years ago, was Mary Sweeney."

McKackney's expression didn't change. "Really."

"I also learned," Mitch continued, watching him closely, "that at the time you and Mary Sweeney were...dating, shall we say, you were arrested for allegedly raping Peggy Bertram, a Mount Vernon College coed, and that shortly after your arrest, Mary Sweeney, alias Gina Lamont, came to the police station and claimed that the two of you had spent the night together."

"She didn't *claim* anything, Detective. She told the truth. And if you did your homework, then you know that I was exonerated."

"Yet Peggy Bertram maintained you raped her."

"Peggy Bertram was nothing but a vindictive bitch who had been after me for months and couldn't take no for an answer."

"Are you saying she decided to get back at you by accusing you of rape?"

"And gain a little publicity for herself in the process." His tone turned cynical. "You did know that she was a drama major, didn't you?"

"Yes, that was in the police report."

"That slut is lucky I didn't sue the pants off her." McKackney almost spat the words. "If I hadn't been with Mary that night, Peggy might have made the charges stick. My career would have been ruined and God only knows what a scandal like that would have done to my father's future as a senator."

"Hmm." Looking thoughtful, Mitch folded his arms. "Do you know what bothers me most about this case?"

"I couldn't possibly imagine."

Mitch pretended not to have heard him. "What bothers me most is that you and Mary Sweeney broke up so soon after that incident. According to an acquaintance of yours," he lied, "you never saw Mary again after that day at the police station. Why is that, Doctor? She was a beautiful girl and obviously quite loyal. Why wouldn't you want to continue the relationship?''

Although the office was kept at a comfortable temperature, small beads of perspiration had formed on the other man's forehead. ''I don't know. I guess she wasn't my type after all.'' He leaned back in his chair in an obvious attempt to look relaxed. ''Why are you asking me all these questions about Mary, Detective? What does her death, or rather the death of... What did you say her other name was?''

''Gina Lamont.''

''Right. What does the death of Gina Lamont have to do with me?''

''Gina had fallen on hard times. In order to survive, she felt it necessary to blackmail some of her customers. I was wondering if she had ever tried to blackmail you.''

He laughed. ''Are you implying that I used her services?''

''No. I'm suggesting that if the alibi she gave you sixteen years ago was false, if she lied to the police in exchange for money, that would make you an excellent candidate for blackmail, wouldn't you say?''

''You're out of your mind!'' McKackney rose, his face livid. ''How dare you come in here and accuse me of God knows what? That alibi was legitimate. Mary came forward because the charges against me were a sham. *I* was the *victim*,'' he added, jabbing himself repeatedly in the chest with his index finger. ''*Not* Peggy Bertram.''

''Are you denying that you, or someone in your family, paid Mary a large sum of money in exchange for that alibi?''

''Of course I'm denying it. There was no reason to pay Mary off. I was with her that night. She was telling the truth.'' He shook his head as if baffled by the possibility that his word wasn't enough. ''I'm a doctor, for Christ's sake. I save lives. I don't end them. That's what you're suggesting, isn't it? That I killed Mary because she was blackmailing me.''

Mitch grinned. ''Since you brought it up, where were you at one o'clock on Tuesday morning?''

McKackney's face turned even paler. ''You can't be serious.''

''Where were you, Doctor?''

He blinked furiously. ''Home. In my own bed. And before you ask, yes, my wife was with me.''

Satisfied that the good doctor was sufficiently shaken, Mitch stood up. He had started the ball rolling. ''Thank you, Doctor. I'll be in touch.''

He was tempted to add, ''Don't leave town,'' just for effect, but didn't. From the look on Sean McKackney's face, the man had had all the excitement he could handle for one day.

At the door, Mitch turned around for one final nod. Still standing, McKackney was holding his desk with both hands and glaring at him.

Sean McKackney waited until Mitch Calhoon had closed the door behind him before allowing his shoulders to sag. The detective's visit had hit him hard. Lucky for him he didn't have a weak heart. The shock might have killed him.

He raked his hands through his hair, forcing himself to calm down, to think of the situation in a rational, unemotional manner. Yes, Calhoon was a smart cop and he didn't look like the type who gave up without a fight, but so what? There were ways to deal with cops—even the stubborn ones.

Taking a deep, calming breath, he walked over to the window overlooking Baltimore Harbor. Five miles to the west, in an exclusive part of the county, was his home, an extravagant white Colonial he had purchased just last year in anticipation of the position he had been coveting for years—chief of surgery.

And now that the position was finally his, he could lose it all—the lavish house, the new title, the seven-figure salary.

He couldn't let that happen. He had to do something. And he had to do it fast.

Walking back to his desk, he picked up the phone and dialed a number. He waited until the person at the other end said hello before speaking. "We've got a problem."

Eighteen

Stifling a yawn, Kate leaned back in her swivel chair and stretched as she glanced at the clock on her office wall. Ten-fifteen. Dear God, had she really been working all that time?

After leaving the Europa Hotel at four, she had driven to Potomac to spend a few moments with Alison and then had come straight to her office to start her preliminary work on the Fox trial. Frankie had offered to stay and help, but Kate had sent her home.

And now it was time for her to go home, as well. Not that she was all that anxious to return to her big empty house and face yet another long, solitary evening. But it had to be better than the office.

Pushing back her chair, she stood up and started transferring her files from her desk to her briefcase. She hoped that one of the other attorneys was still here and wouldn't mind escorting her down to the parking garage. She didn't normally worry about working late, but thanks to Douglas, who hadn't minced his words, and Alison's eerie feeling that she'd been watched at K-Paul's, paranoia was slowly sinking its nasty claws into her.

Fortunately, the light in Don Hatfield's office was still on. Don was a bright young man Ian Baxter had hired right out of law school earlier this year. Eager to pass the bar exams on his first try, he often stayed late to take full advantage of the firm's extensive law library.

"I was just on the way out myself," he said in answer to Kate's request. "I'll be glad to walk down with you." They rode the elevator to the underground garage where the staff of Fairchild Baxter parked their cars. "Coast is clear." Don grinned as they both stepped out of the elevator. "Do you want me to walk you to your car?"

His snappy army green Jeep was parked only a few feet away and Kate shook her head. "No need for that, Don. I'm just down the ramp."

"All right, then. Good night, Kate."

"Good night. And thanks."

She had almost reached her Saab when the young attorney passed her. He beeped his horn once and waved. She waved back.

As the Jeep disappeared around the bend, Kate felt a sudden prickle on her neck. "Come on, girl," she said with a short, nervous laugh. "Don't go soft on me now."

Then she saw it. The shadow against the wall, just to her left. A very large shadow, rising slowly...

A spark of fear leaped in her breast, but before she could scream or even turn her head to see who was there, a black-clad figure sprang at her from behind a van.

Her first impulse was to run, but as she took her first step, a thick arm locked around her windpipe and a gloved hand clamped over her mouth. "Don't move," a rough male voice warned. "And don't scream. If you do, I'll kill you."

Certain he was going to kill her anyway, Kate did the only thing she could think of. She rammed her elbow into his groin. Hard.

"Ahh!" He let go of her instantly, releasing her so quickly, she stumbled forward, nearly losing her balance.

Her briefcase and her purse fell to the ground, but she didn't stop to retrieve them. Willing her shaky legs to support her, she started running down the ramp, screaming as loud as her lungs would allow. In a few leaps, the man had caught up with her. "You bitch," he snarled as he grabbed a handful of hair and pulled her back. "You fucking, no-good bitch. You wanna play games? Huh?"

Kate cried out in pain, but this time he didn't even try to silence her. With an angry grunt, he threw her against the concrete wall. She hit it with a thud.

Pain shot through her and she slid slowly to the ground, her cheek scraping against the hard, grainy surface. Turning her head, she saw the man coming toward her, both arms hanging at his sides, shoulders low. It was the first chance she had had to take a good look at him.

What she saw sent a chill down her spine. He was huge, dressed in black from head to toe. A ski mask from which only his eyes and mouth could be seen concealed his face. His stance was that of a wrestler, readying for another round.

"What—what do you want?" she stammered. "If it's money—"

His mouth pulling into a sneer, he lifted her off the floor as though she were a rag doll. One hand curled into her coat, he shoved her against the wall, pinning her there. His other hand seized her jaw in a talonlike grip, slowly squeezing it. "Stop yapping, bitch, or you're gonna get hurt."

She stared into his eyes. They were small and dark. And mean. The eyes of a killer, she thought with a shiver.

"You've been a big pain in the ass," he continued in that rough, chilling whisper of his. "You stick your nose where it don't belong, and you ask too many fucking questions. You gotta stop. You hear me, bitch?"

Kate tried to nod, but his grip was like a vise. She imagined that huge hand sliding down to her throat, squeezing the life out of her.

"You hear me?" he repeated.

She made a strangled sound. He released the hold on her jaw just enough for Kate to nod her head very slowly, very carefully. She half expected something to crack in the process, or a handful of teeth to fall out of her mouth. But nothing happened.

"Good."

He brought his face to within an inch of hers, and for an insane moment, she thought he was going to kiss her. She could smell his breath, a mixture of stale cigarettes and garlic. Repulsed, but knowing there was no way of escaping him, she flattened herself against the wall.

"If you don't stop asking so many damned questions about Gina Lamont, or if you go shooting your mouth off to the cops about you and me talking, I'm gonna come back and hurt you real bad." He thrust his pelvis against her. "Or maybe next time, I'll go after that sexy daughter of yours. I saw her with you the other day. She's real pretty. I could have some real fun with a number like that."

It was him. *He* was the one who had been watching them at K-Paul's on Saturday. The blood rushed to her ears. "If you touch her, I'll kill you," she snarled from deep in her throat.

The pressure on her jaw tightened again. "You smart-mouth little bitch, you ain't gonna do nothin'."

Suddenly, he let go of her face, then her coat. Sliding to the ground, Kate watched as he slowly backed away. Her well-trained mind took mental notes. His size: about six-four. His weight: two hundred and fifty pounds. Also, a Brooklyn accent, foul breath. And a fixation with the word "bitch."

He pointed a finger at her in a last, silent warning, then, moving with surprising speed for such a big man, he ran down the ramp and disappeared.

Not waiting for the nervous churning in her stomach to subside, Kate pushed herself up, holding on to the wall for support. If she could only see the car he was driving, memorize the license plate...

From the level below, she heard a car door slam shut, an engine start. Before she could even move, the car had taken off in a squeal of tires. "Damn."

She had to get out of here, make sure Alison was safe. Breathing hard, she took a step, waited a beat, then took another, testing her balance. She experienced no dizziness. That was good. No doubt she'd be black-and-blue by morning, but nothing seemed to be broken. She was all right.

Moving slowly and with great care, she walked back to her car, stopping to pick up her briefcase and her purse from where she had dropped them.

Lowering herself into the driver's seat and turning around to lock the door required some effort, but she managed it. Once settled, she waited until she felt certain she could talk coherently before picking up her phone and dialing the Fairchilds' number.

Joseph, who never went to bed until everyone else had retired, put her through to Douglas immediately.

"Douglas, listen to me and don't ask any questions." She paused to take a breath, then grimaced. "I want you to go check on Alison, make sure she's all right."

"Of course she's all right—"

"Go check on her," she snapped. "Now." Her voice softened. "Please, Douglas, do as I say. I'll explain later."

Douglas was back within two minutes. "She's fine. Sound asleep. Now will you please tell me what this is all about? Have you heard from Eric?" His voice turned menacing. "Has he threatened you in any way? Or Alison?"

"No." She was so close to losing it that she had to bite her bottom lip to keep from bursting into tears. "Don't let anyone near her, Douglas."

"Kate, for God's sake, tell me what's wrong. Let me help you."

"Nothing's wrong." She leaned against her seat. "No, that's not true. I—I've been attacked, Douglas."

"Dear God! When? Where?"

"Just now. In the office garage."

He muttered a short, harsh oath. "Have you called the police?"

"No!"

"Well, you must. Right now. And then I want you to come and spend the night here."

"That would alarm Alison."

"She doesn't have to know."

"No. I just called to make sure she was all right. He—" Her voice broke. "He threatened her, you see...." This time, she was unable to stop the flow of tears.

"That bastard."

"That's why I can't call the police. He said if I did, he'd be back. And he would go after Alison."

"But who is he? What did he want with you?"

"I'll explain everything in the morning, Douglas. Until then, not a word of this to Alison."

She hung up before he could protest further.

Wearing her Victoria's Secret blue silk pajamas, Kate sat on her living-room sofa, her fingers curled around a steaming cup of tea. The long, hot bath had had a soothing effect, but although she felt the heaviness of fatigue dragging at every muscle, she was too keyed up to go to bed.

She ached in a dozen different places, but nothing felt broken. There was a throbbing along her cheekbone where her face had scraped along the garage wall, and a pounding in her head that was slowly receding, thanks to the two Excedrin she had taken earlier.

The incident kept replaying in her head over and over. She had no doubt that her attacker was the same man Tony had seen outside Lilly's building the night of her murder. The question was, was he acting on his own? Or was he working for someone else? Maddy Mays, for instance. Either way, it was a miracle he hadn't killed her.

She was still pondering over the matter when the doorbell rang.

She froze, instinctively glancing toward the heavy dark green drapes she had pulled shut earlier. The living room overlooked the street, and although no one could see in, whoever was outside must have seen the light filtering through.

The bell rang again, two quick little jabs. "Kate, open the door. It's me. Frankie."

At the familiar voice, Kate heaved a sigh of relief and went to open the door. Her secretary stood on the threshold, the lapels of her orange parka pulled around her face to shield her from the blustery wind.

Standing beside her, a look of concern etched in his handsome features, was Mitch.

Before she could open the door fully, he was inside. "Are you all right?" he asked, gently gripping her shoulders. "Are you hurt?" His gaze took a hasty inventory.

"I'm fine." Being careful not to move too quickly, Kate disengaged herself. "What are you two doing here?"

Frankie walked past her and closed the door. "Douglas called me. He told me what happened and asked if I could stop by to make sure you were all right."

"Did he also tell you to bring the police with you?"

"No, that was my idea."

"And a bad one, Frankie." She looked from her secretary to Mitch. "Having you here could make things worse."

"What things?" Frankie asked as she threw her coat on a chair. "Douglas said you'd been mugged. Is that true?"

Rather than answer her, Kate watched Mitch as he set what looked suspiciously like an overnight bag on the floor. "What's that?"

"A change of clothes. I'll need them in the morning."

"If you think you're staying here, you're crazy."

"God, Boss, look at you." Ignoring Kate's protests, Frankie laid a gentle finger on Kate's scraped cheek. "What did that beast do to you?"

"He roughed me up a little," Kate said irritably as she walked slowly back into the living room. "And I survived, so quit acting as if I were hanging between life and death."

She sat down, pressing her back against the green plaid pillows while Mitch removed his ski jacket. Kate's eyes shifted to the service revolver attached to his belt. "Don't make yourself comfortable, Calhoon," she snapped. "I told you you're not staying."

"I'm afraid you've been overruled, Counselor. Frankie and I have already conferred about this. We both agreed that, at least for tonight, you need someone to watch over you."

"How did you get elected?"

"The law of logic. I'm a better match for the guy who attacked you than Frankie."

"That's silly. You know as well as I do that he won't be back."

"This was no mugging, was it?" Although his voice was calm, the concern in Mitch's eyes was obvious.

"No." She shifted her body, a movement that drew a sharp protest from her battered body. "It was no mugging."

Frankie came to sit next to her. "What happened, Kate? Who did this to you?"

Kate looked at her, then at Mitch. She knew the reliability of the first, but was still unsure about Mitch. Could she trust him with a secret? With her daughter's life?

The look in his eyes, a mixture of worry and contained fury, convinced her that she could. "I couldn't identify him," she said. "He wore a face mask, but I'm certain that he's the same man Tony saw outside Lilly's building the night of her murder. In fact, except for his facial features, which I couldn't see, he fits his description to a T."

"But what did he want with you?" Frankie persisted. "Did he say anything?"

"I think he was upset over the fact that I'm investigating Gina Lamont's murder."

"Is that what he said?" Mitch asked.

Kate gave a small, bitter laugh. "No, he put it in a much cruder way, but I got the message. He also said—" she paused, willing her voice to remain steady "—that if I didn't do as he said, or if I talked to the police about him, he would go after Alison."

Frankie's hands flew to her mouth. "Oh, my God!"

Mitch was beside Kate in an instant. In a gesture that reminded her of his gentleness the night Alison had run

away, he took her hand in his. "That's not going to happen, Kate. He was just trying to scare you."

"Well, he succeeded. Which is why I can't afford to
screw up." After a pause, she added, "If I find out that
you betrayed my trust, I swear I'll skin you alive."

Mitch, his face serious, nodded. "You can trust me. In
fact, we don't even need to talk about it anymore. You
can tell us the details tomorrow. Right now, you need to
see a doctor."

"No." Kate pulled her hand away. "No police and no
doctor."

"Kate, don't be stubborn. You've been battered. You
have to be checked out."

"A doctor will have to report the incident to the police.
Even if I made up a story and told him I fell down a flight
of stairs, he probably wouldn't believe me."

"This doctor won't ask any questions."

Kate threw him a suspicious look. "Why? What is he?
Some kind of quack?"

"Russell is one of the finest doctors around, and he
knows how to keep his mouth shut. When necessary, he
even makes house calls."

Arguing with him would have taken every ounce of
strength Kate had left. With a small sigh, she waved for
him to do as he pleased. She didn't stand a chance anyway, not with that look of determination in his eyes and
Frankie so clearly on his side.

Dr. Russell Blackstone was in his mid-thirties with
windblown brown hair, serious eyes behind dark-rimmed
glasses and a gentle smile. Judging from the blue-striped
pajamas sticking out beneath his trench coat, he had either
forgotten to dress or hadn't wanted to bother.

"Mitch tells me you fell down the stairs," he said after he had sent both his friend and Frankie out of the room.

"Mitch has a warped sense of humor."

"I won't argue with you on that one." Gently lifting Kate's pajama top, he ran his fingers over her rib cage, lingering a little over the tender spots. Then, coming to stand in front of her, he inspected her bruised cheek.

"I washed the area thoroughly and then dabbed it with peroxide," she informed him.

Russell Blackstone smiled. "That's still the best treatment there is for surface wounds." He pulled out a penlight from his bag and shone it into her right eye, then the left. "Are you experiencing dizzy spells? Double vision? Nausea?"

"No, nothing like that. Mitch is making a big deal out of nothing," she said, embarrassed to have dragged a tired doctor out of bed. "He shouldn't have bothered you."

"It's no bother." He took a small plastic container from his bag and handed it to her. "Here's a mild sedative, just for tonight. Take it. You'll sleep better. Tomorrow, try to stay in bed and take Advil as needed. If you need something stronger, give me a call." He walked back into the foyer and called Mitch and Frankie back.

Mitch was the first one in. "How's she doing?"

"There's nothing broken and no concussion. She'll have to take it easy for the next day or two. Other than that, she'll be fine."

"Thanks, pal. I owe you a home-cooked dinner."

Russell winced. "I'll pass. Unless, of course, you plan to have the dinner catered." He winked at Kate. "If at all possible, don't let him near your kitchen."

Laughing, Mitch wrapped an arm around his friend's shoulders. "You're such a pessimist. One of these days, I might just surprise you."

Frankie watched the two men walk out of the room and heaved a dramatic sigh. "Some girls have all the luck. It's not enough that you have a gorgeous cop looking after you, but your doctor is a dead ringer for George Clooney. When I had the flu last month, tender loving care came in the form of my aunt Bernice."

"What happened to Roméro?"

Frankie snorted. "Roméro is a dirty, stinking pig. He's out of my life forever."

Before Kate could ask the reason for the breakup, Mitch was back, carrying Frankie's coat. "Okay, young lady," he said, helping her into it, "you go on and get some sleep. I'll take care of your friend."

Facing Kate, Frankie rolled her eyes skyward as though she was in ecstasy.

"I don't need to be taken care of. So why don't you go, as well?"

"Because if I did, you wouldn't get any rest. You'd worry about that ape all night. You'd come down every ten minutes, check all the doors and all the windows, go back upstairs and stare at the ceiling, waiting for sleep to come. By morning, you'd be a wreck."

Kate fought back a smile as Frankie bent down to kiss her cheek. "Seems to me as if the man's got you all figured out, Boss," she whispered in her ear.

"Oh, shut up."

Mitch walked Frankie to the door and waited until she had safely driven away before returning to the living room. "And now it's your turn to go to bed." Wrapping an arm around Kate's waist, he helped her to her feet.

Kate took her time. As she walked, she could feel the shift of Mitch's hard body against hers. It had been a long time since a man had held her that close, and longer still since she had found the experience pleasant, even mildly arousing.

"I can manage the rest of the way by myself, thank you," she said as they reached the staircase.

"Are you sure?"

"It's going to take a lot more than some goon roughing me up to put me out of commission." She nodded toward the hall. "By the way, there's a guest room in back of the kitchen. Bathroom is next to it." Since he was determined to play bodyguard and would no doubt do an excellent job, the least she could do was make sure he was comfortable.

"Thanks, but if it's all the same to you, I'd rather sleep on the living-room sofa."

She shrugged. "Suit yourself." She started up the stairs, one step at a time. "You'll find bedding in the hall closet."

"Thanks, Counselor. Holler if you need me."

Fat chance of that.

Three hours later, Mitch was still up, surveying the deserted street from Kate's living-room window.

Standing vigil was an old habit, one he had performed dozens of times in various parts of the world. Tonight should have been no different. But it was, and he knew it. Tonight, he was standing vigil for a woman who was beginning to matter a little too much.

Maybe he should put a stop to it before he was in too deep. A small chuckle rose from his throat. Judging from the way his gut had contracted when Frankie had called to say that Kate had been hurt, he was already in too deep.

He tensed as a car went by, relaxing only when it had disappeared.

When had she become so damned important anyway?

He'd thought all he wanted from her was a date or two. A few laughs. And some hot sex. Nothing more complicated than that. And surely nothing lasting.

So why the hell was he still awake at three o'clock in the morning, feeling so damned restless and analyzing himself to death?

Cursing under his breath, he moved away from the window and pulled the drapes shut. The sofa, with the plump pillow and thermal blanket he had found in the hall closet, suddenly looked too inviting to resist. Hoping there would be no interruptions, he stripped down to his shorts, tossed his clothes on a chair and slipped into the makeshift bed.

Arms crossed under his head, he closed his eyes and tried to blank out the intrusive image of Kate in those silky blue pajamas.

Nineteen

Kate woke up to the aroma of freshly brewed coffee and the rattle of pots and pans.

Opening her eyes, she tried to focus on the sounds and smells, wondering at the same time why she was still in bed.

Then she remembered. The attack in the underground garage; Frankie and Mitch coming to the house; Mitch insisting she see a doctor; Mitch announcing he was staying. And now... Now what? What *was* he doing down there anyway?

Holding her breath, she stretched her legs, testing them before swinging them to the side of the bed and pushing herself up. She was still a little groggy from the sedative Dr. Blackstone had given her. But as she slowly made it to the bathroom, she was pleased to note that her body was much more pliant than it had been the night before.

The fine, needlelike shower spray felt good on her tight muscles. Tilting her head back, she let the water run over her hair and tried to keep her mind blank, but that was no easy task. Last night's images were still so fresh in her mind that she could almost feel her assailant's hot breath on her face, feel the bile rising in her throat as he talked about Alison.

After nearly ten minutes under the water, she stepped out of the shower, toweled her hair dry and slipped into the thick white cotton robe she kept on a hook behind the door.

What she needed to clear her mind and steady her nerves was a cup of that wonderful coffee she was smelling. She was worthless in the morning until that first cup.

Focusing on that thought, she walked into the bedroom—and almost collided with Mitch.

"What the devil are you doing up?" he barked.

Kate nearly burst out laughing. His hair still damp from his own shower, he stood in the middle of the room, holding a breakfast tray. On it was a steaming cup of coffee, cream and sugar, toast and a plate of scrambled eggs. Somewhere he had found a champagne flute, then filled it with water and put a red carnation in it. She recognized the flower from the bouquet in the foyer.

It was sweet, unexpected and definitely not something she would have associated with Mitch Calhoon. It was also exciting. Especially since she couldn't remember the last time a man had brought her breakfast in bed. "What's all this?"

"Breakfast. Frankie called to remind me that you probably hadn't eaten a thing since yesterday. So I whipped up something I hope is edible."

"Shouldn't you be at work?"

"My shift doesn't start until noon. Now get back in bed so I can unload this."

Realizing she was starved, Kate slid obediently under the covers, sitting cross-legged so he could set the tray on her lap. "I thought you couldn't cook."

"Don't believe everything you hear." Mitch pulled over a chair and sat down. "I hope you like your eggs scrambled. I don't know how to make them any other way."

"As a matter of fact, I do." She picked up her cup. "And the coffee smells divine."

"You're in luck there. Coffee is one of my specialties." She took a sip, then another. "Mmm. Excellent."

He watched her take a bite of her eggs. The bruise on her cheek was beginning to turn blue and her lower lip was swollen, but besides that, she looked terrific. Even this close and with no makeup, he couldn't find a single flaw in her beautiful face. He would have been perfectly content to stay here all morning and just stare at her.

"Why are you looking at me like that?" she asked, her cheeks coloring slightly.

"Because you amaze me," he said honestly. "Most ex-wives I know wouldn't lift a finger to help a former husband, and here you are, risking your life for yours."

He could tell by her self-conscious chuckle that she wasn't comfortable with compliments. "I wasn't aware that I was risking my life. Now that I do, you can be sure that I'll be a lot more careful."

"I'm glad to hear that." He settled back. "How did you sleep?"

"I don't think I moved. The sedative your friend gave me must have worked." She glanced at him above the rim of her cup. "You?"

Sleep had eluded him for a long time. When it had finally come, it had been restless. "Like a baby," he lied. "Your sofa was very comfortable." That much was true.

"Hmm." Her eyes, so dull the night before, were beginning to sparkle again. "Don't get used to it."

"You're firing me?"

"Let's just say that your talents would be wasted here. It's obvious my attacker accomplished what he set out to do—scare me half to death. I doubt he'll be back. Unless, of course, I give him a reason to."

He was glad to hear her speak with such logic. It would make his solution for ensuring her future safety that much easier for her to accept. "Speaking of your attacker," he said after she had wolfed down the rest of her eggs, "are you up to telling me what happened last night? With as many details as you can possibly remember?"

Kate nodded as she reached for her coffee cup again. "I was working late," she began. "Trying to make up for the time I had lost earlier. It was a little after ten when I left."

"Alone?"

"No. One of the other attorneys walked down with me. He even offered to walk me to my car, but I saw no need for him to do that. The garage was quiet, well lit. My car was only a few feet away."

"You never saw the man who attacked you?"

"Not at first. There was a blue van parked next to the Saab. He must have been hiding behind it." She recounted the attack, the warning, the threats. "I shouldn't have called Douglas," she reflected, worried that her daughter would overhear him talk to Rose. "If I had taken time to collect myself, I wouldn't have done it. But I was frantic about Alison. The thought that such a monster could lay even a finger on her—" Her voice broke. Tears of anger and frustration threatened once again, but this time she was able to fight them off.

"He won't." Mitch took the tray from her lap and carried it to the dresser. "And telling Douglas about the attack isn't going to put Alison in danger. On the contrary, he and Rose will take even greater precautions to protect her now."

"I hope you're right."

He sat down again, hitching his chair a little closer. "Besides looking like the man Tony saw outside Lilly's building, is there anything familiar about that man? Do you have any idea who he might be?"

"No. But I think I know whom he works for."

He looked startled. "Who?"

"Maddy Mays. The owner of the Europa Hotel."

Mitch's reaction wasn't quite what she had expected. There was no shock at the mention of the famous woman's name, no look of surprise. Just a flicker of interest. "What makes you think that?"

Without revealing the identity of her informant, she told him what she had found out about Maddy and about her visit to the Europa Hotel.

"Was Maddy upset by your questions?" Mitch asked. "Or angry?"

"If she was, she didn't show it. As a matter of fact, Mrs. Mays couldn't have been nicer. Or more cooperative."

"She's a charmer all right. But don't you ever make the mistake of trusting her."

Kate's attention perked up. "Why? What do you know about her?"

"Only that her connections extend far and wide and that she was once suspected of killing a man. The charges were later dropped for insufficient evidence."

"I don't remember that."

"It happened in New York, long before she married Henry Mays. She was smart enough to discuss it briefly in her autobiography a few years ago, before some overzealous reporter got wind of the story and made too much of it."

"You wouldn't happen to know if one of her employees fits my attacker's description, would you?"

"No, but it should be easy enough to find out."

"I'm not so sure. If he does work for Maddy and if

she is as smart as you say, she'll ask him to lie low for a while.''

"If he's in Washington, I'll find him." Mitch leaned forward, his expression deadly serious. "But before I do that, you and I have to come to an understanding."

She looked surprised. "About what?"

"Your safety. Last night was just a warning, Kate."

"I told you I would be a lot more careful from now on."

"That's not going to be enough. You're dealing with killers here, people who have gone to great lengths to cover up whatever it is they're covering up."

"If you're about to ask me to drop the case—"

"I'd be wasting my breath," he finished, giving her that lopsided, and rather endearing, smile of his. "But you can let them *think* that you've dropped the case, both cases—Tony's appeal and Gina's murder—since it's now obvious that they're connected. But for the ploy to work, you'll have to make everyone believe that you've withdrawn. And I mean everyone, Kate—Rencheck, Tony, Douglas, Rose, even Frankie."

"Frankie is my right hand," she protested. "My friend. She knows as much about my cases as I do. And Douglas is family. I could never lie to him about something like that."

"I didn't say it would be easy. Just remember that the more people who know about your decision, the more believable it will sound to the people who are after you. And the safer you'll be."

"How do you expect me to conduct an investigation if I can't come and go as I please?"

"By working covertly. And by letting me do most of the legwork."

Kate studied him with renewed interest. She may have

been risking her life for an ex-husband, but Mitch Calhoon was risking his career for someone he hardly knew. "Are you sure you want to do that? When I was working in the U.S. attorney's office, such chivalry toward a defense attorney would have been frowned upon."

"Oh, I'm well aware of the adversarial nature within our legal system. But I also believe that both sides seek the same goal—justice. And if in order to achieve that goal, a police officer must occasionally team up with a defense counsel..." He shrugged. "I see nothing wrong with that."

She brushed toast crumbs from the sheet. "Is that what we've become, then? A team?"

He smiled. "Too challenging for you?"

"Just intriguing." She cocked her head to the side. "You no longer believe Eric killed Gina, do you?"

Mitch shook his head. "Too many things don't add up."

"Like what?"

"Like Winslow's death for one thing, and that mysterious ape attacking you last night. Someone is scared, Kate. Very scared."

"Did you tell that to the U.S. attorney?"

"The man is stubborn as a mule. He won't listen to a word I say until Eric turns himself in."

Kate sighed. "I wish there was a way I could tell Eric that. He must be a wreck."

"He hasn't called back since the other morning?"

Under his amused gaze, she felt her cheeks color again. "How did you know it was him?"

"Oh, come on, you didn't think I bought that secretary act, did you?"

Kate felt like a ten-year-old caught with her hand in

the cookie jar. "I'm sorry about that. I didn't know what to do."

"Don't worry about it. We have more important matters to discuss."

"Like what? What did you find out?"

"Do you remember an alleged rape case several years ago involving a college woman and the son of Senator McKackney?"

"Quite well. I was a freshman at Georgetown U at the time. When my mother heard the news, she wanted me to come home. When I wouldn't do it, she made me swear never to go out on a date without thoroughly checking the man." Kate frowned. "What does that have to do with anything?"

"Maybe a lot." He told her about his visit to the Carteris Modeling Agency and his conversation with Sean McKackney.

Kate's eyes widened. "Gina Lamont was Sean McKackney's alibi?"

"You see the implications here, Kate? And why someone would kill to keep it all under wraps?" He gave her a moment to digest the news, then asked, "Did you know that Douglas was Sean McKackney's attorney at the time?"

"No, but I'm not surprised. Douglas and Senator McKackney are old friends. They went to law school together."

"If I'm right, and Mary Sweeney's alibi was fabricated, do you think Douglas could have been in on it?"

Kate didn't even have to think about that question. "Not Douglas. He has too much respect for his profession to be part of such a deception. Even for a friend. On the other hand..." She tapped her index finger against her chin. "I wouldn't be a bit surprised if McKackney senior engineered that scheme and then convinced Douglas it was the truth. It wouldn't be the first time that a smart, conniving client pulled the wool over his attorney's eyes."

From downstairs came the sound of the front door closing.

"That's Maria," Kate said, glancing at the clock on her bedside table.

"Good. You can start by telling her that you'll no longer be working on Tony's appeal."

He saw Kate's eyes fill with panic. "Not Maria. Mitch, I can't. She's gone through too much."

Standing up, he squeezed her hand. "You have to do it, Kate. It's the only way to guarantee your safety. And Alison's."

"Madre de Dios!"

Sitting in the chair Mitch had occupied a few minutes earlier, Maria crossed her hands over her breast as Kate finished telling her about last night's attack.

"Are you sure you are all right?" Her soft brown eyes filled with worry. "And Alison?"

"I'm fine, Maria. And so is Alison. To make sure she stays safe, however, starting today, she will be driven to and from school by either Rose, Douglas or Joseph, and she'll be allowed to visit only a few of her friends. She won't like it, but I can't help that."

Still looking troubled, Maria nodded. Kate bit her bottom lip, at a sudden loss for words. Maria had placed so much faith in Kate, in her ability to free Tony. How could she destroy that faith and maintain their friendship at the same time?

"Can I bring you anything before I start the wash?" Maria asked, rising. "More coffee or—"

"No." Kate took Maria's hand and held it. "There is something else I need to tell you. I'm afraid you're not going to like it, Maria."

Maria sat down again. "Is it about Tonio? About the appeal?"

"In a way." She continued to look at her housekeeper, feeling miserable. "That man frightened me very much last night, Maria, but even more frightening was what he threatened to do to Alison."

"Of course. She is your baby." It was obvious from the look of concern on Maria's face that she hadn't yet realized what Kate was trying to tell her.

"If it were only me," Kate continued, "I wouldn't care. But I can't take a chance with my daughter. Even with all the additional precautions I've taken, they could still get to her if they wanted to. If I gave them a reason to."

Maria's hand went to her throat. "You won't be working on Tony's appeal anymore, will you?" Her voice trembled with sudden panic. "That's what you are trying to tell me."

"Yes." The single word came out as a shameful whisper. "I'm sorry, Maria. I wish there was another way of handling this, but there isn't. The man who attacked me made that very clear. Either I stop investigating those two cases, Tony's and Eric's, or he'll hurt Alison."

"What is going to happen to Tonio?"

"I was talking to Douglas before you came up. He gave me the name of an excellent attorney, one who specializes in appellate law. And he'll do it pro bono, as a favor to Douglas."

"I don't want his charity." Maria pulled herself up straight. "It was bad enough that you would not take any money. I'm not going to let a stranger do the same."

"But, Maria, attorneys do that all the time—"

"I want to pay him," she said stubbornly. "I have some money saved. And if it's not enough, I can pay him a little each week. Otherwise, I will find a lawyer of my own."

Knowing that Maria's pride was as unshakable as the woman herself, Kate didn't argue. She would make it up to her later, in the form of a bonus. "Then you're not upset with me?" she asked. "You understand that I have no choice?"

Maria nodded. "I'm upset, but not with you. I know that Alison has always come first in your life, just as my Tonio comes first in mine." She walked over to the dresser and picked up the breakfast tray. "I'd better get to work. I have a lot to do."

"All right, Maria." Kate watched her leave and hoped Tony would be just as understanding.

"The lieutenant wants to see you," Tom Spivak said as Mitch arrived at the station a few minutes before noon. "And he's in a foul mood."

"So what else is new?" Mitch muttered as he headed toward the glassed-in office at the other end of the room.

Jarvis was standing in front of the door, the jacket of his navy blue suit open. His fists were on his hips and he looked as though he was about to pounce on anyone who came through the door. "What the fuck have you done now, Calhoon?"

Annoyed that half the squad room had heard the crude greeting, Mitch slammed the door shut. "I don't know. Why don't you tell me?" It wasn't the most diplomatic way to handle a superior officer, but what the hell, he was tired of being treated like a bumbling rookie.

"I just got a call from Senator McKackney. He's practically foaming at the mouth. He said you accused his son of having killed Gina Lamont."

"I didn't accuse him of anything. I merely questioned him."

"What the hell for?"

"I found out that Gina Lamont and Mary Sweeney were one and the same. You remember Mary Sweeney, don't you, Lieutenant? The sweet girl who gave Sean McKackney that convenient alibi after he was arrested on suspicion of rape sixteen years ago?"

"If by convenient you mean phony, you're dead wrong, my friend. Mary Sweeney told the truth that night. I should know. I was the arresting officer."

"The same Mary Sweeney who later became a hooker? And a blackmailer? Come on, Lieutenant, don't tell me you don't smell a rat here."

"The operative word is 'later,'" Jarvis snapped. "What the girl became is irrelevant. At the time she made her statement, she was clean. That's all that counts."

"That's not as I see it. And I'll be damned if I'm going to let some high-powered senator tell me how to do my job. This is my case and I'll investigate it any damn way I please."

Jarvis turned red. "The hell you will. Effective right now, you're off this case."

Stunned, Mitch stared at him. "What did you say?"

"You heard me. You're off the Lamont murder case. I'm giving it to Spivak."

"Why are you doing this? Are you that scared of McKackney?"

"You're out of line, Calhoon."

"And you're not being fair. You're letting—"

"You want fair?" Jarvis banged his fist on his desk. "I'll give you fair. Senator McKackney wanted you suspended. He told me that if I didn't fire you, he would sue you and this department for defamation of character and everything else he could think of. And don't think for one moment that he couldn't have made it stick. The only way I could get him to back off was to agree to give the case to someone else. So instead of accusing me of being unfair, show a little gratitude, will you? I saved your job. Maybe even your ass.''

''You can shove the job, Lieutenant,'' Mitch snapped. ''I don't want it.'' Reaching into his breast pocket, he pulled out his shield and slammed it on Jarvis's desk. Then, removing his service revolver, he laid it next to the shield. ''Tell the senator that some cops can't be scared off.''

Then as Jarvis, whose mouth had dropped open, started to say something, Mitch stormed out of his office.

Twenty

Situated within sight of the U.S. Capitol, the Irish Times was a Celtic pub in the true Irish tradition, and a favorite of young, hip lobbyists and congressional aids who liked to be seen.

Standing just inside the door, Mitch surveyed the already crowded room as waiters rushed by carrying bowls of steaming Irish stew and pints of foaming Guinness.

Tom, whom he had called earlier and invited to lunch, was sitting at a table on the other side of the room, nursing a club soda.

Mitch came up behind him and laid a hand on his shoulder. "Hey."

His old friend turned around. "There you are." He gave Mitch a troubled look. "What's this I hear about your resigning?" he asked as Mitch sat down. "It's bullshit, isn't it?"

"It's no bullshit." Catching the eye of a waiter, he called out for a Harp beer and two bowls of Irish stew before returning his attention to Tom. He told the detective about his argument with Jarvis.

At the mention of his unceremonious handling of the lieutenant, Tom's lips twitched. "You'll never get a commendation for diplomacy, that's for sure."

"I never claimed to be a diplomat. And if Jarvis didn't

have marshmallows for balls, none of this would have happened."

"McKackney must have come down hard on him."

"So what? We all have to deal with overbearing politicians at one time or another, especially in this town. Since when do we let them dictate how we run an investigation?" He looked across the table at his friend. "Is there anything you need to know about the case? Anything Jarvis may have left out?"

Tom waved his hand. "We can talk about that later. You're not out of the force yet. In fact, if I were to talk to Landers, you'd be reinstated in a minute. I bet he doesn't even know what happened. If he did, you'd have heard from him by now. The old man likes you, Mitch. And he hates losing good cops."

Mitch shook his head. The last thing he wanted was to involve the chief of police. Landers was a good man, and a Mason, the fraternal organization Tom belonged to, which explained their friendship. But going over a superior's head and using a friend to do it wasn't Mitch's style. "Let's not bring Landers into this," he said flatly. "Not just yet anyway."

Tom's shrewd eyes narrowed. "What are you up to, Mitch?"

Mitch feigned innocence. "Who says I'm up to anything?"

"Like I said before, I know you. And I know McKackney. He's not going to like having some stubborn cop revive that old rape case."

"Tough. I'm a private citizen now. I don't have to answer to anyone." A customer had just dropped a quarter in the jukebox and Mitch leaned across the table, trying to be heard over the strains of "Danny Boy." "However, I'm not too proud to ask for help from a buddy."

Tom let out an exaggerated sigh. "How did I know there were strings attached to this lunch?"

"Just a small one." Mitch glanced both ways to make sure there were no eavesdroppers. "It's about Maddy Mays, the owner of the Europa Hotel. There was a rumor a few years back that she was running a call-girl ring. I wasn't in D.C. at the time, but you were. Is there any truth to that story?"

As their lunch arrived, Tom attacked his stew with great gusto. "I heard something to that effect," he said between mouthfuls. "But that was a long time ago, around the time Maddy opened the hotel." He tore off a piece of bread and dunked it in the thick brown gravy. "Why are you so interested in Maddy Mays?"

"Because if the rumor is true, Gina Lamont could have been working for her."

"Hmm." Tom chewed slowly as he thought about that possibility. "So what do you want from me?"

"You have friends on the vice squad. Find out who ordered the investigation on Maddy stopped and why."

Tom lowered his glass. "What are you saying? That the department is dirty?"

"It wouldn't be the first time. All it takes is one bad apple."

"Okay, I'll see what I can find out." Tom pushed his bowl aside. "With one condition."

Mitch grinned. "How did I know there were strings attached to this favor?" He made a grand gesture. "But go ahead. Anything for a friend."

"Is it true that you've been seeing quite a lot of Kate Logan lately?"

Mitch held his friend's gaze. "If by 'seeing' you mean sleeping with, then the answer is no."

"You didn't spend last night at her house?"

"How do you know about that?"

"Povich from the *Chronicle* has been watching Kate's house, hoping Logan would show up. He told his cousin that he saw you going in there at about eleven last night."

"Did that vermin bother to mention that Kate's secretary was with me?"

"He did, but he also said that she left thirty minutes later and you stayed. He claims he resumed his watch at six o'clock this morning and your car was still there. Needless to say, the U.S. attorney wasn't happy to hear that. If you hadn't left in such a hurry this morning, he probably would have called you in and demanded an explanation. He may still do that."

On the table, Mitch's hands balled into fists. "One of these days I'm going to have to shut that sleazy reporter's mouth."

"Then it's true."

"It's not what you think." Remembering his promise to Kate not to mention her attack, he added, "Kate was sick last night and didn't have anyone to take care of her."

"Come on, Mitch, don't play me for a fool. What's going on between you and Kate Logan? Are you falling for her?"

"I wasn't aware that being my friend entitled you to every detail of my personal life," Mitch said defensively.

Tom laughed. "Go tell that to Mary Beth. Her theory is that since you saved my life once, I'm now responsible for yours—every facet of it."

Mitch shot his friend a startled look. "Mary Beth knows about Kate?"

"Uh-huh. She found out from Lucy Yeardon whose sister works in the U.S. attorney's office."

"Christ."

"You've got another problem. A small one."

"What now?"

"Mary Beth wants to meet Kate." He laughed. "She wants to make sure you're not letting another Ava sink her claws into you."

Mitch groaned, knowing that once Mary Beth had made up her mind about something, she hardly ever changed it. The only reason he tolerated her intrusions into his life was that he knew her actions stemmed more from a need to protect than a desire to meddle. Convinced she could never repay Mitch enough for saving her husband's life, she showed her appreciation in the only way she knew—with an outpouring of love and affection.

"I tell you what," Tom said. "Why don't you bring Kate by this afternoon? Mary Beth is baking one of her famous pumpkin pies and I get off duty at four. I may even have something on Maddy Mays by then."

There was no getting around it. To try would simply make Mary Beth more suspicious.

"I'll mention it to Kate," Mitch said noncommittally.

By the time Mitch returned to Kate's house at two o'clock that afternoon, he found her dressed in a loose khaki jumpsuit and moving much better than she had earlier. A tantalizing vanilla smell wafted from the kitchen.

"What are you doing here?" she asked as she let him in. "I thought you had the twelve to eight shift."

"I did." He climbed on a kitchen stool and glanced at the bowls, wooden spoons and other baking apparatus spread out on the island. "I thought Russell told you to stay in bed."

"I told Alison I'd bake her a batch of her favorite Christmas cookies." She dipped a finger in the thick, creamy dough and licked it. "That's more rewarding than staying in bed." She picked up a cookie gun from the island and waved it in front of his nose. "And you didn't answer my question. What are you doing here?"

"I handed in my shield. I'm no longer on the force."

"You did *what?*"

"You heard me. I'm no longer on the force. I quit."

"But why? What happened?"

"Jarvis found out that I went to Baltimore to question Sean McKackney. On the senator's orders, he took me off the case. I didn't like that, so I walked."

The Christmas cookies temporarily forgotten, Kate leaned against the sink. "Took you off the case! Isn't that as good as an admission of guilt on his part?"

"It depends how you look at it, and who's doing the looking."

"Mitch, you have to do something. Go over Jarvis's head—"

"Bad idea," he broke in. "McKackney's accusation that I'm harassing his son could be regarded as justified. I need actual proof of his participation in Sean's alibi before I do anything rash."

"Do you think he'd be stupid enough to have left proof?"

"I'm counting on it." He watched her as she wiped her hands on a kitchen towel. "How well do you know McKackney?"

"Not very well. He and Douglas often go hunting together at the senator's cabin in the Catoctin Mountains. He was always charming, but for some reason, I've never cared much for him. Neither does Rose. Too overbearing perhaps. And phony."

They looked at each other. "So the question is," Mitch mused, "how far would Senator McKackney go to save his son's ass?"

"I think you already know the answer to that question, or you wouldn't have gone to Baltimore."

Mitch continued to look at her. How did she manage to look so sexy in such a bland outfit? "What do *you* think?"

Kate picked up the cookie gun again and started to fill it with the dough. "My scenario is a bit too wild for a conservative cop like you, but here it is." She worked as she talked, her movements quick and precise. "Let's assume that the call-girl ring Gina worked for *was* run by Maddy Mays. If Gina, alias Mary Sweeney, was already working for Maddy at the time of Sean's arrest, Maddy could have provided the girl *and* the alibi as a favor to the senator."

"How would Maddy Mays know the senator?"

Kate laughed. "Come on, Mitch. This is Washington, D.C., where sex and debauchery rival that of ancient Rome. You really have to ask that question?"

"You think the senator was a client of Maddy Mays?"

"It's only a theory, but yes, I think that's quite possible. He could even have been a *valued* customer—one Maddy would have been only too glad to help."

Mitch chuckled. "Counselor, I like the way you think."

"Thanks." She picked up the tray, which was now filled with wreath-shaped cookies waiting to be baked, and slid it into the hot oven. "The problem is, how do we prove it?"

"By probing deeper into the McKackneys' background."

"That could get you arrested."

He gave her a disarming grin. "If it does, I know a great lawyer."

"Just be careful, okay?"

An amused gleam danced in his eyes. "Why, Counselor, if I didn't know better, I'd swear you cared."

Kate felt it safer to avert her eyes. "I don't want to see you getting into more trouble, that's all. I feel bad enough that you lost your job."

"Don't worry about that."

"What do you mean 'don't worry about that'? Your job is your livelihood, isn't it?"

"Not really. After I left the force the first time, I went to work for Vargas World Wide, an investigative agency that specializes in finding and rescuing missing children. I made more money there than I'll ever need. Besides, I've always been pretty resourceful. I'll find something else."

"But you love the force, or you wouldn't have given up such a lucrative position to return to it." Suddenly curious to know more about him, she leaned both elbows on the island. "Why did you leave Vargas anyway? Or is that none of my business?" That same expression Kate had seen in his eyes a few days ago clouded his face again, making her regret the question. "I'm sorry, I didn't mean to pry."

"You didn't." He shrugged. "Something happened that made me realize I was no longer qualified for the job, so I left."

"I find that hard to believe. I heard some of the comments that were made about you when you came back to Metro P.D. a year ago. All of them were very complimentary. Some people even called you a hero."

He was silent for a while, lost in his thoughts, then unexpectedly, he began to talk. "Three years ago, I went out to rescue a child—a little girl. It was something I had done dozens of time—successfully."

"From what I hear, you were very good at it."

Bitterness tightened the corners of Mitch's mouth. "Not that day."

"You weren't able to rescue her?"

He looked at her. His eyes, usually so expressive, had gone flat. She felt as though she was staring into the eyes of a stranger.

"I got her killed."

"Oh, no." As her heart filled with sorrow and compassion, she tried desperately to offer comfort, but couldn't find the right words. "What happened?"

"I let my emotions get the best of me, something I never should have done."

"Did it happen abroad? Or here?"

"In California. I had her in my arms, almost over the wall of the property where she'd been living. In my haste to get her out of there, I didn't see a second armed guard running toward us."

"He *shot* her?"

"He tried to shoot me. And missed. He got her instead."

Kate swallowed the lump in her throat. "Oh, Mitch." This time, her hand moved to touch his. He took it, as one might grab a lifeline, and held it.

"She was only seven years old. A beautiful child, loving and trusting. And I let her down."

"Don't do this to yourself, Mitch. I'm sure you did everything you could."

He didn't answer. And he didn't tell her that the child was his daughter. Thanks to Ava, who hadn't wanted the publicity, and the California authorities, who had agreed to keep the story out of the national media, only a handful of people knew the identity of the little girl who had been killed that awful day.

He glanced at Kate, aware that the story of Gabrielle's

death had shaken her badly. Her eyes were moist and her voice unsteady when she spoke again.

"If you left Vargas World Wide shortly after that little girl died and you only came back to Washington last year, what did you do in the interim?"

"I traveled. I wasn't sure where I wanted to settle down, or what I wanted to do, so I tried a number of locations and jobs." He laughed. "I even worked as a New York P.I. for a while."

"But you came back to Washington."

He shrugged. "You know what they say. Sooner or later, everyone returns to their roots."

"You don't have any family? A mother? Brother or sister?"

"My father was a cop. He died a long time ago, killed in the line of duty. My mother moved to Florida in 1993." He smiled. "You'd like her, Kate. She's one hell of a lady."

"I'm sure she is." There was more to Mitch Calhoon than he had told her, Kate thought as she studied him, but now was not the time to press him for more information.

The timer she had set for twenty minutes rang and she walked over to the stove. As she pulled out the tray, Mitch reached over and stole a fragrant cookie. "I was wondering," he said as he chewed, "are you up to taking a little ride?"

She gave him a startled look. "I don't know. Where to?"

"The Spivaks. Tom is a homicide detective and a good friend of mine. Mary Beth is his wife. I asked Tom to run a check on Maddy Mays and find out whether or not that rumor was true. He may know something by now."

"I know Tom. He and I worked together on a couple

of cases when I was in the U.S. attorney's office. He's a good man."

"You'll like Mary Beth, too."

"Wouldn't I be intruding?"

"I don't think so." He smiled and decided to tell her the truth. "Actually, Mary Beth wants to meet you." He cleared his throat, feeling a little awkward. "You see, she heard from another policeman's wife that you and I were romantically involved and—"

Kate's mouth dropped open. *"What?"*

"I know. That was my reaction, too, but it's just a rumor, Kate. It'll die down in a few days."

"Who started it?"

"Povich. Apparently, he's been watching your house for signs of Eric. Anyway, he knows I spent the night here and he told his cousin."

"Damn." Kate threw her oven mitt on the counter. "One of these days I'm going to take that man's scrawny little neck between my hands and squeeze until he expels his last breath."

Mitch laughed, remembering his own threat to kill the weasel. "You'll have to take a number, lady." He waited a few moments before adding, "If you don't want to go, I'll understand."

Kate thought about her choices—staying home with her aches and pains, or spending the rest of the afternoon with Mitch. The decision took no time at all. "As a matter of fact, I'd love to meet Tom's wife." She gave Mitch a teasing smile. "Someone has to set those rumors straight."

Twenty-One

The moment Kate saw Tom and Mary Beth's two little girls hurl themselves into Mitch's arms, she knew that the detective's relationship with the Spivak family was even more special than she had realized.

"Uncle Mitch, look at my new Barney puppet!" Six-year-old Amy, her hand concealed inside a purple mitt, wiggled the puppet in Mitch's face.

Not one to be upstaged by her big sister, four-year-old Sandy tugged at Mitch's sleeve. "Look at *me*, Uncle Mitch. I can stand on my toes." Eager to demonstrate and show off her new ballet slippers, she pulled herself up and held the pose for an impressive five seconds.

"All right, you two." Laughing, Mary Beth pulled the girls away. "Give your uncle Mitch some breathing room, will you? He just got here."

She was an attractive brunette with a friendly smile and an easy manner that made Kate feel instantly at home.

"They're crazy about him," she told Kate as she led her into a wood-paneled family room strewn with toys. "And of course, he spoils them rotten." As Mitch and Tom disappeared down the hall for a private talk, she removed a huge stuffed panda from the sofa and set it on the floor. "Do you have any children, Kate?"

"A daughter." Smiling, Kate watched Amy and Sandy

as they settled on the floor to play. "She's thirteen and more of a handful than your two girls put together."

"This must be a difficult time for her. With all this publicity going on."

"It hasn't been easy. That's why I'm letting her get away with so much." Kate's eyes laughed as they met Mary Beth's. "As soon as everything is back to normal, I'll start cracking the whip again."

Bending over a tray on the cocktail table, Mary Beth poured coffee. "Somehow you don't look like the whip-cracking type."

Kate laughed. "Couldn't fool you, either, huh?"

"Not one bit."

Kate took the cup that was offered and waited until Mary Beth was seated before asking, "You've known Mitch a long time, haven't you?"

"Eighteen years. He was best man at our wedding." She glanced toward the girls to make sure they weren't listening and lowered her voice. "He also saved Tom's life once."

"I didn't know that."

"It happened a long time ago. Tom and Mitch were partners then, two rookies, fresh out of the academy. They were on patrol when a call came in on the radio about a robbery in progress. Their cruiser was only a block away, so they were the first to respond. When they arrived at the scene, Tom ran out of the car and immediately found himself under fire." She looked briefly into the distance before returning her gaze to Kate. "If it hadn't been for Mitch's quick action, I'd be a widow right now."

"I can see why you care for him so much."

"He's like a brother to us. There's nothing Tom and I wouldn't do for him." Casually, Mary Beth tucked a dark curl behind her ear. "What about you? Have you known Mitch long?"

"Not really. I first met him six months ago when he and I worked on the Tony Fuente case."

"On opposite sides."

Kate smiled. "Yes. And we were still on opposite sides when he was assigned to the Gina Lamont murder, which makes my being here with him rather odd, I suppose."

Mary Beth stared at her hands for a moment. "I have to make a confession," she said, looking up and smiling sheepishly. "I was rather curious about you, Kate. Tongues are wagging like crazy about the two of you, especially since Mitch resigned so abruptly, yet he's never said a word about you."

Kate found the young woman's candor refreshing. "Maybe that's because there's nothing to say. Mitch and I are not involved. Not romantically anyway."

"He seems quite taken by you."

"Did he say that?"

"No, but I have eyes. I can see the way he looks at you. He's never looked at a woman that way before. Not even Ava."

Kate felt a sudden and inexplicable pang of jealousy. "Who's Ava?"

"His ex-wife."

Kate heard the chill in Mary Beth's voice. "You don't seem very fond of her."

"I'm not." She glanced toward the girls again. "I hated her on sight. She was spoiled, immature and self-centered. But Mitch was in love, so Tom and I kept our mouths shut. We were hoping marriage would change her, make her realize that the whole world didn't revolve around her, but it didn't. If anything, she got worse. And she hated Mitch's job."

"That's not too surprising, is it? It takes a special kind of woman to be a policeman's wife, not to let the worry interfere with the relationship."

Mary Beth shook her head. "That's not why Ava hated the force. She wasn't worried about Mitch's safety. She was upset because he wasn't making enough money. That's why he went to work for Vargas World Wide."

"Where is Ava now?"

"California. She remarried…"

She stopped as if suddenly realizing she had said too much. Kate didn't press her. She couldn't have anyway. Mitch and Tom were returning, demanding pumpkin pie.

"So what did you think of Mary Beth?" Mitch asked as they drove across town toward Kate's house. Night had fallen, bringing with it a fine drizzle that enveloped the city in a soft mist.

"She's lovely." Kate looked at him sideways. "And very protective of you."

Mitch groaned. "Oh, no. She didn't put you through the third degree, did she?"

"Not really. She just wanted to make sure that I wasn't some cold-blooded wench out to break your heart."

"Tell me she didn't say that."

Kate laughed. "She didn't. We got along very well as a matter of fact. She was almost disappointed to hear there was nothing between us." Serious again, she asked, "Was Tom able to find out anything about Maddy Mays?"

"Not yet. The two officers who headed the vice squad at that time have long since retired, and others he's talked to don't remember an investigation."

"Could Maddy have been telling the truth?"

"Somehow I doubt it." He turned the Ford onto Porter Street and pulled in behind the Saab. "Tom is trying to track down the retired officers. He'll let me know as soon as he hears something." He saw her stifle a yawn with the back of her hand. "Tired?"

"A little. It's been quite a day." She smiled, feeling suddenly self-conscious. It was getting more and more difficult to deny the attraction she felt for this fascinating man whose life was slowly unfolding in front of her very eyes. And it wasn't helping that they sat in such close proximity. "Thanks for the unexpected afternoon, Mitch. I—"

The rest of the sentence died on her lips. Without warning, and before she had a chance to protest, Mitch pulled her to him and kissed her.

Under the onslaught, Kate felt her body stiffen, then unexpectedly, almost shamefully, she let herself go limp. She couldn't remember anyone ever kissing her that way before. It was a wild, heated kiss that took her breath away and turned her knees to jelly.

Dazed, she found herself responding, moaning, fisting her hands into his hair. Emotions she had no idea she possessed ripped through her, sapping her willpower and all the promises she had made.

Mitch's hands cupped her face. "God, you taste good," he murmured against her mouth. "Just like I imagined." His lips moved to the hollow of her throat, where her pulse was beating wildly. "Let's go inside, Kate."

She never had a chance to answer. As she tilted her head back in surrender, she caught sight of a car coming up the street. It was moving slowly, its lights off. At the intersection, it turned left and disappeared.

"What's the matter?" Mitch pulled away, his gaze following hers. "What did you see?"

"A car." She was trembling. "Driving with the lights off." Mitch threw the Ford in gear, but Kate stopped him.

"No! Let him go." She gripped his arm. "It's probably Povich again. And catching him would only make things worse."

"I'll stay with you, and if he comes back, I swear I'll—"

"No." She said it quickly before her heart, aching for him to stay, had a chance to say otherwise. "Don't you see, that's exactly what he's hoping you'll do. It was only his word against ours before, but I'm willing to bet that tonight, he came with a camera." She glanced up and down the street. "Let's not give him any more ammunition than he already has."

Mitch's thumb brushed lightly against her lip. "All right, Kate, but let the record show that I object."

Breathing slowly and deeply, Kate waited until her heartbeat had quieted a bit before opening the car door. "Objection noted. Good night, Mitch."

"Good night, Kate."

Sam Cory's Gym on M Street was nearly deserted at this early-morning hour, which was why Mitch often chose this time to do his daily workout.

He always began his routine with a three-mile run along the indoor track. The deep breathing helped clear his mind, and occasionally, it even helped him sort through his problems.

But this morning, logical thoughts seemed beyond him. Kate—and the way she had felt in his arms yesterday evening—was the reason.

He was approaching the end of the first lap when he was suddenly joined by another runner. It only took Mitch a quick glance to recognize Senator Sander McKackney. Mitch smiled inwardly as he spotted two Secret Service men, also in running gear, fall in several feet behind McKackney.

Although he had expected the senator to make some kind of move, he hadn't expected to see him here in a fairly public place. Odd that he hadn't realized he was being tailed. Either those government men were getting better, or he was slipping.

"Good morning, Detective," the senator said as he caught up with Mitch.

In his early sixties, the longtime politician was a big, well-preserved man with broad shoulders, muscular thighs and a flat stomach Mitch suspected was as hard as his own. Every strand of his famous pewter gray hair in place, the good-old-boy image was as charismatic as ever.

"You can drop the title, Senator. You know damn well I'm no longer on the force."

"A pity." Although Mitch had increased his speed, the older man kept up with him with hardly a change in his breathing. "Good cops are hard to come by these days."

"Yeah." Mitch chuckled. "And at this rate, they might even become an extinct species."

"Detective, please believe me, I had nothing to do with Lieutenant Jarvis's decision to take you off the case." The Southern accent was much more pronounced now that he was off camera. Or was it due to the fact that he was lying shamelessly? "I merely expressed concern for my son whom you seem to have targeted unfairly. Sean has nothing to hide."

"Then why worry?"

"Because I was concerned, and so was Sean, by your determination to dredge up an old scandal that had nothing whatsoever to do with the case you were investigating."

"You have your opinions. I have mine."

McKackney negotiated a curve, his gait as strong as when he had entered the track. "My son is a brilliant surgeon, Detective, and the father of two wonderful daughters. I ask you, do those two little girls deserve to be exposed to a scandal the country has long since forgotten?"

It was easy to see why the man was being reelected time after time. Not only did he lie with astonishing conviction, but his delivery was flawless.

"You'll have to ask Detective Spivak that question, Senator. He's in charge of the case now. I'm just an average citizen."

"But an obstinate one, I'm told. Which is not a bad thing, mind you." He laughed, suddenly going into buddy mode. "I'm an obstinate man myself, and it hasn't hurt me any, has it?"

It was time to put on the pressure. "Is there a point to this conversation, Senator?"

Their eyes met. For an instant, the TV image disappeared, replaced by a hard-as-steel expression that would have intimidated many men. It did not intimidate Mitch. He had dealt with tougher guys than McKackney.

"The point is," the senator said in a voice that had suddenly turned as smooth as honey, "that if you continue to harass my son, as I'm inclined to think you might, you will regret it."

Mitch gave him a thin smile. "You wouldn't be threatening me, would you, Senator?"

"Take it any damn way you please, Calhoon." The gloves were off now. "Just don't say I didn't warn you."

Mitch watched as the senator smoothly got off the track, the two Secret Service men right behind him. When all three had disappeared, Mitch finished his run.

He had heard many rumors about the senator from Tennessee, but none had ever hinted at the ruthlessness that lay deep within the man. Mitch had recognized it instantly and would have been a fool to dismiss it. Senator Mc-Kackney was definitely a man to watch out for.

Feeling much better after a good night's sleep, Kate hummed softly as she arranged the cookies she had baked the day before in a festive tin. If that didn't bring a smile to Alison's face, nothing would.

As she stepped out her front door a few minutes later, she was greeted by the unwelcome sight of Eddy Povich.

"I have nothing to say to you, Povich," she said, brushing past the reporter. "Not that it will stop you. I suppose you can always make up something to fill your column."

"Kate, Kate." He trotted after her with a hand over his breast. "You know you're breaking my heart when you say those things."

Your balls are what I'd like to break. For a moment, an almost irresistible moment, she actually considered shoving her knee in his crotch for the pure pleasure of seeing him squirm in pain.

"I'm just a hardworking man trying to do his job," he continued, almost running to keep up with her. "So why don't you help me out, okay? Tell me if there's any truth to the rumor that you're no longer representing your ex-husband."

Kate struggled to keep her panic from showing. If Povich wrote about her withdrawal from the case, Alison would see it. She had always been a news buff, but these days, she pored over every page of the *Washington Post* in hopes of seeing something about her father.

Rather than insult Povich again, which seemed to have no effect on him anyway, Kate decided to change tactics, remembering the saying about catching more flies with honey than with vinegar.

"Yes, that's true," she said as if the matter was of no importance to her. "But I wouldn't waste my time writing about it if I were you. Your readers wouldn't be interested."

"How do you know?"

"Because Eric Logan is old news." Hoping to score a point or two with the reporter, she added, "Now if you want a real scoop, you should concentrate on the Fox case that goes to trial in April. You do know that I'm representing William Fox, don't you?"

The thought that she had just implied she would provide him with daily sound bites for the duration of the Fox trial made her want to throw up. But if the unspoken promise kept her name out of the papers, it would be worth it.

Povich's suspicious little eyes narrowed as he studied her face, and for a moment she was afraid he would notice her bruised cheek, which was heavily covered with concealer.

"Or maybe," the reporter said with a smile that was almost obscene, "the reason you dropped Eric Logan is because you didn't want to jeopardize your love affair with Mitch Calhoon."

Kate felt her heart give a little jump. "That's ridiculous," she said defensively, too defensively perhaps. "I'm not having an affair with Mitch Calhoon."

"Then what would you call it? After all, he did spend Monday night at your house, didn't he? *All* night?"

"No, he didn't," she lied. "He had car trouble and took a cab home."

Povich threw his head back and laughed. "That's good, Kate. You should get an Oscar for that one." He moved a little closer. "Except that I'm not buying it. Calhoon was here all right. He didn't leave until eleven o'clock the following morning." The reporter rubbed his hands together. "Oh, Kate, my readers are going to love this."

It took all of Kate's willpower not to slap him. "So that's what you have sunk to now, Povich. Spying? Have you so little faith in your own abilities that you feel it necessary to resort to yellow journalism in order to sell newspapers?"

Unfazed, Povich leaned a shoulder against the side of her car. "I have an obligation to my readers, Kate. You know that."

"Then go cover something worthy of being called news."

"But you *are* news, Kate." He chuckled. "And you'll be even bigger news once the public finds out you've been playing house with the detective in charge of investigating a murder in which your ex-husband is a prime suspect. Talk about a breach of ethics. No wonder the poor guy was fired."

"Get off my property, Povich. Or I swear I'll have you arrested."

The threat went right over his head. "I'm not on private property, Kate. I'm on the sidewalk, covering a murder case." Pulling a pad and pencil from his pocket, he plowed on, "I'm right, aren't I? Calhoon was let go because the two of you are having an affair."

"That's completely false," she said, striving to keep her voice level. "First of all, Detective Calhoon was not fired. He resigned. And second, we are not, I repeat, we are *not* having an affair. And if I see one word alluding to the contrary, I'll sue you."

She might as well have been talking to a brick wall. "Why are you lying, Kate? What are you trying to cover up?'' His grin widened, showing a hint of gold in the back. ''Inquiring minds want to know.''

Pushing him aside, Kate yanked her car door open. ''You make me sick, Povich. Why don't you print that in your filthy paper?''

He was still grinning when she backed out of her parking space, nearly crashing into the neighbor's trash can.

Twenty-Two

Kate's first thought as she drove to Potomac following her confrontation with Povich, was to tell Alison about withdrawing from the Lamont case before she read it in the papers and hope the teenager wouldn't hate her for it.

Halfway to Douglas's house, she changed her mind. Who was she kidding? Alison would be furious with her, and totally devastated. Whatever progress the two of them had made would become nonexistent. Kate had no choice but to keep the matter to herself as she had planned to do all along. There was still a chance Povich wouldn't print the story anyway, and even if he did, the chances that Alison would see it were practically nil. The only papers Douglas allowed in his house were the *Washington Post*, the *New York Times* and the *Wall Street Journal*. Kate's secret would be safe.

When she pulled up in front of the Fairchilds' house ten minutes later, and saw Alison waving at her from her bedroom window, Kate knew she had made the right decision.

It was one o'clock that afternoon when Frankie buzzed Kate. "Guess who's on line three?"

Kate laughed. She had a pretty good idea, but didn't want to deprive Frankie of the pleasure of telling her. "I haven't got a clue. Who?"

Frankie's lusty sigh was clearly audible. "Mitch Calhoon."

"Tell him I don't have time right now."

"*Boss!*"

Kate laughed. "Just kidding, Frankie. Put him through."

As she heard Mitch say, "Hi, Kate," in that low, sexy voice of his, her heart did a little flip.

"Hello, Mitch." Forcing the memory of last night's kiss aside, she tried to sound casual. "What's up?"

"It looks as if your hunch about Chuck Winslow paid off after all," he said.

"Why? What did you find out?"

"Jim Faber, that private detective I sent to Myrtle Beach to watch the Winslows, finally came through for me."

"How?"

"Cora Winslow just bought a brand new Toyota with a price tag of fourteen thousand dollars. And paid cash for it."

Kate fell back against her chair. "I knew it. They had the money all along."

"Looks that way."

"Where was it? How is Cora explaining the sudden windfall?"

"Jim hasn't had a chance to talk to her, so I'm flying down there tonight. That neighborhood should be ripe with excitement right about now."

"Will you call me the moment you get back?"

"Only if you promise to go home early tonight. I'm not sure you should have gone to work at all."

Kate smiled. "Okay, Boss."

The rest of the afternoon passed with surprising speed and relatively few interruptions. At four o'clock, Kate made her daily phone call to Alison, and an hour later, Frankie walked into her office, a bag filled with groceries in her arms.

"Come on, Boss, time to leave."

Kate glanced at the clock. "I hadn't realized it was already five o'clock."

"Now you do." She took Kate's coat from a hanger behind the door and handed it to her. "Come on, I'm going home with you."

Kate's brows lifted. "Why?"

"Because Mitch Calhoon said so. He was afraid you'd welsh on your promise, so he asked me to make sure you left at five and went straight home." She patted the brown bag. "I'm throwing in a bonus, too."

Kate's eyebrows went up. "You're cooking for me?"

"Uh-huh. Your favorite dinner—my aunt Bernice's stuffed peppers. It'll take a while, but it'll be worth it."

Kate, who had only nibbled on a package of cheese crackers for lunch, felt her mouth water. Glad of the chance to share a delicious meal with her vivacious friend instead of facing the evening alone, she pushed away from her desk and stood up. "In that case, what are we waiting for? Let's go."

By nine o'clock, Frankie was gone, the dishes were washed, and Kate was looking forward to going to bed. But as she was setting the burglar alarm, the phone rang.

At the sound of the raspy, breathless voice, Kate almost hung up. She wasn't in the mood for an obscene caller in search of cheap thrills. A feeling she couldn't quite explain, however, made her stay on the line. "Who is this?"

There was a low groan, then the voice spoke again, a little louder this time. "LuAnn."

Kate stiffened. "LuAnn. What's wrong?"

"Someone...broke into my apartment...and beat me up."

"Oh, no." Kate went still as the fear she had experienced only two nights ago replayed in her head. "Who was it?"

"Couldn't tell. He wore a mask." She let out a small whimper. "He hurt me bad, Kate."

"Where are you?"

"Home."

Kate tore a sheet of paper from the block she kept on the kitchen counter. "Give me the address."

"It's 226 Georgia Avenue. Second floor. The door on the left."

Kate wrote quickly. It wasn't the safest address in town at this time of night, but what choice did she have? It was her fault that LuAnn had been hurt. "Give me fifteen minutes or so. Can you get yourself to the door and unlock it?"

"It's unlocked. He broke in while I was in the shower."

Imagining the terrifying scene, Kate briefly closed her eyes. "I'll be there as fast as I can. Hang in there, girl."

Kate found LuAnn huddled on a sofa, a faded green chenille robe wrapped around her. Her left eye was swollen shut and she pressed a balled-up, bloody handkerchief against her mouth.

Holding back a gasp, Kate ran to her. "LuAnn. Oh, my God."

LuAnn started to cry.

"Shh." Kneeling in front of her, Kate gently pushed back the woman's wet hair. "Can you describe the man? Did he look like the sketch I showed you in the museum the other day?"

LuAnn took the clean tissue Kate handed her and dabbed it against each eye. "Yes. He looked just like it. Right down to the ski mask. I was in the shower, all soaped up, and then, without warning…he was there, yanking me out by the hair and slapping me so hard… I thought he was going to kill me."

Kate took LuAnn's left hand in hers and held it tight. "Did he say anything to you?"

"All he said was that he was going to teach me a lesson." She blew her nose. "I'm scared, Kate. I feel like taking the first bus out of town without even asking where it's going. I would, too, if I didn't have Holly and Brian to hold me back."

"Let's get out of here," Kate said. "Can you walk?"

LuAnn bit her bottom lip and nodded.

It took them a little over ten minutes to reach the Saab in the dimly lit parking lot. Although Kate hadn't seen anything suspicious when she arrived, she half expected someone to jump out of the shadows, as he had in the garage, and kill them both. But the area was deserted, and within moments they were safely locked inside the car and on their way.

Once home, Kate helped LuAnn into the downstairs guest room and waited until she was under the covers before going into the kitchen to call Dr. Russell Blackstone.

Half an hour later, Mitch's friend was ringing her doorbell. A snappy gray suit and an abstract tie in various shades of red and gray had replaced the striped pajamas. His friendly smile disappeared the moment he saw LuAnn.

When he was finished examining her, he joined Kate in the kitchen where she had prepared a pot of coffee.

"I'm going to have to put your friend in the hospital," he said gravely.

"It's that bad?"

"I'm afraid so. She has a concussion, two broken ribs and some pelvic damage. I gave her something for the pain, but I'm worried there might be some internal bleeding, which is why I want her in the hospital. Unfortunately, she's giving me a hard time about that."

"Why?"

"She has no insurance. And no money."

Kate waved an impatient hand. "I'll take care of her bills. Just get her there and back on her feet."

He looked at her with his serious brown eyes. "This one will have to be reported, Kate. Hospital rules."

She nodded. "I understand."

"How are *you* doing?" he asked as he dialed the number of an ambulance service.

"Compared to LuAnn, I could probably start training for the New York marathon."

A smile tugged at his lips. "You two ladies need to find different jobs. The ones you have now have become hazardous to your health."

To Kate's dismay, the leading news in the next morning's issue of the *Washington Chronicle* was a nearly complete account of Kate's conversation with the assistant U.S. attorney regarding her withdrawal from the Lamont murder case. Thankfully, there was no mention of Mitch having spent the night at her house. Povich, for whatever reason, must have had second thoughts about that.

As she read the inflammatory article and Ted Rencheck's statement to the press, "Mrs. Logan finally realized she had no case," Kate threw the paper aside.

"That bastard," she seethed. "Why didn't I realize that

he would turn anything I said into a golden opportunity for himself?''

Kate's anger with the prosecutor was quickly forgotten when Frankie buzzed her to say that Rose was on the line.

"Oh, Kate," Rose said, her voice filled with dismay. "Alison just found out you withdrew from the Lamont case. She read it in the *Chronicle*."

Kate felt herself go numb. "I thought you didn't subscribe to that paper."

"We don't. Douglas hates it, but apparently, Alison asked Joseph to get it for her every day. I didn't find out until just now."

"Did she say anything?"

"I tried to tell her that there were circumstances she just didn't understand," Rose continued, "but she wouldn't listen. She left the dining room without touching her breakfast and went upstairs to her room. I'm not even sure she'll be going to school."

"Keep her there, Rose. I'm on my way."

Alison was standing at her bedroom window, looking out. Her arms were folded and her back rigid.

"Alison."

Her daughter didn't turn around. "Is it true?" Her voice shook as though she was on the verge of tears. "You've dropped the Lamont case?"

"Alison, please turn around and look at me. I can't talk to your back."

"You said you would help Daddy!" she cried, spinning around and giving Kate the full impact of her fury. "You swore you wouldn't let him go to prison. And it was all a lie!"

"It wasn't a lie. It's just that...something happened."

"What? What happened? What could be more important than Daddy?"

"I can't tell you...."

The contempt in Alison's voice was like a slap in the face. "You can't tell me because there's nothing to tell. You're lying again."

For a moment, Kate was tempted to tell her the truth and deal with the consequences later. Then she remembered her assailant's threat and what he had done to Lu-Ann. She couldn't take a chance on his doing the same to Alison. Or worse. If Alison had been older, Kate might have confided in her. But she was just a child. She could let something slip at school. It was just too risky.

"I have to go," Alison said abruptly. "Joseph is waiting for me."

Kate glanced out the window and saw Joseph standing beside the Mercedes station wagon he used to run errands. "I'll come and pick you up at school," Kate said. "We can talk then."

"Don't bother. And don't pretend that you care about me, either."

"Alison, I do care." Tears of frustration pressed behind Kate's lids. "Why else would I be here?"

Her head held high, Alison brushed by Kate and left the room.

From Alison's window, Kate watched her daughter get into the station wagon. How could she have let things get out of hand the way they had? All she had wanted was to keep her daughter safe—and to win her back. Instead, she had managed to drive her further away. Feeling the weight of the world on her shoulders, she walked down the stairs, shook her head at Rose's offer of breakfast and left.

* * *

From Potomac, Kate drove directly to Washington Memorial Hospital where LuAnn had been transferred the night before.

As per Kate's instructions, LuAnn had been given a private room and around-the-clock nursing. She had also requested that no one, with the exception of herself, LuAnn's nurses and doctors, and the police, be allowed to visit her. As Kate stepped into the sterile room, she held back a gasp. The left side of LuAnn's face was bandaged as was the upper part of her torso. She lay very still, her eyes closed.

"How is she doing?" Kate whispered to the nurse as LuAnn began to stir.

Nurse Holt was a no-nonsense woman with a chest like a sumo wrestler, short curly hair and alert brown eyes. "The night nurse told me she had a restless night. Other than that, she seems to be doing fine."

"Is she still bleeding?"

"Some. And that's her fault." She glanced at LuAnn over Kate's shoulder, a stern expression on her face. "She's been told to lie still, but does she listen? No, sirree. She keeps moving around, not giving a rat's behind what anybody says to her."

LuAnn, fully awake now, made a snickering sound. "Don't listen to the warden, Kate. She's spoiling for a fight."

Kate walked over to the bed, glad that her worst fears hadn't been realized. "Well, I see you're in good spirits." She handed LuAnn the huge bouquet of yellow roses she had bought at the flower shop downstairs. "These are for you."

"Oh, Kate, you shouldn't have." LuAnn brought the flowers to her face, but was careful not to inhale too deeply. "You've done so much already—the room, the nurse... It must be costing you a fortune."

Kate pulled up a chair and sat down. "Don't worry about it. It's only money, as they say."

At Kate's remark, LuAnn chuckled, then winced.

"Are you in pain?"

"Only when I laugh. The good nurse here has a pocket full of pretty purple pills, but they make me dopey as hell, so I'm not taking them anymore."

"See what I mean?" the nurse said before burying her nose in a crossword puzzle.

"Maybe you should take the pills, LuAnn. Why suffer if you don't have to?"

"No way. If that bastard decides to come back for me, I want to be ready for him." She made a fist of her right hand, then, pressing her head back against the pillows, she sighed. "Who am I kidding? He'd break my arm before I could even blink." She glanced at Kate. "How does he know you and I talked, Kate? And how did he find me?"

Kate held back a sigh of frustration. "I don't know. Do you think you were followed that day at the museum?"

LuAnn's expression remained worried. "I must have been. I told Brad I thought someone was watching me at the cemetery, but he said I was imagining things." She turned to look at Kate. "What if that man knows where I am and comes back for me?"

"He can't get to you in here, LuAnn. There are always two nurses on duty at the nurses' station and one here in your room. You're safe."

"I'm glad to hear that." Her gaze rested on Kate's left cheek. "I was feeling too lousy last night to ask, but... Is that a bruise I see? Our friend wouldn't have paid you a visit, too, would he?"

"As a matter of fact, he did." Before LuAnn could ask another question, Kate placed a finger on her lips and looked at the nurse, indicating that she didn't want to discuss the incident with a third party in the room.

LuAnn nodded.

"Has anyone been in to see you?" Kate asked.

"One of Washington's finest was here—a detective by the name of Carl Cook."

"What did you tell him?"

LuAnn's voice dropped to a whisper again. "That I fell down a flight of stairs." She looked sheepish. "Pretty unimaginative, huh?"

Kate smiled, remembering she had been ready to use the same excuse. "Did he believe you?"

"Nope. And you know what? I don't give a damn. I'm not about to give the brute who beat me up a reason to come back and teach me another lesson."

Kate laid a hand on LuAnn's arm and squeezed it gently. "You did fine, LuAnn. Just don't worry anymore, okay?"

"Okay."

As LuAnn moved her legs, a copy of *The Washingtonian,* folded to a page, fell to the floor. Kate bent to pick it up. "Can I get you anything else to read?" she asked, putting it back on the bed. "Another magazine? A newspaper?"

"No, thank you." LuAnn glanced above Kate's shoulder. "Nurse Holt," she said sweetly as she held the flowers out to her, "would you be a dear and put these in water for me? And if it's not too much trouble, could I have another cup of tea? With milk this time. Not lemon."

The nurse rolled her eyes toward the ceiling, but stoically did as she was asked. LuAnn waited until they were alone before picking up *The Washingtonian.*

"I wanted you to see this," she said, handing the magazine to Kate. "And tell me if you think it means anything."

"You wanted me to see what?"

"This picture." She pointed at a color photograph. "I know this man. I mean...I've seen him before. At the Europa Hotel. With Maddy Mays."

Openmouthed, Kate stared at a photograph of Douglas.

Twenty-Three

Kate looked from the photograph to LuAnn. "Are you sure?"

"Positive. It was June 16 of this year. I remember the date because it's my birthday. Holly came to Washington that afternoon and took me to the Europa Hotel for high tea. We do that sometimes," she added with a small smile. "You know, play hoity-toity, as Holly calls it."

"And you saw that man there?"

LuAnn nodded. "I was looking for the ladies' room when I heard people coming out of an elevator way in the back. Knowing it was the penthouse elevator, and being a little starstruck, I hid behind a wall and watched to see who it was." She let out a small laugh. "In a classy joint like that, you never know when you're going to run into Paul Newman. Or Harrison Ford."

"But you saw this man instead." Puzzled, Kate gazed down at the photograph again. In anticipation of the Washingtonian of the Year Award presentation in January, the magazine had published the photos of the fifteen winners along with a couple of paragraphs listing their accomplishments. Douglas shared page sixty-nine with a former Redskins running back who had funded a football clinic for underprivileged children.

"Yes," LuAnn said. "He had his arm around Maddy's shoulders. They were laughing."

"Did they see you?"

"They couldn't. I told you I sneaked behind a wall."

"Where did they go?"

"Nowhere. The man kissed Maddy on the cheek and left through a back door that said Garage. The woman went back to the elevator."

"Why didn't you tell me this before?"

She shrugged. "It never occurred to me to mention it. And I wouldn't have if it hadn't been for that magazine photo. Then this morning, I heard one of the doctors say something about Douglas Fairchild being your ex-father-in-law." LuAnn glanced toward the door before asking, "Is that true, Kate?"

"Yes, it's true." Still stunned by what she had heard, Kate returned her gaze to the photograph. What was going on here? Was Maddy Mays a friend of Douglas's? Or one of his clients? If so, why had he never mentioned her to Kate?

Nurse Holt had returned. She carried a glass vase in one hand and a cup of tea in the other. "Here you are, Your Highness," she said, handing the cup to LuAnn.

As the nurse went into the bathroom to fill up the vase, Kate bent over to kiss LuAnn's cheek. "Do me a favor, LuAnn. Don't mention this to anyone."

LuAnn gripped her sheet with both hands. "Why? Is he the one who—"

Kate shook her head. "No, no, of course not, but I need to talk to him. Until then, not a word, okay?"

LuAnn nodded. "Okay."

Moments later, Kate was on her way back to the office. As she drove, she remembered something Eric had said about Douglas once. "With Mother having lost her zest for sex, I wonder where the old man gets it now?"

It had been one of Eric's typically crude remarks, one

she hadn't even dignified with an answer. Now, she couldn't get it out of her mind.

"Douglas? You have a minute?"

Douglas looked up from a stack of papers and smiled as he waved Kate in. "How are you, Kate? Beginning to feel better?"

"Physically, yes."

At the gravity of her tone, a look of surprise flickered across his face. "Something wrong?"

"I'm afraid so." She gazed at him in silence, unable to imagine that the man she had known for almost fifteen years could be a friend of Maddy Mays without her knowing about it.

"Well, Kate?" Douglas said a little impatiently. "What is it?"

She dived right in. "Do you know a woman by the name of Maddy Mays?"

Fear, just a flash of it, was the first expression she saw in Douglas's eyes. As quickly as it had come, however, it was gone. "The hotel owner?" he asked, frowning slightly. "I know *of* her, but I don't know her personally, no."

"You've never been to the Europa Hotel?"

"Of course I've been to the Europa Hotel. Many times. I've been there for drinks, for dinner meetings, even for a luncheon or two."

"That's not what I meant."

His eyes narrowed. "Then what *do* you mean, Kate?"

"Someone I can't name saw your picture in *The Washingtonian* this morning. That same person told me you were at the Europa Hotel on June 16 of this year, but not under the circumstances you just described."

"What circumstances might we be talking about?"

"You and Maddy Mays had just come out of the pent-house elevator. And I must say, for someone who claims not to know her, the two of you were apparently pretty chummy. You had your arm wrapped around her shoulders and you kissed her goodbye."

As Douglas's complexion turned gray, Kate felt a lump form in her throat. She had come here desperately hoping that LuAnn had made a mistake, that it hadn't been Douglas she had seen at the Europa, but someone who only looked like him.

Judging from Douglas's reaction, LuAnn hadn't been mistaken at all.

"What were you doing there, Douglas? And why did you lie about knowing Maddy Mays?"

"Because it's no one's business."

"Wrong, Douglas. It's very much my business. You see, there is a very strong possibility that Maddy Mays was involved in Gina Lamont's murder. And Lilly's." Briefly, she told him about her visit to the Europa a few days ago. "That visit," she continued, "is probably the reason I was attacked the other night."

Douglas's eyes grew wide with shock. "My God, Kate, are you saying that *I'm* involved in those two murders, as well?"

"No, that's not what I'm saying. But I want to know why you lied to me."

"What's with all the questions anyway?" he asked, brushing a stack of phone messages aside with an angry sweep of his hand. "I thought you were no longer work-ing on that case."

"I'm not," she lied, averting her eyes. "I found out about your visit to Maddy Mays by accident. Naturally, I got curious."

"My knowing Maddy has nothing to do with Gina's or

Lilly's murders." There was a new strain in his voice, as if he already knew he had lost the battle.

"Then tell me why you lied to me. If you don't, I'll have to find out myself, even if I have to spend every waking hour searching for the answer."

She waited for him to say something, to fly into a rage, or to give her an explanation that would make her breathe a sigh of relief. But he remained silent, his eyes focused on the wall behind her.

Kate leaned forward. "What is it, Douglas? What's going on between you and Maddy Mays?"

Bringing his gaze back, he stared at her for the longest time, his expression a mixture of anger and despair. Then, unexpectedly, he dropped his head in his hands. "Oh, Kate."

She had never seen him like this, frightened and defeated. Although sorrow was not an emotion one usually felt for a man like Douglas Fairchild, that's exactly what she felt now. "Talk to me, Douglas," she said gently.

At last, he looked up and ran his hands down his face. "If anyone else had stumbled upon the information, I could have lied and gotten away with it. There aren't too many people in this town I can't bluff once I set my mind to it." He gave a short, brittle laugh. "But it had to be you, Kate, the brightest and most stubborn attorney I've ever hired." He shook his head. "Who would have thought that the qualities I admired so much in you would be my downfall."

"My God, Douglas. What have you done?"

He clasped his hands and rested them on his desk. He didn't look at her as he spoke. "Maddy and her husband were my neighbors before they moved to Middleton. After Henry's death, I lost track of her. Then, about a year ago, I was at the Europa having a drink with an old friend when I ran into Maddy. After my friend left, she bought me a drink and we talked about old times. A few minutes later, she suggested we continue our conversation in more comfortable surroundings—her penthouse.''

"Did you go?"

He shook his head. "Not then."

Kate stiffened, unable to believe what Douglas was trying to tell her. "Are you saying that you eventually had an affair with that woman? You cheated on Rose?"

"I didn't mean to," he said in a defeated voice. "But one afternoon last June, Maddy called me here at the office. She said she had a legal problem she needed help with. I half knew she was making an excuse to see me, but…" He shrugged. "I went anyway." He ran his fingers through his hair and held them there. "I don't know what came over me that day. Maybe I was just curious. I knew about her past, her reputation, the men she had known. I guess it all went to my head."

"You mean…you were attracted to her not in spite of what she was, but because of it?"

He nodded. "Something like that. I can't explain it. To you, or to myself. But it was just that one time," he added earnestly. "Nothing like that had ever happened before. Or since. And I never saw Maddy again after that day." His eyes were bright with tears. "You must believe me, Kate. I love Rose with all my heart."

Kate fell back in her chair. "Oh, Douglas."

"I know. It was a despicable thing to do. If I could take that day back, I would, but…"

"Does Rose know?"

He shook his head. "No. I almost told her once, but I couldn't do it. I was afraid of what it would do to her, to our marriage."

Kate knew his fears were justified. Rose adored her

husband. After twenty-two years of marriage, she was as much in love with Douglas now as she had been the day she had married him. She would be devastated if she knew he had betrayed her.

"Please, Kate, don't tell her."

Kate looked at the man in front of her. She felt angry and disappointed. But she wasn't the one whose life would be destroyed by the truth. Rose was.

"I won't," she murmured.

"Thank you."

After a minute of awkward silence, Kate stood up and left.

It was six o'clock by the time Kate got home. She went to her answering machine to see if Mitch had called, but the single red dot was still. There were no messages.

Still shaken from her conversation with Douglas, she poured herself a glass of chilled Chardonnay and walked over to the bay window. She wished Mitch was here. She had become accustomed to his presence, his calm reasoning, the way he made her smile.

When the phone rang, she ran to it, spilling her wine in her haste. "Mitch?"

"No, Kate, this is Russell Blackstone. We're taking LuAnn to surgery."

Kate's glass almost slipped from her hand. "Why? What's wrong with her?"

"She has a ruptured spleen and started hemorrhaging."

"Oh, God."

"Don't panic, Kate. She's a strong woman, and her surgeon is one of the best in his field. I'll be assisting and I promise I'll call you the moment I—"

"Never mind that," Kate interrupted. "I'm coming to the hospital."

* * *

In the waiting room, where she had been pacing for over an hour, Kate watched the double doors that led to the operating room in the hope that Dr. Blackstone would walk through them, the bearer of good news. From time to time, she took another sip of the bitter coffee she kept buying from a nearby vending machine.

This was all her fault. If she hadn't bribed LuAnn into confiding in her, the woman wouldn't be fighting for her life right now.

What if she didn't make it? Kate thought as she glanced at the wall clock for the hundredth time. How would she explain LuAnn's death to her daughter and to her little grandson?

Just before 8:00 p.m., Russell Blackstone, his surgical greens splattered with blood, walked through the swinging doors, saw Kate and hurried toward her.

"We stopped the bleeding," he said, pulling down his mask. "And she's resting comfortably."

"Is she going to be all right?"

"It's too early to say. She lost a lot of blood, but the operation was a success. Now we have to wait. The next twenty-four hours will be crucial."

"When can I see her?"

"Tomorrow." As she started to protest, Dr. Blackstone wrapped an arm around her shoulders and gently led her toward the elevators. "LuAnn needs her sleep. And so do you. You look exhausted."

It took Kate all her willpower not to cry on the way home. She was sick of this case. Everything that could possibly go wrong with it had. Her daughter had turned against her, innocent people were being hurt, and the guilty continued to remain free.

The phone was ringing when she walked into her house.

Praying that nothing had happened to LuAnn in that short period of time, she picked it up. "Hello?"

"Hi, gorgeous," Mitch said in a playful tone. "Have you eaten yet?"

"I'm not hungry."

"Oh, come on. Aren't you the least bit curious about how I made out in Myrtle Beach?"

"Mitch, could we talk about that in the morning?"

The cheerfulness went out of Mitch's voice. "What's wrong?"

"Nothing—"

"Don't give me that. You sound upset. I can't believe I didn't pick it up right away. You haven't been attacked again, have you?"

"No."

"Then what is it?"

"I can't talk about it."

"Put the coffee on," he said in a tone that left no room for discussion. "I'm on my way."

Twenty-Four

Mitch made the trip from Adams Morgan to Cleveland Park in record-breaking time. He brought the Ford to a stop in a squeal of rubber and sprinted to the house.

He didn't breathe a sigh of relief until Kate opened the front door. She was pale and her eyes were red and tearful, but other than that, she was fine.

"Kate, what's wrong?" He gripped her shoulders and held her steady.

When she looked up, her eyes filled with fresh tears. "Someone I care about was badly beaten up last night. And I'm responsible."

Mitch's pressure on her shoulders increased. "Why are you responsible? Who was hurt?" A cold fear gripped him. "Not Alison?"

"No. It's…the woman who told me about Maddy Mays. Someone broke into her apartment last night and nearly killed her. She's in the hospital. She was doing fine until a couple of hours ago. Then Dr. Blackstone called to—"

"How did Russell get involved?"

"I called him. He came to the house to take a look at her. That's when he told me he had to put her in the hospital."

"And now she's worse?"

Kate slowly walked back into the living room, Mitch

behind her. "She started hemorrhaging and had to be rushed to surgery."

"I'll take you there—"

She shook her head. "No, it's all right. I just got back from the hospital. The surgery is over, but I won't be able to see her until tomorrow."

"What's the prognosis?"

"Guarded, for the moment. We'll have to wait until morning to know more." She looked up. "Oh, Mitch, I'm so worried about her."

"You're talking about LuAnn Chester, aren't you?" he asked. "She's the one who told you about Maddy."

Kate hesitated, then realizing there wasn't much point in keeping LuAnn's identity a secret anymore, especially from Mitch, she nodded. "How did you guess?"

"Who else but a hooker would know so much about Maddy?"

Kate wiped away a tear with the back of her hand. "It's all my fault, Mitch. If I hadn't convinced her to talk to me, she wouldn't be in this mess right now."

"The choice was still hers, Kate. You didn't hold a gun to her head."

"No." Her voice had a dry, bitter edge to it. "I just waved a thousand dollars in her face."

This time, the tears came fast and furious. Mitch gathered her in his arms and drew her close. He knew all about guilt, how deeply it could sink its teeth into one's heart. "It's all right, baby. Let it out."

With a sob that went straight to his heart, she gripped his shoulders and buried her face in his chest. He held her as she wept, aware that the tears weren't for LuAnn only. They were the result of two weeks of nerve-racking tension, of worry and of fear. He had no idea how she had lasted this long without breaking, but he was glad she had waited until now. Until he could be with her.

After a few minutes, the sobs began to subside. With more tenderness than he thought himself capable of, he took her chin between two fingers and lifted it gently. "Feeling better?"

A dry sob caught in her throat and she nodded.

"Good." Smiling, he wiped away a tear with his thumb, then, impulsively, he bent down and kissed her.

Her lips were moist and salty. And to his surprise, they parted instantly as if in anticipation of more than a chaste kiss.

Every instinct told him to pull away. He wanted her so badly, he could have taken her right here, right now, and that wouldn't be fair. She was too distraught and much too vulnerable for him to offer anything more than comfort.

But when her fingers dug into his shoulders, pulling him back to her, all thoughts of fair play vanished, replaced by something much more primal. And much more fierce.

He kissed her again, and this time, Kate responded with a passion that was dangerously out of control. Her body, which she had trained to feel nothing for the past year, seemed to shift into overdrive. She knew what she was doing was wrong, and she knew there would be hell to pay later. But for tonight, just tonight, she didn't want to think about consequences.

Impatient for the feel of his skin, she pushed aside his open ski jacket. With trembling fingers, she unbuttoned his shirt and slid one hand through the opening. His chest was hard, broad and somehow, familiar to the touch, as if she had known all along what it would feel like.

"Oh, Kate."

The desire she heard in his voice, along with the wild thumping of his heart beneath her fingers, made her hungry for more. A little astounded at her boldness, she opened the shirt wider and pressed her mouth where her hand had been.

His hands cupped her bottom, drawing her closer. "You're playing a dangerous game, lady."

Using her tongue, she traced a small, wet circle around his nipple. "I'm willing to risk it if you are."

She was aware of being lifted, carried up the stairs, of Mitch's hot breath against her cheek. She guided him to her room but didn't turn on the light. There was no need for it. Moonlight poured in through the window, spotlighting the big four-poster bed.

The moment they fell onto it, heat and madness took over. They tore at each other, pulling off clothes and discarding them while feeding their passion with hot, greedy kisses. His hands were all over her now, cupping her breasts, circling her waist, moving over the swell of her hips.

"You're beautiful, Kate." He bent to take a taut nipple into his mouth. "Beautiful enough to drive a man mad."

She felt an insistent tug, deep inside the core of her. "Don't stop, Mitch."

He stroked a hand along the length of her leg and continued to feast. "Never."

His mouth moved lower, tracing a slow, scorching path from her breast to the inside of her thigh. His tongue was like a flame, hot, flickering, driving her higher. Every cell in her body seemed to come alive, pulsing with need and passion.

When his tongue found her center, a gasp escaped from

her throat. "Come inside me, Mitch." She pulled him to her, parting her legs. "Otherwise…"

He covered her body with his. "Otherwise what?"

"Otherwise I won't be responsible for what will happen."

With one single thrust, he entered her, moving powerfully, filling her as she had never been filled before. Responding at once, Kate locked her thighs around his hips and clasped him deep within her.

They moved together, slowly at first, then with increasing speed until they'd worked each other into a frenzy.

Climax slapped into her like a huge tidal wave, engulfing her, making her gasp for air, dissolving everything around her, everything but this glorious, exhilarating, earth-shattering moment.

He watched her sleep, astounded that after spending half the night making love to her, the mere sight of her could still arouse him.

The memory of last night brought a tightness to his throat. No woman had ever felt so right, no sensations more powerful as those he had experienced in her arms.

It was pointless to deny his true feelings any longer. He had fallen madly, hopelessly, irrevocably in love with Kate Logan.

A bit shaken at the realization, Mitch traced the delicate contour of Kate's cheek. "You're awake," he said as he saw her mouth twitch into a smile.

"Mmm. How could you tell?"

"Male intuition."

A low, sexy laugh escaped from her throat. "That's an oxymoron."

"And that's a sexist thing for a woman of the nineties

to say." He nuzzled her ear, felt her shift in his arms as she turned to face him. "How do you feel?"

She opened her eyes. "Terrific. I didn't know you had such remarkable healing powers."

He kissed the corner of her mouth. "You ain't seen nothin' yet, lady." Then, because he had to know, he asked, "Any regrets?"

She tilted her head back, looking deep into his eyes. "None whatsoever. You?"

"Are you kidding?" The dimple in his cheek deepened. "I've wanted you since the first day I laid eyes on you."

"I don't believe you."

"It's true. Don't tell me you never knew it. I must have been as subtle as a Sherman tank at times."

She laughed, then coiled a long, slender arm around his neck. "Actually, I did notice something, but I thought it was just a bad case of juvenile infatuation. Who would have guessed it was the real thing?"

"And who would have guessed that the cool, sophisticated Kate Logan could harbor such passion?"

Her fingers began to stroke his neck, awakening in him a desire he could no longer conceal.

"What can I say? You bring out the beast in me." A wicked expression gleamed in her eyes. "And in case you've forgotten how wild this beast can get, I'd be glad to refresh your memory...."

An hour later, they sat at the kitchen table, sharing a pot of coffee and Maria's delicious *surullitos,* small, cigar-shaped corn sticks they ate with great gusto. The news from the hospital, which Kate had called earlier, was good. LuAnn had spent a restful night and showed no signs of adverse reaction to the operation.

As Mitch refilled their cups, Kate watched him. Last night had been ruled by lust and passion, by the needs of two people who hadn't given tomorrow a single thought. It was different now. Lust was taking a back seat to a new feeling, one that left her almost as breathless as she had been last night.

"A penny for your thoughts."

She smiled at him over the rim of her cup. "If you must know, I was enjoying a moment of sheer contentment, mixed with just a bit of anxiety."

He put his cup down. "Anxiety about what?"

"Us." She dunked her *surullito* in her coffee. "Where are we going with this relationship, Mitch? How far do we take it?"

"How far do you want to take it?"

"I don't know. There are…factors that should be taken into consideration."

He pushed his cup aside and rested his arms on the table. "You're referring to Alison, aren't you? And the fact that she doesn't like me very much."

Kate moistened her lips. Hated him was more like it. That was the word she had used. "I love her so much, Mitch. I don't want to hurt her, or make her feel threatened in any way."

He took her hand and brought it to his mouth. "Then why don't we just say nothing for the time being?" The calm tone of his voice melted her fears away. "Who knows? If I can clear her father of a murder charge, she might start to look at me under a new—"

"Oh, my God!" Kate exclaimed. "Cora Winslow!" She yanked her hand from his grasp, nearly falling out of her chair. "With all this excitement, I forgot all about your trip to Myrtle Beach." As he just sat there, clearly amused, she shook his arm. "Come on, tell me what happened down there."

He laughed. "All right, all right." He covered the hand that still held his arm with his own. "Cora found the money in a safe-deposit box. One hundred thousand dollars—in cash."

"Oh, my God! Did she tell you that?"

"No, her neighbor did. A nosy, mean-spirited woman who couldn't wait to tell me that Cora had struck it rich."

"How did you get the neighbor to open up to you?"

He threw her a cocky grin. "Jim and I rented a theodolite and pretended to be land surveyors. She got curious and came out to see what we were doing. When I casually mentioned her new next-door neighbor, it was like opening a floodgate."

"How does Cora explain the money?"

"She doesn't. She assumed her husband had saved it over the years and never told her about it. I don't know how she thinks he could have saved a hundred thousand dollars on a janitor's salary, but that's her story and she's sticking to it."

"Maybe she's lying. Maybe she's known all along about her husband's perjury."

Mitch shook his head. "I doubt it. She may not be the brightest woman in the world, but she's not stupid, either. If she knew where the money had come from, she wouldn't be flaunting it the way she is. And she wouldn't be sharing the news with all her neighbors."

Kate tapped a finger against her bottom lip. "You know what this means, don't you?"

He smiled. "That you were right all along and I was just a dumb cop?"

"That, too." She slanted him a teasing glance. "But

more importantly, Cora Winslow's newfound money could be enough to warrant a new trial."

"That could take months, Kate. Maybe years."

"Or, I could produce the real killer so Tony can be set free and Eric cleared."

Fascinated at how quickly and efficiently her mind worked, Mitch gazed at her admiringly. "You have a theory, don't you?"

"As a matter of fact, Detective Calhoon, I do." She pursed her lips, looking smug. "Want to hear it?"

"Go ahead, Counselor. Dazzle me."

Propping both elbows on the table, she rested her chin on her clasped hands. "Lilly Moore was a brilliant law student and a fanatic researcher. In the three years she clerked for us, she had familiarized herself with nearly all of our criminal cases, even those dating back twenty and thirty years. That must be how she found out about the rape of Peggy Bertram."

"It was never a full-fledged case, remember? Sean McKackney was let go two hours after his arrest."

"Nonetheless, since Douglas was Sean's attorney, the case was recorded in Fairchild Baxter's files, and Lilly found it. What was not widely known about Lilly, however, and irrelevant to her murder at the time, was that she was a feminist, born and bred, and a fierce defender of women's rights."

"And you think she took interest in this particular case because of that?"

"That's precisely what I'm thinking. A rich boy rapes a young coed and gets away with it. That's exactly the kind of injustice a girl like Lilly would want to look into. She could have read Sean and Mary Sweeney's statements and decided to take it one step further."

"I'm with you so far. Especially since we already know that she went to the Carteris Agency and from there went to confront Gina Lamont. But what did she expect Gina to do? Surely not confess to perjury."

"Maybe all she wanted at that point was a reaction, something that would justify her suspicions." Kate's tone was mildly teasing. "Much as you did when you went to see Sean McKackney."

"Would she do something like that without telling Douglas?"

"Maybe she was planning to tell him and never got a chance. Gina could have panicked and gone to Maddy, even though she no longer worked for her. Maddy, in turn, could have contacted Senator McKackney, and somehow the two of them plotted to kill Lilly. And then later, Gina."

"But why wait six months to kill Gina? Why not do it when they killed Lilly?"

Kate sighed. "I don't know. I'm afraid that from that point on, my theory gets fuzzy. Maybe Gina wasn't a threat to them at the time. Maybe she became a threat afterward, when she realized how badly she needed money."

Sliding his chair back, Mitch took Kate's hand and pulled her onto his lap. "I must say I'm impressed, Counselor. It's not a bad theory at all."

Kate sighed. "Now if I could only prove it."

"You might be able to," he said, sliding his hand up and down her back. "I've tracked down one of Sean McKackney's former med-school buddies. He might be able to shed some light on Sean's relationship with Mary Sweeney." He kissed the tip of her nose. "If you'll have lunch with me later, I'll tell you what I found out."

Kate's sigh was heavy with regret. "I won't have any time at all today. Douglas scheduled back-to-back meetings that will most likely last through the lunch hour. I also have a deposition and somehow, during the course of the day, I have to find time to go see LuAnn." She nudged closer. "Maybe tonight?"

"I won't be free until late. I promised Father O'Malley I'd have dinner with him and the boys. And since I'm sure they'll challenge me to a basketball game afterward, I won't be finished until ten or so."

Another layer of his life was being revealed. "Who are Father O'Malley and the boys?"

"Tim is the parish priest at St. John's in Adams Morgan. You'll have to meet him sometime. He's quite a guy. Six months ago, he was attacked at gunpoint by two teenagers high on crack. They clobbered him on the head and ran off with the church's petty cash. Rather than press charges, Tim took the boys under his wing, made sure they cleaned up their act and then invited them back into his home. You wouldn't recognize those two kids today. They worship him. They're drug free, go to school, attend church on Sundays and even help raise money for the community. This past summer they washed cars and this winter they'll be shoveling snow."

"And how did *you* meet Father O'Malley?" Her eyes twinkled. "Somehow you don't strike me as the church-going type."

"I'm not, much to Tim's sorrow. I met him when he came to the police department to bail the kids out. We started to talk and realized we lived in the same neighborhood. I'm still not sure how he got me so involved with those boys, though," he added with a laugh. "Tim has a way of making you do things while believing all along that it was your idea in the first place.''

''Hmm, that's good to know.'' Kate ran her finger along the crease in his cheek. ''Why don't you stop by anyway, no matter how late it is? I might just put that new knowledge of mine to good use.''

He grinned. ''You've got yourself a deal.''

Twenty-Five

Although Megan Hollbrook had been in the public eye all her life, she had never felt comfortable around reporters.

The vigil they had kept outside the Hollbrooks' luxurious home in McLean, Virginia, since Gina Lamont's murder was one of the reasons she had chosen to remain secluded during the past two and a half weeks.

But when her mother had reminded her of the UNICEF fund-raising luncheon at the Village Green Country Club on Wednesday, Megan hadn't had the heart to cancel it.

Fortunately for her, the handful of reporters and television crews outside the house that morning hadn't been prepared to see her come barreling down the driveway at forty miles an hour. By the time they realized who was at the wheel of the green Jaguar, Megan was long gone.

It was a different matter when she left the country club at two o'clock that afternoon. As she emerged from a back entrance, the hungry pack was waiting for her, ready to devour.

"Have you heard from your fiancé, Miss Hollbrook?" The question had come from a bespectacled man who had shouldered his way forward.

"How do you feel about his betrayal?" another one shouted.

"Have you forgiven him his indiscretion?"

"Is the wedding still on?"

As cameras flashed and microphones were pushed in her face, Megan did her best to ignore them and hurried across the parking lot, wishing she had let the valet attendant get her car. "I have nothing to say."

"Oh, come on, Miss Hollbrook. Just a sound bite for the six o'clock news." A woman with a microphone in her hand and a cameraman in tow caught up with her. "It isn't too much to ask, is it?"

"Please leave me alone."

An unpleasant-looking little man with a pallid complexion ran ahead of her, then turned around, blocking access to her car. "Eddy Povich with the *Washington Chronicle,* Miss Hollbrook. Do you believe Eric Logan is guilty or innocent?"

"One hundred percent innocent." The words escaped her lips before she could remember her resolution not to say a word.

"Does that mean you still intend to marry him?"

Encouraged by Megan's reply, the herd closed in around her and started shouting more questions at her.

Tears streaming down her face, Megan pushed past them, nearly knocking down the *Chronicle*'s reporter as she yanked the Jaguar door open.

In the safety of her car, she heaved a sigh of relief and quickly pulled out of the parking lot, keeping her head high as a camera continued to record the scene.

Sitting on the bed in his motel room in Goshen, Eric watched the live broadcast of Megan's hasty flight from the Village Green Country Club on CNN.

He had never seen her look so upset. Or so hopelessly lost. But it was the vehement proclaiming of his innocence that shocked him the most. Her support was the last thing he had expected. And the realization that she still loved him after all he had put her through staggered him.

Talk about an awakening.

As Megan's Jaguar disappeared from sight and the broadcaster invited viewers to stay tuned for further developments, Eric, on a wild impulse, picked up the phone and dialed Megan's car phone.

She answered on the third ring, a weak, tentative hello that made him feel like a total heel. "Megan, it's me. Eric."

"*Oh.*"

He heard the screech of tires as the Jaguar came to an abrupt stop. Then he heard her uncontrollable sobs.

"Megan, please, don't cry. I can't stay on the phone long." He glanced toward the parking lot to make sure a fleet of police cars weren't already storming the building. If Megan's car phone was bugged, they would know his location in a matter of minutes and send the local fuzz after him.

"Oh, Eric." After another few seconds, the sobs began to subside. "Is it really you?"

"It's really me. I saw what happened at the country club on television and I had to call. I'm sorry I put you through this hell, Megan. I wish I could take it all back."

"I love you, Eric." The words were whispered, but he heard them loud and clear.

"You do?"

"With all my heart. I don't care about that woman. And I don't believe for one moment that you killed her. I'd stake my life on that."

"Then you must be the only one."

"No, I'm not. Kate doesn't believe it, either."

Eric let out a bitter laugh. "Is that why she dropped me like a hot potato?"

"How did you find out about that?"

"It made the news, kiddo. Kate is almost as famous as I am now."

"We can get you another attorney. But you have to come back, Eric. You have to turn yourself in and tell the police that you didn't do it."

Eric drew a breath and let it out slowly. Megan was a sweet girl, but she could be so damned naive at times. "They'll never believe me, Megan."

"They will if you tell them the truth."

"No way. I'm not coming back until they find the real killer."

"Then tell me where you are. I want to come and see you."

"No way. It's too dangerous." She started to cry again, a pitiful sound that affected him more than he ever would have believed. "Don't cry."

"Then tell me where you are. I want to be with you, even if it's for just a little while. And I won't tell a soul where you are. I swear it."

Eric hesitated. Should he risk it? It would be good to see Megan, to have a conversation with someone who believed in his innocence instead of always talking to himself. Not to mention that his funds were getting dangerously low. If he could think of a safe place to meet her, she might be able to bring him some money. Enough for him to move farther west. Montana maybe. Who the hell would think of looking for him in Montana?

"Eric, did you hear me?"

"Yeah, I heard you." He paused. "Maybe we can work something out, but you'll have to be very careful. If at any time you think you're being followed, you change course, you understand?"

"I understand. Tell me where to go, Eric."

"Wait a minute." Eric reached for the tricounty map on the nightstand. "There's a better way to get here than the one I took." He spread the map out on the bed and prayed he wouldn't regret this. "Take Route 66 west out of D.C., then 81 south. Follow the signs to Goshen, Virginia. At some point, you'll see an old, faded wooden sign with Abbot Farms written on it. The road leading to the property is barely visible under the brush, but it's there. You have to look for it."

"Can my car get through?"

"Yes. There are lots of twists and turns, but it's wide enough for the Jag. At the end of that road and up on a hill, you'll see an old, abandoned farmhouse. I'll be there, waiting for you."

"How long will it take me?"

"About four hours. Maybe less. Oh, and Megan, I'm nearly broke so...could you bring me some money? As much as you can withdraw?"

"All right. I love you, Eric."

"I love you, too." He said it automatically as he had dozens of other times. When he hung up, he was wondering, too late, of course, if he had just made the worst mistake of his life. One that could cost him his freedom.

At seven o'clock that night, Eric finally spotted the headlights of Megan's car coming up the narrow, winding road.

The camping lantern he had brought with him stood on a tree stump, illuminating a twenty-foot radius. He had discovered the abandoned farmhouse a couple of days ago during a foray through the countryside in search of a safe place to hide in case he had to leave the motel in a hurry.

When the Jaguar neared the top of the hill, he picked

up the lantern and swung it slowly back and forth until the car turned the bend and stopped.

In an instant, Megan was out of the car and running toward him, half crying and half laughing. "Oh, Eric." She threw herself into his arms. "You're here. You're really here."

"Didn't you think I would be?"

"I wasn't sure. It took me so long. I got lost and had to backtrack. I must have wasted an entire hour."

"You didn't see anyone following you, did you?"

"Not a soul. In fact, the last couple miles or so, I was the only one on the road." She stopped abruptly and took a step back.

"What's the matter? What's wrong?" he asked.

"You look different." She touched his hair, his beard.

"With my picture in all the papers and on television, I had to do something to fool the cops."

She giggled. "You look like my late grandfather."

"Well, at least I know it works. I passed a cruiser on my way here and the cop behind the wheel didn't even blink."

"I would recognize you anywhere." Taking his face between her hands, she kissed him with a passion he never knew she possessed. Or maybe he had never noticed.

"Did you bring the money?" he asked when she finally let him go.

"Yes. Ten thousand dollars. That's all I could withdraw without having to fill out a lot of forms. Even then, the manager, who knows me, came out when he heard I was taking all that cash out of the bank."

"What did you tell him?"

"That it was a personal matter."

"What if he calls your mother?"

"Let him. I'm not going back anyway."

"What?"

Megan seemed much calmer now, and her face looked more serene than he had seen it in months. "I'm not going back. I'm staying with you."

"Absolutely not."

"You can't make me go back."

He took her hands and held them tight. "Megan, listen to me. I live in a crummy motel. I eat sandwiches from a goddamned vending machine and I spend all my time looking over my shoulder, afraid some cop is going to grab me from behind. When I travel, I'm either on foot or in the back of some foul-smelling pickup truck."

"We have my car now."

"Oh, sure. How long do you think it will be until the cops spot it?"

"We can have it painted. And we can put an old set of license plates on it. I passed a junkyard not too long ago. We could go there late at night and just...take what we need."

Astounded, Eric looked at her. "I can't believe what I'm hearing. Five minutes with me and you're already talking like a fugitive."

"I had several hours to think about it," she said.

He gave a slow, incredulous shake of his head. "How can you choose a lifetime on the run over what you have at home?" Given the same circumstances, Eric wasn't sure what he would have done. No, that wasn't quite true, he thought with a twinge of remorse. He knew exactly what he would have done.

"It's easy." In the glow of the lantern, her eyes looked luminous. "I love you."

"Your mother will never forgive you," Eric insisted.

"I don't give a damn about my mother! This is *my* life. And I'll live it any way I please."

Stunned, Eric took a step back and stared at her intently. He had never seen her like this. This girl, who had taken orders since the day she was born, who only knew how to be sweet and obedient, even submissive at times, was changing before his very eyes.

"Megan, this is crazy. I have nothing to offer you."

"You're all I want. I would rather die than spend another day without you."

"And you're all *I* want." To his amazement, he realized that he truly meant it. It may even have been the one true statement he had ever made in his life. His feelings for Megan were changing, not because of her money, not because of what she could do for him, but because of what she had already done, because of her total faith and her unconditional love.

Taking her in his arms, he kissed her, aware that his whole body was yearning for a lot more than this passionate embrace.

"Come on," he said, afraid he'd ravish her right there. "Let's go before we both freeze to death."

She leaned her head on his shoulder as they made their way toward the car.

Twenty-Six

Nothing Megan had ever imagined about being with a man could have compared to the feeling of total elation she was experiencing now, the morning after making love with Eric.

Memories of last night brought a flush to her cheeks. She had been a little apprehensive at first, afraid of disappointing him. But the moment Eric had begun to undress her, slowly and lovingly, all her fears had melted away.

With an inner chuckle, she remembered the day she had set the boundaries of their relationship, explaining that her virginity was important to her. It was a gift she had chosen to give to only one man—her husband.

Eric had been upset at first, calling her old-fashioned, but eventually, he had understood. Maybe her request was the reason he had never been overly affectionate with her after his first few attempts to seduce her. He didn't want to start something he knew he wouldn't be allowed to finish.

But last night had been different. Last night, up on the hill and then later during the short drive to the motel, she had given him clear signals, a little astounded with herself at this unexpected boldness.

And now here she was, sitting up in bed beside Eric, munching on a cheese Danish and feeling like a newlywed. Soon, however, too soon, the moment would pass and she would have to face reality. And make a tough choice. To keep on running with Eric, or convince him to turn himself in and risk losing him.

Although watching over her shoulder for the rest of her life didn't particularly appeal to her, she had been sincere when she had told him that she would rather die than live without him.

But she knew him too well to believe that sleeping in dingy roadside motels and eating out of vending machines was a viable compromise. Eric had always enjoyed the finer things in life. He loved expensive clothes, fast cars and traveling to exotic places. While he had, at times, experienced a serious shortage of funds, he always found a way to get back on his feet. Simply put, Eric was a man who couldn't envision life without luxuries.

The fact that he seemed content with his present situation didn't fool her one bit. Weighed against the possibility of spending life behind bars, freedom, even under these conditions, was a luxury in its own right. But how would he be six months from now? Or even three?

Miserable, Megan reflected as she watched him finish the last of his Danish. Eventually, the ten thousand dollars she had brought with her would be gone and they would be penniless. He would hate the life he had created for himself, and in time, because she had become a part of it, he would hate her, too.

She couldn't bear to see that happen. Which left them with only one option. To go back and try to prove his innocence.

"I was thinking about something," she began, handing him what was left of her Danish.

He ate the morsel and washed it down with coffee. "What's that?"

She chose her words carefully, knowing he would rebel at the slightest attempt on her part to pressure him. "I haven't had a chance to tell you yet, but Detective Calhoon resigned last week."

He looked surprised. "No kidding? How come?"

"I don't know. Rose, who plays bridge with the wife of the chief of police, tried to find out, but all Mrs. Landers knew was that Mitch Calhoon and Lieutenant Jarvis had an argument, possibly over the Gina Lamont murder, and Calhoon handed in his badge and walked out."

"So what does that mean?"

"Rose and I thought he may have found another suspect—one with possible connections to the police, which would explain why Jarvis was upset."

Eric stood up and walked over to the window. If Megan was right, he thought as he surveyed the parking lot, this was the first break he'd had in the two and a half weeks since the murder, the first indication that someone in the police department didn't believe he had killed Gina.

"So, I was thinking," Megan went on, "that if we could go back and talk to him, ask him who he was investigating before his argument with Jarvis, we could go to an attorney, or even a private detective, and ask him to look into it."

Eric let out a short laugh. "Sure," he said, turning around. "I can see us now, waltzing into a room full of armed cops and sitting down with Calhoon for a cosy chat."

"I had something else in mind."

"Like what?"

"Like calling him and asking him to meet us somewhere."

"What makes you think he'll agree to it? Or that he won't try to ambush us."

Megan sensed that his resistance was fading. "I have a good feeling about Mitch Calhoon. If he gives us his word that he won't try anything like that, I'd believe him. If he doesn't give us his word, we don't go. It's that simple."

Eric attacked a cuticle on his middle finger and began to bite it furiously, something Megan had never seen him do before. She understood his anxiety, for she had a few of her own. What if she was wrong about Mitch Calhoon and he did turn them in? What would happen to Eric then?

An eternity seemed to pass before Eric spoke again. "I'll think about it." He crushed his empty coffee cup and tossed it in the trash basket. "That's all I can promise you right now."

Megan nodded. For the time being, the decision was out of her hands.

"Hey, Dick Tracy! Right here."

At the nickname Abdul and J.J. had given him, Mitch glanced to his right and saw that Abdul, a small but agile sixteen-year-old, was perfectly positioned under the basket and unguarded. Turning away from J.J., Mitch dribbled the ball twice, then threw it to his partner. With the grace of a swan, Abdul caught it in midair and executed a perfect hook shot.

"Great shot, Abdul." Father Timothy O'Malley, dressed in gray sweats, came forward and slapped the youth's hand in a high five.

At thirty-one, the young priest could easily have passed for one of the many kids he counseled each week. He had the same youthful physique and an endless supply of energy that was the envy of everyone in the neighborhood.

"And you," he said, clasping Mitch's shoulder. "You didn't do too bad, either, for an old man."

"Yeah." J.J., who had teamed with Father O'Malley, winked at Tim as he swept his jacket from the gleaming gymnasium floor and tossed it over his shoulder. "We even heard some bones crack a few times, didn't we, Padre?"

Tim laughed. "Now that you mention it..."

Mitch bent to fix an untied sneaker. "You know what you two are? Sore losers. But that's all right. Any time you want a rematch, Abdul and I will be glad to oblige." He straightened and wrapped his arm around the youth's shoulders. "And this time, we'll *really* kick butt. Right now, however, this old man is beat."

Not to mention, he thought, with a spring to his walk as they started to leave the indoor basketball court, that he was aching to have Kate in his arms again. Maybe that was the reason he had played with such enthusiasm tonight. He had been eager to finish the game early.

Standing outside on the sidewalk beside Tim, he watched as the two boys waved and walked away.

"You've done wonders with those two," Tim said. "When I think how hopeless they both seemed six months ago, I swear the change in them is nothing short of a miracle."

"The miracle was all your doing, Tim. You gave them hope and a friend they could come to in times of need."

"But you're the one who provided the money to build this gymnasium and got them interested in basketball. It may not sound like much to you, but it sure made a big difference in their lives. And it made my work a lot easier." He watched Abdul disappear inside a doorway. "All the kids in this neighborhood are grateful for what you've done, but those two would walk through fire for you, Mitch."

"And I'd do the same for them." He hoped his eagerness to call it a night wasn't too obvious. "But at the moment, all I want to do is take a shower and go to bed."

"Kind of early for you, isn't it? How about a beer?"

"Maybe another time."

"All right. Good night, then, Mitch. And thanks for the game. Next time, give us a break and let us win, huh?"

Mitch laughed. "I'll think about it. Good night, Tim."

As Father O'Malley started walking toward the rectory, Mitch headed for his town house only a block away. Mrs. Bonfield's beagle was already barking, prompting an instant response from another dog down the street.

"It's okay, Bronco," Mitch called out, wondering for the hundredth time what had possessed his neighbor to give that name to such a small, harmless dog. "It's just me."

The beagle answered by barking even more furiously. "Fine," Mitch mumbled as he fished in his jeans pocket for his key. "Blow out your vocal chords. See if I care."

As he reached his house, he realized that the front-porch bulb was out, something he hadn't noticed earlier. There was no time to replace it now. He'd have to do it tomorrow. Using the faint glow from Mrs. Bonfield's light, he inserted the key into the lock and pushed the door open.

He was inside his foyer and about to flip on the lights when he heard a noise behind him. He recognized it instantly. It was the unmistakable click of a switchblade being released.

Not taking time to think, he spun around. Framed in the dark doorway was the bulky figure of a man. As the intruder raised his arm and prepared to leap, Mitch caught the glint of a blade.

This time, the mysterious attacker hadn't come to frighten, or to threaten.

He had come to kill.

Mitch reacted with the speed of lightning. Keeping his leg rigid as a board, he kicked, knocking the knife from the man's hand. Then he kicked again, this time in the stomach and with enough force to send most men to their knees.

To Mitch's surprise, the man stumbled but didn't fall. With his arms hanging at his sides like an ape, he lunged at Mitch, coming in low and wrapping his arms around Mitch's midsection. They went down together in a tangle of limbs and curses. Under their weight, a small table crashed and broke into a dozen pieces.

Mitch was the first one up. Grateful for the advantage, he tried to catch his breath and instantly regretted it. Quick as a whip, the man scrambled to his feet and lunged at Mitch again, slamming him against the wall. Mitch was about to deliver a blow to the solar plexus when he heard voices coming from the doorway.

"Hey, Dick Tracy," Abdul called out, "what's going on in there?"

Before Mitch could shout a warning, Abdul and J.J. had sized up the situation and rushed Mitch's attacker in a blind-side tackle that brought a foul curse from the man's mouth. But the boys, although quick and tough, were no match for the intruder's brute strength. As they made contact, he grabbed them by the seat of their pants and threw them in Mitch's path.

As all three fell to the ground, the man sprang toward the door and disappeared. By the time Mitch had untangled himself and run outside, the rear lights of a car he couldn't identify were disappearing around the corner. A pursuit would have been pointless. In seconds, the car would be lost in the downtown traffic.

Mitch hit the trunk of an oak tree with his fist, cursing himself for not reacting fast enough. "Shit."

In a moment, Abdul was by his side, rubbing his head. "Who the hell was that dude?" he asked, squinting toward the street.

"I wish I knew," Mitch mumbled. He glanced at J.J. who had come to join them. "Are you all right?" He looked from one boy to the other. "Both of you?"

The two teenagers nodded. "I heard some serious pounding in there, and I knew right away you was in trouble, man." Abdul's streetwise talk always seemed to resurface when Father O'Malley wasn't around. "Me and J.J., we tried to deck him, but he was too damned strong. Like he was made of solid rock or somethin'."

"You did fine." Mitch rubbed his stomach where the attacker had rammed his head. Solid rock was exactly what it had felt like. "One more second and I would have been chopped liver, so I'd say you came just in the nick of time." It wasn't quite true, but he didn't want Abdul and J.J. to think they had let him down.

"Where was your gun?" Abdul asked.

"I forgot it." He didn't tell them he was no longer permitted to carry a gun, not even his own .38 revolver, which he kept in a bedroom drawer. "What were you guys doing here anyway? I thought you went home."

Abdul pointed toward the front step where he had dropped a dark blue canvas bag. "You forgot your bag at the gym. I found it when I went back for my ball."

J.J. looked up and down the street as if he expected to have another chance at the man. "What that dude want with you anyway?"

"Offhand," Mitch said, "I'd say he came to kill me."

Tom Spivak, who had been on duty when Mitch's call had come in, stood in his friend's living room. On the coffee table, loosely wrapped in a handkerchief, was the switchblade Mitch had knocked from his assailant's hand. Next to it was a black glove that must have come off during the struggle. Abdul had found it in the foyer among the table debris.

Tom studied the black-handled knife. "This baby could have done some damage."

"You're telling me." Mitch shook his head, still astounded that he had come out of the scuffle without a scratch. "The bastard must have unscrewed the lightbulb and hid in the bushes. That's why the dog kept barking."

Tom made an entry in his book. "What else can you tell me about the man apart from the fact that he was big, masked and mean?"

Despite the close call, Mitch's mouth twitched in a small smile. "It does sound like something out of a comic strip, doesn't it?" Serious again, he added, "I don't know who the guy is, but I'm sure he's the one who killed Lilly Moore. And possibly Gina Lamont and Chuck Winslow."

Tom glanced at the knife again, then the glove. "And you think Senator McKackney sent him to kill you?"

"After McKackney's visit to the gym the other morning and his not too subtle threat, I have no doubt whatsoever that he wants me out of the way."

"Was anyone on the track besides the two of you?"

Mitch shook his head. "The place doesn't start filling up until about six. He must have known that or he would have found another way of approaching me." Restless, Mitch stood up and walked over to the window. "Where the hell is that ident team?"

"Relax, will you? They'll be here." Using the end of his pen, Tom lifted the glove off the table. "I don't know about the knife, but I bet we can lift a couple of decent prints from the inside of that glove.''

Mitch didn't have a chance to agree. Roy Johnson's car had just pulled up in front of his town house.

While the ident team dusted the entire foyer, Mitch called Kate.

"I'm not going to be able to come after all," he said when she answered the phone. Trying to underplay the incident, he told her about his encounter with the masked man.

Kate's gasp was clearly audible. "Mitch, you could have been killed!"

"But I wasn't, so don't lose any sleep over it, okay? What matters now is the man's ID. Once we know who he is, the rest will fall into place. Maybe.''

"Why did he come after you, Mitch? Did Sean McKackney's former classmate tell you anything important?"

"Not a word. The guy suddenly came down with an acute case of memory loss. But he must have been scared enough to call McKackney right after I left and tell him I was snooping around.''

"We've got to go to the U.S. attorney with what we know, Mitch. I can't have you risking your life again. The next time you might not be so lucky.''

Kate's voice betrayed her fears, and he couldn't blame her. If he wasn't so keyed up about this incident, he'd be worried, too. "Let's wait and see what the crime lab comes up with. If we can trace the man to McKackney, we've got a case. Otherwise, any move on our part would be premature.'' Mitch glanced at Roy, who was signaling he was finished. "I've got to go, babe. We'll talk in the morning, okay? I should know something by then.''

"Mitch, wait! I almost forgot. Rose called me earlier. Megan Hollbrook is missing."

"*What?*"

"The manager of the bank where Megan and Abigail do business called to say that Megan had stopped by to withdraw ten thousand dollars from her account—in cash. Abigail is beside herself. She and Douglas are certain Megan heard from Eric and went to join him. For once I agree with them."

Mitch smiled. As much as he disliked Eric for his weaknesses, he was glad Megan was with him. Being on the run, even for a short time, was a lot more pleasant with the woman you loved lying next to you at night.

Twenty-Seven

At eleven o'clock the following morning, Tom called Mitch with the crime-lab results.

"There were only a few useless smudges on the knife," he said, "but Roy picked up a couple of good prints from the glove and from the floor in your foyer."

"You got an ID on the guy?"

"You bet. His name is Bruno Yager. Age fifty-three, six foot four, two hundred and sixty pounds. Profession—maintenance man and bouncer. He used to work for Dom Costa, a Manhattan drug kingpin, and his last known address was 116th Street in New York City. He lived there from 1970 to 1976."

Maddy Mays was from New York City. She, too, had lived there until 1976. What an interesting coincidence.

"Has he done time?"

"Twice. Once for auto theft in 1962 and again in 1965 when he was convicted of assault with a deadly weapon. The weapon, by the way, was a switchblade."

"So where is this sweet prince now?"

"That's a mystery. He left New York and has managed to keep his nose clean ever since."

"Have you checked with the Veterans Administration? He might be receiving some kind of pension."

"I just talked to someone there. Yager never served.

I'm on my way to the DMV now. They should have something.''

Tom called back an hour later. "Bad news, Mitch. There's no one by the name of Bruno Yager registered with the DMV. Maybe he's using an assumed name. It wouldn't be hard to do for a guy with his connections.''

"Great.''

"We'll get him, Mitch. Just be patient. And watch your back.''

After Mitch hung up, he just stood there, staring at the phone. It was obvious, at least to him, that Bruno Yager either worked for McKackney or for Maddy Mays. But unless probable cause could be shown, no judge in his right mind would issue a search warrant.

On the other hand, there was no reason why he couldn't go to the Europa Hotel and do a little searching of his own. Discreetly, of course. The prospect brought a rush of adrenaline—one he hadn't felt in a long time.

In a much better mood now, he threw on his coat, and in another few minutes was on his way to the Europa Hotel.

Alison was bored. Ever since this new safety rule had been implemented a few days ago, she couldn't do anything fun. She couldn't take the bus to school, walk to town with her friends, or even go to a football game at Pine Hill High. All she was permitted to do, outside of regular school hours, was go to her friend Melissa's house and attend rehearsals for her play. And wherever she went, Joseph had to drive her. She was beginning to feel like Miss Daisy.

And the worst part was that no one would tell her why she suddenly had to follow these stupid rules. Her mother had said something about the press being more aggressive, but she hadn't seen a single reporter in days. Which meant her mother had lied. And so had her grandparents.

What was the matter with all of them? Didn't they think she was old enough to know what was going on? Probably not. One of her greatest peeves these days was that everybody treated her like a baby.

Well, she had news for them. She was thirteen years old. And she understood a lot more than people gave her credit for.

At the bottom of the long, curving staircase, she stopped and looked around her, trying to decide what to do with the rest of the afternoon. Melissa, whose father was an attaché at the Canadian Embassy, was attending a birthday party for the ambassador's daughter. Grandpa was at the office, and Grandma was having lunch with Mom.

Except for the slow, rhythmic ticktock of the antique clock in the foyer, the house was totally silent. Alison heaved a deep sigh. An entire afternoon and nothing to do.

Her arms behind her back, she started to walk down the hall. Several doors opened into elegant rooms. The first was the drawing room where her grandparents did most of their entertaining. Next to it was a music room no one ever used, and next to that was her grandfather's study, a grand, wood-paneled, book-filled room that smelled of lemon polish, old leather and rich pipe tobacco.

It was one of Alison's favorite rooms. Years ago, when she was small, she had spent hours in here, doing her homework or reading while her grandfather worked. Sometimes, he even let her play with his Chinese coffer, an antique cabinet full of small, hidden compartments that could slide open at the touch of a finger or remain stubbornly shut for hours.

Casting a furtive glance in both directions, Alison opened the study door. With the exception of the servants, no one was allowed in this room unless her grandfather was here, but surely he wouldn't mind if she went in for just a minute.

The handsome black-and-gold cabinet stood against the far wall. She walked over to it, wondering if she still knew how to open those secret drawers.

Well, there was only one way to find out. Flexing her fingers, she studied the four intricately carved panels, trying to remember where the pressure points were. Then, splaying both hands over the first square, she moved her fingers in a rotating motion, applying pressure every now and then. Nothing happened.

Moving her hands to the second square, she tried again and then again. Frustrated, she moved to the third panel, sliding her fingers in an up-and-down motion instead.

A small cry of surprise escaped her mouth. The panel had swung open, revealing more than a dozen compartments. The first three were empty, but the fourth one contained a small golden box, the kind that might hold an expensive piece of jewelry. Her heart beating a little faster now, Alison took the box out and flipped the lid open.

"Oh." Nestled into folds of shiny yellow satin was a small gold key.

Keys had been Alison's passion once. She had collected them for years, especially those that time and exposure had badly rusted. Fascinated, she would study them, wondering who they had belonged to, what secret door they might unlock. When she felt truly adventurous, she would even try to match some of the keys in her collection to various doors. She had been successful only once, when she had unlocked an old trunk in her grandfather's attic. Oh, the fun she had had that day.

Taking the gold key out of the box, she looked at it closely. There was an engraving on it: PH 4 Europa Hotel.

She knew the Europa Hotel well. It was on Connecticut Avenue, on the way to Union Station where her mother sometimes took her shopping.

But what was her grandfather doing with this key? She had never heard him mention that hotel. "PH 4," she said out loud. PH as in penthouse? Did he have a permanent suite there? No, that couldn't be. He would have mentioned it.

Her curiosity fully aroused now, Alison slid the key into her pocket. The excitement she had experienced as a child filled her again, as powerful as she remembered. She would go to the hotel and solve the mystery. She couldn't think of a better way to salvage a boring afternoon.

After putting the empty box back in the drawer, she closed the panel, making a mental note of the area she would have to press in order to reopen it later.

Then, hurrying out of the room, she went to look for Joseph.

Bistro Lepic on Wisconsin Avenue, where Kate and Rose had decided to meet for lunch today, was already packed when the two women arrived at twelve-thirty.

"Is there any news from Megan?" Kate asked after they were seated.

Rose nodded. "Abigail called me a few minutes before I left. She and Douglas were right after all. Megan is with Eric. She called Abigail this morning, but was very brief. She told her mother not to worry, that she was fine and would call again, although she didn't say when. Then she hung up."

A waiter came to take their orders and disappeared after the two women had each ordered the smoked-trout salad.

Kate smiled. "Abigail must be fit to be tied."

"She's furious. The first thing she wanted to do was contact the police so they could monitor her phone in case Megan called again. It took me nearly half an hour to convince her that if she tried to trap Eric through her daughter, Megan would never forgive her."

"I'm surprised she listened to you at all." Kate took a sip of the water a waiter had just poured. "Abigail doesn't heed advice well, no matter how wise it may be."

Rose gazed fondly at her former daughter-in-law. "You don't like her very much, do you?"

"What is there to like? The woman is pretentious, bossy and boring. And the way she's treated Megan since her engagement to Eric is nothing short of deplorable. Why can't she accept the fact that the girl adores him and leave it at that?"

"Because she's a stubborn old fool." Unfolding her napkin, Rose added, "Speaking of mother-daughter relationships, I have some encouraging news about Alison."

Instantly alert, Kate put her glass down. Since that article in the *Chronicle* last week, the relationship between her and Alison was more strained than ever. Refusing to give up on the child, Kate continued her early-morning visits to Potomac, bringing little peace offerings each time. "What kind of news?"

"I think her rebellious stage may be over sooner than we thought."

"Why are you saying that?"

"The girl is bored out of her mind. She doesn't have enough to do in that big house to keep her occupied. Yesterday afternoon, I found her in the kitchen playing checkers with Joseph. Lord knows what she's going to do today with only half a day of school."

"She'll probably go to Melissa's house."

"She can't. Melissa is attending the ambassador's daughter's birthday party."

Kate's heart went out to her daughter. The month of December had always held a special meaning for Alison. She liked to shop for Christmas presents, bake cookies with Kate and listen to Christmas music. Even last year, when Alison was so upset with the move from Potomac to Cleveland Park, she had cheered up considerably at the prospect of having their very own Christmas tree.

"Maybe I should go pick her up after lunch and take her shopping," Kate said, moving aside as the waiter brought their food. "I know she's still angry with me, but she won't be able to turn down a Christmas shopping spree. Who knows? I might even talk her into moving back home for the holidays."

Rose wrinkled her nose. "I'm not sure I would do that if I were you. She's just now beginning to realize that living with us isn't nearly as much fun as she had thought it would be. If you give her a little more time, I have a feeling that she's going to tell you she wants to move back. But it has to be her own decision, Kate. Otherwise, it won't work."

Kate smiled as she speared a flaky chunk of trout. "Where did you inherit all that wisdom, Rose? I've been a mother for over thirteen years and I still don't have a clue how to handle my daughter."

Rose chuckled. "None of us do. When I was raising Eric, there were times when I was just as lost as you are. We do the best we can until we get it right, I guess."

Her eyes had clouded. Knowing how deeply she loved her son, Kate reached across the table to touch Rose's hand. "Don't worry too much about Eric, Rose. He'll be all right. He's always been able to take care of himself."

"Only because he had people like you and me to always bail him out. But now that he's alone…'' With the tip of her middle finger, she caught a tear at the corner of her eye.

"He's not alone anymore,'' Kate reminded her. "He has Megan now. She's a gentle, sensible young woman who might just have enough stabilizing influence on him to make him do the right thing.''

"I hope so.'' Rose's expression relaxed a little. "Thanks for listening to the ramblings of an old woman, Kate. You have no idea how good it feels to confide in someone who understands.''

"Oh, stop it. You're not old and you're not rambling. You're just another mother worrying about her child. What could be more natural than that?''

"It's very kind of you to say that, dear, but I shouldn't burden you with my problems. You have enough of your own.''

"And when I do, I run to you or to Douglas for advice.'' Knowing how self-absorbed Douglas could be at times, she asked, "Have you tried to talk to Douglas about your feelings, Rose? I know he and Eric don't get along, but if he was aware of how much this has affected you, he'd want to know.''

Rose's mood shifted and she let out a small sigh as she stared down at her plate. "I did try to talk to him, but Douglas hasn't been himself lately. I don't know if this situation with Eric has disturbed him more than I realized, or if it's something else, but whenever I broach the subject, he just blows up.''

"That doesn't sound like Douglas.''

"I know.'' She looked up. "In fact, I was going to talk to you about it. Maybe it's not Eric that has him on edge but something at the office?''

Kate shook her head. "I would know about it.'' Unless,

Kate reflected, he was worried about Sander McKackney. Could he suspect that his old friend had lied to him and feel caught between his loyalty to Sander and his moral duties as an officer of the court? "I'm sure Douglas is suffering from stress as we all are," Kate said, not wanting to worry Rose further. "And what better remedy for such an ailment than a vacation? Especially since yours was cut short recently."

Rose didn't look thrilled at the prospect. "The weather in Bermuda right now is almost as bad as it is here."

"Then go somewhere else. The Orient perhaps. Or Europe. I hear Paris is lovely at this time of year. The *grands boulevards* are all decorated for Christmas, the shop windows brimming with expensive merchandise. Just imagine yourself sipping champagne at La Tour D'Argent and then strolling along the Seine under the moonlight." Her lips twitched in a wry smile. "There is nothing better than moonlight and champagne to put a little fire back into a relationship."

To her surprise, Rose lowered her gaze. "Believe me, Kate, in our case, moonlight and champagne would be a total waste of time."

"Rose, how can you say that? Where is your sense of adventure? Your sense of romance?"

"Oh, my dear." A sad smile briefly twisted the corners of Rose's mouth. "I'm afraid I lost it a long time ago."

Kate blinked in surprise. She had always thought of Douglas and Rose as the perfect couple. Douglas's confession regarding his one-afternoon fling with Maddy Mays hadn't changed that opinion. "But why?" she asked incredulously. "Don't you love him anymore?"

"Oh, of course I do. It's just that..." She took a deep breath as if the words she was about to say weighed heavily on her heart. "Douglas and I no longer have sexual relations."

Kate lowered her fork as she once again recalled Eric's remark about his parents' lack of intimacy. He'd been right after all. "I'm sorry," she said.

Rose's eyes filled with tears. "He would kill me if he knew I discussed this with you, so please, swear you'll never mention it to anyone."

"You know I won't."

Rose glanced around her before leaning forward. "Three years ago, Douglas was diagnosed with prostate cancer and had to be operated on."

Kate sat stock-still. "But that can't be. I would have known. He would have told me—"

"He didn't want anyone to know. That's why he had the procedure done in Vail during our winter vacation."

"Oh, Rose." The thought that her friend had gone through such an ordeal alone filled Kate with sadness. "Why didn't you call me? You know I would have come to stay with you."

"You don't know how much I wanted to do that. But Douglas wouldn't let me. To him, prostate surgery was something too shameful and embarrassing to share with anyone."

Sensing that Rose wasn't finished, Kate waited.

"At the time," Rose continued, "the doctors assured us there wouldn't be any complications. Douglas was a healthy man and there was no reason why his sexual functions couldn't return to normal within a few months. But they never did." Her voice dropped. "He's been impotent ever since."

"*What?*" Kate felt as though she had been sucker punched.

"It's true. We haven't been able to have any kind of sexual relations since the operation three years ago."

Kate's appetite vanished. *Douglas impotent.* How could that be when he had admitted to having had sex with Maddy Mays only last June?

"Are you sure that he really is impotent, Rose?" she asked, anxious to clear the doubts that were forming in her mind. "I mean…you consulted a physician? Together?"

"We consulted half a dozen of them. Some prescribed drugs, a few suggested alternatives Douglas wouldn't even begin to consider, and others simply said that time would eventually remedy the problem. It didn't. A year ago, he went through another series of tests. This time, the diagnosis was definite. Douglas's sexual functions would not return. He was devastated."

Afraid the expression on her face would give her away, Kate took another sip of water. Douglas had lied to her. He hadn't had sex with Maddy on that June afternoon. Or with anyone else. He *couldn't* have.

So what had he been doing at the Europa Hotel with a woman suspected of running a call-girl ring? And why had he lied to her?

"What's the matter?" Rose was suddenly attentive. "You're white as a ghost. Oh, God, I've upset you, haven't I?"

Kate shook her head. "That's not it." She picked up her purse from the floor where she had set it earlier and opened it. "I just remembered a terribly important appointment."

"An appointment?" Rose's eyes widened. "Now?"

"It's about the Fox case," she improvised as she rose from the table. "I was supposed to meet with the U.S. attorney at one o'clock." Not wanting to waste time charging the meal to her credit card, Kate took forty dollars from her wallet and dropped the bills on the table. "I feel awful about this, Rose. I promise I'll make it up to you another time."

"Oh, you don't have to do that." Rose extended her cheek as Kate bent to kiss her. "I know how demanding your job can be, so go on, dear." She smiled. "Do what you have to do and don't worry about me. I'll be just fine."

"Thank you." Kate hurried out of the restaurant. Once outside, she started running.

Twenty-Eight

As always at this time of year, the Europa was busy, which made Mitch's job of exploring the hotel in search of Bruno Yager relatively easy if not as rewarding as he had hoped.

So far, his efforts, which had been confined to the underground engineering control room, hadn't produced anything. The four men who worked the day shift had never heard of Bruno Yager. Either they had been warned to keep their mouths shut or Mitch had been wrong in assuming that Bruno worked at the Europa.

He was about to take the elevator back to the lobby when a heavyset man in a cook's uniform came walking out pushing a cart. A quick glance at the cart, which was loaded with thick sandwiches, coleslaw, potato salad and nachos, told Mitch the man was delivering lunch.

"That's quite a feast you've got there," he said affably. "Feeding time at the zoo?"

The man laughed. "You wonder where they put it, don't you?"

Casually, Mitch positioned himself in front of the cart, making it impossible for the man to go any farther. "You work in the kitchen?"

"Yup. I cook the food we serve in the pub." He looked up. "What about you? You're new here, ain't you?"

"I don't work here." Hands in his pocket, Mitch tried

to look disappointed. "As a matter of fact, I stopped by to visit an old buddy of mine. I thought he told me he worked in maintenance, but—" with a toss of his head, he motioned toward the door behind him "—no one in there seems to know him."

The man looked at him with renewed interest. "Maybe I know him. What's his name?"

"Bruno. Bruno Yager."

"I know a Bruno, but his name ain't Yager. It's Ramsey."

Ramsey. No wonder there had been no record of him. "It could be him," Mitch said with a laugh. "He always said he'd change his name one of these days. Big guy, right?" he asked, holding his hand above his head. "With a low, raspy voice?"

"That's him all right." The man pointed a thumb toward the ceiling. "He works up in the laundry room."

"Where's that?"

"On the main floor, behind the kitchen."

Mitch grinned. "Thanks, pal. I think I'll go on up and surprise him."

He would have loved to do just that, to see the look on Bruno's face as he walked into the laundry room. But without a badge, there was nothing he could do to force him to talk. He might even scare him into taking off.

He had accomplished what he had come to do—verify that Yager worked here. All he had to do now was go back to the station, tell Tom where he could find Bruno and let him make the arrest.

It almost sounded too easy.

Sitting next to Joseph in the station wagon, Alison could barely contain her excitement. Before leaving home, she had ripped the metrorail map from the phone book and highlighted her route from Melissa's house on D Street to the Europa Hotel on Connecticut Avenue. She would take the metro at Foggy Bottom, get off at Farragut North and walk the short distance to the Europa.

It was one o'clock when Joseph, a silver-haired man with impeccable manners and a British accent, pulled up in front of the Franklins' home. "I'll pick you up at three," he said as Alison jumped out of the station wagon.

"Thanks, Joseph." Two hours would give her plenty of time to go to the hotel, solve the golden-key mystery and then return here.

Knowing Joseph wouldn't leave until she was safely inside Melissa's house, she ran up to the front door and rang the bell, waiting patiently until Zina, the Franklins' Pakistani maid opened the door and let her in.

"Melissa not here," Zina said in her thick accent. "She at ambassador daughter party."

Hoping the young woman wouldn't see through her act, Alison slapped her forehead as if she had just remembered. "How stupid of me. I completely forgot." She gave Zina her sweetest smile. "Oh, well, I guess I came for nothing." She turned to leave.

"One moment!" Zina, who clearly had her orders regarding Alison's comings and goings, looked worried. "Where Joseph?"

"He's parked down the road. I wasn't going to stay long, so he said he'd wait for me." God, her heart was beating so fast from all the lies, she was starting to get light-headed.

She opened the door, but Zina stayed right behind her. "I no see him."

"Hc's over there." Alison pointed toward the end of the street. "In front of that UPS van." She pulled her collar up. "I have to run. He doesn't like it when I stand in the street too long."

Before the maid had a chance to voice another protest, Alison was running down the steps to the street. Soon, she was out of sight and able to breathe a sigh of relief.

Walking briskly, she reached the metro station within a few minutes. Because she and her mother were no strangers to public transportation, it only took her a few moments to get herself oriented. She reached the lower platform just as her train was pulling in.

"The hell with a warrant!" Mitch shouted as he and Lieutenant Jarvis faced each other again. "There's no time for that. The guy tried to kill me last night. We've got his fingerprints all over my foyer, and we know he's a convicted criminal. That's probable cause, and you damn well know it."

"Now calm down, will you?" Jarvis said with uncharacteristic diplomacy. "Arresting this guy without a warrant would be a stupid thing to do. Maddy Mays is a powerful, well-connected woman in this town, Mitch. We barge into her hotel without the proper documents and I guarantee you that within the hour, this Bruno Yager or Ramsey or whatever his name is, will be out on bail." His smile was almost friendly. "So calm down, okay? As soon as Spivak comes back, I'll send him to get a warrant. Yager will be behind bars before the next shift. How's that?"

"Where is Tom now?"

"I sent him to Lafayette Park to investigate a shooting."

"Couldn't you have sent Benedetti? Or Haskell?"

At any other time, a remark like that would have earned Mitch a severe reprimand. Today, Jarvis merely shook his head. "They're both out. In case you haven't noticed, we're shorthanded. We always are at this time of year."

Mitch's hands were tied. If Jarvis had just plain refused to arrest Bruno, he would have had a legitimate reason to go over his head. But the lieutenant's argument was justified. If they arrested Bruno without a warrant, Maddy Mays could, and would, have him out on bail faster than he could scream "unlawful arrest." And once he was out on bail, they'd never find him.

"Go on home, Mitch," his former superior suggested with a concern that was definitely not the man's style. "We'll let you know as soon as something breaks."

"If it's all the same to you," Mitch said, "I'll wait out in the squad room."

As Kate walked briskly down the hall of Fairchild Baxter, the words she had repeated over and over during the short ride from the restaurant kept echoing inside her head. *Douglas had lied to her.* And then the question she couldn't answer, didn't want to answer. *Why?*

Douglas's secretary was at his desk, stacking several files into a neat pile. "Where is he?" Kate asked as she barged into his office.

Monica had been working with attorneys long enough not to let anything, or anyone, faze her. She gave Kate a pleasant smile. "Mr. Fairchild is meeting with a client in Alexandria, Mrs. Logan. He said he'd be back by three."

"If he calls in before that, tell him I need to talk to him, will you, Monica? It's urgent."

"Surely."

Back in her office, Kate sank into her chair and dialed Mitch's house. "Damn," she muttered as his machine came on.

"Did you say something, Boss?" Frankie stood at the door, an inquisitive expression in her eyes.

"I was just mumbling to myself." She glanced at her watch. "Mitch didn't call while I was at lunch, did he?"

"No. But Rencheck did. He's got the evidence report you requested on the Fox case. You can pick it up any time after nine o'clock tomorrow morning."

Kate nodded absently. "Take care of it for me, will you, Frankie?"

"Sure, Boss." Still concerned, Frankie came farther into the room. "LuAnn Chester also called, but she didn't leave a message."

LuAnn. She had forgotten all about her promise to go see her after lunch. "Thanks, Frankie. I'll call her right now."

"Kate…"

Feeling Frankie's eyes riveted on her, Kate looked up. "Yes, what is it?"

"About LuAnn. I thought she sounded strange, almost groggy. And there were some odd noises in the background."

Kate busied herself with the Fox case file. "Odd noises?"

"Yes. Announcements through a loudspeaker, doctors being paged." She closed the door and leaned against it, hands behind her back. "Is LuAnn in the hospital, Kate? Did something happen to her?"

Resting her elbows on the desk, Kate closed her eyes and rubbed her throbbing temples. She was tired of lying, tired of playing games, tired of all the secrecy. "Yes," she said without looking up, "LuAnn is in the hospital."

Frankie pulled up a chair and sat down. "What happened?"

"She had an accident."

"A real accident, or the kind of accident you had in the garage last week?"

Kate smiled. That's what she liked about Frankie. She didn't pull her punches.

"I thought we were friends," Frankie persisted when Kate remained silent. "I thought you and I could talk about anything."

"We can—"

"Then why are you keeping secrets from me? And why did you feed me that load of manure the other day about your dropping the Lamont murder case?" As Kate's head snapped up, Frankie's expression turned cocky. "What? You thought that because I didn't say anything, I bought your story?" She laughed. "In a pig's eye. I've known you much too long to believe that you could be scared off. Douglas may have bought it, Maria and Tony may have bought it, but I sure didn't." She leaned forward. "What's going on, Boss? Tell me."

Kate shook her head. "I can't. This case has turned into a complicated cat-and-mouse game, and until I know who the players are, I can't afford to endanger anyone else." She gave her a tired smile. "It'll be over soon, Frankie. Until then, bear with me, will you?"

Not waiting for an answer, she picked up the phone and dialed Mitch's number again.

The lobby of the Europa Hotel was a breathtaking blend of gold silk, gleaming chandeliers and polished marble floors in various shades of gold. In the center of the room, a huge Christmas tree decorated with old-fashioned ornaments twinkled with hundreds of miniature lights.

Dazzled by the opulence surrounding her, Alison felt her mouth open. Everywhere she looked, she saw attractive women in fur coats, small groups of businessmen with cellular phones to their ears, foreigners dressed in the costumes of their native countries. One could spend an entire day in the lobby alone and never be bored.

But she hadn't come here to admire the elegant crowd. She had come here to solve a mystery. And if she didn't get to it right away, she wouldn't make it back to Melissa's house in time to meet Joseph.

Pulling her gaze away, she followed the signs that said Elevators. Once there, she was faced with her first hurdle. To reach any of the four penthouse apartments, all of which were on the eighth floor, a special key was required. Unfortunately, the key to penthouse 4 didn't fit. Which meant she had to find the stairs and climb all the way up.

After circling the lobby three times and getting disoriented, she finally located a door that said Stairs, opened it and started climbing.

It was one-thirty by the time she reached the eighth floor. A little out of breath, she started walking down the carpeted hallway. As she passed penthouses 1 and 2, she admired the elegant decor, the small gilded tables, the Chinese urns filled with golden orchids, the silk-papered walls. Whoever designed this hotel must love gold.

As she reached penthouse 3, Alison stopped abruptly.

Inside the apartment, someone, a woman, had just spoken her mother's name.

Twenty-Nine

Startled to have heard Kate's name spoken with such anger, Alison approached the penthouse door. But as she pressed her ear to it, straining to hear more, the rest of the conversation came out in disjointed sentences she couldn't piece together.

Her heart pounding at her audacity, she gripped the knob and turned it, half-expecting to find the door locked. To her surprise, it wasn't.

Holding her breath, she let herself in. From the foyer, which looked like a small replica of the elegant lobby below, Alison had a broad view of the next room where a woman in a black suit was talking into a cordless phone.

"You want facts?" she asked as she paced. "I'll give you facts. Jarvis just called. Mitch Calhoon was here. He knows that Bruno is the man who tried to kill him last night. And somehow he's found out he works for me.... How the hell do I know how he found out?" she exploded after a brief pause. "He's a cop, isn't he? ...Yes, yes," she added impatiently as she continued her nervous pacing. "Jarvis is stalling him, but for how long? Calhoon isn't stupid. And he sure isn't patient."

There was another pause, but whoever was at the other end of the line apparently failed to reassure the woman. "I'm not the one who fouled things up, you idiot. *You* are. If you had let me kill Kate Logan when she started to poke her nose into my business, we wouldn't be in this mess right now..."

Startled by what she had just heard, Alison backed away—right into a table. She quickly regained her balance but wasn't fast enough to catch a vase that had begun to tilt. Horrified, she watched it crash to the floor.

Before she could make a run for the door, the woman had come out of the other room. "Not so fast, young lady." She grabbed Alison's arm and pulled the girl around to face her. "Who the hell are you?"

"You're hurting me!"

The woman shook Alison's arm. "If you don't tell me who you are and what you're doing here, I'll show you the true meaning of hurt."

Alison swallowed the lump that had formed in her throat. "My name is Alison. Alison Logan."

The woman briefly closed her eyes. "God Almighty." As if she was trying to compose herself, she took a long breath and expelled it slowly. "How long have you been eavesdropping?"

Trembling from head to toe, Alison shook her head. "I wasn't cavesdropping. And I didn't hear anything. I swear."

"You little liar." The woman shook her again, harder this time, causing Alison's head to bob back and forth. "Who the hell do you think you're kidding? What are you doing here? Who sent you?"

"N-no one. I..." As the woman started to drag Alison into the living room, the key she was still holding fell to the floor.

"Well, well, what have we here?" The woman bent to retrieve the key and studied it through narrowed eyes. "Where did you find this?"

Alison was too terrified to lie. "In my grandfather's

desk. His name is Douglas Fairchild,'' she said, hoping the woman would recognize the name and be too impressed to hurt her. "He's a famous attorney."

"I know who he is.'' She put the key in her pocket. "You didn't answer my question. What are you doing here?"

"I was bored." Alison felt her teeth chattering. "So when I found the key in my grandfather's study, I thought I'd come here and...and see what room it belonged to."

"And on the way, you decided to let yourself into *my* penthouse and eavesdrop on my phone conversation."

"I didn't mean to," Alison cried. "I heard my mother's name and..." Too late, she realized her mistake. Shrinking back against the wall, she threw a desperate glance toward the front door. It seemed miles away. "I didn't hear anything else. I swear. Just her name. That's why I came in. I thought...I thought maybe she was here—"

"Shut up." The woman's voice had changed. It was no longer angry, or even afraid. It was cold, empty of all feeling. Still holding Alison's arm, the woman walked over to a desk and pressed a button. "Bruno," she said, leaning over an intercom, "come to my penthouse immediately."

A few minutes later, a huge man dressed in black came in. He was the ugliest, scariest man Alison had ever seen in her life. His head was completely bald, showing unsightly brown warts, and his face was covered with thick acne scars. Small, expressionless eyes stared at her.

"This is Alison Logan, Bruno," the woman said. "Kate Logan's daughter."

The man gave Alison a dirty look. "What she doing here?" He had a low, gruff voice that made him even more menacing.

"The little brat was snooping. And as a result, she heard too much."

"What she hear, Maddy?"

Maddy. Alison tried to remember if her grandfather had ever mentioned someone by that name before, but couldn't. She was too scared to think clearly.

The woman waved an impatient hand. "I'll tell you later. Right now, you need to get out of town. And you're taking the brat with you."

"Where am I going?"

"The senator's cabin." Maddy walked over to a desk and took a set of keys from a drawer. As the man she called Bruno started to take them from Maddy's extended hand, she grabbed his wrist and held it. "Watch her closely, Bruno. She's a tricky one." She released her hold and let him have the keys. "If she tries anything..." She tugged on the French cuffs of her white blouse and skewered Alison with an icy look. "You know what to do."

With a smile that looked more like a sneer, Bruno put the keys in his pocket.

"And be sure to stay under the speed limit," Maddy continued. "The last thing we need is for some cop to stop you for speeding and find her in the back seat." She glanced at her watch. "I'll call you later with further instructions."

"Okay, Maddy." Still smiling, he closed his huge hand around Alison's arm.

"I'm not going anywhere!" Alison screamed, trying to pry her arm free. "And you can't make me. I'll scream and scream—"

She never had a chance to finish. Bruno backhanded her so hard, she felt her eyes roll inside her head and then the world faded to black.

* * *

Sean McKackney was sweating profusely as he dialed his father's office on Capitol Hill at two o'clock that same afternoon. The shit had just hit the fan, and he was right in the middle of it. Unless the old man could perform some sort of miracle, by the time the six o'clock news came on, they'd both be behind bars.

"This is Dr. Sean McKackney," he said to his father's secretary when she answered the phone. "I need to speak to my father right away."

"I'm sorry, Dr. McKackney." The woman's voice had a cultured Boston accent. "Senator McKackney is on his way to the White House to meet with the president. I don't expect him back until late afternoon."

Late afternoon. All hell would have broken loose by then. "I need to speak to him now." Aware that his voice was quivering, he tried to level it. Later, the woman might remember his panic and report it to the police. "It's an extremely urgent matter." There, that was better.

"I'm sorry, Doctor. The senator left strict instructions not to be disturbed—under any circumstances. Would you like to leave a message on his voice mail?"

Oh, sure, wouldn't that be great? *"Dad, Jarvis called. Calhoon's figured out everything—from the phony alibi to Gina's murder. He's pressuring Jarvis to arrest Bruno, and there's a strong possibility that Maddy will be brought in for questioning, as well. If she talks, we're finished."*

"No, thank you. I...I'll call back later."

With a hand he couldn't stop from shaking, he dropped the phone back into its cradle and fell back against his chair. What now? From the tension he'd heard in Lieutenant Jarvis's voice, the situation had reached a critical point. The man was doing his best to stall Calhoon, but at the same time he was demanding to know who the hell Bruno was.

His legs unsteady, Sean stood up, walked over to a cabinet that was filled with liquor and imported mineral water and splashed some Scotch into a glass. He wasn't supposed to drink before surgery, but what the hell, he thought, looking at his hands. Shaking the way he was, he'd never be able to hold a scalpel anyway. He would have to let someone else do the procedure.

The liquor went down his throat like liquid flame. But it felt good. In a minute or so, he'd be able to think rationally.

He glanced at the mirror above the cabinet. He looked awful. He was white as chalk, and he had dark smudges under his eyes from all the sleepless nights he had spent since Calhoon's visit a week ago.

He took another gulp of the Scotch. He had to collect himself. He couldn't let the staff see him looking like this.

Holding the glass against his chest, he walked back to his desk. All right, what was the worst possible scenario? Maddy, whom he had called a little while ago, had assured him that Bruno was safely out of the area. But even if that moron was caught and confessed to the murder of the two women, Maddy would deny any involvement. Who were they going to believe? A convicted criminal with the IQ of a pea, or a respected, upstanding member of the community?

Maddy was a tough broad. There wasn't a cop in the world who could make her do something she didn't want to do.

Was there?

With a hand that was marginally steadier, he brought the Waterford tumbler to his lips again. There was nothing more he could do right now except wait and see what happened next.

And hope to God that his faith in Maddy Mays was justified.

Sitting at his desk, with his shirtsleeves rolled up and his tie undone, Chief of Police Steve Landers leaned back in his chair, steepled his fingers in front of him and gave Mitch a long, hard look. "Are you telling me that Lieutenant Jarvis is a dirty cop?"

"That's what I suspect, sir." Not having been invited to sit down, Mitch remained standing. "Although I have no proof other than the facts I have just stated."

Landers, obviously shaken by what Mitch had told him, bobbed his head a few times. "And you're sure about this Bruno Yager? He was the man who attacked you last night."

"Yes, sir. He's been positively identified. Detective Spivak saw the crime lab report and so did Lieutenant Jarvis. Shortly after that, the lieutenant sent Spivak to investigate a shooting at Lafayette Park, but when Spivak was delayed, Lieutenant Jarvis refused to send someone else to arrest Yager."

Mitch had waited outside Jarvis's office for exactly ten minutes before asking his former boss to send someone else to the Europa. When he refused, Mitch had gone straight to the top.

Suddenly, Landers stood up and started rolling down his sleeves. "I'll have to get Lieutenant Jarvis's version on this," he said, buttoning a cuff. "You come with me."

The first thing Alison was aware of when she finally woke up was a tremendous headache that began at the base of her neck and wrapped around her skull like a vise.

The second thing she was aware of was snow falling down, sticking to the car windows.

Afraid to move for fear her head would split open, she remained perfectly still, moving only her eyes. She was in the back of a car, a smelly car, and Bruno, the animal who had hit her, was driving.

Where was he taking her?

The woman's words came back to her. *The senator's cabin.*

Alison knew only one senator—Sander McKackney. He was an old friend of her grandfather's, and he owned a hunting cabin somewhere in the mountains. Her father had gone hunting with him a few times before finally giving up the sport.

But why was Bruno using the senator's house? How did he even know about it?

Being careful not to make a sound, she pushed herself up on one elbow. Lying on the console between the two front seats was a cellular phone. Closing her eyes, Alison said a silent prayer. She couldn't do anything now, but maybe later, once they arrived at their destination, she would have to find a way to get to that phone.

It was snowing harder now, and the road was getting very narrow. As Bruno kept turning the wheel right and then left to get around the curves, Alison's stomach began to churn. She had never been a good back-seat rider. But she couldn't get sick now. She had to keep pretending that she was passed out. That way, Bruno wouldn't feel as if he had to watch her every second.

She wasn't sure how long the rest of the ride lasted. She was concentrating on her breathing, which she kept deep and even, just in case Bruno was listening to it. It was a little trick she had perfected during the past twelve months. Every night, and especially after an argument, her mother would come up to her room before going to hers, hoping they could have one of those mother-daughter chats she was so fond of. But Alison would pretend to be asleep. After a while, Kate would kiss her on the forehead, tuck the covers around her and leave.

A sob began to press against her throat. She swallowed to push it back. *I'm sorry, Mommy. I wish you were here now.*

The car came to an abrupt stop and Alison's stomach did a somersault. Please, God, she prayed, don't let me throw up. Not now.

The back door opened and she quickly closed her eyes. She thought of everything her drama teacher at Sawmill Academy had told her the day Alison had found out she was going to play the lead in the Christmas play. "Forget that you're acting and that you're on a stage. Let yourself into the skin, the soul, the heart of your character. Don't just *imagine* what it would feel like to be Elena. *Become* Elena."

That's what she had to do now. She had to become that limp, unconscious girl and hope she was as good in this role as she was in Mrs. Gherart's *Elena's Christmas Wish.*

Grunting, Bruno reached into the back and pulled her out feetfirst. Although she hadn't expected him to be gentle, she wished he had been a little more considerate. Then she remembered that she was supposed to be unconscious. Unconscious people didn't gripe about their kidnapper's rough manners.

Letting herself hang from his arms, she tried to relax while at the same time wondering where he was going to dump her. A couch or a bed probably wouldn't bring out so much as a murmur from her. But what if he dropped her on the floor? Would she be able not to cry out in pain?

You'd better if you want a chance to get to that phone.

As she felt herself bounce on something soft and springy, she relaxed.

Bruno's footsteps moved away. Feeling relatively safe, Alison opened her eyes. She was in a log cabin of some sort. A table lamp cast a soft glow on the log walls and rustic furnishings. Directly across from the sofa where she lay was a huge brick fireplace. Above the mantel, the antlers of what must have been a very large buck pointed down at her.

Turning her head slightly, she saw Bruno standing by the window. His broad back blocked out most of the light. In this small room, he looked even bigger than he had in Maddy's penthouse.

How was she going to make a run for the phone with him standing there?

As he started to turn, Alison resumed her pose, letting her right arm dangle over the side of the sofa for effect.

He didn't seem to pay any attention to her. Instead, he started to walk aimlessly around the room. As the minutes passed, he grew more and more restless.

Was he upset because Maddy hadn't called with her new set of instructions?

With a chill in her heart, she remembered the tragic story of Polly Klaas, the California girl who had been abducted from her home a couple of years ago, raped and then killed.

What if she was about to suffer the same fate?

Before she could scare herself even more than she already was, she heard a noise. Opening up her eyes again, she saw that Bruno had picked up the phone, not the cellular, which was hopefully still inside the car, but the one on the small table near the fireplace. His back was to her.

"This is Bruno," he said roughly after a few seconds.

"Let me talk to Maddy." Suddenly, with no warning, Bruno let out an exclamation. "Jail?" he said as Alison watched him intently. "They took Maddy to jail? What the hell for?"

Alison sat up. Maddy in jail? Not sure whether the news was an omen or a greater threat, she moved slowly to the edge of her seat.

"Damn." Bruno ran a hand over his bald head and kept it there. "Did she say anything?" he asked, his voice sounding uncertain. "Did she leave a message for me?"

Alison threw a frantic glance toward the front door, which was no more than eight or ten feet from where she sat. Here was the chance she'd been waiting for. It was now or never.

Standing up, she took a deep breath. God knew when she'd be able to take the next one. Then, ever so slowly, she inched her way toward the door, one cautious step at a time. Bruno continued to talk on the phone, unaware of what was happening behind his back.

She was almost there.

At last, Alison's hand made contact with the doorknob. Her eyes fixed on Bruno, she turned it, opening the door just wide enough to slip through it. Once she was outside, she closed it again.

The snow was still coming down, but she ignored it. She kept focused on the car in the driveway. When she reached it, she said another prayer. "One more favor, God," she whispered as she gripped the handle. "If you grant it, I promise I'll never miss another Sunday service. Don't let the car door be locked."

Pulling on the handle, she felt the door open and almost let out a cry of victory. Then, remembering that time was crucial, she quickly stepped into the car. The phone was still there—on the console.

Leaving the door open, she picked it up and dialed the number of Fairchild Baxter. "This is Alison Logan," she said quickly. "May I speak to my mother, please. It's an emergency."

"Certainly, Alison. Hold on, honey."

"Alison," her mother said when she came on the line, "what emerg—"

"Mom, I've been kidnapped!" Before Kate could reply, the words tumbled out of her mouth. "This big, ugly man took me to some mountain cabin—"

A huge hand fell on hers, knocking the phone to the floor. "Little bitch." Bruno pulled her out of the car so hard, she thought her arm would fall off.

Alison's shout of pain was lost on him. Looking like a madman, he grabbed Alison by her coat and literally dragged her back into the cabin.

This time, he took her to a back bedroom and made her sit on the floor while he yanked a sheet from the bed. With no more effort than it would have taken to tear a page from a newspaper, he ripped a strip from the sheet. Then, holding Alison's hands together, he twisted the makeshift rope around her wrists, made a tight knot, then tied her to the bedpost.

When he was sure she wouldn't be going anywhere, he left the room.

Alison glanced hopelessly around her. How in God's name was she going to get out of this one?

Thirty

Her morale considerably boosted by Kate's encouraging words at lunch, Rose dropped her keys on top of the credenza in the foyer and picked up her mail from a silver dish.

Kate was right. Eric was a big boy now. And he was with the woman he loved. At least she hoped he loved her. After all Megan had risked to be with him, she would be devastated if she found out that her feelings weren't shared.

When the phone rang, Rose picked it up, speaking absently into it as she kept sorting through her mail. "Hello?"

"Hi, Mom."

A strangled sound, halfway between a sob and a laugh escaped from Rose's throat. She gripped the receiver with both hands. "Dear God, Eric, is that really you?"

"It's me, Mom. And I'm coming home."

"Oh, Eric, I'm so glad. But…" She paused. "What about the warrant for your arrest?"

"I'll deal with that when I get there, Mom. And I'll explain everything then."

"When will that be?"

"Megan and I are on the way. Provided we don't get picked up by the police," he added with astounding lightness, "we should be in Potomac in about an hour. But don't tell anyone, okay? Not even Douglas. I've got to do this my own way."

"I won't say a word." She had difficulty remaining calm. "Oh, Eric, I'm so glad you called. Everything is going to be all right. You'll see."

"I know. Look, it's starting to snow here and I've got to concentrate on the road. I'll see you in a bit, okay?"

"Okay, darling. Give my love to Megan."

After hanging up, Rose folded her hands and pressed them against her mouth as tears of relief ran down her cheeks.

She glanced at the phone again, wondering if Eric's warning not to tell "anyone" had included Kate. She never had a chance to finish her thought. The front door opened, and Joseph, looking paler and more agitated than she had ever seen him before, walked in.

"Dear God, Joseph, what's wrong?" Mildly alarmed, she glanced behind him. "Where's Alison?"

Joseph gripped his cap with both hands. "I don't know, ma'am." Making a tremendous effort to keep his voice on an even keel, he added, "She's gone."

Rose's hand shot to her mouth. She could already feel the blood rush to her head as something icy settled in the pit of her stomach. She held on to the credenza. "What do you mean gone? Where did you take her?"

"To Miss Melissa's house, ma'am. It was agreed that I would pick her up at three. But when I went there, the maid told me that Miss Alison had come in for just a few minutes and then left."

"Why would Alison go to Melissa's house when she knew perfectly well that Melissa wouldn't be there?"

"I wasn't aware of that at the time, ma'am. She must have wanted to go somewhere else. She told Zina that I was waiting for her at the curb when she knew that I had already left.''

"She lied to you? She *deliberately* lied?"

Joseph sighed. "Yes, ma'am." Then, his voice stronger, he asked, "Should we call the police?"

"Yes! No!" Rose ran a hand through her hair. "Oh, God, I don't know what to do. I should call her mother first." She picked up the phone. "Yes, that's it. Kate will know what to do."

As Alison's call was abruptly cut off, Kate hit the plunger in a frantic attempt to be reconnected. "Alison! Alison, talk to me!"

But she knew it was useless. The line was dead.

Frankie, whose office door was open, ran in. "Kate, what is it?"

Raw fear shot through Kate's bloodstream. Everything she had ever learned about staying calm in a time of crisis was forgotten.

Some maniac had taken her little girl.

"Kate!" Frankie was shaking her. "Answer me."

"Alison's been kidnapped." She wasn't sure how she got the words out, or how she was able to hear them and not break down completely.

"Oh, my God, no." Frankie's eyes were wide with horror. "Does she know where she is? Or who took her?"

Kate tried to put the questions in order, but her mind, blurry from the shock, refused to function. "Mitch," she said, her speech slurred as if she had been drinking. "Have to contact Mitch."

"I'll do it." Before Frankie could reach the phone on Kate's desk, it shrilled, startling them both. Frankie picked it up, then handed it to Kate. "It's Rose."

"Oh, Kate." Rose's voice was filled with panic. "Alison is missing. She lied to Joseph about going to Melissa's house, and when he went to get her, she wasn't there."

Through a monumental effort, Kate was able to collect herself. "She just called, but we were disconnected."

"Then she's all right!"

"No." Kate pressed a hand over her heart in a futile attempt to stop its erratic beating. "She's been kidnapped." There was a small cry at the other end of the line, followed by hysterical sobbing. Kate could feel the panic mounting again. "Rose, stop it!" she said sharply. "I'm not going to be able to do a single constructive thing if everyone around me falls apart."

The sobbing stopped. "What shall we do?" Rose asked in a trembling voice.

"I'll contact Mitch Calhoon. Then I'll come to your house to talk to Joseph."

"What if Alison calls you again?"

"Frankie will stay here in case she does. And I'll ask Maria to go back to the house and cover that line."

"We should call the police, Kate. Or the FBI."

"No," she said firmly. "Not until we know what the demands are—if there are any."

As she was hanging up, Frankie called from her office. "Kate, I've got Mitch on line two."

Kate hit the button. "Mitch, thank God."

"Frankie said Alison has been kidnapped."

"I don't have a lot of details." Feeling as though she was about to hyperventilate, Kate took a few deep breaths and exhaled slowly. "She just called and said that a big, ugly man took her to some mountain cabin She didn't have a chance to say anything more. We were disconnected. I'm on my way to Douglas's house. Joseph may remember something important."

"I'll meet you there."

Felicia, the housekeeper who had replaced Maria a year ago, was standing in Rose's drawing room, her chubby face clouded with worry. "Joseph told me what happened," she said to Rose. "Is there any news from Miss Alison?"

Rose nodded and tried not to cry. Kate was right. Nothing could be accomplished by falling apart. "She's been kidnapped. Detective Calhoon and Mrs. Logan are on their way here."

Felicia closed her eyes and crossed herself, murmuring something Rose didn't understand.

"Please make some coffee, Felicia, and perhaps some sandwiches. I'm not sure how long we'll..." She couldn't put that last thought together. But Felicia understood.

"*Sí, señora.* Right away."

She ought to try to reach Douglas again, Rose thought as Felicia left the room. His secretary had expected him back at three, but it was well past that now and there was still no sign of him.

Maybe he was with Senator McKackney. Although Rose wasn't aware of any problem, she knew from Sander and Sean's many phone calls these past couple of days, that something was wrong. Maybe Douglas was at Sander's house, discussing whatever was troubling him.

She hurried toward her husband's study to look for Sander's phone number. She would feel much better once Douglas was here. He was so good in a crisis.

She opened the study door, took a few steps inside, then stopped dead in her tracks.

Douglas was there, standing in front of the wall safe where he kept their important papers. "Douglas!"

He whipped around, looking startled.

She heaved a sigh of relief. "Thank God you're here." Her hands twisting in despair, she rushed toward him. "Alison has been kidnapped."

"*What?*"

"She's been kidnapped," Rose repeated. "We don't know by whom or why—"

"Have you called the FBI?"

A sob caught in Rose's throat. "Kate said not to. She's on her way here. So is Detective Calhoon. He'll know..." As Douglas took a step back, she suddenly noticed for the first time the bundle of money he held in his hand. "What are you doing with all that money?"

When he didn't answer, her eyes took in the entire scene detail by detail—the pallor of her husband's cheeks, the open safe, the stack of bills, the passport...

She was filled with an inexplicable sense of dread, a foreboding that something terrible was about to happen. "Douglas?" His hands, still clutching the money and the passport, fell to his sides. His face was ashen now and his eyes spoke of a torment she couldn't even begin to comprehend. "What are you doing with all that money? And your passport?" She searched his eyes, afraid of his answer.

For a moment, he looked at a loss for words. Then, as if he had been suddenly touched by a magic wand, he started to function again. Shocked, Rose watched him walk to his desk and stuff the money into a bag that lay on his desk. "I'm going on a trip, Rose."

"A trip?" She came closer, forcing him to look at her. "I just told you that your granddaughter has been kidnapped and you're going on a trip?"

"My staying here isn't going to change anything. Calhoon is the expert in that department." He slid the passport into his breast pocket. "If the abductors want a ransom, contact the bank and do what has to be done. I left you plenty of money."

In a daze, Rose glanced into his bag. He had packed light clothing, the kind he always took when they went to Bermuda. "Where are you going?"

"That's not important."

"Not important?" She laughed, a short, nervous laugh that caught in her throat. "I come in here, find you with your bags packed, a stack of money in your hands, and when I ask you where you're going, you tell me it's not important? What kind of answer is that?"

He continued to look at her, his mouth set in a tight, stubborn line. But she could be just as stubborn. And he knew it.

"I won't let you go, Douglas. Not until you tell me what's going on. Is it Sander? Or his son? Are they in trouble?"

How many times had he told her, jokingly, that she was too damned smart for her own good, that under that sweet smile and easy disposition was the mind of a shrewd and discerning woman. She had never thought of herself as particularly shrewd. Intuitive perhaps, but not shrewd. It was that intuition that made her realize that the problem was much more serious than she had first thought.

"What did they do, Douglas?" Fragments of recent phone conversations came back to her. She took his hands in hers. "It's about that old rape case, isn't it? Somehow the whole thing has become unraveled and you're right in the middle of it."

Douglas looked down at their entwined hands. "It's more complicated than that."

Although the house was pleasantly warm, she felt a sudden chill. "Then tell me what it is. Let me help you."

He glanced beyond her shoulder, at the clock behind her. "There isn't time."

"You'll have to make time," she said, in a voice she hoped conveyed enough authority. "I'm your wife. If you are in trouble, I want to know about it. I have the *right* to know about it."

Douglas sighed. It was the sigh of a man with a heavy burden on his shoulders. "I guess there's no harm in telling you now. The others will be arrested shortly. I could be next."

"Arrested!"

"Sean McKackney raped that girl," Douglas continued. "And I helped Sander fabricate an alibi for his son."

Although the confession stunned her, Rose tried not to show it. She knew there was more, much more, and she wanted to hear it all. "Helped? How?"

Calmly, Douglas picked up an address book from his desk and slid it into his breast pocket with the passport. "Sander and I had a mutual friend—Maddy Mays. You know her, she was our neighbor for a while." He looked away. "After Henry died, she started a call-girl ring. The young woman I hired to play Sean's girlfriend that night was one of Maddy's girls."

Rose remembered Maddy well. And she knew all about her reputation. To hear her husband admit to a relationship with a former hooker awakened feelings of jealousy she didn't know she had. "Were you a customer of Maddy Mays, Douglas?" she asked sharply. "Did you sleep with her? Or with any of those women?"

"You know that's not my style, Rose. I didn't even know Maddy was running a call-girl ring until Sander told me."

"And that's why you're running away? Because you helped Sander lie?"

He held her gaze. "The girl I hired to help Sean that night was Gina Lamont."

This time, Rose couldn't conceal her shock. "The woman Eric is accused of murdering?"

He zipped his bag shut. "Yes."

Unable to grasp the full meaning of what he had just told her, Rose shook her head slowly from side to side. "You knew Gina Lamont?"

"Yes," Douglas whispered. "I'm the one who briefed her and rehearsed her before we went to the police station."

"Oh, Douglas."

"Don't give me that shocked look, Rose. What was I to do? My best friend was in trouble. Yes, his son had done a terrible thing, but Sander still loved him as much as you love your own son. If he had let Sean face the rape charge, the kid's medical career, and his life, would have been destroyed."

"What about the young woman he raped!" Rose cried. "He destroyed *her* life, didn't he?" Rather than answer, Douglas closed his hand around the bag handle. Rose remained in front of him, determined not to let him go until she had heard everything. "What happened? Did that poor girl finally decide to talk about the rape?"

"No. I never heard from her again."

"Then who—"

"I don't have time to explain, Rose. Maybe later—"

She gripped his wrist and forced him to put the bag down. "You're going to tell me now. Someone must have talked, or threatened to. Surely not Maddy or your other accomplices. They had more to lose than you did."

He yanked his hand away. "Dammit, Rose, let me go."

"Was it Gina?"

"All right!" he shouted. "It was Gina. Are you satisfied now? The bitch was blackmailing me. She was blackmailing all three of us—me, Sander and Maddy."

"Blackmailing you...?"

"That's right. She demanded one million dollars from each one of us."

Rose's next question came on a whisper. "Did you give her the money?" Douglas didn't answer. He didn't have to. She had already guessed the rest. Horrified, she took a step back. "You killed her, didn't you? You're the one who killed Gina Lamont, not Eric."

Then came an even more staggering realization, one that hit her with such force she had to hold on to Douglas's desk for support.

He had let Eric take the blame for Gina's murder.

"Look, Rose, I'm sorry, okay? I never meant for things to go this far."

This time, he was the one who took her arm, but she wrenched it free. All of a sudden, his touch had become unbearable. "You knew Eric was innocent!" she cried. "You knew it all along, and yet you stood in this very house, accusing him of a crime *you* committed, plotting with Abigail to have him captured."

"I wouldn't have let him go to prison, you know that."

"Liar!" Her fury unchained, she threw herself at him and started pounding his chest with her fists. "You framed my son for murder! You were ready to have him stand trial so you could save your skin. And that of your precious friends."

He took all her blows. When he couldn't take any more, he gripped her wrists and held her back until, exhausted, she collapsed onto a chair and buried her face in her hands. Sobs she could no longer hold back poured out of her, draining her, sapping her of all strength. She wasn't

sure how long she cried, or for which of the two men she
loved she cried the most.

When she looked up, Douglas was gone.

Thirty-One

Kate shot onto the busy beltway at fifty miles an hour, ignoring the honks of an angry driver who had barely missed her. Somewhere behind her, the sound of a siren filled the air. A quick glance in the rearview mirror confirmed what she already knew. A police car, lights blazing, was coming after her.

She didn't slow down. Her hands tightly clasped on the steering wheel, she wove the Saab in and out of traffic with an expertise she had never had to test before.

She tried desperately not to give in to the panic, to the paralyzing fear that made her heart pound and turned her throat so dry she couldn't swallow. Forcing her mind to remain blank, she concentrated only on the traffic. And on safely getting to Douglas's house. It wouldn't help matters if she had an accident now. Or if she allowed a highway trooper to stop her.

As the Welcome to Maryland sign came into view, she was relieved to see that the police car was falling back. As she had expected, he had broken off the chase, and she knew why. A regulation that prosecutors had tried to fight for years prohibited District police from pursuing anyone across the state line unless he or she was a suspected murderer. As long as the officer didn't notify the Maryland police, she was safe.

At last, the Fairchilds' mansion came into view, looking

so grand and peaceful it was impossible to imagine the drama that was unfolding within its walls.

At the entrance, Kate slammed on the brakes, coming within inches of Mitch's car. Her heart hammering inside her chest, she ran up the half-dozen steps that led to the front door, then, not bothering to ring the bell, she threw the door open.

She could hear Mitch's voice, strong, calm, reassuring. Pressing a fist against her mouth, she raced down the hall until she reached the drawing room. As she stood on the threshold, all eyes turned toward her, but it was Mitch she ran to. "Oh, Mitch, they took my baby."

His strong arms encircled her. He spoke softly as he buried his face in her hair. "We'll find her, Kate. I promise you, we'll find her."

"Do you really believe that?" Her voice was turning shrill. "I'm sure Bruno is the one who took her. The same beast who tried to kill you, who attacked me—"

Rose, her eyes red from crying, came to stand next to them. "Who is Bruno?"

"He works for Maddy Mays," Mitch replied.

"Then Douglas must know him." Rose looked at the detective. "Oh, Mitch, do you think he could have had something to do with Alison's kidnapping? His own granddaughter?"

"What are you two talking about?" Kate interrupted sharply. "Where is Douglas?"

Gently, Mitch pulled Kate onto a sofa. "All we know is that Douglas is up to his neck in trouble, but there's no time to explain right now." He held her hands in his. "Tell me what Alison said on the phone."

Kate repeated Alison's brief message.

"Sander McKackney has a cabin in the mountains," Rose said in a voice that was barely audible.

Mitch and Kate exchanged a glance. "Do you know where it is?" Mitch asked.

"In the Catoctin Mountains. He and Douglas used to go hunting there. But I'm afraid I don't know the exact address."

Remembering that Eric had gone with them on a couple of occasions, Kate turned to Rose. "Doesn't Douglas have a map with the route to the cabin already traced out?"

"I believe he does. It should be in his study."

"Please get it, Rose. Hurry."

Rose rushed out of the room and returned a few moments later, carrying a large-scale map of Frederick County. She spread it open on the coffee table. "The cabin is on Tower Road," she said, tracing the thick, blue-penciled line with her finger. "A little over an hour from here." She handed him a dozen or so pictures. "I found these with the map. They were taken during a recent trip and show the landscape around the area quite well."

They did, Mitch thought as he flipped through the photographs. The house, an A-frame log structure, sat on a mountain slope and had a large deck overlooking the narrow, winding road below. Not the best rescue conditions if someone was watching from a window, but the wooded area surrounding the house would provide adequate cover.

"Mitch." He felt Kate's fingers sink into his arm. "I waited until now in the hope that someone would call and tell us what they wanted in exchange for Alison, but..." She shook her head. "It's been an hour since Alison called. There's no more time to waste. We have to do something."

"I think we should call the FBI," Rose said again. "When Ellen Faraguay's son disappeared last year—"

Kate cut her short. "We will not call the FBI. It would take them too long to set up a rescue operation." The pressure on Mitch's arm increased. "I want you to do it, Mitch."

Startled, he turned to look at her and was shocked to see the expression on her face. He had seen it many times before—on the faces of other mothers who had entrusted him with the lives of their children. It was a mixture of desperation, hope and absolute trust. Once perhaps, he had been worthy of such blind faith, but not anymore.

"I can't, Kate."

"What do you mean you can't?" She let go of his arm and took a step back. "It's what you've been trained to do. I wouldn't even dream of letting anyone else rescue my daughter."

"If you want a true expert to rescue Alison, then you'll wait for Randy Vargas. I called him from the car on my way here and gave him as many details as I knew. We can fill him in with the rest when he gets here." He glanced at his watch. "That should be any minute now. He's bringing one of his best men with him."

"I don't want Randy Vargas! I want you!"

"I can't do it," he repeated. His face grim, he walked over to the window and pushed the curtains apart. "And you know why."

Kate was at his side again, her voice low and urgent. "Mitch, listen to me. That incident you told me about happened a long time ago. And that little girl, precious though she was, was a stranger. This is Alison we're talking about. *My daughter.* Doesn't that mean anything to you?"

He swung around, his facial muscles taut. "It means *everything* to me!" he flung back. "That's why I can't do it. I can't put her in the same danger I put my..." Realizing he had almost let out the truth, he walked over to the well-stocked bar and poured himself a Perrier.

"It was one mistake, Mitch." Undaunted, Kate followed him. "One mistake out of dozens of successful missions. Don't you think it's time you put it behind you and moved on?"

For a moment, he weighed the odds. Other men had failed missions and gone back into action almost immediately. Maybe he could too—just this one time.

But in the end, Alison's safety came first. "You'll have to wait for Randy."

He saw her stiffen and understood the loathing she must be feeling for him at this very moment. He was letting her down at a time when she needed him the most. No matter how much he tried to make it up to her afterward, there would never be a more significant moment in their lives. Maybe the significance was in the harsh reality that their relationship was over.

Rose came to stand between them. Somehow she had composed herself and was once again the strong, sensible woman Mitch had met six months ago. "Look," she said, her gaze moving back and forth between Mitch and Kate. "I don't know what's going on between you two, or what you're talking about, but maybe Mitch is right, Kate. If he doesn't feel comfortable with the idea of rescuing Alison, then we shouldn't force him."

"Oh, don't worry, Rose." Kate's voice dripped with sarcasm. "I wouldn't dream of forcing him to do something he doesn't want to do." Although her words rang with a chilling finality, the expression in her eyes told Mitch she wasn't through with him yet. She hadn't delivered her coup de grâce. "You know what you are, Mitch Calhoon?" Rage and contempt bubbled up to the surface, spilling into the room like a poison. "You're nothing but a coward."

Then, struggling to control her tears, she turned away from him and went to the sofa to pick up her purse.

Mitch let the angry words roll off his head. "Where are you going?" he called out after her.

"None of your damned business."

Seconds later, the front door slammed shut.

Astounded, Rose turned to Mitch. "What's the matter with you? Why didn't you stop her?"

"Because she didn't want to be stopped." Pulling the curtain aside again, he watched the red Saab speed down the driveway and disappear. "And because she hates me right now."

"But don't you see what she's going to do?"

"No, Rose, I don't." He felt suddenly very tired. "I've never been much of an expert on women. I'm assuming she's going for a drive to clear her head."

"God." Rose rolled her eyes toward the ceiling. "She's going to rescue her daughter herself!"

He spun around. "That's ridiculous."

"Is it?" Rose pointed at the coffee table where a moment ago Douglas's map had been spread out. "Then will you please tell me why she walked out with the map to Sander's cabin? And the photographs?"

"That fool!" Mitch exploded. "She'll get herself killed." He made a mad dash for the door, glad that this time he had his gun with him.

Rose ran after him. "What shall I tell your friend when he gets here?"

Cursing at the delay, Mitch stopped, pulled out his notebook and wrote down the directions to the cabin with as many details as he could remember. "Give him this," he said, tearing the page from his book and handing it to Rose. "And tell him to make it there as fast as he can."

Then he sprinted out of the house, hoping he would catch Kate before she became Bruno Yager's next victim.

Thirty-Two

Rose was sitting on her sofa, the back of her head pressed against the cushions, when she heard the sound of her son's voice.

"Hello, Mom."

Her head snapped up. "Eric!" she cried, rising and rushing into his waiting arms. After hugging him fiercely, she extended an arm toward Megan, bringing her into their embrace. "Megan." She seemed quite incapable of saying anything more than those two names.

"Why is everybody walking around as if they'd just lost their best friend?" Eric asked lightly. "I just saw Joseph and he looked awful. He couldn't even say hello. I haven't been accused of another crime while I was gone, have I?" he asked with a laugh. "I haven't turned into some kind of mass murderer."

"Oh, Eric, you don't know."

Eric's expression sobered instantly. "Know what?"

"Alison's been kidnapped."

He wasn't sure what hit him first—fear or rage. Fear at the thought of his daughter in the hands of an abductor, or rage at himself for not having been here to prevent the abduction.

"When did it happen?" he asked as Megan gripped his arm. "Who took her? What do they want? If it's money—"

Rose shook her head. "It's not money." Taking a deep breath, she told him what she knew, including what Douglas had told her.

To her surprise, Eric made no comment about his stepfather. When he spoke, his voice was remarkably calm. "I'm going up to the cabin."

"No, Eric. You'll only be in the way. Let Detective Calhoon handle it."

"If you think," he said somewhat dramatically, but with no less determination than the most devoted of fathers, "that I'm going to let some hotshot cop who thinks he's Rambo rescue my daughter, you're gravely mistaken."

"Detective Calhoon isn't like that at all. In fact, he didn't want to go. He wanted to wait for his former boss, a Mr. Randy Vargas, who should have been here already," she added, glancing at her watch.

"We won't need Mr. Randy Vargas, either. I'm here now."

Megan, looking worried, squeezed his arm. "Eric, are you sure? Those men are professionals. They know what they're doing, how to approach such a situation."

"And I'm Alison's father." He tilted his chin upward. "I let her down once, but I'm not going to let her down again. She's my responsibility, not that of a bunch of...mercenaries." He kissed Megan's mouth. "I'll be all right, darling, I promise. You stay here with my mother."

The phone rang and Eric sprang to get it. "Hello? No, this is Eric Logan. Who is this?" He relaxed. "Oh, Mr. Vargas. No, he left a little while ago." He listened for another few seconds. "Thanks for calling. Yes, I'll tell him."

He hung up. "Randy Vargas and his associate are tied

up in a major traffic jam fifteen miles from here. Nothing is moving. He has no idea when he'll get here."

"Oh, dear," Rose said.

"Don't worry, Mom." He kissed her cheek. "I'll bring Alison back. Safe and sound."

Holding on to Megan's hand, Rose watched her son walk out of the room. She had never felt more proud of him. Or more frightened for his life.

Please, God, she prayed silently. Keep him safe.

The Catoctin Mountains, some thirty miles northwest of Washington, D.C., were a major component of the Blue Ridge Mountains, extending for a little over thirty-five miles and reaching an altitude, in the northern part of the range, of nearly two thousand feet.

It had taken Kate forty minutes to reach Route 15, also known as Catoctin Mountain Highway. Now, as she drove toward Cunningham Falls and began climbing, she turned her windshield wipers to high speed. Snow had only been a threat on Interstate 270, but up here it was beginning to reach blizzard conditions, making visibility difficult.

She tried not to think of Mitch and of the blunt way he had turned down her request to rescue her daughter. She had to concentrate on her driving and on what she would do once she arrived at McKackney's cabin.

She had no experience in such things. But she had a knowledge of the criminal mind. She knew firsthand how people who fitted a certain profile thought and acted. The fact that Bruno Yager did not seem to be terribly intelligent would be equally helpful. She could divert him away from the house somehow, and once he was busy looking for whatever had caught his attention, she would get inside, grab her daughter and run.

Too easy, she thought. Something was bound to go

wrong. And yet, she couldn't think of any other way to save Alison.

The thought that she should have waited for Randy Vargas came and went. Every minute spent waiting could put her daughter in graver danger. And if Bruno suddenly decided to move her to another location, she might never find her.

Just before Cunningham Falls, she turned left on Catoctin Hollow Road and looked for the two landmarks she had seen in one of the photographs—an abandoned well and a camp site. At the camp site, she turned right. The climb was steeper now and the twisting road barely wide enough for the Saab, but she made it through.

Another photograph, one at which she glanced briefly as she drove, showed a clearing three hundred feet or so from the house. She had no idea if Bruno would be watching from a window, but she couldn't chance it. She would have to stop the car before that clearing and make the rest of the climb on foot.

Suddenly, as she turned a bend, she saw it! A small, A-frame house with a wooden deck jutting over the road.

Guiding the car as far as she could inside the heavy, snow-covered underbrush, she felt it lurch to a stop. "Oh, no."

Opening the door, she looked down. The two front tires had sunk into the snow. She was stuck.

Well, she would have to deal with that problem later. If she didn't feel she had enough time to get the car out, she and Alison would have to walk. She had passed a house not more than ten minutes earlier. They could make it there with no problem.

Wishing she had worn her snow boots instead of flimsy leather-soled flats, she began climbing through the woods, trying to stay out of sight. After ten grueling minutes of slipping and sliding and pulling herself back up, she was exhausted. Her face was scratched from the tree branches and her hands were raw from the cold, but she kept on climbing, glad that the house was getting closer.

"Kate!"

Startled by the sound of her fiercely whispered name, she held on to a sturdy oak and turned around. And saw Mitch. A hundred yards or so behind her, he was climbing the steep, snowy slope with the agility of a mountain cat. Her hopes soared. He had come to help her. He had come to rescue Alison.

Grateful for the chance to catch her breath, she took big gulps of air and waited until he had caught up with her. "Mitch, thank God—"

"Have you seen anyone?" His tone was sharp, his demeanor cool as he observed the house.

"No." Hurt, she took a step back. "But there's a car in the driveway and a light inside the house."

"Okay, here's what I'm going to do. I'll go through the back door—"

"How do you know there's a back door?"

"I saw it in one of the photographs."

She had missed that, but didn't dwell on it too long. "All right. And then what?"

"He'll either have Alison in the front room with him or in one of the back rooms. Once I've located her, I'll signal to her. What do you think? Can she handle the situation without giving me away?"

"She's a born actress. But you'll need help. I'll create a diversion out here. When Bruno comes out—"

"Oh, no, you don't." His gaze remained trained on the house. "He could be armed. And if he's not, there are guns in that house. You make any kind of noise and he'll come out shooting."

"If you think for one moment—"

He turned to look at her. "There's no room for discussion here, Kate. I don't want to have to worry about you while I go after Alison. If I feel that I need you, I'll let you know."

The sharpness of his tone kept her from arguing further. He was the expert. And she trusted him. That's all that mattered. "All right, then. Go."

As Mitch was about to resume his climb toward the house, he heard the roar of an engine. "What the hell…" He turned around and, to his stupefaction, saw a green Jaguar jerk to a stop right there in the open.

A bearded, gray-haired man in a woodsman's jacket jumped out of the car. "Where's Alison?" he shouted. "Where's my daughter?"

"My God," Kate gasped. "It's Eric."

"You stupid jerk!" Mitch shouted back. "Get that damn car out of here. You're going to screw up everything."

The warning came too late. Up on the deck, a door opened, and a huge man, presumably Bruno, stepped out, a high-powered rifle in his hands.

He must have seen Eric at the same time Mitch pulled Kate out of sight. A shot rang out, then a second and a third. A split second later, they heard a scream.

Pushing himself up on his knees, Mitch glanced toward the spot where Eric had stood moments earlier. Holding his thigh and shouting obscenities, Kate's former husband skipped on one foot for a few seconds, then fell to the ground and rolled down an embankment, disappearing from sight.

"He shot him!" Horrified, Kate started to scramble to her feet. "That maniac shot him."

"Shh." Mitch yanked her down. "Don't move. Don't let him know we're here."

Moving farther into the brush, Mitch and Kate watched as Bruno, rifle in hand, came down from the deck and walked toward the embankment. Something icy clutched at Kate's heart. "My God, he's going to kill him."

"Go get Alison," Mitch told Kate, helping her to her feet and pushing her forward. "I'll take care of Bruno."

"He'll kill you, too!" Before she could stop him, Mitch had drawn his gun and was running after Bruno.

Her feet sinking into the snow, Kate started toward the deck. Suddenly, a shot rang out, followed by another. Turning around, she saw Mitch grab his arm as the gun fell from his hand.

"Mitch!"

With an angry grunt, Bruno, who had been firing from behind his car, tossed the rifle aside. Then, coming out in the open, he held himself low, the way he had in the garage when he had come after her, and lunged at Mitch. The two men fell down and rolled onto the snow. Wounded and favoring his left arm, Mitch was clearly at a disadvantage.

"Get the gun, Kate!" he shouted.

She looked wildly around her. "I don't see it!"

The sound of a solid punch made her wince. Knowing she'd never find the gun in all that snow, she started looking around her for some other weapon. Her gaze fell on a stack of firewood under the deck.

Half walking and half crawling, she made her way to the pile, grabbed the biggest log she could find, then went back to where the two men were still wrestling. Holding the log like a baseball bat, she started swinging at Bruno's head. She missed, hitting Mitch's forehead instead.

Mitch fell flat on his back and just lay there.

"Mitch!" Kate cried. "Oh, my God."

At the sound of her voice, Bruno turned around, realized what she had tried to do and came after her, an angry scowl on his face. "Bitch."

Kate dropped the log, stumbled and fell. As the huge man moved toward her, she started to crawl backward like a crab. "Mitch! Help me!"

Her call remained unanswered. Numb with fear, she watched Bruno's long arms reach for her. In a desperate effort to hold him off, she kicked, aiming at his face. The pathetic attempt only made him laugh.

He was going to kill her, she thought as he grabbed her ankles and started to drag her toward the house. He was going to kill them all.

"Let her go, Bruno."

Still holding Kate, the big man turned around. Mitch was standing up, his legs apart, his gun steady as he held it with both hands. There was a bullet hole in the upper part of his left coat sleeve from which blood was seeping out. He wasn't paying attention to it.

"Let her go," he repeated, "or I'll blow your brains out."

There were some things even a stupid man understood quickly. Bruno let her go. Half-dazed with terror, Kate crawled away from him.

Holding the gun with his left hand, Mitch reached behind his back with the other and produced a pair of handcuffs. Then, not taking a chance that Bruno would try something, Mitch hit him on the back of the head with the .38 before cuffing him to the deck.

The moment Kate saw Bruno crumple to the ground, she started running toward the house. "Alison!" she cried, going from room to room. "Alison, baby, it's me. Where are you?"

"Mommy!"

Relief washed over her as she ran toward the sound of her daughter's voice.

"In here, Mommy! At the end of the hall."

Kate threw the door open and let out a small cry. Alison sat on the floor, tied to the bedpost. She was shivering.

"Oh, my baby." Kate was beside her in an instant, struggling to untie her, crying with joy and relief and frustrated that her fingers, stiff from the cold, couldn't work any faster.

In a moment, Alison was in her arms, crying softly. "I'm sorry, Mommy," she kept saying between sobs. "I'm sorry."

"Shh." Kate held her tight, rocking her the way she had when she was a small child. "It's all right, baby. You're all right now." Removing Alison's wet coat, Kate took a blanket from the bed and wrapped her in it. "Did he hurt you, darling? Did he do anything to you?" The thought that he might have raped her made her blood run cold.

Alison shook her head. "No, he was just mean, that's all."

Tears of relief spilled onto Kate's cheeks.

"Where is he, Mommy? Where's Bruno?"

"Mitch Calhoon handcuffed him to the deck." She kissed the top of Alison's head. "He won't hurt you anymore. No one will ever hurt you again."

"I want to go home, Mommy. *Our* home."

"Yes, darling." Kate closed her eyes. "Oh, yes."

Suddenly, Alison pulled away. "Detective Calhoon. You're bleeding."

Kate turned around. Mitch stood in the doorway. His face was pale, but the bloodstain hadn't gotten any bigger.

"Let me help you with that," she said, getting to her feet. "There should be a first-aid kit somewhere in the house."

Mitch shook his head. "Don't bother. It's just a flesh wound."

She looked at the red scrape on his forehead. "What about your head? Did I hit you hard?"

"No, it was just a glancing blow. Fortunately." His expression softened as he looked at Alison. "Are you okay?"

Alison nodded. "I'm fine. I was scared. I heard all those shots."

Suddenly, Kate shot Mitch a panicked look. "Where's Eric?"

"Oh, Christ," Mitch mumbled as he hurried out of the room, "I forgot all about him."

Running past Bruno who was still out, Mitch rushed toward the embankment. Eric sat on the ground, his back against a tree. His left leg was drawn up and the wounded one was stretched out in front of him and bleeding, although not too badly.

Eric glared at Mitch. "About time you got here," he said testily.

"I was busy."

"This is all your fault, you know. If you hadn't shouted so loud, that guy wouldn't have come out with his guns blazing. Some cop you are." Not giving Mitch a chance to reply, he looked toward the house. "Is Alison there? Is she all right?"

"She's fine." Mitch knelt in front of Eric's leg and started to finger the wound. "How bad is it?"

"Bad enough. I can't put any weight on it."

Mitch reached into his back pocket and pulled out a handkerchief. After unfolding it, he grasped it by each end and twirled it around a few times. Then, wrapping it around Eric's leg, just above the wound, he knotted it. "There, that should stop the bleeding." Sliding his good arm around Eric's back, Mitch pulled him up. "Come on, work with me, Logan. I can't carry a dead weight with just one arm."

"I'm trying, all right?" Holding on to Mitch, Eric pushed himself up on one leg.

"Daddy!" Running toward them, Alison threw herself into her father's arms, nearly sending both men into the snow.

"Hello, princess." Standing on one foot, Eric hung on to Mitch with one arm and grabbed his daughter with the other.

"Oh, Daddy, you're shot, too."

"I'll live."

Up on the deck, as snow kept falling and dusk began to change the landscape, Kate watched the scene in silence as tears streamed down her cheeks.

Thirty-Three

Alison, Eric and Kate's arrival at Georgetown University Hospital three hours later had all the drawing power of a major event. Somehow the news of Alison's abduction and dramatic rescue had leaked to the press and dozens of reporters and television crews were already there.

A team of doctors and paramedics had been alerted and were waiting by the emergency entrance when Kate pulled up, driving Megan's Jaguar with Alison in the front seat and Eric stretched out in the back. The Saab, deeply entrenched in the snow, would have to wait for its own rescue.

Mitch had gone directly to the police department with his prisoner and had promised Kate he'd have his arm looked at as soon as Bruno was booked.

"No questions until later," Kate said sharply as a camera crew pushed forward. "Right now, we have an injured man to take care of, so please get out of the way."

Surprisingly, they parted to let them through. Rose, Frankie and Megan were standing together just inside the wide glass doors. Rose saw her granddaughter first and ran to her. "Oh, pumpkin, thank God you're all right." She enfolded her in her arms. "I was never so scared in my entire life." Then, seeing Eric, who had been placed on a gurney, she let out a small cry and rushed to his side.

Frankie came forward and ruffled the top of Alison's

head. "Hey, kid. You're okay?" When Alison nodded, she glanced at Kate. "How about you, Boss? You didn't say much on the car phone."

Kate wasn't in the mood for a long, drawn-out explanation of the afternoon's events. In fact, in spite of her relief at having Alison back safe and sound, she wasn't in the mood for much of anything. Her mind had been preoccupied with Mitch and on how she had fouled things up between them.

"I'm fine," Kate replied as Frankie continued to observe her. "Just tired, that's all."

As Eric was wheeled away to an operating room, one of the doctors, a young intern by the name of Dr. Drucker, took Alison behind a curtained partition and gave her a thorough examination. "She's fine," he told Kate when he came out a little while later. "All she needs is a good night's sleep."

Kate kept her arm around her daughter's shoulders. "Shall we do that, Alison? We can come back in the morning—"

Alison gave an emphatic shake of her head. "I want to stay here until Daddy is out of surgery." She looked up, her gray eyes partly worried and partly apologetic. "I've got to, Mom."

Kate smiled. "All right, then. We'll go on up and wait with Grandma and Megan."

"I'll come with you," Frankie said.

In the waiting room, Alison went to join the other two women, while Kate and Frankie walked over to the coffee machine.

"What's the prognosis on Eric?" Frankie asked as she fed quarters into the slot.

Kate shrugged. "We don't know. Mitch thinks the bullet is still in there. But Eric was in good spirits during the entire trip.''

"I guess he should be. He's no longer a suspect, is he?''

"Not really, but nothing can be finalized until there's actual proof that someone else killed Gina and Lilly. It all depends on how much they can get out of Bruno.''

"They have more than Bruno, Boss. Didn't Mitch tell you?''

"Tell me what?''

"Maddy Mays was arrested. And Lieutenant Jarvis, who's apparently been on her payroll for years, was suspended pending an investigation by Internal Affairs. Oh, and Mitch was reinstated. He and Detective Spivak are working on the case together now.''

"What about the McKackneys?''

"In custody. Both of them. The senator was at the White House meeting with the president when all hell broke loose. The U.S. attorney called the president and told him that McKackney was about to be arrested and why. Needless to say, both the White House and the Senate are in a state of shock, and our phones haven't stopped ringing since the news broke out. Not even Washington was prepared for a scandal like this, Boss. Everything else pales in comparison.'' They sipped their coffee in silence. Then Frankie, her face grave, asked, "Did Rose tell you about Douglas?''

Kate nodded. "I haven't said anything to Alison yet.''

"I can't believe it,'' Frankie continued. "What in the name of God could he have been thinking of? A lawyer of his reputation, involved in murder.''

"Any word on him?''

"The last I heard, the police had an all points bulletin out, but other than that, there's been nothing.''

Kate glanced at Alison, whose head was resting on Rose's shoulder, and felt a pinch in her heart. She looked so innocent, so trusting. How in the world was she going to explain to that sweet child what Douglas had done and not shatter that trust forever?

Looking slightly less glamorous than she had at the time of her arrest three hours ago, Maddy Mays glowered at Mitch as she was escorted into an interrogation room.

"You're going to pay dearly for this, Detective Calhoon. In fact, it'd be safe to say that you're going to curse the day you ever met me." She glanced at Tom Spivak, who had just laid a tape recorder on the table. "And the same goes for you. You're all going to pay."

His arm in a sling, Mitch waited until she was seated before doing the same. "You're in no position to make threats, Maddy. Bruno is in custody, we have Alison Logan's statement that you ordered her abduction, and your good buddy, Lieutenant Jarvis, is singing like a canary."

Although Jarvis had, in fact, come clean about his dealings with Maddy Mays and his involvement in Sean McKackney's release, he had sworn he had no knowledge of her participation in any of the murders or who Bruno was. As for Bruno, he hadn't uttered a word since that last grunt at McKackney's cabin. Unless Mitch could somehow convince Maddy to confess, he wouldn't have enough to charge McKackney or Douglas with conspiracy to murder.

"You're lying," Maddy said.

"No, I'm not. He's already told us some pretty incriminating stuff."

The color left Maddy's face. "I've never even met Lieutenant Jarvis."

A corner of Mitch's mouth twisted into a smile. His

eyes still on Maddy, he leaned toward the tape recorder and pushed a button. Jarvis's voice, although not nearly as offensive as it used to be, came out loud and clear.

"I met Maddy Mays at a police benefit in 1978," he began. "After about five minutes of small talk, she asked me point-blank if I would like to earn some extra money in exchange for protection when and if she ever needed it. The amount she quoted me at the time was twice what I was making as a detective. I guess the thought of making so much money blinded me. I know what I did was wrong, but I had three kids and another on the way…"

Mitch shut off the machine. "Heard enough, Maddy?"

"What the hell did you do to him to get him to say that crap?"

"We made a deal with him. Information in exchange for leniency. We do that all the time—provided, of course, the suspect has something valuable to offer."

Tom rolled up his sleeve, as if he was readying himself for a long, tedious session and had all the time in the world. "The kidnapping charges alone will get you fifteen to twenty," he threw in casually. "Then there's bribery, prostitution and, most likely, conspiracy to murder." He started to roll up the other sleeve. "I'd say you're looking at a hundred years."

Maddy gave Tom a hate-filled look. "I want to see my attorney," she said, folding her arms across her chest.

"Well, you see…" Mitch scratched his head. "We've got a little problem locating him, just as you did when you tried to call him earlier." He smiled innocently. "Mr. Fairchild, it would seem, has flown the coop."

A little vein in Maddy's right temple began to pulse rapidly. "What the hell are you talking about?"

"According to his wife, Douglas went home at about three o'clock this afternoon, packed a few clothes, took a pile of money from his safe along with his passport, then took off. We've got APBs out for him all over the East Coast, but so far we haven't been able to locate him.''

That wasn't quite true. On his way back from Mc-Kackney's cabin, Mitch had gotten word that Douglas had been apprehended by the Miami police as he was about to board a plane bound for Buenos Aires and was being escorted back to Washington.

''Rose thinks he's gone to Argentina,'' Mitch continued, noting with satisfaction how Maddy's eyes were beginning to narrow. ''Where there's no extradition treaty.'' He studied her carefully, wondering how close she was to her breaking point. ''Looks like he's left you to take the fall, Maddy.''

''That son of a bitch.'' The insult hissed out of her mouth like venom. ''That two-timing, backstabbing, good-for-nothing son of a bitch.''

''You ought to choose your friends more carefully, Maddy,'' Tom commented.

''Oh, shut up, why don't you?'' Maddy shouted as she finally lost control. ''You're beginning to get on my nerves.''

Tom and Mitch exchanged an amused glance.

There was a fierce, vengeful look on Maddy's face as she leaned forward. Looking from Mitch to Tom, she slapped her palms on the table. ''All right. You two jackasses want details? You want to know who masterminded the murder of those two women? And Chuck Winslow? I'll tell you, but not until I get some guarantees.''

Mitch, who had already been told by the U.S. attorney to make whatever deal was necessary to nail the murderer, or murderers, began to relax. ''Kidnapping is a federal offense, Maddy, so the U.S. attorney won't be able to help you there, but even the FBI has been known to be lenient in certain cases. Now, about the other charges Detective Spivak mentioned, the U.S. attorney is prepared to drop them, provided you give us the information we need.''

"Will I still go to prison?"

"I'm afraid so, Maddy. But the sentence will be considerably reduced. Of course, you'll have to prove that what you're telling us is true.''

"Oh, I can prove it all right. I've got recordings of conversations that'll make your head spin.'' She gave him a thin smile. "I wasn't born yesterday, you know.''

Mitch smiled back. "I'm all ears, Maddy.''

She looked from one detective to the other. "Shouldn't I have an attorney present?''

Mitch shrugged. "You can call one if you want to. Or we can provide one for you. But I'm telling you, Maddy, all an attorney is going to do at this point is advise you not to say a word, which, of course, would negate our deal.''

Maddy was silent for a moment, as if mulling the thought over, then, having made her decision, she nodded. "All right. What do you want to know?''

Tom removed the tape with Jarvis's confession on it and replaced it with a blank one.

"Let's start with Lilly Moore,'' Mitch said as soon as Tom had pressed the Record button. "Who killed her and why?''

Maddy lowered her gaze to her hands, which were loosely clasped on the table. "Lilly had a habit of poking around Fairchild Baxter's old case files. One day, she found one that intrigued her—the rape charge against Sean McKackney—and decided to look into it. Before long, she had found out that Mary Sweeney and Gina Lamont were the same girl.'' She looked at Mitch. "But you already know that, don't you, Detective?''

Mitch nodded. "Did Lilly suspect that Douglas was involved in the conspiracy?"

"No, but she told him she had enough for him to re-open the case. She said she wanted justice, not just for Peggy Bertram, but for all of womankind." She barked a short laugh. "Have you ever heard such a load of crap?"

"What did Douglas do?"

"He got scared. We all did."

"Can you tell us, for the record, who you mean by 'all'?"

"Me, Douglas Fairchild, Senator Sander McKackney and Dr. Sean McKackney."

"Go on."

"That same morning, Douglas came to see me and told me we had to kill Lilly. That scared me even more. I didn't want anything to do with murder. I was prepared to pay Lilly anything she wanted, but Douglas said she wasn't interested in money. So that afternoon, Douglas took Lilly's keys from her purse, made a copy of her apartment key and gave it to me."

"And you gave it to Bruno."

"I didn't want to. I argued with Douglas until I was hoarse. I've got it all on tape."

"Why did you feel you had to tape your conversations with Douglas?"

"Because I didn't trust him. Or Sander for that matter. They both agreed that Lilly had to be killed, but they didn't want to hear how it was going to be done. They said I should handle that part. That's when I became suspicious."

"They knew Bruno worked for you?"

"Yeah. And they knew he was devoted to me, that he would do anything I told him to. Bruno and I go way back, when we both worked for Dom Costa."

"Where are the tapes?"

"In my office safe. With copies in my safe-deposit box at First Federal."

Mitch wrote the information in his notebook. "Whose idea was it to buy Winslow's testimony?"

"Douglas's. He talked to all of Lilly's neighbors before selecting Winslow. The poor bastard might as well have signed his death warrant that day."

"What do you mean?"

"Douglas had planned to kill him a week or two after the trial was over. He was afraid he'd start spending that hundred grand all at once and give the whole thing away. When Kate Logan told him she was going to question Winslow again, Douglas decided to speed things up."

"What about Gina?"

"Ah, Gina." Maddy's smile was a mixture of pride and regret. "My best girl. I taught her everything she knew. The problem with her, however, was that she wasn't very bright. Imaginative, but not bright, otherwise she never would have tried to blackmail me."

"How much did she hit you for?" Tom asked.

"A total of three million bucks. One million from me, one from Douglas and one from Sander. She said if we didn't give it to her, she would go to the police and tell them everything."

"Why didn't she try to do that sooner?"

"She didn't have to. First of all, her payment for agreeing to help Sean was very generous. She could have retired on that money alone. Second, as one of my most popular girls, Gina was swimming in money. Until eighteen months ago when she got hooked on coke." She gave a sad shake of her head. "She was no good to me then. And worse, she was beginning to give my operation a bad name. I had to let her go."

"I'm surprised she didn't try to blackmail you then."

"I was afraid she would, but I don't think she even thought of it. She was having a great time with her new drug habit and her trendy friends. Besides, I had given her the phone numbers of a few clients—those I didn't mind losing, and she was able to keep on working. I don't think she got the idea of blackmailing anybody until she really hit the skids two or three months ago."

"Was killing her Douglas's idea, also?"

Maddy nodded. "He said that with her drug habit and her lifestyle, the three million wouldn't last long. He was afraid she would keep on blackmailing us until she bled us dry."

"What about Kate Logan's beating last week? Whose idea was that?" Mitch's easy manner had vanished.

"We had another argument about that one, but not because I wanted to spare Kate Logan's life." She tugged at a shirtsleeve. "I knew that broad was trouble the moment she walked into my office. I told that to Douglas, but he wouldn't listen. He said that all she needed was a warning. But he was wrong on that one." When Maddy looked up at Mitch, her eyes were cold and hard. "Kate Logan should have died."

Mitch had never had the urge to strike a woman before, not even when he had found Ava making love to another man. But in Maddy's case, he would gladly have made an exception.

As if sensing his frustration, Tom looked at Maddy. "What about LuAnn? Was she supposed to die, too?"

"No. We just wanted to teach anybody who might be tempted to talk a lesson."

A uniformed officer came in and leaned toward Mitch, talking low.

Mitch rose. "I'm going to have to send you back to

your cell for now, Maddy.'' He nodded to the guard at the door. ''We'll finish this a little later, okay?'' He shut off the recorder.

''Why?'' Maddy was suddenly alert, glancing from Mitch to the officer who was standing beside him, waiting. ''What did he tell you? What's going on? If it's about me, I have a right to know.''

''It isn't about you, Maddy.''

Mitch waited until she had left the interrogation room before nodding to the young officer.

''Okay, Art, you can bring Douglas Fairchild in.''

Thirty-Four

"Are you comfortable, darling?" Megan, who hadn't stopped fussing since Eric had returned from surgery, fluffed another pillow and tucked it behind his head.

Eric leaned back and smiled. Both his mother and Megan had been smothering him with attention. But he wasn't complaining. After the two and a half weeks he'd endured, he deserved a little pampering.

"I'm fine," he said as Megan refilled his water glass. "The local anesthetic they gave me hasn't had a chance to wear off yet, so there's no pain." He patted the bed. "Stop moving around. Come here." Megan sat down and let him take her hands in his. "Did you hear from Calhoon?" he asked. "Have I been cleared of that stupid murder charge?"

Megan beamed. "Totally. Mitch called while you were in surgery. Douglas killed Gina. Well, he didn't actually *do* the killing, but he ordered it. And the others, as well."

"What others?"

"Lilly Moore and Chuck Winslow. He's even responsible for an attack on Kate."

"That bastard." Happy though Eric was to be a free man again, his hatred of Douglas almost choked him. The man his mother had loved for twenty-one years, the stepfather who had preached honesty, hard work and integrity, the attorney an entire town respected and admired, was nothing but a cold-blooded killer. "That bastard," he repeated between clenched teeth. "I hope he rots in jail for a long time."

Megan's fingertips, soft as feathers, brushed against his skin. "I don't want to talk about Douglas anymore," she said, her expression serious.

He brought her hand to his mouth and kissed it. "What do you want to talk about?"

She drew a breath and released it slowly. "Mother."

"*Your* mother?"

Megan nodded. "She called. She wants to see you." She moistened her lips. "I think she wants to apologize."

Eric laughed. "Your mother apologize? She doesn't know the meaning of the word."

"She's learning, Eric. And she's trying. Please give her another chance. I promise you won't regret it."

He grinned and pulled her to him. "What do you mean by that?"

"I mean," Megan said, blushing as she settled against him, "that I'll be forever grateful."

"How about giving me a sample of that gratitude right now?" He started playing with a button on her blouse.

She laughed and gave his hand a gentle slap. "Stop that. What if someone came in and saw us?"

"No one will if you lock the door."

"Eric, what did they give you in that operating room anyway?"

He pulled her closer. "Make love to me, Megan."

"Not here."

He cupped her breast and heard the little catch in her throat. "If you do, I'll welcome Mother Hollbrook with wide-open arms."

"This is crazy—"

"Go lock the door, Megan."

Her breath coming a little quicker, Megan stood up and went to lock the door.

"That horrible woman wanted to kill you, Mom." Alison almost choked on the words. "I heard her say it on the phone."

Kate tucked the covers around Alison's neck and kissed her cheek. "That's all behind us now, darling. Maddy Mays can't harm us. And neither can Bruno." She pushed back a golden strand of hair, enjoying the simple pleasure of touching and looking at her daughter.

"Who was she talking to on the phone, Mom?"

It was the second time tonight that Alison had made reference to that call. She had also inquired about her grandfather, wanting to know why he hadn't been at the hospital. Kate had hinted at an unexpected out-of-town trip, hoping the small white lie would temporarily satisfy her. It had, but considering how every newspaper and television station in the country had pounced on the story, it was a miracle that Alison hadn't already heard about her grandfather's involvement in this lurid affair.

Tomorrow would be time enough to tell her the truth, Kate thought as Alison stifled a yawn. "Let's talk in the morning, baby, okay? You've had enough excitement for one day."

Alison took her mother's hand. "First, I want to tell you how sorry I am that I said those terrible things to you the other day. I really thought you weren't going to help Daddy anymore."

"I know. I wish I could have told you the truth."

"You should have trusted me." There was a trace of reproach in Alison's voice. "If I had known that you were only pretending not to be working on the case and that

Detective Calhoon was helping you, I would have kept your secret. I'm not a kid, you know.''

Kate smiled. "I do now. Next big secret, I promise I'll share it with you.''

"'Kay." Alison was thoughtful for a moment. "How's Detective Calhoon?''

"He's fine. The bullet went through and there's no permanent damage. He'll have to wear a sling for a few days, but that's all.''

"Daddy said Detective Calhoon tried to save him and that's how he got shot. He could have been killed.''

"Fortunately for Detective Calhoon, and for your father," Kate said in an attempt to insert a little lightness into the conversation, "Bruno was a lousy shot." Kate was relieved to see her daughter smile. "Go to sleep, sweetie," she said, turning off the bedside lamp. "We'll talk in the morning.''

"I changed my mind about Detective Calhoon, Mom." The sleepy gray eyes filled with youthful mischief. "He's okay. And it's okay if you like him. You can even invite him to dinner if you want to.''

Kate bent to kiss her daughter. "That's a great idea, darling. I'll ask him when I see him tomorrow.''

She walked out of Alison's room, certain that Mitch would never want to step into this house again. For any reason.

She had wanted so badly to go to the station and talk to him, but by the time Eric had come out of surgery, Alison was so exhausted that Kate had had only one thing in mind—to take her home.

Maybe it was just as well that she hadn't seen him, she thought as she began to undress. Mitch needed time, time to understand how desperate she'd been, time to realize she hadn't meant any of the things she'd said to him.

She slid between the sheets and thought about the night they'd spent in this bed together. It seemed like years ago. After a while, she took the pillow Mitch had used, held it against her chest and closed her eyes.

It had been a busy morning.

Only an hour ago, Tony had been released from jail, and he, Maria and half the Latino population were celebrating. Eric had been cleared of all charges, and Maddy Mays had somehow managed to become the woman of the hour. The press, quick to sensationalize the incident, had dubbed her "The East Coast Madam." There was even talk of a television movie.

Now, sitting at Mitch's desk, next to Rose, Kate watched the detective as he returned from the cell area.

"I'm sorry, Rose," Mitch said, sitting on the edge of his desk, facing the two women. "Douglas doesn't want to see you."

Rose raised stricken eyes toward him. "But why? I'm his wife. I want to be with him...." She opened her purse and pulled out a handkerchief. "He's upset because I betrayed his confidence, isn't he?" she asked, blotting her eyes. "He doesn't think I should have told you that he was leaving the country."

"Don't blame yourself, Rose." Mitch's voice was gentle. "You did nothing wrong. You had a choice to make—to clear your son or to let your husband go free. You chose your son. Millions of mothers all over this planet would have done the same thing." Mitch turned to Kate. "However, he did ask to see you."

Kate wasn't surprised. Although she hadn't offered to talk to Douglas, she had suspected he would want to see her. The problem was, she wasn't sure she wanted to see him.

"Please, Kate." Sensing her hesitation, Rose touched her hand. "Go. Do it for me."

After a few more seconds of indecision, Kate stood up and nodded to Mitch. As a guard unlocked the cell door, Mitch glanced at her. "You want me to stay?"

She shook her head. "No, I'll be all right."

He nodded. "Call the guard when you're ready."

Douglas, looking as if he had just returned from a business trip, sat on the cot in his shirtsleeves. Always the perfect gentleman, he rose as she walked in. "Thanks for coming, Kate. I wasn't sure you would."

"I didn't do it for you." She pulled a chair away from the dingy wall and sat down. Then, crossing her legs, she leaned back and just looked at him, waiting.

"I want to explain... But I'm not sure where to begin."

She remained silent, her eyes fixed on him. It was an unnerving tactic, one he had taught her himself. From the brief smile that curved his lips, she could see that he remembered that.

"I won't bore you with the details regarding Sean's alibi. I'm told that Maddy has been quite explicit about that, and other things."

He looked past her at the wall where former occupants had scrawled dirty messages and phone numbers. She wondered if he was thinking of all the times he had been in here counseling others, and how different it felt now that things were reversed.

"I'm sorry about Alison's ordeal," he said, staring at his hands. "I take full blame for that. If I had found a better hiding place for that damn key, she wouldn't have been kidnapped."

Curiosity got the best of her. "What exactly was that key?"

"It belonged to one of the penthouses Maddy had put at my disposal."

"Did it come complete with a hooker?"

The contempt in her voice was thick enough to cut, but he ignored it. "Occasionally, yes. It was a little perk some of my clients appreciated. But I never used the penthouse myself, Kate. You've got to believe that."

"Why should I ever believe you again?"

"Because I no longer have anything to lose by telling the truth."

She looked at him for a long, measuring second. "How could you do it, Douglas? How could you have had all those people killed?"

"They pushed me into a corner."

"You pushed yourself into a corner the night you fabricated that phony alibi for Sean McKackney."

He stared at a spot on the ceiling and didn't answer.

"It was a high price to pay for friendship, wasn't it?"

"I didn't do it for friendship alone." He returned his gaze to her. "Sander offered me a lot of money. He told me that if I found a way to help Sean, he'd give me a million dollars—in cash. *In cash,* Kate," he repeated as if that justified everything. "Cash I could put in a Grand Cayman bank and watch grow, which is exactly what I did."

Money. He had done it all for money. "But you were a successful attorney. Why would you—"

"No, I wasn't." He stood up, jammed his hands in his pockets and started to walk around the cell. "After my father was appointed to the Supreme Court and I was left in charge of the firm, things changed. A lot of his old clients didn't like my methods. They said I wasn't as good as the old man, that I didn't have enough know-how, enough clout. So they left, one by one." His tone turned bitter. "And my father never let me forget it."

Although Kate had never met Douglas's father, she knew about his intolerance for human failures, including those made by his only son.

"When Sander came to me with that offer," Douglas continued, "I couldn't turn it down. Not only did I stand to make a lot of money, but Sander had also promised to send me the kind of high-profile clients who would change the way others perceived me—as a lawyer lucky enough to have inherited his daddy's firm. I could finally show my father that I was every bit as good as he was."

"And in the process, your values got blown to hell."

"I never meant for things to get that far."

She watched him as he stopped in front of the cell door, his back to her. "Maddy said you were responsible for what happened to me in the garage last week. She said that *you* ordered the attack. Is that true?"

He spun around. "Did that bitch also tell you she wanted to have you killed?" His eyes were so bright and hot, he looked as though he had suddenly come down with a fever. "Did she tell you that she wanted to send Bruno to your house and have him do to you what he did to Gina? I'm the one who stopped her, Kate. If it weren't for me, you'd be dead."

"And that's supposed to make me feel grateful?" she flung back, springing from her chair. "I'm supposed to turn my head the other way and not even flinch at the thought of all you've done? My daughter was kidnapped, Douglas. She could have been killed."

"I had nothing to do with that. I didn't even know Bruno had her until the police took me off the plane in Miami."

"But you had a good idea, didn't you? And what if

you *had* known? What would you have done? Would you have come back and tried to save her? Or would you have boarded your plane to Buenos Aires?'' After a few seconds of heavy silence, Kate laughed. ''The answer is so damned obvious, you can't even lie about it, can you, Douglas?''

''Mitch Calhoon was an expert in rescue operations. I couldn't have done anything more for her.''

''What about all the other people you betrayed? Maria, Rose, Tony. How do you explain the hell you put that young man through? You even had the gall to sit in my office the day of the verdict and question his innocence.'' Still bewildered at the thought, she shook her head. ''My God, Douglas, when did you become that good an actor?''

''I'm not proud of what I did.''

''It's too late for regrets.''

''But it's not too late to start making it up to all those I've hurt, including that prostitute Bruno beat up so badly. I understand she's in the hospital.''

''That's right. She, too, could have died.''

''I want to pay her bills, Kate. You just tell me what to do and I'll do it, no matter how much it costs.'' For a moment, the old Douglas was back, full of spunk and authority. ''And I want to take care of Tony's college tuition, as well.''

''I'm taking care of LuAnn's bills.'' Kate's voice was harsh, causing Douglas's eyebrows to arch. ''And I doubt Tony will accept your offer.''

''I'm only trying to help.''

''You're in no position to help anyone. You're going to prison, Douglas. Or hasn't that sunk in yet?''

''I'm not going anywhere. Not if I pick the right attorney.'' He held her hard gaze. ''That attorney is you, Kate. I want you to represent me.''

Thirty-Five

If he hadn't spoken so clearly, Kate would have thought she'd heard him wrong. *"Represent you?"* She stared at him in total disbelief.

"I'll pay you whatever you want. I have close to five million dollars in Grand Cayman. And if that's not enough, I'll sell the Potomac house and the one in Bermuda. Whatever it takes to get me off, I'll pay it. All we have to do is find one or two jurors we can buy—"

"Are you talking about jury tampering now?"

He gave a small snort of laughter. "It's done all the time. You know that."

She took a step back. "Have you ever done it?"

He waved her question aside and started to pace again. "I can show you how to pick them. They have to be hungry, but strong, the kind of jurors the others will listen to. Of course, we'll have to be careful. An error in judgment could be disastrous…"

He was so absorbed in his planning that he never heard Kate call the guard.

He was still talking and pacing when she walked out.

Rose looked up as Kate returned to Mitch's desk, her expression hopeful. "How is he?" she asked. "What did he say?"

Kate sat back down. "He's fine. Planning his defense."

"Defense?" Rose's eyes widened. "Isn't he going to plead guilty?"

"It doesn't look like it. But whatever he decides to do, that's not my problem, Rose."

Kate could tell from the look in Rose's eyes that she had already guessed what Kate was about to tell her. "You're not going to represent him, are you?"

Kate shook her head. "No, I'm not. I hope you understand, Rose. And I hope it won't change anything between us."

"Never," Rose said earnestly. "I despise him for what he did, but at the same time…" She closed her eyes. "I still love him, Kate. Does that make me a terrible woman?"

"No. It only proves that you're human." She patted Rose's hand. "But don't worry too much about Douglas. I'm sure that before the day is over, he'll have hired a very competent attorney—one that will be only too glad to take his money." She glanced around the busy squad room. "Where's Mitch?"

"I don't know. He was here a minute ago."

"I have to find him." She stood up. "You don't mind taking a cab home, do you?"

"Of course not."

As soon as Rose had left, Kate walked over to the next desk where a young detective was busy typing a report. "Do you know where I can find Mitch Calhoon?" she asked. "He was here a moment ago."

"He just left." The detective looked apologetic. "He didn't say where he was going. I'm sorry, Mrs. Logan."

"What about Detective Spivak? Is he in?"

"His shift doesn't begin until noon."

"Thank you."

Moments later, she was behind the wheel of Frankie's

red Camaro, heading for the Spivaks' home on Fulton Street.

"Kate." Mary Beth embraced her the moment she opened the door. "Tom told me what happened. I was going to call you, but Sandy came down with an awful cold." She pulled her inside. "Come in, please. Is your daughter all right?"

"She's fine, thank you. And back in school like a real trouper." She followed Mary Beth into a cheery yellow kitchen, catching a glimpse of a huge Christmas tree as she passed the family room. "I was hoping to talk to Tom."

"He came in very late last night, so I don't think he'll get up until he has to." Mary Beth glanced at her watch. "Which won't be for another hour." She untied her apron and tossed it on the counter. "Can I do anything for you?"

"Well…" Feeling suddenly awkward, she stopped. She had only known Mary Beth a short while and here she was, ready to discuss her most private thoughts with her.

"Kate, what is it?"

The gentleness in the woman's voice chased some of Kate's apprehensions away. She had to find Mitch, and at the moment, only one person could help her do that. "Do you have any idea where Mitch is?" she asked.

"Why, no. I thought he was at the station. Tom said he had to take a statement from you and Rose."

"He did. Then he took me to see Douglas, and when I came out, he was gone and no one knows where he went."

"I see." Mary Beth sat back in her chair. "You two have a fight or something?"

"I'm afraid it's more than that."

"I'm surprised. The other day when you and Mitch

came to the house, I had the impression there was something very special between the two of you." She smiled. "Even though you denied it."

"I didn't lie to you. There was nothing between Mitch and me at the time." Then, because the strain of the past day was finally beginning to catch up with her, she added, "Oh, Mary Beth, I'm afraid I did something terrible."

"What did you do?"

"I said some awful things to Mitch. I didn't mean any of them. I just blurted them out when he refused to rescue my daughter. I was just so angry."

Mary Beth's smile disappeared. "What did you say to him?"

"I called him a coward."

Mary Beth recoiled as if Kate had hit her. Her eyes, so soft and gentle a moment ago, filled with an anger she was having a hard time controlling. "Mitch is one of the bravest, most courageous men I know. He risked his life up there, for you, for your daughter and for your ex-husband. How many men do you know who would have done that?"

"I told you I was upset. He didn't want to rescue my daughter because of what happened in California and it made me crazy. All I wanted was for him to forget about that little girl and save mine."

"Oh, Kate." Mary Beth leaned back in her chair. "You hit below the belt with that one, but you couldn't have known, so I won't hold it against you."

"I couldn't have known what?"

Mary Beth hesitated. "I'm not sure I should be the one to tell you this."

Kate gripped the woman's hands. "Mary Beth, I love Mitch. I didn't expect to fall in love so soon after my divorce, but I did. And I think he's in love with me. So if there's anything you can do to help me understand him better, please tell me."

Mary Beth gave her a long, speculative look, then nodded. "The reason I said you hit him below the belt..." Her eyes misted. "Was because that little girl who died in San Luis Obispo that day, that little girl you told him to forget, was his daughter."

"No!" Kate cried in a shocked whisper.

Mary Beth nodded. "Only a handful of people in the entire country know that, and that's the way he wants it, so please don't tell anyone. The only reason I told you is that despite the fact I wanted to smack you a minute ago, I still think you're good for Mitch. So if you don't mind eating a little crow, you should get your ass out to his place, assuming he's there, and see what you can do to get him back. Believe me, Kate, you can roam the earth from here to kingdom come and you won't find a finer man than Mitch Calhoon."

Feeling numb, Kate stood up. "Where does he live?"

"114 Kalorama Road." She walked Kate to the door. "Let me know what happens, will you? I've got a stake in this."

"I will."

Ten minutes later, Kate was driving down Kalorama Road in the Adams Morgan neighborhood of northwest D.C. in search of a parking space. She finally found one at the intersection of 18th Street and Columbia Road.

Once a posh district of Washington, somewhere along the way, Adams Morgan had become D.C.'s Latin Quarter and Greenwich Village rolled into one. Throughout the year, residents and tourists alike delighted in the neighborhood's lively street parties, music festivals and the display of handmade crafts from all over the world.

Three weeks ago, Kate would have wondered why a man of Mitch Calhoon's means would choose to live anywhere but posh Georgetown. But now that she knew him better, knew the kind of man he truly was, she understood why he had chosen this mecca of ethnic diversity and bohemian good times as his home.

Unfortunately, Mitch wasn't there. After fifteen minutes, she gave up the wait and started rummaging inside her purse in search of pen and paper.

"Good morning."

At the friendly greeting, Kate looked up. A dark-haired man in a clerical collar was smiling at her. He was young, no more than twenty-five or so, and very handsome. A large, Christmas-wrapped package was tucked under his left arm.

Recalling Mitch's story about his friend, she smiled back. "Good morning, Father O'Malley."

The brown eyes registered surprise. "We couldn't possibly have met," he said, coming up the steps to the front porch, "or I would have remembered."

She laughed as she extended her hand. "My name is Kate Logan. And no, we haven't met, but Mitch has told me all about you, including your fondness for basketball."

"Ah, then he must have also told you that I'm a poor loser."

"No, only that you like to give him a run for his money."

"Kate Logan," he said, pursing his lips in concentration. "You're the mother of that young girl who was kidnapped."

Kate nodded. "I am. And I'm glad to report that Alison is safe and sound, thanks to Mitch." She glanced up and down the street, hoping to see the familiar Ford. "I need to talk to him, but no one seems to know where he is."

Father O'Malley studied her for a moment, as if trying to make up his mind about her. "You might want to try Habanita on 18th Street," he said at last.

She lowered the pad she had pulled out of her purse. "Habanita?"

"It's a neighborhood bar Mitch frequents occasionally."

"And you think he's there now?"

"I *know* he's there now. I ran into him about ten minutes ago and he invited me to go with him." He patted the package under his arm. "But I still had a couple of parishioners to visit, so I had to decline."

Kate stuffed her notepad back into her purse. "Thank you, Father." She beamed. Maybe her luck was finally changing. "You've been a tremendous help."

"I'm always glad to hear that," he said as he watched her go.

Habanita, in the heart of Adams Morgan, was already packed with a trendy crowd when Kate arrived. Men in designer jeans and women in short black sheaths stood at the banana-shaped bar drinking wine and munching on skewered shrimp. Salsa music pulsed from the overhead speakers, making anything more than casual conversation a near impossibility.

Mitch sat at the far end of the bar. He had taken the sling off and was staring into the glass of beer in front of him. As Kate made her way toward his stool, he saw her and stood up.

"What are you doing here?"

"I ran into Father O'Malley." She shook her head at the bartender who had come to take her order, then returned her gaze to Mitch. "He told me where I could find you."

The music changed to a softer, more tolerable beat. "You didn't have to come looking for me," Mitch said. "I was going to call you."

"I wanted a chance to talk to you first." She watched his profile as he sipped his beer, but his expression gave nothing away. "I know I hurt you, Mitch, maybe beyond repair, but I was beside myself yesterday. You were my only hope, the only man I trusted to save my daughter, and when you refused to go..." She waited for him to say something, to give her some sort of encouragement. He didn't. "I had no right to talk to you that way, and I wouldn't have if I had known about...your daughter."

He turned to look at her. His eyes were impenetrable. "How did you find out about her?"

"Mary Beth told me. But only because I gave her no choice." When he returned his attention to some point at the far end of the bar, she forged ahead. "I'm so sorry, Mitch. I had no idea that the little girl you talked about that day was your daughter. Now that I do, I wish I could take the pain you're feeling and bear it for you. But I can't do that, any more than I can take back what I said."

She glanced at a young couple across the bar. The man, no more than twenty or so, was whispering something in the girl's ear and she was giggling. Kate would have done anything to feel that carefree again.

Tearing her gaze away, she looked at Mitch. "I came looking for you..." Her voice shook with emotion and she fought to steady it. "Because I feel that what we have is worth saving. I love you, Mitch. I never thought I'd say those words again, but here they are. I hope they mean something to you." Instead of getting smaller, the abyss between them seemed to grow wider. "You gave me my daughter back yesterday, and for that I'll never be able to thank you enough, but if you'll let me try..."

She couldn't go any further. If she did she would make a spectacle of herself and embarrass Mitch. So she just stood there, looking at his profile, while her unfinished promise hung in the air. Her heart was heavy with words she couldn't say. Why did she need words anyway? Why couldn't she just say the hell with everything and throw her arms around him and kiss him senseless?

Because he doesn't want you anymore and you know it.

After an excruciating moment that seemed to stretch forever, she stood up. "I guess coming here wasn't such a good idea after all."

He didn't answer her. She wasn't even sure he was still listening to her.

Fighting back the tears, she picked up her purse from the counter, hooked the strap around her shoulder and hurried out of the bar.

Hillside Cemetery in Fairfax, Virginia, where Gabrielle was buried, was relatively quiet on this wet Friday afternoon.

Bending down on one knee, Mitch laid the bouquet of pink roses on Gabrielle's grave and let his gaze drift across the inscription on the stone: Gabrielle Marie Calhoon 1986–1993. The pain was still there. It would always be there, but he knew now that in time, it would become more tolerable. The process had already begun, and the demons he had been fighting for the past few years were gone, thanks to a persistent, wonderful woman named Kate Logan and her spunky daughter.

He wanted Kate to know that, if it wasn't too late.

After a while, he stood up, said a silent goodbye to the daughter he would always love and walked back toward his car.

* * *

It was two o'clock by the time he arrived at Kate's house. He had called her office first and found out that she had taken the next two days off. "I think she and Alison are home," Frankie had told him. "Kate even said something about buying a Christmas tree today."

Mitch smiled as he pulled up along the curb. Propped against the front door was a seven-foot fir tree, still wrapped in string.

Alison opened the door and he was relieved to see that all trace of resentment was gone. She gave him a bright smile. "Hi."

"Hi yourself, young lady." There was a gleam in her eyes, and although her resemblance to Eric was indisputable, the expression reminded him a lot of Kate. "Is your mother home?"

She nodded and opened the door wider. "She's in the kitchen." Then, with a look that told him this little girl had done a lot of growing up in the past twenty-four hours, she added, "I'll be upstairs."

Kate sat in the window seat, her knees drawn up.

Nerves taut at the thought that he might be too late, he came up behind her. Before she could turn around, he closed his arms around her. "I was wondering," he whispered in her hair, "if you could use a couple of strong arms to bring that Christmas tree in. Because if you do, I've got a fairly decent set right here."

So she wouldn't have any doubts, he tightened his hold, favoring his wounded arm a little. At the sound of that slow, sexy laugh rising from her throat, he breathed a sigh of relief.

"And later," he continued, "if you ask me real nice, I might even break into my special rendition of 'Jingle Bells.' Just to set the mood."

As he released her, Kate stood up and turned around. The loving look in his eyes brought a lump to her throat. She wrapped her arms around his neck. "Mmm," she said, pretending to be deadly serious. "There's only one problem with that offer, Detective."

"And what is that, Counselor?"

"Whenever a man sings to me, especially Christmas carols, I start to feel incredibly sexy." She tilted her head back as she gazed into his blue eyes. "Would you happen to have a remedy for such an ailment?"

He lowered his mouth to hers. "You bet I do, lady."